To Find You

A Novel by Linda Schmalz

Also by Linda Schmalz:

A Lonely Sky

What Dead Women Want

The Magic in a Dress (short story)

Acknowledgements

To my wonderful mother, Camille Siedelmann, who instilled in me a passion for reading and books. Your love and support makes all things possible.

To my fabulous critique partners: Sarah Bradley, Jenafer Dance, Nancy Dillman, Betsy Norman, Camille Siedelmann and Angie Stanton, your knowledge, critiques and support encourage and enlighten me every day. Thanks for sharing in the journey!

Special thanks to Andrew Siedelmann, Jenafer Dance and Geri Gibbons for help with research! Your wisdom brought Brigid's and Thomas's world to life! Special thanks to James Proce, Sr. who figured out the mystery of why great-grandma had snails in her sink.

This is a work of fiction. The characters, entities, incidents and dialogues are the product of the author's imagination. Any similarity to actual events, entities or persons (living or dead) is coincidental and not intended by the author. Although some actual figures and locations from history are mentioned, all are used fictitiously.

Chapter One

Brigid Mary O'Brien noted the date - April 18th, 1912 - and tried not to cry. Today should have been her wedding to David Cavanaugh. But instead of standing before a New York City justice of the peace, she stood on Pier 54 in the cold and drizzle, while David's sister, Clara, clenched her arm in a vise-like grip.

Not that Brigid could blame Clara, nor think to ask her to let go, even though she was fairly certain her arm would be bruised within hours. That didn't matter. None of it did anymore. Not the wedding, not the weather, not even the homesickness in Brigid's heart for her beloved County Donegal. The only thing that mattered now was seeing David Cavanaugh walk off the *Carpathia* and home to safety.

Deep in her heart, however, Brigid knew the chances of David surviving the sinking of the *Titanic* were slim. The latest reports on the ship's disaster said that only seven hundred people or so had been saved, mostly women and children. Thousands perished in the early morning hours of April 15th when *Titanic* sank, and Brigid prayed that David was not one of them. But, given the thousands of people on and near the pier, each waiting for a relative or friend as she and Clara did, Brigid knew odds were against them.

"Here they come!" A man a few rows ahead shouted and pointed at the *Carpathia* now docked against the pier. Brigid lifted her eyes from the rosary she held between her chilled fingers. The gigantic ship stood magnificent, illuminated by the many powder flashes from photographers who perched aboard a trailing tugboat.

Passengers crammed the *Carpathia's* deck. Brigid's heart wrenched as a gangplank lowered and they began to disembark. The crowd strained and stretched in hope of finding a loved one.

Brigid said a silent prayer that David was among the passengers. Beside her, Clara stifled a sob. Brigid patted Clara's hand, but remained silent, for what words would comfort this woman who most likely lost a brother? She was also afraid that if she tried to help Clara, her own emotion would boil up and erupt, and she might say something to upset Clara further. For, should David be dead, not only would Brigid not marry, but she'd be dependent on Clara's kindness and generosity to help her adjust to this new country. She did not know a soul here, and she didn't wish to be a burden, especially if Clara would be grieving. But without David, Brigid would be lost. He was her future. Her past was in County Donegal, to which she certainly could not return. Those bridges had been burned.

Brigid pushed the memories of home far into the recesses of her mind and returned her attention to the *Carpathia.*

"Those aren't the *Titanic* survivors." A baritone voice startled her from her thoughts. Brigid looked to her left. The voice belonged to a tall man with sun-streaked, light-brown hair, a tailored overcoat and dark bowler hat.

"No, I be supposin' not," Brigid answered.

"How do *you* know?" From somewhere behind Brigid, a woman spoke, her voice choked with accusatory anger and angst.

"They have luggage." Brigid and the gentleman spoke in unison. They turned sad glances on each other, and their eyes locked. Brigid could not help but be drawn to the compassion the man's brilliant light blue eyes conveyed. She didn't even know him, yet his sympathetic expression seemed to say he understood what was in her heart at this moment. She forced her gaze back on the ship.

Brigid watched as more passengers descended. From what she could see, the original *Carpathia* passengers wore furs or stylish coats like the one David had bought her in England. He had wanted her to look smart when she sailed with Clara on their earlier voyage over on the *Olympic*. He had given her so much in the brief time she knew him, not only a fancy coat, hat and dresses, but his unwavering love. And she hoped that one day, she'd return that love with her own. In time she'd fall in love with David Cavanaugh and repay him for helping her escape a marriage to a man of her parents' choice. But perhaps now, it was too late. If David had perished, he did so believing she loved him. She had truly wanted to.

As the last of the original *Carpathia* passengers left the ship, Brigid felt her toes begin to numb in her new, tight-fitting button shoes. Her stomach growled with hunger.

"Here come the *Titanic* survivors," said the man beside her. She nodded in acknowledgement as her throat clenched tight and her eyes welled. Many bedraggled looking women and children, and too few men, left the ship. They carried no luggage and wore makeshift clothing, most likely borrowed from *Carpathia's* passengers.

The crowd around Brigid wailed and sobbed as each survivor descended the gangplank. Waiting officers escorted the weary travelers to a nearby building.

"I don't see David." Clara spoke softly, her grip on Brigid's arm loosening.

"I don't either." Brigid blinked back tears. She could barely see the faces of the survivors, but it was heartbreakingly easy to discern that none were David. They didn't fit his height or form. He had been, or was, Brigid corrected herself, unusually tall.

"Where will they go if they have no family here?" asked woman in the crowd.

Brigid wondered the same thing and praised the saints above that she, at least, had Clara.

"Well, if they have no family or friends in America to greet them, The Travelers' Aid Society of New York, the Women's Relief Committee and other organizations are on hand to provide clothing and transportation to shelters." Again, the answer came from the man at her side. She looked at him again.

"How do you know all this?" she asked.

"I'm a medical man." He offered a kind smile. "Came to the pier to help out, but with this crowd, I can't get near the building or ship to offer my assistance." He turned his mesmerizing blue eyes on Brigid, and his voice softened. "Did you have someone on the *Titanic*?"

She glanced at the *Carpathia* and found she could not answer. She simply nodded as her tears began to fall, for David's fate now revealed itself on the ship's empty deck. The crowd around her thinned; the sounds of their heart wrenching sobs would haunt her forever.

She felt Clara let go of her arm, and Brigid hastily wiped her own tears. She must help Clara now. Whereas she had lost a future, Clara had lost a brother. And, with a most deserved rush of horrendous guilt, Brigid knew Clara's grief would be the greater.

She turned to offer Clara comfort, but to Brigid's horror, Clara slumped to a sitting position on the ground, ready to topple over.

"Clara!" Brigid stooped to catch her, but her slight frame could barely manage to keep the taller woman righted. The gentleman at Brigid's side rushed to help. He knelt beside Clara, held her upright, and gently patted her cheek to keep her from fainting full on.

Brigid knelt beside her as well and rubbed Clara's arms to keep her warm.

Brigid was relieved to find her friend conscious. "Don't worry, Clara. I'm here."

David's sister, who had treated her with nothing but kindness since they left England, slapped Brigid's hands away. She glared as if Brigid herself killed David. And when Clara finally spoke, she spewed more malice and hatred than Brigid had ever heard in her twenty-three years.

"Get your filthy hands off me, you money-grubbing Irish whore!"

~~~~~~~~~~~~~~~

Thomas Ashton felt as if he'd been slapped even though the vile insult was clearly hurled at the pretty, Irish woman. His own face burned with
~~~~~~~~~~~~~~~

embarrassment, and the shocked and hurt expression she now wore made him sorrier for her than the woman he braced upright on the wet ground.

Others on the pier turned to see who could be the recipient of these cruel words at such a mournful time. As if feeling the weight of the stares, the Irish woman rose from beside her accuser. Thomas watched helplessly as the poor thing stood frozen in her humiliation.

His heart bled for this pretty stranger. He knew the pain of loss, the look of hurt and abandonment, and a face strained from fending off tears. He'd seen it too many times in the city hospitals where he trained, and he felt as useless now as he did then. He wanted to leave the black-haired woman sitting on the pier and take the other lady into his arms. What could she possibly have done to deserve such venom?

Only a moment or two had passed since the woman's words stunned them all, but she now composed herself and glanced around. Her dark eyes flew open wide and her cheeks flushed as if shocked and surprised to discover Thomas a witness to her cruelty.

"Oh!" She pulled away from his kneeling form and sat up on her own. "I didn't realize someone was behind me."

Obviously not, Thomas thought, for her demeanor had switched in a flash. She brought a gloved hand to the back of her head and patted her hair, most of it tucked neatly under a wide- brimmed, feathered, black hat. "Forgive me. I must have fainted."

Thomas surmised not. She hadn't lost consciousness at any time, and her color was good. Too good, in fact.

"You didn't faint." He forced a small, sympathetic smile. "You may have fallen, however, as a reaction to shock." He glanced at the other woman who remained planted on the deck as if stuck in cement. He addressed her delicately. "Which might explain a few things."

He couldn't help but contrast the two women, for they could not be less alike. The one sitting had hair black as coal with eyes to match. Her tall frame was wiry thin. Her eyes were small, yet set far apart by an unfortunate hooked nose. Her alabaster skin was her only redeeming physical quality.

The other woman appeared a gentle flower in comparison. She stood about five-foot-five, and from what he could tell, filled out her coat rather pleasantly. Her hair was a wheat-colored blonde, and her almond-shaped green eyes, high cheekbones, smallish nose and rosebud shaped mouth, set a very pretty countenance indeed. Her faint accent sounded Irish, but she was far fairer than any Irish lass he'd met.

His eyes met hers. She took a deep breath, seemingly relieved by his explanation for her friend's wickedness. He wished he could do more to soothe her.

"Might you help me up, my dear fellow?" The dark-haired woman shoved a gloved hand his direction.

"Of course." He helped her to her feet, an easy task, since she was light as a hummingbird. He held her by the forearms until he was certain she'd be steady on her feet.

"Thank you." Her beady little eyes studied him as she offered a slight smile. "You must forgive my outburst. As you stated, I suppose I am in shock." The woman glanced back at the *Carpathia*. She turned wounded eyes to him. "You see, I know now that my dear brother, David, has most likely perished."

"Yes," he answered, his compassion unfeigned. "Understandable. My deepest condolences." He glanced again at the other woman who didn't move nor speak. "But, if I may be so bold, it isn't me to whom an apology is due."

The woman before him either missed his meaning or chose to ignore it. Instead, she inspected the back of her fur-collared coat. "Oh, dear. I'm terribly drenched from falling on the pier."

Thomas glanced at her coat. It was wet, but no more so than his pants or the other woman's clothing. He resisted the urge to roll his eyes and force the woman to apologize to her friend. Why was the condition of her coat more important?

The dark-haired woman suddenly seemed to regain enough strength to set aside her wardrobe concerns. She extended her hand to him. "I'm Clara Cavanaugh. To whom do I owe my gratitude for rescuing me from my own possible demise upon the pier?"

Thomas tried not to laugh at the self-imposed drama Miss Cavanaugh drafted. "You were never in danger of death. Had you hit your head, you may have acquired an unsightly bruise to the forehead, but no more than that."

"Oh." She seemed disappointed her fall hadn't been more perilous. Thomas hid a half-smile. He removed his hat and addressed both women. "I'm Thomas Ashton, and as I explained earlier to-" he turned to the blonde woman. "Forgive me, but I didn't get your name."

"Brigid's her name," Clara spat before the other woman could reply. "She was to marry David." She acknowledged the other woman with a smirk and tilt of the head. "But that's over now, too. Isn't it, Brigid?"

The blonde woman stared at her feet like a schoolgirl being reprimanded. Thomas wondered how Miss Cavanaugh could be so insensitive to her once future sister-in-law. He surmised that this Brigid not only lost her fiancé, but based on Miss Cavanaugh's rich attire, a wealthy future as well.

Thomas tried to catch Brigid's eye, but she kept her head lowered, so he talked to the top of her hat. "I'm sorry for your loss as well, miss."

She finally raised her head, her emerald eyes brimming with tears. She nodded in response and then looked away as if embarrassed by her grief.

Miss Cavanaugh continued to chatter on. Grief and shock clearly didn't stop her mouth. "Mr. Ashton, I simply must repay you for your kindness this evening."

He shook his head. "No, no, you mustn't. It was nothing."

"You saved me from hitting my head."

"But you see, Miss Cavanaugh, that's what I do. I'm studying to be a doctor."

"*Really*?" His occupation seemed to interest her more than her own brother's death.

"Really." His disdain for this woman grew ever more. "Actually, medical school is not all that impressive. In fact, it's hard as hell, but rewarding, just the same." Realizing what he just said, he made amends. "Excuse my profanity, ladies."

Miss Cavanaugh donned a smile nearly wider than her hat. "As a student, you must be starved for a good meal." She lowered her voice and spoke in a hushed whisper. "Once the mourning period is done for my dear David, you simply must come to the house for dinner. I live with my cousins, Grace and Leopold Cavanaugh, on Park Avenue. Perhaps you know of them?"

Poor dead David's body was probably lying at the bottom of the Atlantic, and his sister was setting up dinner parties? Thomas couldn't believe his ears, and from the look of disbelief on Brigid's face, neither could she.

He grit his teeth and tried to remain polite. "Yes, I've heard of your cousins." The Cavanaugh family came from "old money" and was rich as sin. "I won't hold you to that invitation, however. You'll have enough on your mind without feeling the need to repay a simple courtesy."

Was it his imagination, or did Miss Cavanaugh look more dejected at his refusal than she did about her brother's death? Either way, he would try not to pass judgment at a time like this. He knew people responded to grief in odd ways, and if inviting him to dinner took her mind off her brother for a moment, he'd let it be. And yet, he could not forgive the cruelness she had hurled at her companion.

He turned to Brigid. "And you, miss? Are you holding up all right?"

She startled, as if shocked by being addressed at all. Her voice came soft and sweet. "As well as can be expected, sir. Thank you." But, again, she would not meet his eye. He longed to hold her gaze for more than an instant.

"Brigid and I must go." Miss Cavanaugh spoke more to him than Brigid. "There's nothing more for us here." She walked with determination past them, and then quickly spun around as if realizing she'd left the forlorn woman behind.

But it was Thomas she addressed. "I do hope you'll take me up on my invitation, Mr. Ashton." She shot Brigid an irritated look. "Come, Brigid." She spoke as if Brigid were her mongrel dog. Thomas cringed.

Miss Cavanaugh headed toward the pier entrance, but Thomas stood steadfast, waiting for Brigid to pass. She took a few steps and paused, glancing up at him from under her hat. Her eyes harbored gratitude.

"Thank you," she said.

"If you need anything...well, I'm difficult to reach as I'm not home much due to my work at the hospital, Cranston, that is." He sounded like a confused idiot, and his words didn't seem to register with the woman. She stared at him, her expression blank.

He continued on, hurried and unabashed. "If you need assistance, you could send me a note at the hospital. I'm more likely to receive it there. Or, I suppose, if you have access to a telephone, you could try to call."

A slight, but grateful, smile appeared. "You're very kind."

"Brigid, the motor car is waiting!" The Cavanaugh woman yelled, although only a few feet away.

"Excuse me." Brigid brushed past him, the sleeve of her coat lightly grazing his own. He watched as she hurried to catch up with Miss Cavanaugh, and then he quietly followed behind.

A driver escorted them into one of those new Hupp-Yeats electric cars Thomas admired. Thomas could barely see Brigid through the car's windows, but as the vehicle pulled under a gaslight, he noticed her look out the window. Her expression was one of uncertainty and sorrow. He'd known her only briefly, and spoken to her even less, yet in that short time, in those few words, Thomas felt drawn to her.

The rustle and shouts of passersby jolted him back to his senses. He chided himself for thinking there could be more between him and this woman. He didn't even know her, and even worse, she'd just lost her fiancé. The last thing she needed right now was to be bothered by some medical student with nothing to offer. For all he knew, she'd disappear into the throng of New Yorkers, and he'd never see her again.

He walked to his borrowed Model T motorcar, compliments of his now deceased father. Once inside, he tried to forget the evening and his encounter with both women. Thinking of Brigid, however, helped push away the images of the *Titanic* survivors, the despair of the crowd, and his studies waiting at home.

As the car headed past Park Avenue, an idea struck, which made him happier than he deserved to be tonight.

He *would* take Miss Cavanaugh up on her dinner invitation.

If only to see Brigid again.

Chapter Two

Brigid and Clara did not speak on the ride home. As they entered the Cavanaughs' parlor, cousin Leopold, and his wife, Grace, sat fidgeting, awaiting the news. They rose from their seats, their eyes filled with hope, only to have it dashed with two words.

"David's gone." Clara's words rang somber.

Grace collapsed into sobs upon a fainting couch. Leopold knelt at her side and consoled her while wiping his own tears with a handkerchief. A young parlor maid turned pale at the news, her face screwed up as if she, too, might burst into tears.

"Fetch the brandy!" Clara snapped at the poor soul, causing her to scurry off faster than a frightened field mouse.

Brigid felt for the girl, but her heart broke for the Cavanaughs. She stepped forward to help, but Clara's hand shot out, halting her mid-step.

"This is a private matter. For family only!" Clara hissed, her words audible only to Brigid.

Brigid retreated, her every nerve awakened by Clara's cruelty. Back home, she would have spat right back, demanding to know what was wrong, but here, on foreign soil, in someone else's home, she knew best to hold her tongue. Her willfulness had brought her enough trouble before she left, and she vowed that in her new life, she'd, well… temper her temper.

But Clara's actions pained her. She couldn't believe this was the same woman she met in England and traveled with on the *Olympic.* David's sister had been nothing but kind to her, even honoring his request that Brigid stay at the Cavanaughs' until he arrived in New York. But now, Clara had changed, and Brigid couldn't imagine what she'd done to deserve her wrath.

"I was only wantin' to help." Brigid kept her voice steady and kind, no easy task. Her plea fell on deaf ears.

"Go to your room." Clara pointed at the stairwell as if Brigid were twelve, not twenty-three. "I'll speak with you in the morning."

Brigid willed her feet to turn and walk away. She was not one to flee a fight, but she did know when to surrender the battle. Still, she couldn't ignore the burning in her cheeks or the tears welling at the admonishment. She hated herself for the thought, but she was beginning to suspect that Clara was not the kindly woman she pretended to be in front of David.

A wave of fatigue engulfed her as she reluctantly climbed the staircase. Grief had certainly taken its toll on all of them. Maybe more so on Clara? Perhaps all Clara needed was a good night's sleep to be herself again. Brigid could only hope.

The next morning, Brigid stood at the guest bedroom window, pulled back the chintz drapes and peered down upon the dingy, city streets. She watched the hustle and bustle of motorcars, horse-drawn carriages, and well-dressed men walking by, presumably on their way to work. Men greeted each other with a tip of their hats; fashionably dressed women wearing long coats, feathered or flowered hats, and carrying parasols nodded politely to each other. A few men stopped to share their newspapers, pointing to the headlines, most likely more news about the sinking. They shook their heads in disbelief.

A boy rode past on a bicycle and hurled a paper toward a house across the street. As he rounded the corner, nearly skidding on the wet pavement, Brigid noted that she hadn't seen a blade of grass in nearly two weeks, not since she sailed with Clara from England. She missed the brilliant green landscapes and rolling hills of her homeland. She missed azure skies, and ominous cliffs draping the ocean. She missed the smell of an Irish spring rain. She missed the music from her father's violin at bedtime. She even missed the sheep she sheared on her parents' farm.

Perhaps she might have liked New York, had David survived to be her companion and guide to the city. But faced with only busy streets, hazy air, the stench of rotting trash and dirty pigeons, her loss compounded. She lost David, her future with him, and the country and family she abandoned an ocean away. The homesickness she ignored now raged full force. New York was dirty and gray. Ireland was color and warmth - and very far away.

Most of all, she missed her parents, six brothers and sisters and their small, stone farmhouse.

Tears threatened again, and she willed herself not to cry over the decision she had felt forced to make. Had she stayed in Ireland, her parents would have married her off to an aged, corpulent, foul-smelling farmer, Percival McGowan.

"Tis for the good of the family," her ma had pleaded against Brigid's vehement protests. "If you marry him, he'll pay all your da's debts and pay for the education of your brothers and sisters!" Oh, the guilt! But now, with poor David lost to the sea, Brigid wondered whether her decision to run might have been the wrong one.

What was it Ma used to say? Ah yes. "It is a bad hen that does not scratch for itself." Funny how angry her parents became when she told them she was leaving with David. They couldn't fathom it. David wasn't overly handsome, and while not as old as Mr. McGowan, he was still older than Brigid by a good ten years. How to explain to them that David was kind, loved her, and would save her from an awful marriage to Percival? How to explain that she hoped to love David one day? She had certainly scratched for herself, all to her ma's dismay.

Brigid straightened her shoulders and held her head high. Yes, her stubbornness certainly led her into this situation, and now, she needed to somehow peck her way out.

She turned from the window, and once again, admired the bedroom she'd been assigned to by the Cavanaughs. She sat on the edge of the huge, four-poster bed. The bedspread was pretty - white with pink and green flowers, and matching curtains. The mahogany wood of the posts matched the small vanity next to the window, as well as the chest of drawers, tall wardrobe and full-length mirror.

The Cavanaugh home, and this bedroom, the most luxurious Brigid had ever seen, were the only things she liked about New York. This house even surpassed the wealth and luxuriousness of Aunt Mildred's London home where Brigid first met David.

Brigid sighed. If she had married David, she might have lived in a house like this, with a family to fill it.

She brushed that happy time from her thoughts. Not only would the memory deepen her sorrow, but also dwelling on the past would not help her concentrate on the future and plan her survival.

Yet, here she sat, alone. She hadn't even been called to breakfast; a serving girl brought her morning meal on a plain, wooden tray. Oatmeal porridge and coffee, nothing more. Not even a biscuit or egg.

Brigid startled as the bedroom door burst opened without knock or announcement. Clara marched in, closing the door firmly behind her. Her face was expressionless, her hair parted in the middle, drawn up and fastened on each side. She wore a long-sleeved, high-collared dress of black crepe and, although clearly a mourning dress for David, Brigid couldn't help but admire the style.

"Good morning, Clara. I hope you slept well?" She tried to diminish her brogue as much as possible, remembering how David and Clara wanted her to sound more like a proper English lady, and how the accent irritated Clara in particular.

Clara did not respond, her face still a blank slate.

Brigid stood and smoothed her skirt. "I'm sorry. I don't have a proper mourning dress." She wore one of her own dark skirts and modest white blouses, hoping it was appropriate enough. She had nothing else close to suitable; her wardrobe consisted of so little - the skirts, blouses and undergarments she brought from home, and the items David bought her -three fancy dresses, a coat, shoes and a shiny black valise.

"Whatever would you need a mourning dress for?" Clara stared at her with such disdain, one would have thought Brigid killed the family cat.

A chill ran up Brigid's spine. She chose to ignore it and press on. "For the proper mourning period for David, of course."

Clara sighed, folded her hands in front of her and spoke as if explaining etiquette to a child. "You are not David's family."

Brigid felt her ire rise. She shoved it back down and spoke as if Clara's words didn't burn her soul. "I was going to be his *wife*."

"And now, you are *not*." Clara unfolded her hands, walked to the wardrobe and opened it. Brigid watched, curious, as she pulled out the dresses and coat that David had bought her. Clara draped them over her arm and turned back to Brigid. "These belong to me now, as the sole heir of my father's estate."

Brigid blinked in disbelief. "Those were gifts to me." She looked down at her plain skirt and blouse. "I'll have nothin' left but two skirts and blouses."

"Then that's all you have." Clara walked to the bedroom door, opened it, and from the hall, pulled in a worn, brown valise. It was not the lovely one David bought. "Although you can have this. I have no need for it."

Brigid glanced from her near empty wardrobe to the valise. "Where am I goin'?"

"You tell me." Clara finally smiled as if she knew some secret Brigid was supposed to guess.

Brigid shook her head. A small tendril of her hair fell from the loose knot she secured to the back of her head this morning. "Are you tossin' me out?"

"No. You're leaving." Clara kicked the valise closer to her.

Brigid felt her face flush hot, as if concealing her temper might cause her skin to burst into flames. "But I'd be havin' nowhere to go. I know not a soul here, save for you." She bit back her anger one more time and tried to appeal to the Clara who accompanied her on the trip. "Clara, what has happened? You were nearly a sister to me. For the love of God, what have I done?"

"Simple." Clara didn't move. "You didn't marry my brother. Which is just as I hoped. The last thing he needed was some poor, Irish-" Clara seemed to catch her words, "-*girl* for a wife. I don't know what he saw in you and I still don't."

"He loved me," Brigid said, her only defense. David knew she had nothing to offer him dowry-wise, but he had loved her anyway. He'd been her salvation from a horrible marriage, yet he didn't know that, and now, never would.

Clara's eyes narrowed. "David was my brother and only sibling. With our parents dead, we only had each other. Our father's recent death shook him, but then you came along. You made him happier than he'd been in a while, so I ignored my true feelings - that he was marrying a lowly farm girl with an ugly accent, ghastly manners and the social graces of a kitchen maid. I was your friend only because David asked me to be. And now, he's gone, and my little charade is done."

Brigid sat on the bed. A fight still raged within her, but the truth smacked her down. Why hadn't she seen this in Clara? Was she so blinded by David's promise of a happy and bright future in America that all she thought about was her new life?

She couldn't speak, but didn't have to.

Clara spewed forth more wrath. "And now, the family inheritance falls to me. Every penny of it." She glanced around the room. "This house becomes mine. Our father bought it for cousin Leopold when he and Grace first came here. You see, Leopold is a drunk and can't always earn a living. My father was extremely kind and forgiving that way."

Brigid wanted to retort that Clara didn't seem to take much after her father, but held her tongue. She didn't know where this conversation was headed. Brigid remembered the insult on the pier, when she'd been called 'a money-grubbing Irish whore'. Clara was wrong. Brigid hadn't agreed to marry David for his money. She needed to marry him to escape marrying Mr. McGowan. And David fell in love with her. His wealth was an unasked-for blessing.

Clara rambled on, her pace nearly manic, as if she simply thought aloud and spoke to no one in particular. "Of course, I'm not cruel. I won't boot Leopold and Grace from their home. But I will live here and manage the purse strings until I find a husband and we can buy our own home." She looked off in the distance, and Brigid wondered if Clara had a certain gentleman in mind. Then, as if remembering Brigid existed, she said, "I still don't know how the likes of you could appeal to someone as refined as my brother. He's the type of man who marries someone like *me*."

Brigid wondered if Clara was jealous that she would marry since Clara didn't have any prospects.

As if realizing she had said too much, Clara spoke between clenched teeth. "You will leave this morning."

Brigid couldn't believe Clara's words. She knew she must leave, but so soon? "But where will I go? Surely you'll let me stay here a few more days until I can figure out what to do?"

"There are the Irish tenements over on Thompson, Elizabeth and McDougal streets. Pick one." Clara reached into her dress sleeve and removed something. She walked to Brigid and held out a few small bills. "This should help you bribe one of your kind for a bed and some food. After that, I'm sure you'll know how to get by." The smirk on Clara's face told Brigid exactly how Clara expected her to "get by".

Brigid resisted the urge box her ears, but despite her money-poor upbringing, she had pride and knew how to be a lady.

She stood and stared Clara down. "I'll not be takin' your money."

Clara smiled. "Suit yourself, you proud, stupid girl." She turned on her heels and marched to the door, clearly thinking herself the victor.

Brigid could not help but get in a parting shot. Her proper lady took a back seat to her true Irish soul. "You're a lying, old spinster!" It wasn't the best of insults, but it hit home. Clara stopped, her hand on the doorknob.

Brigid waited for more verbal daggers to soar her way, but to her surprise, Clara drew a deep breath, righted her shoulders and, without another word, walked out.

For several long moments, Brigid stared at the closed door, the events of these past two weeks replaying over and over in her head. Finally, the emotional turmoil - the excitement, happiness, then tragedy, despair and now devastation, took its toll. She threw herself upon the beautiful, expensive bedspread and cried.

Chapter Three

Brigid was unaware how long she had cried, but when a gentle knock sounded on the guest bedroom door, she pulled her head off the wet pillow, wiped her eyes and tried to gather strength. She expected the visitor to be Clara, demanding she leave at once.

"Come in." Her throat weak from crying, she barely croaked the words.

To Brigid's surprise, plump Grace Cavanaugh, not spindly Clara, entered and closed the door softly behind her. She walked to the bed, handed Brigid a handkerchief and offered a sympathetic smile.

"Thank you," Brigid sniffled. She managed to right herself to a sitting position. "I'm sorry I'm still here. I know I'm supposed to be goin'."

"There, there." The woman patted her hand and sat down next to her on the bed's edge. Her warm, soft touch reminded Brigid of her ma. "Don't worry about leaving just yet. I'm not here to toss you out."

Brigid wiped the last of her tears as Grace continued. "Clara went out with Leopold to the White Star offices to see if a passenger roster might confirm that David had been aboard the Titanic. It's futile, I suspect. David would have been in contact with us by now if he wasn't."

Brigid nodded in agreement, and her heart hurt for David. He was a kind, generous spirit, and didn't deserve this tragic fate. Brigid missed his friendship and wished she could have loved him. He deserved that.

"But," Grace said, patting Brigid's hand again. "It's good for those two to have something to do. And I'm sure that office will be full with inquiries today, so I doubt Clara will return for an hour or two." She took Brigid's hand between her own. "That will give us time to talk."

Brigid could only nod while her throat clenched tight with apprehension. She wanted to trust Grace, but her recent encounter with Clara left her wary. Dare she confide in this seemingly caring woman? She and Grace had barely conversed since Brigid met her a few days ago. Although they dined together at the house these past weeks, Clara dominated the conversations, even when Grace or Leopold directly asked Brigid a question. But Grace had always seemed open to Brigid, as if, had Clara allowed her a word, she'd like to get to know her. Grace seemed about sixty; her graying hair swept up into various puffs, rolls and twists, all held together by a jeweled comb. Her eyes were round, bright and ready with empathy and understanding.

Brigid swallowed her fear and forged ahead. After all, she had nothing left to lose.

"Clara says I must leave." She gripped the handkerchief with her free hand. "I'm to go to the Irish tenements."

Grace nodded. "I know. I heard."

"Clara told you?"

"No." Grace smiled as if a child with a secret. "I stood outside in the hall this morning. I couldn't help myself. I was passing by and heard the conversation and wondered why my old valise was outside your door."

"Oh." Brigid's cheeks burned. To think that someone else heard that awful row! She hung her head. "I wasn't any better than Clara, I fear, and may the dear Lord forgive me. I called her a spinster."

"Well, it won't be long until she is one, poor thing."

"Oh." Brigid tried to feel sorry for Clara, but couldn't. Not after the way the spinster had treated her.

Grace continued on, as if thinking aloud. "I imagine it makes Clara bitter. Several times she's been close to a proposal, only to have her suitor snatched away by a prettier thing."

"Oh, I see," Brigid said, thinking she'd gladly trade Percival McGowan to Clara in exchange for room and board. "I'm sorry." She would need to go to confession for that lie.

Her eyes fell on the ugly valise that still sat in the middle of the floor. "You can have your valise back, if you want it." She looked the other way.

"There, there," Grace said, and let go of Brigid's hand. "The bag is not my concern here, dear." She cupped Brigid's chin and turned her face until Brigid met her compassionate eyes. "I was wicked for eavesdropping, but I'm mighty pleased I did." She laughed, remembering. "And when Clara suddenly opened the door to grab that valise, oh my!" Grace laughed harder and fanned a hand in front of her face. "I had to flatten myself against the wall so she wouldn't see me! Imagine!" Grace tittered with laughter and Brigid could not help but smile at the image of the round woman trying to inhale herself thin.

Grace calmed herself. "Anyhow, I've come to help you. You were David's fiancé. If he loved you, Leopold and I love you. I can't imagine why Clara is treating you so poorly."

"Thank you." Grace's words touched her heart. Brigid took a deep breath and exhaled what felt like two weeks worth of emotional turmoil. "I just need a few days to figure out where to go and what to do."

"Are you thinking of returning to Ireland?" Grace said. "Or perhaps England? I know that's where you met David. I'm a bit confused as to your exact origins, my dear."

"It is confusing," Brigid said. "My family is from Ireland. The town of Donegal in County Donegal to be exact. But I have an aunt who lived in London. I stayed with her there, as her companion." Brigid sighed, remembering. She hated those visits, for even though Aunt Mildred treated her kindly, her uncle never ceased to remind her that she was just a poor relation.

"I see," Grace said. "And how did you meet David then? Oh wait, it must have been when he visited his father in England?"

"Yes, we met at a flower show. David's father was healthy then. He knew my uncle. When David's father heard my aunt took sick, he and David paid visits."

"Ah," Grace said, a smile of satisfaction forming on her full lips. "And that's when you and David fell in love."

Brigid fell silent wishing to go no further with this conversation. Yes, her story should be that she and David fell in love, but of course, that wasn't true. She didn't fall for David, but he fell in love with her.

Grace continued, seemingly nonplussed by Brigid's silence. "So then, David proposed and off you came to America! I'm sure your parents were thrilled to have you make such a fine match!"

Brigid folded her hands together in her lap and looked down. "No, they weren't happy at all."

"Why? Whatever was the matter with David?"

Brigid smiled. "Oh, there was nothin' wrong with David, except he wasn't the man they wanted me marryin'. They expected me to marry some old farmer friend of theirs."

"But I thought those arranged marriages were a thing of the past!" Grace's eyes opened wide with surprise.

"Mostly they are," Brigid said. "But my family is poor. We own a farm, but my da isn't much of a farmer." *He's more of a drinker*, she wanted to say, but kept the secret to herself. "My ma helps out with the farmin', does most of the work, but she also has my younger brothers and sisters to take care of."

"Was the man they wanted you to marry wealthy?" Grace seemed genuinely interested in Brigid's background, so Brigid continued.

"Yes, very. His farm was very prosperous." Brigid turned to Grace hoping she might understand her situation. "But he was nearin' fifty, fat and smelled!"

Grace nodded sympathetically. "Did you explain your feelings to your parents?"

"Jesus, Mary and Joseph, I did!" Brigid had not been able to control her temper that day, hollerin' and wailin' at her parents when she heard the news. "But, you see, in exchange for me as his bride, he offered to pay off my da's debts and for the learnin' of my five younger brothers and sisters, a deal too good for my parents to be passin' up."

"I see," Grace said. "But, you ended up with David, instead. Good choice." Grace suddenly gasped, her eyes welling with tears. "Oh dear! I mean you didn't! I'm so sorry."

It was Brigid's turn to comfort the older woman. She took Grace's hand in her own. "It's all right. I know your meanin'."

"I just don't understand why Clara is being so cruel to you," Grace said, both women obviously relieved to have the conversation directed back to the current problem. "The tenements, really! I was so shocked and angered when she said that to you, I nearly marched in the room and slapped my cousin."

Brigid tried not to laugh at the image of the plump and petite Grace Cavanaugh knockin' Clara a good one.

"I've done something for you, my dear." Grace pulled a piece of paper from her pocket. "Whatever you decide to do, you'll need money. I'd give you some myself, but as Clara so 'delicately' told you, Leopold keeps our funds tied up."

"Oh, no, that's quite all right," Brigid said, thinking of her da and understanding completely how taking to the drink ruins things. She accepted the folded piece of paper and opened it to find an address written on it.

"After I quit my eavesdropping, I spoke with the household staff to see about finding you employment."

A flicker of hope ignited in Brigid's heart.

Grace continued and pointed to the paper. "That the address for a Mr. Charles Ransom, on Fifth Avenue, across from Central Park. Lovely home, I hear. I don't know the family, but our cook says they're in dire need of a maid, someone to watch over the missus, who, rumor has it, is not quite right in the mind."

Brigid paused. How had things come to this? Three weeks ago she looked forward to a new life as David's wife, a life full with promise - and now the best she could hope for was a maid position? Perhaps it served her right. Perhaps she was never meant to have more than she could find in Ireland, and this was God's way of sending her home? Still, why would David need to suffer because of her sinful ways?

Brigid felt ill. No matter what she faced, her fate would never be worse than David's. She should be lucky to secure a lady's maid job. She should be grateful to be alive.

She smiled at dear Mrs. Cavanaugh. "Thank you! Do you really think they'll hire me?"

"Chances are good." Grace rose from the bed. "Cook says they are desperate to find someone. I guess no one wants to tend a crazy lady."

"I'll do it!" Brigid jumped off the bed and grabbed the valise. "I'll go right away." She turned to Grace who began to remove Brigid's sparse belongings from the wardrobe. "You have been so kind, Mrs. Cavanaugh. I don't know how I'll ever repay you."

"Be happy, my dear. That's how." The woman smiled cheerfully as she helped Brigid pack the valise.

Hope bloomed in Brigid's heart. Perhaps if she saved enough money, she could buy a ticket back home!

Or not. All would depend on her parents. She needed to write them.

"Mrs. Cavanaugh, I need to be askin' another favor."

"Please ask." Grace turned from folding Brigid's old nightgown.

"May I be borrowin' pencil, paper and postage? I'll pay you back when I can."

Grace studied Brigid's face. "Yes, but that's hardly a favor to be nervous about asking." She turned back to the closet. "You don't have a coat?" Grace searched the closet as if Brigid hid it.

She hung her head. "No, Clara took it." The absent coat reminded her again of how very little she actually owned and the last time she wore it. The image of the handsome man with the brilliant blue eyes at the dock flashed through Brigid's mind. Hadn't he mentioned something about an organization that aided *Titanic* victims? Perhaps they might help her, but she couldn't recall the organization's name.

She turned to Grace again. "May I be sendin' two letters?" She would write to the nice man. She remembered his name, Thomas Ashton. At Cranston Hospital, he had said.

"Of course." Grace finished the last of the packing. "You can come into my bedroom and write your letters. I will post them in the morning for you. When you've finished, I'll have our driver take you to Ransom House."

"Thank you." Brigid picked up the valise. She would be forever grateful to Grace Cavanaugh and God for answering her prayers.

Grace linked her arm through Brigid's as they walked to the door. "I suppose you'll be writing your folks?"

"I will write my parents." She wanted to go home, but only on one condition.

She would not marry Percival McGowan. If her parents could not agree, then by Heaven, she'd stay in New York and somehow create a life for herself.

But, it was that "somehow" that scared her witless.

Chapter Four

The Cavanaugh's chauffeur helped Brigid from the motorcar and handed her the valise. He nodded at the corner mansion. "That's the house then, miss."

"Thank you." Brigid stared at the vast expanse of home that stood seven stories tall. Despite its grand and imposing appearance, she inwardly denounced it as vulgar. The formal brick building with its many-paned windows, rooftop balustrade, scrolled stone doorframe and sidewalk moat deemed cold and unwelcoming.

"Good-day then." The chauffeur tipped his hat and hurried back into the car.

Brigid opened the valise to retrieve a letter of reference Grace wrote for her. It had been awfully kind of Mrs. Cavanaugh to write it, considering she barely knew Brigid, but Grace insisted. As Brigid reached for the letter, she found yet another envelope hidden in the valise. Curious, she opened it to discover a few dollars, another note from Mrs. Cavanaugh and the address of a women's boarding house. Grace wrote that Brigid was to use the money for a few nights' rent.

Brigid nearly wept. Grace must have parted with some of her own scarce money to do this. She vowed to pay the dear lady back.

She tucked the money back in the bag and retrieved the letter of reference. She was to hand it to a Mrs. Latimer who, the Cavanaughs' cook said, hired the maids. Brigid stared at the massive house and said a silent prayer. She needed this job more than anything. She thought back to the letters she left with Mrs. Cavanaugh to post, hoping that, should this interview fail, she still had Mr. Ashton's or her parents' help to rely on. Unsure of her lodgings for the next few days, she had asked them to post their replies to Mrs. Cavanaugh.

Battling the butterflies in her stomach, Brigid gathered her courage and walked to the cement steps. Rain fell once more, and she sighed, wondering if she would ever see a sunny day again.

She reached the landing and rang the bell. She waited several long moments in her rain-dampened dress before the doors opened.

An elderly man, tall, willowy and balding, whom Brigid assumed by his waistcoat, vest and black tie to be the butler, looked her up and down.

"Yes?"

"My name is Brigid Mary O'Brien, and I've come for the lady's maid position."

The man said nothing, but stared down his patrician nose as if she smelled bad.

She continued, praying words would not fail her, and hoping for admittance out of the rain. "I'm to see Mrs. Latimer." She held out the reference note. Her hand shook, betraying her false confidence. "I have a-"

"You'll need to use the servants' entrance."

"Pardon?"

"The likes of you can't enter through *this* door." He looked at her as if she were an irritating fly he'd sooner swat than allow into the elegant home.

Brigid looked to her left and right. She couldn't see any servants' entrance. She swallowed, her voice failing her. She'd meant to be strong, show what a brave and upstanding lady's maid she could be, but now she could barely stand up to this snobby butler.

"I don't know where that entrance is, sir." She feared getting lost on the property.

The man bent close to her. He smelled like mothballs, and his breath reeked foul as he shouted. "What did you say? Speak up, miss!" He pointed to his right ear. "I can't hear very well."

"I said," she yelled, fueled by adrenaline and frustration, *"that I don't be knowin' where the servants' entrance is!"*

The butler stepped back so fast, Brigid was certain he'd fall right over. She almost wished he would. Then she'd step over him, march into the house and …and…she had no idea what she'd do.

"Good Lord, Henry, what's all the commotion?" A deep voice roared from somewhere in the dark hall behind them.

"Nothing, sir," Henry replied over his shoulder. "No need to concern yourself. Just someone for the lady's maid position. I'll take care of it." He turned back to her. "Go back outside the gate and follow it around the corner and to the courtyard. You'll see steps leading down to a door. *That* will be *your* entrance."

Brigid glanced down the block. She'd look like a wet rat by the time she made it to *her* door, assuming she'd find it at all in this rain. Tears threatened to betray her pent up frustration. It had already been a long, emotional day and her temper fused short. Still, she needed to stay calm if she had any hope of being hired.

Perhaps it was her welling tears, but Henry suddenly seemed to take pity on her. "I'll get you an umbrella."

He walked away leaving the door slightly ajar. She heard a bang and loud clattering from the hall. She was tempted to peer in, but didn't want to risk her unworthy head appearing in the *wrong* door.

Henry returned, totally flustered, and shoved a black umbrella at her. "Here. I knocked the entire umbrella stand over getting you this."

"I'm extremely grateful," Brigid said, biting back her sarcasm.

"For Heaven's sake, Henry, what is all the racket?" The angry, menacing voice boomed again as a tall, broad-shouldered man with thick black hair and mustache, bushy eyebrows and deep-set blue eyes, appeared at Henry's side. The man's six-foot three stature was regal, his presence imposing, his expression unsmiling. Brigid fought the urge to turn and run. Even Henry seemed to visibly quake in this man's presence.

"My apologies, sir," Henry said, his face turning ashen and his voice shaky. "I was just informing this young woman to go around back and use the servants' door to see Mrs. Latimer."

The door opened wider and the man stepped forward. He sized Brigid up and down with a glance that lingered too long on her hips and chest. She felt her cheeks burn despite the chill in the air. She willed her hands not to shake.

"Is that our umbrella, Henry?"

Henry's eyes went wide. "I lent it to her so she wouldn't get wet walking around the building, sir."

"I don't be needin' it!" Brigid thrust the umbrella toward the men. They'd not be getting into an argument about whether or not she could borrow a stupid umbrella!

It was the dark-haired man's turn to look startled. He took the umbrella and burst into amused laughter. "You stupid woman! Get out of the rain!" He took her by the forearm and firmly pulled her through the door. He shot the butler an exasperated glance. "Really, Henry. Did you expect this mouse to walk to the back in this weather, umbrella or not? She'll catch her death! The last thing we need is another sick servant."

Henry's face flushed. Brigid actually felt sorry that he'd been admonished on her behalf. He looked at Brigid. "Forgive me, miss. I was just following house protocol."

"Yes, yes you were, my good man," the other man said. "But in this case, I think exceptions can be made." He smiled at Brigid. "I'm Charles Ransom, owner of Ransom House. You are seeking employment?"

Brigid nodded.

"I assume you've been referred?"

Her stomach a flutter, she dropped the valise and showed him the note. "Yes, from Mrs. Grace Cavanaugh. Her cook knows your cook."

"Humph." The man took the note, his fingers brushing her own. Brigid quickly pulled her hand away.

Mr. Ransom skimmed the note. "I don't know Grace Cavanaugh personally, I did know Clara Cavanaugh, briefly. Any relation?"

She'd rather not go into that story…at least not right now. But she certainly didn't want him talking to Clara about her. "Yes, Grace Cavanaugh is Clara's cousin. But I don't really know her," she lied. "Just Mrs. Cavanaugh, sir."

"Ah." Mr. Ransom read the note again and then his cobalt blue eyes settled on her. His glance traveled from her wet and disheveled hair, to the frayed and soaked hem of her skirt. When his eyes met hers again, his smile sent a chill up her spine. She knew she should take this feeling as a warning. Her ma always said she had a good sense of others. And Brigid usually did…that is, until she met Clara. Maybe her sixth-sense didn't work with Americans? What was it Ma always said? Oh yes, "Seeing is believing, but feeling is God's own truth. Go with your feelings, Brigid Mary!"

"You don't have a coat, Miss O'Brien?" Mr. Ransom's observation interrupted her suspicious musing. He didn't seem lecherous now, just concerned about her lack of a coat. Perhaps fatigue overwhelmed the best of her senses?

"I must have left it in the Cavanaugh's motor car," she lied. No need to let on how piss poor she really was, or how desperate. She heard of people using information like that to their own advantage against the downtrodden. She prided herself for being smarter than that.

"I see." Charles Ransom turned to Henry. "I'll interview Miss O'Brien in my study." He turned to Brigid, his manner business-like. "Henry will bring your bag along."

"But, sir," Henry said, his expression aghast. "I'm sure Mrs. Latimer would be happy to interview the woman."

"Were my orders not clear, Henry? Bring Miss O'Brien's valise into my study and bring us tea. Mrs. Latimer need not concern herself at present. Should the girl be hired, we'll contact her then."

"Yes, sir." Henry picked up Brigid's bag and headed down the hall.

"Now then." Charles turned intense eyes on Brigid and offered a reassuring smile. He motioned for her to follow him down the long, marble-floored hall. Brigid hesitated. Something told her to turn and run, yet her dire situation forced her to stay. After all, where would she run to? And with what? Henry now held her valise, and the small bit of money hidden within, hostage.

Mr. Ransom realized she hadn't immediately followed. He turned and snapped, "Are you coming?"

She had no choice. She moved quickly to follow him into a room on the right.

Charles slid open the heavy, wood-paneled doors, each disappearing into the adjacent walls. His study was luxurious, magnificent and immaculate. One wall was made up entirely of shelves and held more books than Brigid thought existed in the whole of Ireland. On another wall, rose-colored damask curtains covered floor-to-ceiling windows; giant portraits of men in powdered wigs lined another. Brigid tried to appear unimpressed, but the warmth from a roaring fireplace could not be ignored. How she wished to sit in front of it and dry her dress!

As if reading her mind, Mr. Ransom pulled a high-backed, winged chair from behind a large mahogany desk and placed it near the fire.

"Sit, Miss O'Brien," he commanded.

She sat. If he didn't care that she dampened his velvet cushions, neither would she.

He pulled up an identical chair and placed it opposite her. Henry arrived with the tea set, a silver pot with matching tray, and delicately painted white china cups with a floral pattern. Henry poured and offered the first cup to Mr. Ransom, who deferred it to Brigid. She accepted the warm liquid whole-heartedly, wishing to gulp it down and squash her chill. But, remembering her parlor manners, she sipped it lady-like.

Charles Ransom's eyes followed her every move, but he didn't speak until Henry left the room.

"So, Miss O'Brien," he began as he seated himself. "Tell me about yourself and why you want this position. I detect an Irish accent, yes?"

"Yes. I'm from County Donegal." She placed her teacup and spoon back on the tray Henry left and tried to organize her thoughts. The last thing she wanted Mr. Ransom to know was that she planned to work for him only long enough to afford a ticket home.

"An immigrant, then?" His words were kind, as if he really took interest in her.

She looked at her hands. "Yes."

"I see." He paused as if pondering the next question. "Are you here with family?"

She thought of Clara.

"No." It wasn't a lie. Clara never was family in the legal sense.

"Ah. Excellent."

His answer confused Brigid, and her puzzlement must have shown, for Mr. Ransom quickly explained, "Nothing to distract you from your work here, then, you see."

She smiled in response. So far, so good.

"How do you know Grace Cavanaugh?"

She had to think fast. If she said her fiancé recently died, Mr. Ransom might suspect she'd be returning to Ireland. "I worked for Mrs. Cavanaugh," she lied. Heck, if Grace could lend her a fake reference, Brigid could certainly invent the fake lady's maid position to go along with it.

"Then, you must have met Clara Cavanaugh," Mr. Ransom surmised. Brigid felt her frustration grow. What did her relations with the Cavanaughs have to do with hiring her?

"Yes." She answered politely, keeping her anxiety in check.

"Are you close with Clara?"

Brigid stifled a sarcastic laugh, but answered honestly. "No, we don't speak as I am below her station, and she wants nothin' to do with me."

"That's the Clara I knew!" Charles laughed. "So, I know you're not lying to me."

"No sir." *Not quite.*

"She had a brother, didn't she? A rather nice fellow…David, I think?" Charles looked her straight in the eye. "And how is he?"

Brigid's breath caught in her throat. Mr. Ransom would never know how difficult this innocent question was for her to answer.

Her words came out in a whisper. "He died, sir. On the *Titanic*."

"Oh!" Charles's eyes went wide with what appeared to be genuine shock. "I hadn't heard about him being aboard. I've been away."

It took all Brigid's will power not to tear up. But she couldn't betray her feelings. Too much depended on her staying strong.

Mr. Ransom cleared his throat. "And, you're not married? No children?"

Why did he keep harping on her relations? Didn't he want to know her qualifications, of which of course, she didn't have many. "No. No husband or children."

"Where are you living?"

Another strange question. As long as she could do the job, what did it matter where she lived?

"A ladies' boarding house." *Which hopefully, is near a church and confessional, with all this lyin' I'm doin'.*

Mr. Ransom's mustache twitched as if the answer displeased him. He looked from her wet dress to her valise. "The boarding houses are a bit far from here."

Well, she had no idea.

"I'd be wary of you traveling back and forth. Seems to me the weather or other hazards might make you late for the job each day."

She hadn't thought of that when she lied.

"Would you consider taking a room in my home in the servants' quarters instead?" He smiled. "That is, if I offer you the position."

She bit back her enthusiasm over a decent place to live, and pretended to consider the offer. "Yes, I suppose I could be doin' that."

"How old are you, Miss O'Brien?"

"Twenty-four."

Mr. Ransom smiled. "When can you start?"

She fell silent and chewed her lip, thinking. She said she lived at a boarding house. Would it seem awkward if she asked to start her employment right now? Surely, Mr. Ransom must be desperate for someone to look after his insane wife.

Again, as if reading her thoughts, Charles Ransom said, "We could use you right away."

"Yes, of course." She smiled, grateful, wondering what kind of life he led with a mentally unstable wife. Part of her pitied him, but another part warned her to stay wary.

He rose and motioned Brigid to follow. "Grab your things. I'll send for Henry and he can take you to the kitchen to meet the cook, Mrs. Duffy."

Brigid nearly skipped to the door. "Thank you, but I'm really not hungry."

Charles Ransom turned, and his smile faded. "I'm not offering you a meal. You'll be working there as a kitchen maid."

Brigid felt the blood drain from her face. A kitchen maid! The lowest of the low and the most poorly paid! It would take her forever to save for a ticket home! She'd be stuck in this dismal, ugly city forever!

"A kitchen maid?" She could barely speak. "But I came for the lady's maid position!"

"Tsk, tsk." Charles shook his head and smiled, but this time his smile bordered on wicked. "No lady's maid job is available for your sort, I'm afraid. You will scrub the pots and pans like the rest of your kind, but…" He looked her up and down again. "You do have potential."

With that, Charles Ransom exited the room, leaving Brigid alone, shocked and wondering what the devil he meant. She looked longingly down the hall at the front door. She then looked in the opposite direction to find Henry approaching to escort her to the kitchen.

She needed to decide to stay or leave. It was then she remembered the letters she wrote. She hoped either her parents or Mr. Ashton might soon respond, but they needed to know where to find her.

She pondered trying to find a boarding house this evening now that dusk had fallen. The money she had would not pay for both a carriage and a night's rent, and she doubted she had the strength left to walk in the pouring rain and find the boarding house.

Her immediate future looked bleak.

Brigid made the only decision she could. She picked up her valise and marched down the hall, meeting old Henry halfway.

Chapter Five

Charles Abraham Ransom III didn't believe he was an evil man. He thought himself a very good man, a hard-working man, a man who simply wanted and procured the best. Money afforded him this privilege; he had earned his fortune through banking and railroad investments.

He liked to think, however, that he put his socks and shoes on just like every other fellow in New York, but of course, *his* socks and garters were imported from a small shop in Rome, and his shoes, the finest patent leather. He'd have it no other way.

His home reflected his style too, of course. Ransom House, handed down to Charles by his father, was an opulent seven story, fourteen-bedroom mansion, standing proudly on Millionaire's Row. Socially, he and his beautiful wife, the former Eliza Markeson, an heiress in her own right, rubbed elbows with New York's finest and wealthiest: J. P. Morgan, Andrew Carnegie, Henry Clay Frick, and, up until the *Titanic* disaster, the Astors. Unfortunately John J. Astor had perished in the sinking, leaving his vast fortune to his young, pregnant wife.

As if losing his friend was bad enough, the *Titanic* tragedy reminded Charles of his own pressing need for an heir, for there was no one, save Eliza, to inherit his vast fortune. And, given Eliza's fragile state, her greedy Markeson relatives might swoop in, declare her mentally unfit and take charge. Before he'd let that happen, he'd personally return from the grave and murder them all.

This need for a son or daughter pervaded his every waking thought. And, until Brigid O'Brien appeared on his doorstep penniless and desperate, he'd seen no way to solve the problem.

As if confirming that yesterday's woes and rain were a thing of the past, a ray of sunlight peeped through Charles's bedroom curtains, encouraging him to rise and begin his day. A moment later, at exactly at seven-thirty sharp, Theodore Glass, Charles's valet, knocked lightly on the bedroom door and entered with a breakfast tray, coffee and newspaper. While Charles ate and read, Glass laid out Charles's suit, tie and shoes.

Conversation with the valet covered the latest news stories in paper, mostly all related to the Titanic tragedy.

With breakfast finished, Charles dressed. Satisfied he looked his best, he left the room, leaving Glass to tidy it. The next order of business brought him to his wife's room for a good morning kiss and a check with Mrs. Archer, her nurse, to see how Eliza's night had been. He hoped she had slept, but a quick shake of the nurse's head told him that once again, sleep eluded Eliza. She had, instead, roamed the halls of Ransom House, a slave to melancholia and insomnia.

This morning, however, she slept. He walked to her bed, pulled away the wisps of dark auburn hair that fell across her alabaster skin and kissed her cheek lightly so as not to wake her. *Eliza.* How he loved his beautiful, but lost, Eliza. She was the one broken thing that he could not fix. He would do anything to bring back the bright-eyed, whimsical, carefree woman he married. He missed his delightful and intelligent wife. She'd been the perfect complement to him, her ethereal beauty stood out against his dark good looks; her kindness, laughter and wit making her the perfect hostess to their high-society friends. The men were jealous of him, the women wanted to be her. She was everything, but most importantly, *his* everything, the one thing he truly loved. But, in one tragic moment, he had lost her through his own folly and stubbornness, and lost her to grief.

The clock on Eliza's fireplace mantle chimed the time, reminding Charles he was due at the bank. After a few words with Mrs. Archer, he left Ransom House in his chauffeur-driven car and headed to the First Financial Bank of New York, which he owned.

His business day was filled with meetings, but his mind could not stay focused. After two years, Eliza was no better than the day she learned their tragic news.

After his unproductive day at work, Charles dined with business associates, followed by drinks and cigars. Finally, he headed home to sit with Eliza. Perhaps he'd read poetry to her this evening. Emily Dickinson and T.S. Eliot were her favorites, but whether or not she enjoyed listening to Charles read, he never knew. Still, he read.

He found Eliza in her room, sitting in her rocking chair by the fire. Her long, copper curls were drawn back into a loose, white ribbon, and she still wore the ivory-colored nightgown from this morning. A crocheted beige shawl draped across her shoulders. She looked up as he walked in, her large eyes sad and haunting, but she quickly returned her attention to the fire.

"She hasn't said a word at all today, sir." Mrs. Archer's voice startled him. He turned to find the nurse replacing Eliza's water pitcher.

"I see." She wouldn't speak to him either, of course. There was no use trying. He walked over. Her hand lay on the armrest, and he covered it gently with his own. She pulled hers away.

Charles turned back to the nurse.

"Perhaps we won't read this evening after all." He put his hands in his pockets as if Eliza's withdrawal had burned them.

"It's best, sir," Mrs. Archer answered. "I think she could do with the quiet."

He glanced at his wife a final time. "I'll be in my study," he said, as if she might care.

Charles headed to his sanctuary, his study. Henry had started a roaring fire in the hearth. Charles drew his chair near and lit a cigar. A brandy also had been set on a nearby table and he was grateful. It would help him make sense of what he needed to do.

He took up the glass and swirled the dark amber liquid. Slowly he took a sip, the warmth of both drink and fire relaxing him, encouraging his thoughts.

Eliza's melancholia was no better. Dr. Stouch had tried everything to break her illness, but to no avail. He had even suggested institutionalizing her temporarily, but Charles would not hear of it. He couldn't bear to have her away from him.

Nagging thoughts that he was to blame for her condition rose up like a viper from its nest. Another sip of brandy helped quell the thoughts, replacing them instead with his own plan on how to cure Eliza.

The solution became clear the moment the pretty, yet demure, Brigid O'Brien entered Ransom House. She had walked off the New York City streets as if an angel sent to answer his prayers. One glance at the alluring blonde, who appeared to be older and more sensible than his other maids, and his plan formed. She would give him and Eliza the one thing they needed most, another child.

A rush of guilt stormed his mind, for Eliza *had* given him an heir - a son, Tobias, two years ago. Her pregnancy had been such a happy time for them both until Tobias's birth. One look at his son, with his short fingers, space between the toes, low set ears and other disconcerting features, and Charles's worst fears materialized. His son was a mongoloid. Dr. Stouch confirmed that Tobias would never function at a normal intellectual level, and Charles had stormed out of the house unable to hear the rest. He could not accept this child as his son. He was an embarrassment, a flaw in Charles's otherwise perfect world.

Unknown to Eliza, he signed papers to have the baby institutionalized. Eliza awoke the next day to an empty crib and the news that her son had unexpectedly died. She didn't believe Charles or Dr. Stouch. She begged and cried for them to tell her where her baby was. Charles tried to soothe her with the promise of other children, but she was not, nor would she ever be, consoled. Eliza failed to conceive again, eventually refusing to share the marriage bed. Adoption was out of the question. Charles couldn't imagine leaving his fortune to someone not of his own bloodline. He needed to accept that he'd have no heir. But of course, he couldn't. Charles Ransom always got what he wanted, and what he wanted was his own child and to make Eliza whole again.

Brigid O'Brien could give him that child. He would get his heir, and Eliza would have another baby. She could forget Tobias and be happy again. As for Miss O'Brien? Well, she was poor, desperate and all alone. The promise of money should lure her into doing as he asked.

Of course, she might refuse. Which would be unfortunate for her. He would get what he wanted or simply take it.

But Charles Ransom was not an evil man.

At least *he* didn't think so.

Chapter Six

Thomas Ashton adjusted his black bow tie for the tenth time since arriving at Cavanaugh House, one of the smaller homes in the wealthy Park Avenue district. He double-checked his clothing, making sure his trousers only sported the creases he put into them with a trouser press. He straightened his checkered waistcoat and verified that the wings of his white shirt collar lay flat. When satisfied that he could no longer improve one iota of his appearance, he touched his silk top hat for good luck and rang the bell.

Within minutes, a young maid answered the door.

He removed his hat. "Good afternoon. I'm Thomas Ash-"

Before he could finish his introduction, the maid, with a frantic wave of her hand, motioned him into the modest-sized, but pristinely decorated home. "I know who you are, Mr. Ashton, sir. The lady of the house has been practically climbing the curtains waiting for you!" She took his hat and overcoat and all but pushed him into the parlor. "But you never heard that from me."

"My lips are sealed." Thomas smiled at the frantic, little redheaded woman who scurried about in uniform and apron like a nervous chicken.

"I'll tell Miss Cavanaugh you're here." She bustled toward a door on the other side of the room. "She'll probably knock the others over in a rush to see you. Oh the extra fuss we had to make over dinner tonight!" The maid turned, a horrified look upon her face. "Oh, don't be telling her I said that either!"

Thomas laughed. "I won't."

The maid relaxed and returned the smile, her cherubic face blushing a deep pink. "I can see why she likes you, Mr. Ashton." She curtsied quickly and left the room.

Alone in the parlor, Thomas's stomach rumbled but he wasn't sure if it was from hunger, excitement, nerves or all three.

The hunger was easily explained. He had classes at the hospital early today, no time for breakfast and barely enough time to change into his evening clothes. His excitement was in anticipation of seeing Miss O'Brien again, and his nervousness stemmed from his false pretense in accepting dinner with the off-putting Miss Cavanaugh, when it was only Brigid he longed to see.

Brigid's woeful eyes that night on the pier still haunted him. A few days after that first meeting, he'd been excited to hear from her. He carried the letter with him now and removed it from his trousers' pocket. Her words left him curious because she asked for the names and addresses of the organizations he mentioned on the dock. From her dress and manners that evening, he thought her to be somewhat wealthy. Yet her letter was written in broken English and her request for help seemed odd. She'd been David Cavanaugh's fiancée, so surely his family would take care of her after Mr. Cavanaugh's passing. Perhaps her inquiry was for others left desperate in the aftermath of the *Titanic's* sinking? The thought touched his heart. He'd like to think she was like him, someone who truly cared for the less fortunate.

Thomas had planned to write her back and ask if he could pay her a visit. But before his studies allowed him the time to do so, another letter came, the dinner invitation from Clara. He'd been shocked to receive it, for the invitation arrived less than a week after David's funeral mass. A friend at the hospital who knew David had attended the service.

Thomas's stomach rumbled again. He returned Brigid's letter to his pocket and pulled his timepiece from his waistcoat. For someone so eager to see him, Miss Cavanaugh certainly took her time welcoming him.

No sooner had he returned the watch to his pocket, and she entered the room. Thomas tried to hide his shock. The mourning period for her dear brother was certainly over.

Clara wore a sleeveless, pink silk dress with floral embroidery, over which draped a black tulle cape decorated with black and crystal beads, silver sequins, and tassels flowing from the shoulders. An ebony lace flower cinched the sheer fabric at her waist. Her black hair was swept up and curled under a beaded, tulled cap, and her make-up was simple.

Thomas had to admit that she looked halfway alluring, and perhaps a better man would be drawn to her, but his attraction remained for Brigid. He wondered where she was.

"Good evening, Mr. Ashton." Clara walked to him and extended her arm and relaxed hand as if she expected him to kiss it.

He held it lightly. "Thank you for the dinner invitation, Miss Cavanaugh."

"I'm delighted you could come." She smiled, closed-lipped. "I would offer you a sherry, but we don't keep libations in the house."

"That's quite all right," Thomas said, trying not to look past her for Brigid. "I must return to the hospital after our engagement this evening, so it would be best without sherry."

"I see," Clara said. "I apologize if I kept you waiting."

"Oh, certainly not," Thomas lied.

Clara smiled coyly. "Well then, I'm pleased. I hope you are pleased as well." She glanced demurely at her dress. "To be here, I mean."

Thomas swallowed. What to say? Yes, the dress was lovely, but he simply didn't find this woman attractive either in appearance or personality. She seemed to be the gatekeeper to Brigid, however, so he played along.

"You look splendid." It was the best he could manage.

It worked. She smiled like a schoolgirl whose crush just pulled her pigtails.

"Shall we go to dinner, then?"

"That would be grand." Thomas walked to her side, and she locked her arm in his. She stood just an inch or two shorter than his six feet, and smelled of gardenias.

Clara led him through the sitting room door, past a massive library and into a hall. As she chatted about the weather, they walked into a dining room of modest size with expensive, dark furnishings.

An ornate sideboard decorated one wall, and a built-in buffet, another. The room boasted a fireplace, and floor- to-ceiling windows covered with dark green tapestries and gold cording. The wallpaper was done in earthy hues and topped off with a border of stylized leaf and floral patterns.

A two-tiered crystal chandelier hung over the white linen-covered dining table. An extravagant floral centerpiece and two silver candelabras completed the perfectly set table.

Despite this elegance, it was the place settings that caught Thomas's eye - delicate white china, finely polished silver and clear crystal water goblets…set for four.

Four? Who, beside Brigid, would be joining them?

At that moment, a man and a woman entered the room. Clara released Thomas's arm. "Mr. Ashton, may I introduce my cousin, Mr. Leopold Cavanaugh, and his wife, Grace."

"Good to meet you!" Leopold smiled wide and, with a hearty grip, shook Thomas's hand. He appeared to be a jolly, rotund fellow about sixty, with sparse, dark hair combed to one side. His eyebrows were bushy and his nose a shade of cherry, but his eyes sparkled with humor. His wife was short, pleasantly plump, her face sweet, set with inquisitive blue eyes. Her dinner dress was an understated deep blue.

"I'm pleased to meet you both," Thomas said, and although not begrudging this friendly couple, he realized that if they were his and Clara's dinner companions, then Brigid was not.

"Shall we sit?" Clara said.

They sat, but not before Thomas held Clara's chair for her, and Leopold helped Grace into hers. Clara resided at the head of the table with Thomas to her right. Grace sat across from him, and Leopold took his place at the foot. Clara led a quick prayer and then rang a small dinner bell. Two servants brought in the first course, oysters on the half shell, accompanied by Tabasco sauce and buttered brown bread.

"Clara tells us she met you on Pier 54 waiting for the *Carpathia*?" Grace said as a maid served the oysters to each individual.

"Yes," Thomas said. "I was there to lend a hand, if I could, to the *Titanic* survivors."

"He ended up aiding me, however," Clara said, her eyes never straying from him. She watched as he removed his oyster from its shell with an oyster fork. He quickly downed the appetizer, although the taste was not to his liking.

"Yes." He directed his words to the Cavanaughs. "I'm terribly sorry about the loss of your cousin, David."

Grace teared up and looked away. Leopold shook his head. "Terrible year for the Cavanaughs, I'm afraid."

"Besides David, who do you mean?" Thomas said, panic rising inside of him. Had something happened to Brigid?

"My father passed away in January of this year," Clara said, her voice flat. "He was in England at our family estate when he collapsed from a weak heart."

"My sincerest condolences," Thomas said.

"David and I sailed to England immediately, but it was too late."

"That is tragic," Thomas said. "May I inquire as to -" *Miss O'Brien* he was about to say, when Clara interrupted.

"Yes, you may inquire about my mother. She is dead also."

The conversation paused while the servants replaced the oyster dishes with oxtail consommé and Custard Royale. Again, not Thomas's favorite. He preferred more simpler dishes, like his mother's homemade ravioli. Still, he had to admit, the soup smelled much better than the oysters had tasted.

"I'm sorry to hear about your mother, Miss Cavanaugh," Thomas said as the servants departed. "Was this recent?"

"No." Clara spoke without emotion. "She died when I was eight, and David, ten."

"A growth in her womb," Leopold blurted. "I mean, that's what she died from, not that David was a growth in her womb, then again, of course, at one time he was."

Clara sighed, her exasperation with her cousin apparent, although Thomas rather liked the fellow.

"Cousin Leopold, that's not appropriate table conversation." Clara reprimanded the older gentleman as if he were a child of eight. Thomas cringed.

"But you said that Mr. Ashton's a doctor!" Leopold shot back. "Certainly he's heard worse!"

"Yes, but not at dinner, dear." Grace's soothing voice seemed to calm her husband. She patted his hand across the table corner.

Thomas cleared his throat, hoping to lead the conversation to Brigid's whereabouts. "So, Miss Cavanaugh, you grew up in London? I don't detect an accent."

"No, you see, Father brought David and me here when we were very young. He wanted to get in on the steel business while it was booming and further his fortune."

"And he kindly brought Leopold and me over to take care of the children here in New York when Clara's mother died," Grace added.

"Ah," Thomas said. He turned to Clara. "You have had your share of loss, and I'm sorry." He finished his soup and set down his spoon. "There was another woman with you on the pier-"

His inquiry was interrupted while the servants replaced the consommé dishes with a delicious smelling platter of baked fish and hollandaise sauce.

"Your surname is Ashton," Clara said, as if she'd not heard his last question. "It's of English origin, is it not?"

"Yes." Who cared? "My father is English. My parents emigrated to New York when they were young. I was born here."

"For living in such close proximity to each other, Mr. Ashton, I'm surprised we haven't met before," Clara said. "What does your father do?"

Thomas offered up a sad smile. "He died ten years ago. Pneumonia."

"Now it is our turn to be sorry," Grace said.

"Dreadfully," Leopold added.

"Thank you." Thomas took a bite of his fish, his frustration growing as the conversation veered away from Brigid's whereabouts once again. "My father was in real estate. He made a rather good living which affords me the ability to support my mother and go through medical training."

"What area of medicine interests you, Mr. Ashton?" Grace asked.

"I'm currently interested in the work being done on infectious diseases," Thomas answered, a burst of pride enveloping him. "I'd love to discover a cure for yellow fever, or educate people on the importance of sanitation in avoiding typhoid. I so admire the brilliant men who work diligently to fight these deadly diseases."

"And your mother, is she a great lady?" Clara said, seemingly not interested in his career or the bettering of humanity.

"I'd say so," Thomas said, smiling. "She ran our household, raised me, helped my father when she could, and for extra income she used to make artificial flowers out of silk and wire for manufacturers. Now that she's elderly, she volunteers her time by baking breads and pastries and donating them to-"

"It sounds as if you come from a lovely family," Clara said, as if bored by his conversation. "I'm surprised I haven't heard of the Ashton family before."

"I think your choice of profession is quite noble, Mr. Ashton," Grace said.

"Here, here!" Leopold raised his water glass to Thomas.

Clara placed her fork next to her plate. "More doctors are certainly needed in New York with all the disease those filthy immigrants bring to our fine city. They treat the ones that are here, but then more arrive and the diseases begin anew."

Thomas felt his blood boil, but tried to keep his voice steady and his manner respectful. "Well, we must remember that all our ancestors were immigrants once and most left their countries perfectly healthy, only to acquire illnesses like dysentery, cholera or measles on the ships. I remember my own mother telling me how…" Thomas caught himself before he blurted out the miseries of dysentery in hot and cramped steerage quarters with only buckets for latrines. "Forgive me," he said. "This isn't suitable dinner conversation. But let me suggest that if the shipping industry improved travel conditions for the poor, they'd arrive healthier, and better yet, *more* of them would arrive."

Clara took a sip of water from her crystal goblet. "Well, it's a good thing most of those unwashed Irish and Italians have their own neighborhoods and tenements. I'm surprised you'd want to bother with them, Mr. Ashton. I think they're a hopeless cause."

The room fell silent. Thomas dared not open his mouth, as he wasn't sure what spiteful words might spew in light of Clara's ignorance and prejudice.

She sat smug in her opinion. The Cavanaughs would not look him in the eye, but seemed to take an overwhelming interest in their dinner plate.

Thomas's appetite was ruined.

"What are your plans after your medical training, Mr. Ashton?" Clara spoke as if the horrible awkward silence had been but a blip in the conversation.

Despite his desire to walk out of this house forever, Thomas knew he must continue a while longer. "I hope to earn a good enough living to send my mother back to her beloved home country."

"Oh? Where is that?" Clara smiled.

"Italy."

A maid who had been replacing the fish platters with a cheese soufflé and salads dropped an empty plate on the floor, startling them all. "My apologies," she said, as she hurried to scoop up the broken pieces. She practically ran from the room.

"You're *Italian*?" Leopold let out a hearty guffaw, and Grace smiled quietly behind her napkin. Thomas waited for Clara's reaction. Her faced flamed hotter than the soufflé, but her expression remained stoic, as if he'd not said anything at all.

"Yes, half." Thomas said, addressing Clara directly. "My mother is Italian, from the southern region of Italy. Calabria, to be exact."

Clara remained undaunted, but her eyes flashed so much heated anger, Thomas felt they could melt the iceberg that befell the *Titanic*.

"And, as we discussed, my father is English," he continued, hating himself for feeling amused at Clara's discomfort. "He met my mother when they both sailed to America in 1885. My father first saw my mother from afar as she boarded the boat for steerage, but says her dark, exotic beauty drew him to her like a moth to the flame."

Clara cleared her throat. "He actually said that?"

"I embellish a little." He smiled.

His answer broke the angry ice between them, and Clara allowed herself a light laugh. "I apologize for my earlier comments. I had no idea. You don't look Ital-like your mother, do you?"

"No. No dark exotic beauty here, I'm afraid." Thomas relaxed, ready to try yet again to get the information he sought. "How is your brother's fiancé?" He feigned forgetfulness. "What was her name? Brigid, was it?"

Leopold continued to make good on his cheese soufflé while Clara and Grace suddenly quit eating, their faces both turning pale, their immediate silence, unnerving.

Thomas feared the worst. "Miss O'Brien's all right, isn't she?"

"She went back to Ireland," Clara said quickly.

"She did?" Thomas and Grace spoke in unison, and he noticed that Grace looked as shocked as he felt.

"When did she leave?" he asked. "Why?"

"She is from Ireland. And she went back home the day after the *Carpathia* arrived without David." Clara picked at her salad and avoided eye contact. Thomas looked to Mrs. Cavanaugh for confirmation of this news, but she looked away. Something was clearly amiss. He reached into his pocket and pulled out Brigid's letter.

"Well, then, I'm confused," Thomas said, sounding a bit too accusatory for his own liking, but unable to help it. "Why would Brigid send me a letter asking for help on the very day she boarded a ship to Ireland?"

He was awarded Clara's full attention. And Grace's too. The poor woman's face went white as a bleached sheet, and she dropped her utensil onto her salad plate.

"Let me see that." Clara held out her hand, and Thomas passed her the letter. He knew that Brigid must have been at the Cavanaughs' house when she wrote it, for the stationery had the initials *GMC* embossed in gold lettering at the top.

Clara read the letter and then, very slowly cast a long, hard look at Grace. Clara's beady black eyes and determined demeanor reminded Thomas of a ravenous hawk stalking its prey.

"Oh, dear!" Grace quickly stood, waving her hand frantically in front of her face. "I'm not feeling very well. If I may beg your pardon?" Thomas and Leopold both stood.

"Are you all right, dear?" Leopold held her lightly by the elbow.

"Yes, yes," she assured him. "I just need some air." She glanced at them all. "By myself."

Grace bustled out the door without a backward glance. Thomas and Leopold sat, Leopold returning his attention to his plate, and Thomas returning his to Clara. She hadn't moved an inch. She sat still as stone staring at the door through which Grace left.

As if realizing Thomas watched her, she came to life. She folded the letter in the manner it was handed to her and returned it to him. "*That* was an interesting letter." She smiled as she spoke, but seemed to weigh each word. "It gives one pause."

"Well, it doesn't sound to me like Miss O'Brien had the means to travel," Thomas contested. "These organizations she inquires about help the destitute. You, Miss Cavanaugh, were her family…or would have been. Surely she spoke of her plans with you?"

Clara took a deep breath, her face taut, and straightened her shoulders. "Mr. Ashton. I'm sorry to say that Miss O'Brien and I were never close. Although I offered her my help and home, she outright rejected my generous offer, packed her bags and left here the day I said she did."

Leopold cleared his throat as if to interrupt. Clara shot him a look that could cut glass. Mr. Cavanaugh promptly hung his head and returned to his meal.

Clara continued. "Miss O'Brien didn't even have the decency to attend David's funeral services, Mr. Ashton. That, in itself, confirmed for me that she never really loved him and was only after our family fortune."

"Well, was she aware that you were having a service? I didn't see any announcement of anything for David in the paper," Thomas said.

"No. I didn't tell her. It was a private affair," Clara retorted. "Family only. And Brigid wasn't family anymore."

"Now wait a minute," Leopold said, looking at both of them. "Brigid *was* family and the service wasn't pri-"

Clara cut him off. "Leopold, I think you should check on Grace, *don't you*?" It was a command, not a suggestion.

Leopold huffed and threw his napkin on the table. He stood. "I can't drink in my own home, and now I can't even talk in my own home! I'll just be taking my leave, then." He nodded to Thomas. "Best of luck to you, sir."

"Thank you," Thomas said as Leopold left the room.

He suddenly felt uncomfortable alone with Clara. He hadn't believed a malicious word out of her mouth. It made no sense that Brigid would ask for his help and then suddenly leave for Ireland. And if Clara was so certain she'd left for Ireland the day after he met them, why had she expected Brigid to show at the mass? And why did Clara say the mass had been for family only, when Thomas's hospital friend, who certainly was not related to the Cavanaughs, attended? Two and two weren't adding up to four.

There was no point wasting more time. He hadn't found Brigid, he had sick patients to visit, and he certainly had lost all other patience with Clara.

The silence between them became most uncomfortable.

The servants entered again, but Clara waved them away.

"I seem to have lost my appetite," she said, staring at her salad. A look of melancholy shadowed her face. She looked as defeated as Thomas felt.

She rubbed her forehead as if it pained her and turned vacant eyes on him. The rate at which her moods changed unnerved him.

"Perhaps we should retire to the sitting room for coffee? I'd like to know more about you, Mr. Ashton." Her voice was hopeful, but her face resigned, as if she suspected his answer in advance.

Thomas tried to feel sorry for this hopeless woman, but at the same time, he knew she'd sooner send his own mother to the tenements than invite her for tea. He pulled out his timepiece and feigned studying it. The time didn't matter; he was leaving.

"I should return to my patients." He pushed back his chair and stood. "Dinner was delicious," he lied. "Thank you."

Clara rose, her ghostly white skin nearly transparent in the candlelight. "I'll see you to the door."

"I wouldn't dream of it," Thomas said, truthfully. "I can find my way out."

She clasped her hands in front of her. "Perhaps, under less stressful times, we'll meet again?"

Over his half-Italian dead body.

He pretended not to hear her, as she'd done many times to him throughout dinner. "Could you have your maid meet me at the door with my coat and hat?" He turned and left Clara standing in the dining room, the snake beheaded.

The maid met him as requested, handed him his belongings and hurried off. He turned to leave when someone called his name, a voice so soft he nearly missed it.

"Mr. Ashton!" The whisper grew louder.

He turned to find Mrs. Cavanaugh descending the stairwell, a finger to her lips to warn him not to talk.

"Mr. Ashton," she said, glancing in all directions as if the walls had ears. "I know where Brigid is." She handed him a piece of paper hidden in the palm of her hand. "The poor dear. Clara was going to send her to the tenements, but I found her employment. It's true…she hasn't a penny to her name."

Thomas read the address and offered the sweet lady his most gracious smile. "Thank you."

Worry filled her eyes. "Can you check on the dear girl? She's all alone. She's got no one."

Thomas put his hat atop his head and touched Grace lightly on the shoulder. "She's got me, Mrs. Cavanaugh. She's got me."

He turned and walked out the door, determined to find Miss Brigid O'Brien.

Chapter Seven

Brigid returned the last of the pots, pans and crockery to their rightful places and glanced at the kitchen wall clock. Half-past two and her morning and early afternoon duties were complete. With late afternoon and evening responsibilities yet to come, the next hour and a half would be hers to enjoy. That is, if lying down and resting to regain strength for more work could be called enjoyment. But after a morning that began at five forty-five with washing and dressing, followed by a multitude of never-ending kitchen tasks with only a short lunch break, a midday rest was certainly needed. Work would then resume until half-past nine.

Brigid sighed with weariness as she removed her cap and wet, dirty apron. Today's duties had been more taxing than usual, for the scullery maid, Anna, was in bed with a fever, and the other maid, Ruthie, afoot with laziness. Thus, Brigid had to help with scullery chores as well as her own kitchen work, which much to her dissatisfaction, did not involve cooking. Although Mr. Ransom had hired her as a kitchen maid, her position changed on that first day, and not for the better, when Mrs. Dorothea Duffy, the cook, discovered that Brigid knew nothing about gas stoves or American food.

"Why in the Lord's name Mr. Ransom would make you a kitchen maid when you can't cook defies all logic," Mrs. Duffy had complained on Brigid's first day. His decision defied Brigid's logic as well, considering he hadn't asked her one question about skills she did or did not have.

Worse yet, and what caused Mrs. Duffy to gasp and roll her eyes, was when Brigid admitted not knowing how to cook French dishes. According to Mrs. Duffy, *grand* houses such as Ransom house prided themselves on serving impeccable French cuisine to their most honored guests, and Mrs. Duffy would "not tarnish the upstanding reputations of Mr. and Mrs. Charles Ransom by serving anything less exquisite."

"But I *can* cook," Brigid had pleaded, explaining that as an eldest daughter she helped her mother cook for her younger siblings. "And, I can follow recipes!" She prayed her plea would keep her from scullery duty. "I just need to know how to be workin' the stove. I've never seen the likes of that one." She pointed at the modern range with its odd gadgets. "We use coal stoves back home."

Mrs. Duffy had waved away her comments. "I don't need any help with the cooking, and Mr. Ransom well knows that! I need help with the cleaning and the scrubbing and the running of errands. Can you do that, girl?"

Brigid nodded. Yes, she could do that, she just didn't want to. She'd gone from the hopeful ranks of lady's maid, to kitchen maid, to something in between that and a scullery maid. Her Irish blood boiled with each lowering in rank, but she needed this job. She had nowhere else to go.

Mrs. Duffy had eyed her. "You sure? It's a lot of hard work."

Brigid hesitated as her mother's voice invaded her thoughts. "*Brigid Mary! If you do not sow in the spring, you will not reap in the autumn!*" And spring, it was.

She held her head high. "I *can* do the job, Mrs. Duffy."

"Good." Mrs. Duffy studied Brigid from head to toe with curious eyes that crinkled at the corners when she smiled. "Well. I'm sure you'll do fine, here. I am grateful to Mr. Ransom for the help. I've been asking for another girl for months. An extra pair of hands is always better than ones that don't seem good for anything." She cast a long, reprimanding look toward young Ruthie.

Brigid warmed to the chatty, yet slightly gruff cook who reminded her of own grandmother. Mrs. Duffy was of average height, yet the years had thickened her middle considerably. She was pretty of face, with a rosy complexion, twinkling blue-gray eyes and dark, curly hair woven with strands of silver.

Mrs. Duffy had turned to the eavesdropping pair of scullery maids standing in the entryway to the scullery. "Ruthie, take Miss O'Brien to the upstairs quarters and show her where she'll sleep." She turned back to Brigid. "It's late. I'll have a uniform brought to you by morning. Be down here promptly at half-past six, if not earlier, dressed, washed and awake. Oh, and later this week the doctor will drop by to give you an inspection."

Brigid startled. "An inspection? Whatever for? I was given a clean bill of health after I departed the *Olympic* only two weeks ago!"

Mrs. Duffy sighed. "It's Mr. Ransom's orders, miss. Ever since typhoid and yellow fever and the like ran amuck years back, he won't take the risk of any immigrant bringing disease into his home."

"I never 'ad any check-up," Anna piped up, her cockney accent recognizable to Brigid.

"Me neither," Ruthie added. "And I'm from Ireland, too."

Mrs. Duffy rolled her eyes, her exasperation clear. "You two aren't around the food." She turned to Brigid. "Since he hired you as a kitchen maid, I guess you get the examination."

Brigid sighed. "Yes, ma'am."

And now, two weeks later, Brigid felt no better off than she'd been that first day. The doctor's appointment had been humiliating. Dr. Stouch asked her all sorts of embarrassing questions regarding every disease known to man, whether she or anyone back in Ireland had it, or knew someone with it. She told him the only diseases that afflicted her family were German measles, which had taken a baby brother, and scarlet fever, which both she and a younger sister had suffered as children. But most embarrassing was when Dr. Stouch inquired into her female matters, how often her monthly bleeding occurred, when it occurred last, and when she expected it again. She saw no reason why this would affect her ability to clean pots and scrub floors, and she had angrily informed the doctor so.

"Some women are unable to work during their monthly course, miss," Dr. Stouch explained not looking up from his paperwork. "Your employer wouldn't want to hire someone who might miss so much work."

Brigid supposed that made sense, but the questions still made her uncomfortable. Luckily, the physical exam was not as probing, for Brigid was allowed to remain dressed. Dr. Stouch inspected her hair, eyes, ears, throat and listened to her heart and lungs. He then declared her "fit as a fiddle", smiled and sent her on her way.

She did not have to pay the doctor, which had worried her. She didn't know how such things worked in America, but the doctor explained that Mr. Ransom paid him. Brigid had sighed with relief, for she hadn't much money yet, and her earnings were meager. Her long work hours left no time to look for a better paying job. Stuck in the kitchen all day, she barely heard word of the outside world, save from what the other servants gossiped about at mealtime. She could go out with them in the evenings to the saloons and such, but if she spent her money there, it'd take even longer to save for passage home - if her parents would even take her back.

Each day she hoped Grace Cavanaugh might arrive with a letter from her mother saying that she could come home. Perhaps her parents might even send some money for her ticket, although she doubted they had the means. Mr. Ashton, that handsome and compassionate man from the dock, also remained in the forefront of her thoughts. Brigid knew chances were slim that her letter found him at the hospital, and if so, that he'd make good on his offer to help. He probably didn't even remember her. And, even if he did, why would he want to help someone he met once and for only a few minutes? Still, she couldn't shake the memory of meeting him, or the feeling that he truly cared about people, perhaps even her. Something in his crystal clear blue eyes had told her so. She couldn't forget him.

Brigid wiped her forehead with the back of her hand. She must stop thinking of Mr. Ashton or another trip to the confessional would come due. Poor David was only weeks in his ocean grave.

She pushed away the sad thought and surveyed the kitchen one last time. Satisfied that she had cleaned it as best she could, she headed for the servants' stairwell.

"Brigid!" Mrs. Duffy's high-pitched wail penetrated the quiet of the empty hall.

Brigid glanced to her right to find the cook scurrying toward her, hands flailing every which way, her fire engine red face contorted with panic.

"Brigid, wait!"

She met Mrs. Duffy halfway down the hall. "What is it?" From the look on the woman's face, surely someone had died.

"I just counted my bread loaves. There's not enough for the evening meal or tomorrow's breakfast!"

Jesus, Mary and Joseph! If a bread shortage harried the dear woman so, Brigid could only imagine what a real crisis might do.

Between gasps for air, Mrs. Duffy continued. "I think someone around here has been taking a share or two up to their rooms!" She placed her hand against the wall for support while catching her breath.

"Mrs. Duffy, I would never-" Brigid started.

"No, no, not you." Mrs. Duffy waved her other hand as if shooing Brigid away. "I meant that awful Ruthie. I've been short on bread and pastries often as of late, and Ruthie's uniform is growing a bit too snug if you ask me."

Brigid suspected Ruthie as well. More than once, Brigid had caught the young maid slipping a little "something" into her apron pockets, but Brigid was no snitch. She had enough problems with the other maids not liking her without adding fuel to the fire by ratting on one of them.

Mrs. Duffy grabbed her by the wrist, her voice desperate. "You must do something for me."

"Yes, ma'am." Brigid waited while the woman calmed her fluster and collected her thoughts.

"You must go to the bakery and buy more bread loaves. I haven't the time to make them myself nor the extra ingredients to bake them, and I can't get to the market until next week."

"The bakery?" Brigid asked. "Now?" She was so exhausted and didn't even know where the bakery was. She hadn't left the Ransom House grounds except to stroll around the block or walk to the nearby Catholic church. She hadn't even explored Central Park right across the street.

"Yes, now!" Mrs. Duffy pulled a fifty-cent piece from her apron pocket and shoved the coin into Brigid's hand. "The bakery is about six blocks south and then around the corner. You must hurry, and be sure to select only the freshest loaves!"

Brigid feigned a cheerful smile. So much for a rest. "I'll be needin' my coat."

"Yes, yes!" Mrs. Duffy turned and hurried back down the hall, disappearing into the pantry.

Brigid hustled up flights of stairs to the attic where she, Anna, Ruthie and a few other kitchen and housemaids slept. Brigid entered her tiny and cramped room, which contained only a small bed, dresser, washbasin and tiny window. Although she'd been assigned the smallest of all the servant rooms, Brigid still earned jealous remarks from the other maids who shared rooms. She was bothered at first by the snide comments, for she wouldn't have minded a roommate and someone to talk to at night. And, as if she needed another reason for the others not to like her, Mrs. Ransom, upon hearing of Brigid's meager wardrobe, immediately provided her with a coat and two simple day-dresses. The maids hadn't talked to her since.

Brigid donned the new coat and hat, rushed downstairs, and exited through the servants' entrance. She hurried in the direction Mrs. Duffy suggested, nervous to walk the unfamiliar city streets alone, and afraid of becoming lost.

A few blocks down, she passed St. Andrew's, the Catholic church she attended for mass and confession. The priest there had given her a harsh penance when she told him the circumstances surrounding her arrival in New York, but her confession felt like a cleansing of her soul. She told Father Cipriatti how she disobeyed her parents, ran away, and told David she loved him, even though she didn't, but hoped to. She even confessed about those few times when, as a young girl, she spent a sinful hour or two in the barn hayloft with a boy, kissing and doing a lot more than a good girl should. To atone for these sins, Father Cipriatti made sure she spent another good hour in the church, on her knees, reciting the Lord's Prayer many, many times.

Another three blocks west and one right turn later, Brigid located the bakery. The aroma of freshly baked bread greeted her as she entered the store, her stomach growled. She purchased the required five "fresh-as-you-can-get-them" loaves, placed the change in her pocket, and, sack of bread in hand, started the journey back.

As she turned onto Fifth Avenue, she heard someone call her name.

"Miss O'Brien!"

There it was again. She hadn't heard wrong. As she looked toward the street, a motorcar pulled to the curb and idled. A tall man with light brown hair emerged from it. He looked directly at her and smiled wide.

"Miss O'Brien! There you are!"

Brigid smiled back, her heart filling with hope for the first time in weeks.

She'd know those brilliant blue eyes anywhere.

Chapter Eight

"I almost didn't recognize you behind all that bread!" Thomas said as he removed his driving gloves.

Brigid's heart raced with delighted excitement.

He was as handsome as she remembered, tall with broad shoulders and lean physique.

"Mr. Ashton." She smiled brightly. His sudden appearance excited her, yet she wished they met under different circumstances. Why on earth must she be carrying all this bread? Why couldn't she be holding something elegant instead, like flowers?

"I was on my way to Ransom House to see you. Mrs. Cavanaugh gave me your new address." His voice fell to a hush. "She told me what happened with Clara. I'm very sorry."

Brigid's smile faded as her face flushed crimson. Thank God she thought to throw a coat over her kitchen uniform and switched from her work cap to her hat. It was bad enough Mr. Ashton knew that instead of marrying an upstanding gentleman, she now worked for one. He needn't know that she was barely a step above the scullery maids as well.

"Thank you." The silence grew uncomfortable. Brigid couldn't force words past her tangled tongue. Why did he have to be so unnervingly good-looking?

"I received your letter," he said. He pulled it from his overcoat pocket. "I tried to find you sooner, but I thought you were at the Cavanaughs'."

She fought through her embarrassment to explain. "I wasn't there very long. When we realized David wasn't comin' back, Clara asked me to leave." Which was putting it mildly. "I'm workin' at Ransom House…as a lady's maid."

The lie slipped out faster than her brain could process it. She hated lying to Mr. Ashton, but couldn't bear for him to witness how far she'd fallen. When she first met him, she was nearly a lady of means.

His glance fell to the brown bag of bread loaves. "I suspect that the kitchen must be short on help if the lady's maid has to run for bread?"

"Yes." Brigid defended her lie, even though she suspected he knew better, but her Irish pride slugged her honesty with a one-two punch. "Mrs. Ransom went down for a nap, and Mrs. Duffy, that's the cook, ran out of bread and the other maids…" she searched for what possibly might keep them from shopping "…are all ill." Well, Anna, was, but not the rest of them. Back to the confessional for her!

"I see." Thomas seemed intrigued by the lie. "Shall I stop by? I'm a doctor, if you recall. Well, almost one."

Blast! How could she forget he was a doctor? Because she was too busy fibbing, that's why.

"No, no need," she answered. "Thank you, though. Dr. Stouch has been by." Which was true, although he'd come to see *her* on another day, not the other maids.

"Well, all right then," Thomas said, matter-of-fact. "We'll let Dr. Stouch handle it." He paused, and then furrowed his brow. "Wait a minute. Dr. *Rupert* Stouch visited?"

"I don't know his first name." Another truth.

"Is he tall and thin, with glasses and a huge mole by his left nostril?"

"Yes," Brigid answered. There was no forgetting that grotesque black bump.

Thomas seemed amused. "Why did they send for him in particular?"

"I don't know."

"Doctor Stouch is an obstetrician."

"An obstetrician? What is that?" She'd never heard the word.

"He's a doctor that delivers babies. Is one of the maids in a family way?"

Brigid's eyes flew open wide and her face flamed hot. "No!" Well, at least she didn't think so, and she certainly didn't want to be the one caught starting *that* rumor. Worse yet, she wondered why Dr. Stouch had examined *her*. She certainly wasn't having a baby!

Brigid grasped for a way out of the new mess she created. "Well, I'd be supposin' that maybe obstetricians might see women for other conditions as well? Like, supposin' the family doctor had an emergency and couldn't come?"

"Well, certainly," Thomas said. "What did Dr. Stouch say is wrong with the maids?"

"Influenza." There wouldn't be a confessional kneeler heavy enough to support all the lying she was doing. But, she needed to dispel any untoward rumors she may have put in Mr. Ashton's mind. If the girls heard what she said, and told Mrs. Duffy, she'd find herself unemployed faster than her father could down a pint of Guinness.

"Influenza," Thomas repeated. "Well, I'm sure they'll be fine soon, and it was very nice of you to get the bread for them."

"I suppose." Stupid bread. She needed to change the subject and quick. "Mr. Ashton, you said you received my letter?"

"Please call me Thomas, or Tom, if you like."

"All right. And you may call me Brigid." She liked this exchange of first names very much. It gave her a sense of familiarity with someone here in America.

Thomas continued. "I came to talk with you about these organizations you inquired about. Do you have a moment?"

A glimmer of hope lit in her heart. Perhaps one of the charities could help her get to Ireland sooner? But as a passer-by checked his timepiece, she was reminded of the hour and that she needed to return for afternoon duties.

"I do wish to talk with you, Thomas, but I must be gettin' back with the bread."

"I see." He looked up the street and then back at her. "May I offer you a ride?"

Brigid knew, no matter the distance left to walk, that getting in Thomas's car would not be proper. She barely knew him. Then again, who was she to judge propriety after her run-away excursion across the ocean to marry a man she didn't love? And, look how that turned out. She'd vowed never to take that sort of wild chance again.

"Thank you, but I only have a short distance to walk, and even so, I'm not certain it's proper."

A faint blush appeared on his cheeks. "Oh, do forgive me, Brigid. I meant nothing by it. You're correct, of course. You don't know me. I shouldn't have suggested it."

She hadn't meant to offend him so, but his reaction was so strong, one might have thought he'd suggested a kiss! Brigid couldn't help but wish he had offered that kiss instead of the ride, propriety be damned!

His mere presence caused her thoughts to scatter and her emotions to swirl. Where had her mind gone? *I'm so sorry, David. Why couldn't I have been attracted to you the way I am to Thomas?*

And yet, she didn't want to be attracted to Thomas. She barely knew him. For all she knew he might be like Clara, all goodness and sweetness until he suddenly turned on a dime. She couldn't take that chance. She'd have to ignore these feelings and carry on. Plus, she was going home. There was no time to fall in love with this breathtaking, admirable American doctor.

"It's quite all right, Thomas," she said, adopting a nonchalant air. "I know you were only tryin' to help."

"Well, may I walk the rest of the way with you?" He held out his arms. "I'll carry the bread, which will keep my hands busy, and thus, we shall remain proper."

Brigid laughed. She ignored her anxiety and handed over the bread. He carried it in one arm and walked beside her.

"I'm glad you wrote me," Thomas said. "Unfortunately, I don't have very good news for you."

Brigid's heart sank.

"The organizations I mentioned on the pier help women and children who are *survivors* of the *Titanic*. They receive clothing and transportation to shelters," he said.

"I see." Brigid tried to keep disappointment out of her voice. "So my circumstances are different than those women who were actually on the ship and lost someone? Even though I lost someone on the *Titanic*, too? I don't see how my comin' over on a different ship makes my situation less tragic. I'm still alone."

Thomas stopped walking and turned to her. "The thing is, you have housing and employment. The Travelers Aid Society protects stranded women and children from others who would…" he paused for a moment…"victimize them or force them into … unsavory relations. The Women's Relief Committee helps with the immediate needs of the *Titanic's* survivors - warm clothing, money, temporary homes and arrangement for employment."

Brigid still didn't understand why she couldn't get help from these places, especially the Women's Relief Committee. Her ears had perked up when Thomas suggested they provided money. Considering her dire circumstances, perhaps they might provide her with a ticket back to Ireland?

But before she could suggest this, Thomas inadvertently dashed her hopes. "I'm afraid, Brigid, with you already here for…what is it now?"

"Nearly a month," Brigid answered, her hope vanishing by the minute. "I came over with Clara on the first of April, about two weeks before David would have arrived."

"Oh." Thomas sounded as dejected as Brigid felt. "That makes it worse. You see, your needs aren't as immediate as the others. And you've already accomplished what the committees would do for you. You have shelter, food, clothing and a job."

"Curse my blessed luck." She didn't care how sarcastic she sounded, for her words rang mild compared to how she really felt. The Irish in her wanted to holler, throw a good old fit, shake her fist in the air and then go have a whiskey.

"But I don't any have money," she said, grasping at invisible straws. "Certainly that should qualify me for somethin'?"

Thomas continued. "The committees won't see it that way, Brigid. And even if they did, your needs would fall last on their list. You weren't on the *Titanic.* You would need some way to prove that the sinking caused you harm."

Brigid knew she was stuck. She had zero proof that she came to America to marry David, other than Clara's word. And Clara wasn't about to run to Brigid's defense and explain that Brigid was destitute because she kicked her out.

"If you tell the organizations you know the Cavanaughs," Thomas said, as if reading Brigid's mind, "they won't even consider you, assuming you have wealthy friends."

Brigid fought back tears. She was stuck between the proverbial rock and a hard place.

"I'm truly sorry," Thomas said.

"Thank you." Brigid said. "You have helped. I'm knowin' now that I won't be gettin' any aid, so, should I be thinkin' of leavin' my job, I shouldn't. It makes that choice easier."

"I see."

Thomas said nothing further as they approached Ransom House in all its magnificent wealth and dark splendor, a mammoth monster against a clear, blue sky.

As they walked closer to the courtyard, Brigid stopped and turned to Thomas. "I appreciate you comin'." She hoped to sound grateful even though his news disheartened her. "I'll be takin' the bread now. Thank you for carryin' it."

But Thomas wouldn't let the sack go. "I-". He paused and suddenly seemed ill at ease. Good Lord, could he have more bad news?

He looked her square in the eye. Brigid braced for the worst.

"I wanted to let you know," he began. "That I haven't forgotten you. Not after we met on the pier, and not after Mrs. Cavanaugh told me about your…circumstances." He glanced at Ransom House.

She was flattered speechless by his comment. She should say something, but his kind remark took her off-guard.

"Well, you see," he continued, seeming to choose each word carefully. "I was hoping I might see you again…I mean, other than now?"

Brigid startled. This, she hadn't expected. She couldn't contain her smile. "I'd be likin' that, too," she said. "I mean, I could use a friend," she added quickly, just in case Thomas was merely concerned with her welfare and didn't have courting on his mind. She did not wish to be presumptive or forward. She wasn't even sure she would remain in New York.

"Excellent. And we shall be only the most *proper* of friends, right?" Thomas said, seemingly relieved by her answer.

She could give as good as she got. "Well, I *suppose*." She pretended to mull the idea over, as if having a friend this congenial and so fine in face and form needed any thought whatsoever. "I don't have any friends just yet, and since no relief committee seems to be offerin' me up one…"

They both broke into quiet laughter. Thomas handed Brigid back the bag of bread.

"When can I see you again, my friend?" he said.

Her all-consuming work schedule brought her sad reality back into focus. "Well," she thought quickly. "I could meet you tomorrow afternoon. I have my break from two to three-thirty and Sundays off." She thought to also suggest that her evenings were free after nine, but realized that sounded too forward.

"I could work that into my schedule." Thomas tipped his hat to her. "Then shall we meet here tomorrow afternoon?"

Oh no. That wouldn't do. He'd have to come to the servants' entrance and then someone would slip that she was a kitchen maid, not a lady's maid.

"Let's meet across the street at Central Park, the carriage entrance?" she said.

"Very well!" Thomas smiled and turned to leave. "Till tomorrow?"

"Till tomorrow." Brigid hated to leave him, but knew she must get to work. As she hurried across the courtyard, she glanced back, sad to see him walking away. But tomorrow wasn't far off.

"*Brigid Mary O'Brien!*"

She swore her mother's ghost called from across the sea. Ma would be so furious with her right now for meeting yet another man. But as Brigid turned toward the voice, she discovered it belonged to Mrs. Duffy, who huffed and puffed her way up the cement steps and across the courtyard.

"Where have you been, girl?" She took the bread from Brigid and started back toward the servants' entrance. "Come on! You're late."

Brigid hurried after the cook, but her spirits remained buoyant. Nothing could break the happy spell Thomas had cast.

Once inside, Brigid removed her coat and hung it on the hall hook, not wanting to waste more time by returning to her room. She donned a clean apron and prepared for work.

As she entered the kitchen, Mrs. Duffy smiled. "You did well selecting the bread, Brigid."

Holy heavens! A compliment from Mrs. Duffy? This was turning out to be a wonderful day indeed!

Mrs. Duffy stopped poking at the bread and reached into her pocket. "While you were gone, a Mrs. Cavanaugh stopped by." She pulled an envelope from her pocket and handed it to Brigid. "She left you this letter."

Brigid's heart leapt as she accepted the envelope. It came from Ireland! Could more good news be heading her way? She ripped open the envelope, not caring that the little shards of paper fell onto Mrs. Duffy's pristine floors.

She read the contents and burst into tears.

She'd not be wanted at home.

Chapter Nine

Brigid read Mrs. Duffy the letter from home, and then cried in the cook's arms for the next ten minutes. Although the woman could be gruff, Mrs. Duffy could also be a dear when she wanted, and this was one of those times. She offered Brigid the opportunity to skip afternoon duties and get some much needed rest.

The woman's thoughtfulness melted Brigid's heart. Sleep would indeed put her mind right again, but at the same time, Mrs. Duffy was still short on help. She thanked the cook for her kindness, but tucked away her self-pity and worked through the evening without sniffle or tear. About nine, when Mrs. Duffy headed home to her husband, and the other servants sat down for their evening supper, Brigid excused herself from the meal and headed upstairs. She checked on Anna, as she had promised Mrs. Duffy she would. The girl's fever had broken, and she slept. Brigid went to her own room, shut the door, plopped face down on her bed and muffled overdue sobs into her thin pillow.

When her tears finally ceased, Brigid lifted her head from the pillow and dried her cheeks. Exhausted, she mustered the strength to change into her plain, cotton nightgown. She sat up, swung her legs over the side of the bed, lit her oil lamp and gasped.

The ghost-like figure of Eliza Ransom stood in her doorway, her large, hollow eyes and translucent skin illuminated against the dark by the lamp she held.

"Shh." Mrs. Ransom raised a forefinger to her lips.

Her heart raced. Brigid couldn't have said a word if she wanted to. She could only sit and watch as the lady of the house entered the bedroom and quietly closed the door.

Mrs. Ransom appeared to glide to Brigid's bed like a ghost from a dream, yet one who wore the most beautiful peach-colored, silk dressing gown and robe. Without invitation, she placed her oil lamp on the end table and sat next to Brigid. Mrs. Ransom studied her intently with curious, gray eyes. Brigid remained frozen, not knowing what to make of her visitor.

She had never met Eliza Ransom in person. Although Mrs. Ransom had bought her a new coat and a few dresses, the items had been left on her bed. She saw Mrs. Ransom only occasionally in passing, or during formal dinners when Brigid filled in for another maid.

Mrs. Ransom's hand moved toward Brigid and it was all Brigid could do not to flinch or back away. The woman was supposedly mad, leaving Brigid unsure how to respond. She remained still, but studied Mrs. Ransom out the corner of her eye. Brigid noted the woman's beauty, but she also knew that beautiful women could be as off their nut as plain ones. The murderous Mary Geary from Ireland, who was stunning as a Donegal dawn and madder than a sack of rabid barn bats came to mind. Beautiful women could slap, pinch or strangle along with the best of them. Brigid stayed on her guard.

Yet all Mrs. Ransom did was place a lock of Brigid's hair behind her ear, like Brigid's mother used to do.

"You've been crying a long while." Mrs. Ransom's voice was gentle and sweet. Her eyes searched Brigid's face, as if waiting for an answer. “I heard you from outside the door.”

Brigid’s cheeks burned with embarrassment. How long had the woman listened to her cry? She had tried to keep so quiet!

She nodded and found the courage to look at the woman full on. Mrs. Ransom didn’t look wild-eyed or raving mad. Her expression was one of concern, sad yet caring. Brigid guessed her to be somewhere in her thirties, maybe younger, but she was so beautiful it was hard to tell. Dark auburn locks spiraled loose and wild past her shoulders, and her frame was so light and delicate that Brigid was pretty sure she could lay her flat, should the need arise. She hoped that wouldn’t be necessary.

“Why were you crying?” Mrs. Ransom’s asked gently.

Brigid knew she must answer, but wondered if it was proper to burden her employer with her troubles, especially a lady rumored to have her own troubles.

“Don’t be afraid,” Mrs. Ransom encouraged, as if reading Brigid’s mind. “I know you’re new here. Are you homesick?”

At the word ‘homesick’, Brigid’s heart broke a little further, and a fresh round of tears welled. She turned away, but Mrs. Ransom gently cupped Brigid’s chin and turned her head back to face her.

“You must tell me what’s wrong,” Mrs. Ransom implored. “Perhaps I can help?”

Brigid doubted anyone could or would help her. She was tired, alone and wanted to go to bed. She wanted to start fresh tomorrow and figure a way out of the mess she had made of her life. But Mrs. Ransom didn't appear anxious to leave.

Perhaps if she told Mrs. Ransom her pathetic story, the woman would see her for the peasant she was and leave her alone.

"I received a letter from my family," Brigid started, pulling the offending piece of paper from her bedside table. "I was hopin' to return to Ireland, but they won't have me."

"I'm so sorry." Mrs. Ransom said. "Why not?"

"I left against their wishes." That simplified it, but she wasn't sure how much Mrs. Ransom really cared to know.

"Hm." The lady seemed to ponder Brigid's answer for a moment. "Well, it seems to me most parents would be relieved to know their child is safe."

Brigid agreed. One would think that, but not in her case. "I left because they wanted me to marry someone I didn't want to."

"An arranged marriage?"

"Sort of."

Mrs. Ransom smiled. "I thought those were a thing of the past."

"Well, my family is desperate, you see. The man is very wealthy, but nearly fifty! He promised to help my family financially in exchange for-"

"You." Mrs. Ransom finished her sentence.

Brigid wiped away her tears with her sleeve. "And now, the situation is even worse. My sister, Cecelia, she's the one who wrote the letter for my mother, she's only seventeen and they've made *her* marry Mr. McGowan!" A fresh set of tears began. "It's all my fault. My poor sister!"

"Oh dear," Mrs. Ransom said.

Brigid had to admit that despite the constant onslaught of tears, it actually felt cathartic to spill her story. "My sister writes that my mother wants me home, but my father won't be havin' none of it. I'm to stay where I journeyed and good luck and Godspeed. And I'm not to write again, lest my father be findin' out."

"Your mother's heart must be broken," Mrs. Ransom said and gently rubbed Brigid's arm. Brigid wasn't afraid of her touch this time. She couldn't believe Mrs. Ransom to be crazy. The lady understood Brigid, sympathized with her and talked intelligently. She looked more melancholy than anything, but insane? Brigid didn't see it.

An awkward silence ensued, and Brigid felt unsure what to do. Mrs. Ransom looked away to the tiny window.

"I had a child," she said.

Brigid didn't know how to respond. The Ransoms had a child? Although it was frowned upon for the staff to talk about their employers, occasionally a morsel of gossip would spread amongst the servants. This was one tidbit Brigid had not been privy to, however.

"Two years ago," Eliza continued, and turned to face Brigid again, her voice steady and determined but kept just above a whisper. "A boy. I still miss him, just as your mother will always miss you no matter what you've done."

A painful lump formed in Brigid's throat. "Thank you." She wondered what happened to the child but didn't have to wait long for an answer. Mrs. Ransom seemed eager to tell.

"I named my boy Tobias," she said, her eyes fixed on Brigid. "He wasn't born quite right, however. But when I held him, I thought he was the most beautiful baby in the world. I loved him so much."

Brigid didn't doubt Mrs. Ransom's baby would be beautiful.

"But the next day, they told me he died during the night!" A calm anger laced Eliza's words and her eyes grew dark. She stared straight ahead now, as if speaking to the darkness. "But how could that be? He was healthy at birth. I held him! He had the bluest eyes, his cheeks were so pink, and he had a shocking tuft of red hair that I'll never forget." She paused. "And, he had the oddest shaped birthmark on the inside of his left wrist. It was the shape of a heart."

Eliza looked down at her hands in her lap, and Brigid noticed her lashes wet with tears. "I'll never forget that strange, but lovely, birthmark."

"I'm so sorry," Brigid said, wanting to reach out and comfort her, but she held back, not knowing if it was proper to touch one's employer.

"They said it was a respiratory infection that took his life." Mrs. Ransom stared at the wall as if seeing that awful day replay before her. "I became hysterical because I knew the baby's lungs were healthy just the day before." She paused and drew a deep breath, turning her attention back to Brigid. "I knew Charles was to blame for my baby being gone. He says I'm wrong, but I saw the look on his face when he saw Tobias for the first time. He could not accept that our baby wasn't perfect. Well, *I* won't accept that my baby is dead."

Brigid shifted uncomfortably. She felt so sorry for Mrs. Ransom but at the same time wondered why the lady confided in her, a lowly kitchen maid. Was it proper for a servant to be privy to so much personal information? And yet, Mrs. Ransom talked on.

"I've never gotten over the loss of my son," she said. "I never will. I will be sad until I see him again, be it here on earth or in Heaven." She sighed. "I don't believe he's dead. Tobias was healthy. And, I know Charles. He'd never have an infant killed."

Brigid gasped. Was this why Mrs. Ransom was rumored to be mad? Was she telling people her baby wasn't dead and that Charles was to blame for the baby's disappearance?

"Charles showed me Tobias's death certificate, signed by Dr. Stouch," she continued, unaware of Brigid's discomfort with the conversation. "But, I still don't believe it." She stood and paced. "I'm just so miserable and trapped. I can't stand the sight of Charles. I want to leave him, but if I do…" she paused as if deciding whether or not to continue, but forged ahead. "If I leave him, I will never find my son."

Brigid drew a breath, uncertain what to say, uncertain as to why Mrs. Ransom had opened up to her. Was her tragic story supposed to make Brigid feel better about her own troubles? If so, it wasn't helping. She felt worse, but for Mrs. Ransom; and totally exhausted and confused. Mrs. Ransom's story sounded puzzling, yet she did not seem crazy. And what if Mr. Ransom *had* done something to his son? Sent him away or… Brigid pushed away the horrible thought. She didn't care for Charles Ransom either. She found him condescending, but she couldn't imagine him doing something harmful to his own baby. No one could be that evil.

Mrs. Ransom didn't seem to notice that Brigid hadn't commented. She turned and took Brigid's hand. Her eyes held excitement, and Brigid had to admit that this animated Mrs. Ransom unnerved her a bit.

"Everyone thinks I'm crazy, but I want you to know, and it's important that you do, that it is merely pretense and the only way for me to avoid Charles while I secretly search for my baby."

Brigid nodded, lost for a response. At this point she didn't know what to think about Mr. Ransom or why Mrs. Ransom would spill her soul to a servant.

"It's been two years since Tobias was born," Mrs. Ransom said. "I've sent private inquiries to all the hospitals and orphanages in the area looking for him, but to no avail."

"I'm sorry," Brigid said, knowing how heartbreaking this must be for this sweet lady. A thought occurred. "I don't mean to be cruel, ma'am, but was there a burial?" Brigid wondered how Mrs. Ransom could deny the baby's death if there had been a service and cemetery plot.

"They sedated me after telling me the baby died. I was asleep for several days…"

"Days?" That sounded odd to Brigid.

"Yes. And when I awoke, Charles told me he had the baby c-c-cremated." Mrs. Ransom stopped to catch her breath, then continued even though it obviously pained her to recall the memory. "I was told there was no service, just a blessing in the hospital chapel. The next day they handed me a box with Tobias's ashes."

Brigid felt nauseated, her heart pained. What an awful thing to do to a new mother.

Mrs. Ransom's voice dropped to a whisper. "Please don't think ill of me when I tell you this, but a week later, when I was well enough, I took those ashes and tossed them in the river. That's how certain I am that my baby is alive."

Brigid gasped and held onto the side of the bed, lest she fall off in her shock. What if Charles *hadn't* been lying and the baby actually died? Did that thought ever cross Mrs. Ransom's mind? Poor little Tobias may not only have been cremated, but also tossed like someone's day old garbage into the Hudson! Brigid pinched herself in disbelief. This had to be some horrible nightmare, and she wanted to wake up.

Unfortunately, the pinch hurt. She was wide awake, but terribly tired. She'd been through enough for one day and night. She was tired from running the bakery errand, from meeting Thomas again, from receiving the heartbreaking news from home and now *this*. She wished Mrs. Ransom would leave her, but it became quite obvious that the lady was here for a reason.

"I need your help, Brigid."

"Me?" Brigid's eyes flew open wide. What could *she* possibly do for Mrs. Ransom?

"Yes. You're the perfect person to help me." Mrs. Ransom stopped her pacing and returned to the bed. She squeezed Brigid's hand. "I knew it the minute Charles told me he hired you."

"I don't understand."

"You're older than most of the other maids, so you can be out on your own. I feel you can be trusted because Mrs. Duffy says you can and says you're a hard worker. And, you're pretty. People will respond to you."

Brigid shook her head back and forth. She didn't understand.

"Miss O'Brien." Mrs. Ransom's eyes lit up like fireworks. "*You* can find my baby!"

Brigid drew her hand away. Perhaps the lady *was* insane.

"Now, just how in the world would I be doin' that?" She didn't mean to sound angry or disrespectful, but exhaustion and shock got the best of her.

Mrs. Ransom's face fell.

Brigid hurried to explain. "I'm sorry, I didn't mean to sound upset." But the idea was preposterous. "I just don't know how I could find your baby."

"I have given this a lot of thought. Believe me, I wish I could stop thinking, but until I find Tobias, my mind will forever race. I'm certain Charles sent the baby to an institution or orphanage. He may have sent him far away, but I must start looking near."

"You can't go?" Brigid knew she sounded like a timid coward, but it couldn't be helped.

"Not with my reputation for being ill," she said, with a sarcastic laugh. "They don't let me out of the house."

"Oh yes, that would be right." Brigid realized her fatigue was getting the best of her thinking.

"My hope as a mother is, if I can't have him, then someone adopted him. But given his troubles, I fear they've put him in one of those horrid institutions."

"Yes, I see." Brigid said, sad for the young child.

Eliza continued. "Anyway, I'm hoping you might search for Tobias at the nearby institutions and orphanages."

Brigid shook her head. "I don't feel I could be of much help, Mrs. Ransom," she said, honestly. "I don't know New York City at all. I don't know what your baby looks like, and I don't know how I'd go about getting' into these places."

But, Mrs. Ransom would not be deterred. "Tobias would no longer be an infant. He'd be two. He most likely has red hair. And…" she paused, her memories casting a shadow across her face. "He's a mongoloid. Do you know what that is?"

Brigid nodded her head. A woman in another town near Donegal had given birth to a child with the condition, and against all advice to give the child away, kept her. That Charles would want to give his son away because of this malady bothered Brigid greatly. That little girl was the sweetest, most affectionate and loving babe. Charles had the means to care for such a child. It angered her that he may have sent his own son away.

"I'd like you to use your afternoon breaks and check out a few places that Tobias might be," Mrs. Ransom said. "It's possible that Charles sent my boy far away. On the other hand, he may have kept him near. After all, despite Tobias's flaws, he is Charles's flesh and blood."

Flesh and blood be damned, Brigid simply did not like Mr. Ransom. She could not stick up for him, whether it was to Mrs. Ransom's liking or not. "I don't know how you can say he's not an awful man when he'd tell you the baby died if he didn't," Brigid said. "That makes him plain horrid to me."

Mrs. Ransom clasped her hands together in her lap. She hung her head. “It’s complicated.” She looked up again. “Please tell me I can count on your help?”

Brigid wanted to refuse. After all, only today she had promised Thomas she’d meet with him every afternoon. And, she really liked Thomas. He was her only friend.

“I really don’t think I’m the right person for this, Mrs. Ransom,” Brigid said, honestly. “There must be someone better suited, someone who at least knows the city?”

“There is no one. The male servants are very devoted to Charles, so they’d never help me. The other maids are too young to be running about on their own, plus they’re a bunch of gossips.”

“What about a trusted friend?” Brigid suggested. Surely this rich, beautiful woman had friends who would help her.

“No.” She shook her head. “Again, they are loyal to the man, to our money. They’d never do anything to jeopardize losing the friendship of the wealthy Charles Ransom. I’m sorry. You probably don’t understand what I mean. ” She turned her gray, pleading eyes on Brigid. “I’m desperate. I can’t go forward with my life because I don’t know whether to trust Charles or not. I need to know the truth about my baby.” Her voice fell to a whisper again. “I’ll make it very worth your while.”

Brigid sat up straight. “What are you meanin’?” She tried to sound curious, not greedy. But when you have nothing, hoping for anything seems to be asking for a lot.

“Whatever you want.”

Brigid was taken aback. “Whatever I be wantin’?”

“Yes.” Mrs. Ransom smiled. “What is it you would like most in the world right now, Miss O’Brien?”

A good night’s sleep was the first thing to pop into Brigid’s head, but instead she answered, “I’d like to be your lady’s maid instead of workin’ in the kitchen.”

“Miss O’Brien!” Mrs. Ransom tittered softly. “You don’t seem to understand. You can have *anything* you want.”

“Well, the lady’s maid position pays more. It’s the money I’m needin’. I’d like to get my own place in New York, since I won’t be going to Ireland now.”

“But I could give you all the money you want! You wouldn’t have to be my maid!”

“Really?” The nightmare had turned into some unexpected dream. “I could actually rent a room somewhere?”

“Darling, I could buy you an entire house!”

Brigid sat stunned. *Her own home*? All for the price of looking for a baby? “But what if I can’t find the child?”

“Then you’ll at least provide me peace of mind,” Mrs. Ransom answered. “And that will still be worth the price I pay.”

Brigid thought the offer too good to be true. She reminded herself that Mrs. Ransom really might be mentally deranged and may have invented this entire story, but then again, what if her story was true?

“May I have a day to think on it?”

Mrs. Ransom stood, but her smile was bright. For the first time that evening, she seemed happy and alive. “Of course. I’ll come back tomorrow night for your answer.”

"All right."

Mrs. Ransom let herself out of Brigid's room. Brigid sat for a moment and contemplated her choices. She truly had no idea what to do.

She turned down the wick on her lamp, blew out the flame and rested her head on her pillow. It didn't take long for her eyelids to grow heavy. The events from her long day played across her mind like those picture shows she'd heard about. Bread loaves, Mrs. Duffy, her parents, Eliza Ransom and babies flashed across her mind as her eyes closed.

Her last thought was of Thomas Ashton. *Thomas...oh yes, handsome Thomas. Tomorrow, I'll ask Thomas what to do. Thomas will know.*

He likes to help people.

Chapter Ten

Brigid couldn't keep from staring at the kitchen clock. She was to meet Thomas on her afternoon break, and time moved slower than a snail. Even as she plowed through her morning duties, which were more numerous than usual due to the Ransoms' dinner party that evening, the minutes still dragged. But, finally, those stubborn clock hands landed on the appointed hour.

The other maids, butlers and Mrs. Duffy departed for their breaks about five minutes earlier, and the kitchen was quiet. It was Brigid's job alone to ready the kitchen for the afternoon cooking, and she hurried to finish her final inspection. Someone had left a pitcher of cream on the counter, but she deemed everything else satisfactory. She would put away the cream and then hurry upstairs to change into one of her white blouses and a clean, black skirt. She'd then head out to meet Thomas.

Brigid rounded the worktable, walked to the icebox and returned the cream. As she closed the door and turned, she gasped, and her heart nearly leapt from her chest. Mr. Ransom, dressed in a pinstriped suit and shiny shoes, stood in her path. How had he entered the kitchen without making any noise? Had she been so lost in her desire to see Thomas that she simply hadn't heard her employer come in? And what *was* it with these Ransoms sneaking about the house and scaring her out of her wits? Mrs. Ransom had appeared all ghost-like in her bedroom doorway the evening before, and now Mr. Ransom snuck up on her in the kitchen.

As his tall and solid frame towered in front of her, she backed against the cool icebox.

"G-good afternoon, sir," she stammered. He stood way too close for her liking and he smelled nauseatingly of old cigars and stale spirits. Her gaze darted every which way in search of an escape route, should the need arise.

"Good day, Miss O'Brien." His sapphire blue eyes bore into hers. He offered a slight smile. "I was hoping to find you here." His tone was smooth, friendly even, but Brigid noticed dark circles under his eyes and an anxiousness about him.

"This is where I usually am, sir." She edged away from the icebox and took a few steps to her right. "Excuse me," she explained. "My back is gettin' cold."

"Well, we can't be having *that*," he said with a laugh and turned toward her. "Can we?"

Brigid didn't answer, not comfortable at all with how his eyes roamed her body.

"Mrs. Duffy says you've settled in well?"

"I'm supposin' I have. I'm gettin' on fine, thank you." If all he wanted was to check on her welfare, she wished he would hurry up. Time was wasting for her to see Thomas.

Mr. Ransom placed his hand on her shoulder and gave it a light squeeze. Brigid flinched, unsure whether to move away or remain. Was it proper in America for one's employer to touch you? She didn't know, but didn't like the eerie chills his fingers sent careening up her spine.

His hand moved down her arm in a soft, slow caress. *This*, she knew, was not appropriate. She yanked her arm away from his intrusive fingers, but he resumed the caress, a threatening look in his eyes warning her not to move again.

"If there's *anything* you need, Miss O'Brien, I want you to come see me, *personally*."

She bit her lip and nodded. *Please, please go away!* A wave of nausea rose within her.

"If you continue to do well, Miss O'Brien," Mr. Ransom said, moving his hand to her face and stroking her cheek with the back of his fingers. "I may just consider you for an upstairs position."

Had she not been so disgusted by his touch, she might have laughed in his face. To think of him bribing her with an upstairs position when he was the one who stuck her in the kitchen in the first place! She wanted to pull away and tell him that she'd be needing no stinking upstairs job, because *his wife* was going to buy her a house! She held her tongue however, and tried to back away, but a metal counter thwarted her attempt.

"You must prove yourself worthy, Miss O'Brien," Mr. Ransom said, his tone soft. "Do you understand?" He played with a ringlet of her hair that had fallen out from under her cap.

She wanted to slap his hand away, turn and run, but fright had turned her legs to lead.

"What on earth-?" Mrs. Duffy stood in the arched kitchen doorway.

Mr. Ransom removed his hand as if Brigid's hair had burst into flame. When he turned and addressed the cook, his manner was calm and collected, as if she had only interrupted a game of cards. "Ah. Mrs. Duffy. There you are!"

Brigid's body fell limp with relief, and perspiration moistened her brow. She only now became aware of her racing heart. Thank heavens for Mrs. Duffy!

The cook's eyes flitted between Brigid and Mr. Ransom. Brigid tried to send her a mental distress signal.

"I remembered I forgot to put the cream away," Mrs. Duffy said. "Whatever brings you to the kitchen, Mr. Ransom?" Her eyes narrowed and her lips pursed and then, as if aware of her suspicious tone, she seemed to backpedal fast. "I mean, I'm honored to find you in my kitchen, Mr. Ransom, of course. It's just such a surprise."

She stepped further into the room and glanced Brigid's way. Brigid tried to speak, but when she opened her mouth, no sound came; her throat still constricted with fear.

Mrs. Duffy offered her an overly reassuring smile but addressed Mr. Ransom again. "Is there something you're needing in my kitchen, sir?"

Mr. Ransom turned toward the cook, swaying to and fro on his expensive heels as if he had all the time in the world. "Seems to me, Mrs. Duffy, that this is *my* kitchen, now isn't it? And I suppose I can meander down to check up on a few things now and then, can't I?" He offered the cook an amused smile. "Or do I need *your* permission, Mrs. Duffy?"

Mrs. Duffy's smile fell into a straight line, her cheeks grew rosy, and Brigid expected steam to pour from her ears. "Well, of course you don't, sir. It's just that you usually send Mrs. Latimer on such matters."

"Yes, well," Mr. Ransom cleared his throat. "Our housekeeper seems to be down with whatever fever seems to be ailing the servants as of late."

Mrs. Duffy snorted. "Mrs. Latimer's illness must have come on rather quickly." Brigid silently agreed. They'd both seen Mrs. Latimer just this morning barking orders at the housekeeping staff.

"Yes, it seems so." As if lost in thought, Mr. Ransom stepped away from Brigid and headed for the door. "Anyhow," he said, scratching his head as he passed Mrs. Duffy. "Due to the staff dropping like flies, I came downstairs to assure we have enough servants to serve dinner."

"We're all fine and healthy down here, sir," Mrs. Duffy said. "Anna is back on her feet and no one else has taken ill."

Mr. Ransom stopped at the doorway and turned back, his eyes fastening on Brigid once again. She looked away, bristling under his stare.

"Thank you, Mrs. Duffy," he said. "Be assured, you shouldn't find me down here again."

Mrs. Duffy seemed to feign a smile, but her voice remained flat. "That's quite all right, sir. After all, it is *your* kitchen."

Mr. Ransom chuckled, turned, and headed back to the hall and toward the stairs. Brigid released a breath she hadn't realized she held.

Mrs. Duffy scurried her plump body around the worktable and over to Brigid. "Are you all right? You're quite flush. Are you coming down with the fever?" She paused. "Or is it something else?" She glanced at the doorway.

Brigid pulled herself together as best she could. "I'm fine, ma'am, thank you." She forced her wobbly legs to take a few steps. "Like you, I was just rattled to find Mr. Ransom in the kitchen. I hadn't heard him come in. He caught me off guard." Yes, he had, and Brigid chided herself for not being able to stick up for herself. Now that the incident was over, she wished she had decked him a good one. Then again, it was a good thing she hadn't. She wouldn't be standing here still employed.

Mrs. Duffy studied her intently as if trying to read her mind. Brigid wished she had more time, or the inclination, to tell her what happened, but all she really wanted was to leave Ransom House and see Thomas. Mrs. Duffy, however, seemed intent on assuring her well being, and although it delayed her further, Brigid found the gesture very kind,

"Mr. Ransom cuts quite the commanding figure, doesn't he?" Mrs. Duffy said, raising her eyebrows as if expecting Brigid to follow her lead and talk about their employer. But Brigid wanted to forget the incident or what other ugliness might have occurred if Mrs. Duffy hadn't interrupted. She shivered and tried to put the thought from her mind.

"I'm sorry, Mrs. Duffy," she said. "But I must be goin'. I'm meetin' a friend on my break."

Mrs. Duffy stepped to the side to let her pass. "Take an extra ten minutes then," she said. "For the time Mr. Ransom detained you."

"Thank you!" Brigid hurried past Mrs. Duffy and into the hall, grateful to the dear woman for not pushing the subject further. Even with the extra time granted, she couldn't waste another minute. She removed her apron, hung it on a hook and surveyed her work dress. It would have to do. There was no time left to change. She removed her cap, grabbed her coat and wide-brimmed hat, and quickly put them on. Even though the weather had warmed, her coat still looked nicer than her dress.

And, Mr. Ransom had given her a chill she couldn't shake.

Chapter Eleven

Brigid hurried across Fifth Avenue, dodging motor cars, bicyclists and horse-drawn carriages. She spotted Thomas waiting for her at the Central Park carriage entrance. As she hurried down 59th street, he saw her too. He smiled and waved.

Her heart skipped a beat and butterflies took flight in her belly. Thomas seemed more attractive than ever in his brown cutaway coat, matching trousers and top hat. She was immediately drawn to his twinkling blue eyes, so light she felt she could almost see through them. He was clean shaven, as usual, a fashion she found particularly attractive; it set him apart from those men who wore those ridiculous handlebar mustaches.

"Good afternoon, Thomas," she said, securing her hat, which had become jostled in her hurriedness. With her smile wide, her face flush and her heart racing, she could not contain her happiness to see him again. "I'm so sorry I'm late."

"Not at all!" He presented her with a brown paper bag. "I brought you something."

Brigid's excitement mounted. A gift? She accepted the bag. "Shall I open it here?"

"Of course!"

Brigid opened the sack and peeked inside. She looked up at Thomas, confused, but delighted. "Briosca!"

"Well, here in America, we call them biscuits." He smiled again. "But these are not just *any* biscuits! They're called Oreos and are new!"

Brigid laughed. "I would love to try them!"

Thomas motioned toward the park. "Why don't we find a bench to sit on and enjoy our feast?"

"That would be lovely."

Walking alongside Thomas, Brigid felt the tension from her horrible morning flow from her body. The biscuits had been such a sweet and thoughtful gift. She felt as if she might smile forever.

They located a bench at the edge of a walkway, across from a pond. Thomas took a handkerchief from his suit and wiped the seat.

"Thank you." She sat and took her first good look at the park. She was a bit disappointed. Central Park, at least this section, was not well cared for. Dead trees sporting broken and bare limbs, and shrubs with untamed branches grew haphazardly within the confines of sparse spring grass and ready-to-bloom bushes. Litter was strewn hither and yon, and walking paths were cracked and unkempt scattered with winter's leftover dirt and dead, wet leaves.

Thomas glanced to where she stared and spoke as if reading her mind. "It's not the grand park it used to be. We have our city politicians to blame for that. They won't allocate the funds to take care of the park."

"It's fine," Brigid lied, but suddenly missed the plush greenery of her homeland. In a Donegal springtime, one could run free through flowered meadows where an angry mama sheep might be your only foe. Here it seemed a simple walk might send one cascading to the dirty ground over a forlorn tree branch.

Brigid sighed softly and reminded herself that New York City *was* her home now, not Donegal, and she needed to make the best of things. Being with Thomas certainly made that easier.

He joined her on the bench. Brigid opened the bag and pulled out the four biscuits. She handed two to Thomas and bit into her own. They were deliciously chocolaty and sweet.

Thomas nodded his agreement.

"I'm glad the weather held so we could meet," he said in between bites. "How are things going at Ransom House? Are the maids feeling better?"

Oh yes, that was right. Yesterday she had told him the kitchen maids were sick.

"Anna is much better," she said, knowing it to be true. "The others are well, too." Again, very true since they were never sick to begin with, but guilt still gnawed at her. Thomas had been so nice to bring her a treat, and yesterday she had lied to him. She very much wished to reveal her true position at Ransom House, but feared losing his friendship due to either her fibbing or her employment status.

Thomas seemed like a fair man, however, and should he leave because of her lies, she only had herself to blame. If he left because she was a lowly kitchen maid, then maybe he wasn't a good person to begin with, which she'd find hard to believe. She hated the lie between them; it weighed heavy on her heart. Her relationship with David had been based on a lie. Granted, she had hoped to fall in love with him, but look how that turned out.

No, she would not begin another relationship by fibbing. What was it her ma always said? Ah, yes. *A hen grows heavy when carried far.* It was time to put down her hen. She would make amends with Thomas and pray that the Heavenly Father would see fit to keep him as her friend.

They finished their last Oreo and brushed crumbs from their clothing. A few gray-brown sparrows took advantage of the unexpected treat.

Brigid turned to Thomas, her heart in her throat. "I need to apologize to you, Thomas."

"Oh?" His eyes searched hers, but his smile remained intact.

She looked at her hands, red and raw from helping with the scullery work. They seemed to goad her into telling her truth. "I'm not a lady's maid. I said that to make you think better of me, but I work in the kitchen."

She half expected him to yell at her for her betrayal, or, at the very least, walk away. He did neither.

"That's all right, Brigid," he said, his voice kind. "Why were you afraid to tell me? I think no less of you whether a kitchen maid or lady's maid." He turned on the bench to face her, his face taut, his expression serious. "Brigid, regardless of your station, you are still *the lady* I met on the pier, whether you wear a fine dress or whether you wear an apron." He took her hand in his, it's warmth sensual yet comforting and protective, so unlike Mr. Ransom's touch which had nauseated her to the core.

Thomas continued. "In the short time I've known you, I have come to like you better than the upper-class women I've met."

How could this be? She wanted to believe him, mostly because her feelings for him had grown stronger, but she barely knew him. Yet she felt more affection and attraction for Thomas in the few weeks they had known each other than she ever felt for David over the past year.

"But Thomas, what if the more you get to know me, the less you think of me?"

"I don't believe that could ever happen, Brigid," Thomas said. "I saw everything I needed to that night on the pier. You were so kind to Miss Cavanaugh, and then later, after I learned how she turned you out, you had every reason to be bitter. And yet, you're still as sweet as the day is long."

She felt herself blush from head to toes. "Thank you." Thank heavens he didn't know how much she hated life in New York. Sweet, his arse, he would think.

As if reading her mind, he asked, "So. Other than your job, how are you liking the city? I hope it's working its magic and convincing you to stay."

She looked at the forlorn park. What to say? How to answer? Yes, she was staying, but only because circumstances forced the situation, not because she liked it here. She hated the crowded streets, the constant noise, the unusual smells, and found the people odd - the exceptions being Thomas, Grace Cavanaugh and Mrs. Duffy.

She chose her words carefully.

"I've decided to stay," she said, not elaborating that she hadn't any other choice. "I'm goin' to save my money and then decide what to do. I'm not sure city livin' is for me."

"I suppose New York City would take some getting used to coming from the Irish countryside," Thomas said. "My mother has never been fond of the city either, and she emigrated from Italy. I grew up here, though. There are a lot of good things about this place."

"Besides you?" Brigid said, hoping to sound playful and not too flirtatious. Then again, he still held her hand. "Name one."

The twinkle in his eyes and boyish smile told her he was up for the game.

"Well, let me think." He put his other hand to his chin. "Oh, I know! On New Year's Eve, in Times Square, a huge ball is lit with a thousand or so lights and it falls from the sky during the last sixty seconds of the year!"

"They drop a huge ball?" Brigid couldn't fathom it. "Don't the people below get hurt? Does it shatter?"

Thomas laughed. "I'm not explaining this correctly. No, the ball doesn't actually fall. It's lowered on wires. The crowd goes ecstatic at midnight."

"Oh." She didn't understand the excitement about a falling ball or standing in a crowd of smelly New Yorkers in the cold, but Thomas thought it wonderful, so she let it go. She'd probably be long gone from New York by New Year's Eve anyhow. The thought saddened her, and that feeling confused her.

"Let's try something else," Thomas said, as if sensing her sudden melancholy. "Perhaps you need to get out more."

"I don't get out at all," Brigid said. "Except for bread."

They both laughed.

"Well," Thomas said, sitting up straight and holding her hand a bit tighter. "Perhaps you might like to come for dinner at my mother's on Sunday night? I'd love for you to meet her. You said you don't work on Sundays. Is that right?"

Brigid's eyes flew wide open, despite her efforts not to look surprised. Although very pleased at the invitation, she wondered if meeting his mother might be more awkward than pleasant. Thomas owned a car, studied medicine and dressed well. She assumed his family had money. The last thing she wanted was to sit at dinner with another woman who looked down her nose at her.

Her quiet indecision seemed to unnerve him, and to her dismay, he backed off from the idea. He cleared his throat and looked away. "I apologize. I shouldn't have been so forward. It may be too soon after your loss…to further our friendship by having you meet my mother, I mean."

"Oh, my loss," Brigid said, realizing Thomas's thoughts had taken a completely different path than her own. "David Cavanaugh." He was the last thing on her mind right now. "Yes, well, thank you." She let go of his hand and crinkled the paper bag she still held. Unfortunately, the pain of losing David was fading faster than her Catholic guilt approved of.

"You must think me awful," she said, turning toward him. "Meetin' with you so soon after."

"But, *I* invited you."

"But, *I* came." She also stared straight ahead.

"Then, we'll rot in Hell together," Thomas said, deadpan.

Their simultaneous laughter broke the somber mood and set them both right again.

"I'll be goin' to Hell first, I fear," Brigid said, thinking of her past.

Thomas turned toward her again and smiled. "Now, how could that possibly be?"

She drew a deep breath. To tell or not to tell? But she had promised herself no more secrets. It was bad enough Mrs. Ransom forced her to keep one, a biggie, at that. Best to tell of her horrid past and let him judge for himself.

"I didn't love David," she began and took the next several minutes to spill her sad tale of abandoning her family for a marriage she hoped to find in love in, only to have David die. Thomas remained quiet, letting her ramble without interruption. "Clara thought I had been after David's money, but I wasn't. I was after a happy life, and I thought I'd find it with him. He was a nice man." She stopped there and waited like a prisoner for Thomas's sentencing. Worse yet, she feared he might feel she was using him in the same way she used David. How to explain that this was not the case, that she hoped to make enough money to move on with her life. Then again, that would mean Thomas might not be in it. All these conflicting feelings made her head spin.

His eyes were kind, not accusing. "I still think Miss Cavanaugh should have helped and not turned you out."

"Thank you," Brigid said, figuring it a good a time as any to tell the rest. "But, there's more." She told him about the letter from home and why she could not return to Ireland.

"And so you see," she concluded. "I would love to be meetin' your mother, but I'm afraid I would only disappoint her. I'm sure she'd rather you brought home someone more suit-"

He cut off her words. "Brigid. I'm so very sorry for all you've been through. I can't imagine starting over in a new country."

"Thank you."

"Now, about my mother…"

Brigid's heart dropped to her feet.

"…she will love you." Thomas winked, and his playful smile returned. Brigid realized he had toyed with her. "Please say you'll come on Sunday. I'll pick you up on 57th Street outside Ransom House."

"Only if you bring me more Oreos when we meet again tomorrow." Two could play at this game! But then, Brigid's smile faded as she remembered her conversation with Eliza Ransom. "Oh, I forgot to tell you. I've got a problem with meetin' you on my afternoon breaks."

"What is it?" Thomas's face fell.

Brigid paused. She'd meant to tell him earlier about Mrs. Ransom and her missing baby, but now, asking for his help in the matter seemed like almost too much to ask. After all, he'd just invited her to dinner. She didn't want to abuse his kindness. And dare she trust Mrs. Ransom's secret with him? But if she didn't tell, she'd have to make up yet another lie about why she couldn't meet him on her breaks, and she was done lying.

She sighed and hoped she wasn't making a huge mistake. "I need to be helpin' Mrs. Ransom with somethin' that might take a while." She told Thomas what Mrs. Ransom had said about Tobias and Mr. Ransom. Talking about Charles Ransom sent a chill through her. She didn't mention this morning's encounter.

"The thing is," Brigid explained, hoping he'd see the logic in her decision to help Mrs. Ransom. "She's goin' to pay me handsomely to find out what happened to the child. I was thinkin' last night that I could use that money to help my family back in Ireland and maybe they'd let me come home."

Thomas sat back and whistled low under his breath. "I heard Eliza Ransom is unstable."

"I don't think so," Brigid said, and then second-guessed herself. "Then again, I trusted Clara, so I don't have the best judgment."

Thomas laughed.

"I'm supposed to be goin' to all these institutions and orphanages to see if anyone has heard of or seen the babe," Brigid explained.

"I see." Thomas leaned forward, rested his elbow on his knee, and his chin in his palm. "I'm thinking it might be easier if you give me the list."

"Why? What can you do?"

He patted his knees as if pleased with himself and sat back again against the bench. "You seem to forget that I just might have a bit more access to the folks on that list than you would."

Brigid couldn't believe what she heard. "You'd do that for Mrs. Ransom?"

Thomas laughed lightly. "I'd do it for *you.* And me, if it means I can see you on your breaks."

She wanted to squeal, jump, and clap her hands, but she remained lady-like and proper. "That would be wonderful. I'd be forever grateful."

"Bring me the list on Sunday," he said. "Unfortunately, my own schedule won't allow me to meet you tomorrow. I was afraid to tell you that earlier, afraid you might think I had no interest in meeting you again, which is why I brought up Sunday early on."

She nodded. Everything seemed as if it would work out. Thomas would help her with investigating, Mrs.

Ransom would pay her for the work, and she'd get to see Thomas on Sunday for dinner. Dinner. In a real home, with a real family.

"I would like that very much!" She reached into her pocket and retrieved the list that Mrs. Ransom had slipped under her door that morning. "I can give you the list now. I was afraid to leave it at the house in case someone might snoop in my room." She handed him the paper.

"Very good, then!" He rose and offered her his hand. She accepted, excited again by his touch.

"Would noon on Sunday do?"

"Yes." Tomorrow would be a long day knowing she'd not see Thomas on her break. "I'll wait outside the Ransom House gate on 57th Street." She could have invited him to the servants' entrance to pick her up, but she didn't want everyone at Ransom House knowing her business.

"Very well, Brigid." He took her lightly by the elbow. "May I escort you back to the house?"

"Of course! Thank you for everything, Thomas."

They hurried from Central Park to the corner where Ransom House stood massive and looming.

"Until Sunday, then?" he said, with a slight tip of his hat.

"Until Sunday," Brigid answered.

She turned and headed toward her entrance. For the first time in weeks, she felt her life might actually be heading in the right direction, and she had Thomas to thank for that. With his help, she'd solve the mystery of little Tobias and earn her due from Mrs. Ransom. With the money, she'd have the freedom to choose between returning to Ireland and staying in New York.

The thought startled her. *She actually might want to stay here.* Deep in her heart she knew the reason why.

Thomas.

Chapter Twelve

The next day, Thomas stood at the bedside of Patient 2025 and waited. Waited for the old man to either wake from a coma or die, a decision this unfortunate victim of trampling by carriage horse seemed unwilling to make. The man had arrived with no identification, and no family came running to claim him. Surgery had been necessary to relieve pressure from a skull fracture, but Patient 2025 hadn't regained consciousness prior to, nor after, the operation.

Being a first year medical student, Thomas was under the supervision of Archibald Hack, a physician notorious for not trusting his underlings to empty a bedpan let alone actually treat a patient. Thus, the nurses tended to the injured man's physical needs, and Thomas found himself mainly "babysitting" Patient 2025. His job was to be present if the man woke or died, but Patient 2025's condition remained as steady as a surgeon's practiced hand. There was no quickening or declining of the pulse, no fluttering of the eyelids, nor any telltale death rattle from the lungs. Patient 2025 was a stubborn one.

With nothing to do but wait or study other medical cases for his classes, Thomas sat in the otherwise empty ward. He finished reviewing the last of his charts, pulled out his pocket watch and glanced at the time. At least three hours to go before Dr. Hack would meet with his students in the lecture hall. Thomas returned the watch to his pocket, his fingers brushing against a piece of paper. He pulled it out. It was the list of orphanages and institutions Eliza Ransom wanted Brigid to search for her son in, as well as notes Eliza jotted regarding Tobias's birth, description and disappearance.

Now *this* he found interesting. He couldn't help but be intrigued by what Eliza Ransom wrote about her husband and son. Everyone in New York City believed the Ransom baby had died, and that Eliza went insane with grief. As Thomas reread Eliza's notes, however, it was clear to him that Eliza believed her baby to be alive. But, was Eliza reliable? Why would she ask *Brigid* to help her? Brigid could have no idea how to find or travel to the organizations on Eliza's list. And yet, Brigid was eager to help. Of course, she'd also been very upfront with her reason: she needed the money Eliza offered. But what if this was some wild goose chase invented by a crazy woman who had no means or intention of actually paying her?

Thomas was glad Brigid brought the matter to his attention. Not only could he help, but by knowing what was going on at Ransom House, he might also keep her out of harm's way should Mrs. Ransom's plan, or Mrs. Ransom for that matter, go awry. He'd become protective of his new friend.

Protective. Thomas stifled an inner laugh. Who was he kidding? He'd been *enamored* with her since the first time they met. She was beautiful in an understated way, her hair the color of summer wheat, her eyes cat-like and emerald-green, her cheekbones prominent and pink. She was neither tall nor short, her figure tending toward the thin side, but from what he could tell, as he'd never seen her without a coat on, she possessed all the right curves. She didn't seem to have a clue to her beauty and she was kind to a fault, hence her misguided trust of Clara Cavanaugh. Yes, she hid her employment status from him, but for pride's sake, which he understood. He felt that she was honest, good-hearted and not looking for anything other than a way out of her desperate situation. He'd never fault her that. And, try as he might, for he knew she might return to Ireland someday, he couldn't stop thinking about her.

He forced his attention back to the paper she entrusted to him. The first hospital on the list was Baybridge, the best and newest hospital in the city. Eliza noted that she delivered at home, under the care of Dr. Rupert Stouch. When the baby supposedly became ill, Charles took him to Baybridge. If Tobias Ransom had indeed died from a respiratory ailment the day after his birth, the information would be found there in his records.

Thomas checked his pocket watch again and glanced at Patient 2025. He hadn't moved a muscle in hours, except involuntarily when the nurses turned him. Thomas calculated the time it would take for a quick rail ride to Baybridge and back. He added in a good hour to get into the hospital, find the records library and study Tobias's file. The entire process should take no more than two hours, allowing him time to return for Dr. Hack's lecture.

He picked up his study materials, rose from his chair and walked to the nurses' station. Two were on duty, one on the telephone, and the other at the medication cart.

He approached the elderly woman at the cart.

"I'm off to retrieve more records and may stay in the library for a while," he lied, feigning a stretch. "I need to move around. Send for me if there's any change in our patient."

"Of course." The gray-haired woman smiled kindly and glanced through the glass that separated the nurses from the ward. "He's pretty well behaved, though."

Thomas laughed, thanked her and made a hasty exit.

The rail car ride, although speedy, allowed Thomas time to collect his wits and form a plan about how to gain entry into the records room at Baybridge. Luckily, Saturday was a busy day for hospitals with visitors milling about. With his white coat, medical badge and stethoscope, he should easily blend into the hospital environment.

He entered through Baybridge's main entrance. The lobby buzzed as busily as he had hoped, and the waiting room overflowed with patients to be admitted. A nurse behind the lobby desk glanced up, but nodded as he flashed his credentials. He hurried down the first hall he saw. He then found himself completely lost, not having any idea where the records room might be. If this hospital was designed like Cranston, archived records would be in the basement.

He found a stairwell at the end of the hall, and proceeded down a level. A large metal door opened onto another long corridor with stark white walls and a shiny, tiled floor. A few hospital employees walked by but paid him no heed.

Thomas had to admit he was impressed with Baybridge. A sign hanging from the ceiling with an arrow painted on it pointed to an x-ray and laboratory department. Many hospitals in New York had no such departments and sent samples out, delaying diagnoses and treatment.

He walked to the end of the hall and rounded the corner, nearly colliding with a young, brunette nurse.

"Oh, excuse me," she said, her brown eyes opening wide.

"My fault entirely," Thomas said, although he knew they were equally at fault, him for looking up as he rounded the corner, her for looking down.

The nurse stopped dead in her tracks, her large eyes reminding him of a surprised doe. "No, the fault was *clearly* mine." She glanced at his nametag. "Dr. Ashton." She cocked her hip, batted her eyelashes and stood directly in his way.

"I'm sorry," he said, having no time or desire to flirt. "I'm in a hurry. Could you tell me where old patient records are kept? I'm new here."

"Of course you are." She smiled demurely and softened her voice. "I would have remembered seeing *you* before." She crooked her index finger and turned. "Follow me. You're almost there." As she turned and headed back in the direction she came, Thomas could not help but notice the extra little hip sway she added to her walk. He rolled his eyes. The only thing he wanted from this hospital was information.

They turned another corner, and the records library came into view.

"Voila'!" the nurse said, extending her upturned hand and turning to face him. "You've arrived. Can I help you with *anything* else?"

"No, and thank you," he said. He headed for the door.

"Perhaps another time?" he heard her suggest as he entered the room through swinging metal doors. Yes, perhaps in his younger, more carefree days, he'd respond to the nurse's flirtations, but not now. Now he wanted nothing more than to help Brigid and win her trust, and time was of the essence.

The records room was rather large, more like a library, which he expected. A wooden desk, nearly the length of the room stood before him, and on his right, another set of swinging doors. He suspected the records were kept behind them.

A young woman with reddish hair pulled into a bun, sat behind the counter, typing faster than he'd known fingers could fly. He approached the desk. Glancing up through round, wire spectacles, she stopped her finger-fury. "May I help you?"

She offered no smile and seemed irritated by the intrusion. Thomas sensed his charisma would not work on this one.

He flashed his sincerest smile, but she remained unmoved. "I'm Dr. Ashton, a medical student from Cranston."

She remained still as stone.

"I study under Dr. Archibald Hack…"

"And…?" She tapped her fingers on the desk. "Please get on with it. I have work to finish." She nodded toward the typewriter.

"I need to research cases to present," Thomas said. It was true, except he wasn't supposed to be looking for them at Baybridge.

"Why aren't you at Cranston then? You have a records library there, do you not?"

"That we do," Thomas said, relieved to have invented this story during his rail ride over. "But I hear that Baybridge's library is *far* superior to Cranston's."

"It is." The woman didn't even have the modesty to blink.

"Which is why I hoped I might find more interesting cases here to present to Dr. Hack. Surely you've had other students search your archives?"

The woman removed her glasses and glared. "Yes, but they are students at *this* hospital."

He was getting nowhere, and time ticked. He dropped the smile, sighed audibly and tried another approach.

"The truth is I'm failing my first year. Miserably." He nearly choked on the words, knowing he was doing exceptionally well in his studies. How could he fail when he was never allowed to touch a patient? "Becoming a doctor is all I ever wanted." Again, not true. When he was little he thought he might become a priest, but adolescence and a keen interest in girls changed all that.

"Uh-huh." The woman stifled a yawn.

"If I could just find one truly *unique* case and present it to Dr. Hack, a case that might just knock his knickers off…"

Still no reaction. He couldn't even make the woman blush! He pressed on. "I mean, if I could just impress Dr. Hack with one-"

"Oh, for Heaven's sake. Just go in." The woman waved him away as if he was an irritating gnat. "I need to work."

"Thank you!" He hurried toward the doors. The woman obviously had little patience for whining medical students, and luckily that worked to his advantage.

Thomas entered the room and whistled low under his breath. File cabinet upon file cabinet stood before him in long rows. Baybridge was only about five years old and had fewer archived charts than other area hospitals, but finding one specific chart amongst this many would be daunting. He pulled a few charts from the top drawer of the nearest cabinet. As he had hoped, the charts were filed in order by year of patient's admission. Estimating the number of files per year, and multiplying by two, one for each year since Tobias's birth, he quickly located the 1910 files. Thomas then figured that, with Tobias being born in January, his record should be at the beginning of those files. He pulled a few, noted the date of admissions and worked backward to January 4th, the day Tobias was brought to Baybridge. He located Tobias's record within minutes.

He opened the thin file that consisted of a death certificate and one page of handwritten notes:

Date: January 4, 1910
Patient: Tobias Charles Ransom
Date of Birth: January 3, 1910
Attending Physician: Rupert C. Stouch, M.D.
Reason for Admission: Acute Respiratory Failure

Notes: Infant born at home via vaginal delivery, January 3, 1910, 10:15 am. Delivered by myself. No others in attendance. Normal birth, full-term, born with signs of Down's Syndrome, i.e. "Mongoloid Syndrome". Small head circumference, flattened and broad face, small chin, poor muscle tone. Weight: 5 pounds, 12 ounces. Length: 16 1/2 in. Color good, respirations 50, normal and steady. Heart rate 150. Infant alert. Breastfed well.

January 4, 1910: At approximately 12:15 a.m. Charles Ransom called me at my home. The infant had developed unknown acute respiratory distress with blue skin, wheezing and labored breathing. I informed Mr. Ransom to meet me with infant at hospital. Tobias Ransom was deceased upon arrival.

Vitals on admittance: No pulse, no respirations, unresponsive. Attempts to revive child unsuccessful.

Time of Death: 12:30 a.m.

Autopsy declined by Charles Ransom, father.

Cause of Death: Unknown respiratory disease, possible sudden pneumonia. Immediate cremation requested by father.

Rupert C. Stouch, M.D.

A death certificate had also been filled out and signed by Dr. Stouch. Thomas found it odd that no cremation date was given, nor had any undertaker signed for the cremation. All other sections had been filled in.

Thomas felt sick to his stomach. Little Tobias Ransom died on the way to the hospital? Thomas flipped the page thinking there had to be more. What attempts took place to save the infant? Why weren't they listed? What if the baby had been poisoned? Granted, that would be a rarity indeed, but Thomas knew that among the wealthy, the sudden and unexplained death of an heir apparent was always suspect. Had someone tried to smother the boy? None of these possibilities seemed to concern Dr. Stouch or Charles, as nothing was noted in the record. It seemed Tobias Ransom just quit breathing and neither his father nor the doctor deemed his short life worthy of further examination or autopsy. Had this been Thomas's child, he'd be devastated by this sudden death. He'd demand answers about his baby boy. But it seemed Charles Ransom accepted "possible pneumonia" as explanation enough and moved on, even having his baby cremated without autopsy.

End of case. Little Tobias Ransom's entire existence was reduced to about fifteen sentences in an archived chart.

Thomas pulled Eliza's paper from his pocket for comparison. According to her memory, Tobias was born healthy, albeit a mongoloid child, and was breathing and pink. Dr. Stouch's notes confirmed this. She wrote that she never heard any noise in the house the night Tobias supposedly took ill and was brought to the hospital by Charles. Nor had any of the household staff heard anything, not even Charles's call to Dr. Stouch. Charles didn't even bother to wake their chauffeur. He drove himself and the baby to the hospital.

Thomas paused. How had Charles managed that? How does one drive a car with a gasping, dying baby in your arms? Why not call for an ambulance?

A cough from the other room reminded Thomas that he had limited time. He needed to get back to Cranston soon. He returned the record and skimmed Eliza's notes again. She wanted Brigid to look for Tobias in nearby orphanages and institutions. She was certain he wasn't dead. As a medical professional, Thomas leaned toward believing the file notes, that the baby had died. Yet, he had a nagging feeling about the death, mostly about how quickly Tobias's health had turned, and how even quicker his body was whisked away for cremation. Why hadn't Charles given his beloved wife one last chance to hold her son? Things didn't make sense.

He'd have to continue his search another day, however. He hurried from the records library and found his way back to the first floor. As he headed for the lobby, he nearly collided with a short, stout man washing the floor with mop and pail.

"Oh, pardon me," Thomas said.

The man turned. "Mr. Ashton!"

Thomas couldn't believe his eyes. "Mr. Cavanaugh!" He shook hands with Clara Cavanaugh's cousin, the man he'd met at her dinner. "What on earth are you doing working at Baybridge?"

Chapter Thirteen

Leopold Cavanaugh's shocked expression mirrored Thomas's own.

"Just cleaning up a little mess, you see," Mr. Cavanaugh replied. A faint blush stained the man's sturdy cheeks.

"I can see that." Thomas tried not to stare at the swirl of discolored liquid in the bucket. "I meant, *why* are you working here?" From what Clara had said at dinner that night, Leopold and Grace had been living in Cavanaugh House since Clara was little, per her father's wishes. They came from a wealthy family. Surely, Mr. Cavanaugh could find more meaningful employment than janitorial duties.

Leopold stopped swishing his wet mop and ran the back of his hand across his forehead. He now appeared quite flushed, and droplets of sweat adorned his brow. He rested the mop against the wall, took a handkerchief from his gray workpants pocket and dabbed his face.

"I want to help Clara with the bills." H looked away, his answer sounding rehearsed.

"But Clara is a woman of means!" Thomas didn't mean to pry, but this obviously unwell, older gentleman should not be washing floors. "Surely she doesn't need the meager income you must make at this job!" Another thought came to mind. "What happened to the inheritance from Clara's father and brother? Didn't that come through?"

"Not that I am aware of, sir." He would not look Thomas in the eye.

"Please, call me Thomas, or Tom. I'm nobody's sir, especially yours, Mr. Cavanaugh. And what of Mrs. Cavanaugh? Has Clara put her to work as well?"

"No," Leopold said, finally raising bloodshot and tired eyes to Thomas. "Just me. I've been working here for about two years. I don't mind it. Gets me out of the house, gives me something to do, and Clara says it keeps me from the drink." He laughed, winked and pulled a small flask from his shirt pocket. "Don't tell her." He looked around, and when satisfied the hall was empty, took a sip. He offered the bottle to Thomas.

"No thank you." Thomas recalled that Clara had mentioned that Mr. Cavanaugh liked his liquor. "I'm on duty."

"Well, so am I." Leopold laughed again. He took a step closer. He smelled of gin and slurred his speech ever so slightly.

"As to why Clara found me this job," he continued as if Thomas had pressed the matter. "It just might be that she wants me to keep an eye on a certain doctor." He winked again and nudged Thomas playfully in the ribs. "If you know what I mean."

"Actually, I don't, Mr. Cavanaugh." Thomas was confused. He thought he made it clear at dinner that he had no designs for Miss Cavanaugh. It made no sense that's she send her cousin to work to spy on him!

"Oh come on, Thomas, my boy!" He slapped Thomas a tad too exuberantly on the back. "You mean to tell me you never heard about Clara and Dr. Stouch's little romance a few years back?"

Dr. Stouch? "Dr. *Rupert* Stouch?" Thomas wanted to laugh at his own inflated ego.

"You know any other Dr. Stouch?"

A nurse wheeling a patient turned down the hall toward them. Leopold quickly put his flask back in his pocket and both men nodded to them as they passed.

After the nurse and her charge disappeared down another corridor, Leopold continued. "Dr. Stouch courted Clara a few years back. You'd never seen the girl so happy in all her life. She doesn't get many gentleman callers, you know, even being as wealthy as she is. She was certain Stouch was going to marry her! He even planned a little get-a-way for them, she said. She was certain he'd propose beforehand. Then, at the last minute, the doctor said he couldn't go, and insisted she go anyway. Alone! Can you imagine? And she did! She was only gone a week or so, and when she came back, Stouch was engaged to Louisa Twyne. Now, you must have heard of *her*?"

"Louisa Tywne? No." Thomas felt as if he'd been living under a rock. And he may as well have been as he devoted his life entirely to his studies and taking care of his mother. He'd heard of Dr. Stouch prior to reading Eliza's notes, however. One could not be in medical training without knowing of the renowned physician to the wealthy.

Thomas was anxious to get to his lecture on time, but held captive by Mr. Cavanaugh's words. "Do you really think Clara still carries a torch for Dr. Stouch?"

And if so, maybe she could answer a few questions for him. But then again, hadn't Clara appeared to flirt with *him* at dinner? Why invite him to dinner if she really desired Stouch? And why *Stouch* of all people? The doctor was at least twice Clara's age, warty and as skinny as a poor man's wallet.

"I'm not entirely sure," Leopold said. "I remember her ranting aloud to a friend that Dr. Stouch came into a lot of money."

"If she wanted to marry him, I think she'd be happy he was wealthy," Thomas said.

Leopold waved a finger in front of Thomas's face. "No." He stumbled a few clumsy steps backward. Thomas grabbed him by the arm and righted the poor fellow.

"You see," Leopold continued as if he hadn't just nearly toppled over. "Dr. Stouch came into the money right after he left Clara." Leopold laughed again, and then quickly stopped. "I shouldn't laugh. That wasn't funny. My poor cousin. All she wants is to be married and have a family." He pulled his flask back out and took another sip. "I thought for a bit that she took a fancy to you, inviting you to dinner and such."

Thomas needed to end the conversation before it went further. He certainly didn't want to discuss his less than flattering feelings toward Miss Cavanaugh, nor did he wish her to know of his friendship with Brigid. He had a slight suspicion that if he told Mr. Cavanaugh anything, it might leak back to Clara. "Perhaps I should find a cab to take you home? I could tell your supervisor you're sick."

"God no!" Leopold shoved the flask into his pocket. "I'll sober up, Thomas, I will. Especially before my shift ends. Can't have that cousin of mine seeing me like this or it's off to the inebriate asylum again for me!"

"Clara sent you to an inebriate asylum?" Thomas cringed. Mr. Cavanaugh might be a drunkard, but he seemed a mild-tempered one, albeit a bit loose with the tongue. But an inebriate asylum was no place for an elderly gentleman, and Thomas had never heard of any asylum patients actually cured of the drink. Besides best rest, a healthy diet, and therapeutic baths, the patients also partook in highly structured and disciplined labor, which Thomas felt too stringent a treatment for a rest home. He preferred newer ideologies, those of the mental hygienists who felt that inebriety might be a hereditary biological defect and therefore incurable. Mental hygienists stressed the importance of family, friends, and occupation in creating a beneficial environment, not locking the poor souls away involuntarily. It also bothered Thomas greatly that most of the original asylums now housed the insane.

"Clara sent me away right after she returned from her trip without Stouch. One moment I'm falling into my bed, the next I know, Gracie is crying, and men are hauling me off!"

"What did you do to make her commit you?" Thomas couldn't imagine Mr. Cavanaugh as a mean drunk. Perhaps Clara felt this might truly help her cousin?

"I don't know." Leopold rubbed his forehead as if this would make him remember. "Gracie came to visit me there and said I had mumbled something to Clara during one of my episodes about seeing her at the train station."

"What did you say to Clara?"

"For the life I me, I don't remember. I've got myself a poor memory on top of everything else. You could ask Grace."

"I just might." Thomas wished he had more time to delve into the Cavanaughs' problems, but made a mental note to try. He dearly liked both Mr. and Mrs. Cavanaugh. For now though, he needed to attend his lecture.

"Promise me you won't drink anymore today so I don't have to worry about you getting home?" Thomas held out his hand hoping Mr. Cavanaugh would hand over the bottle, but Leopold ignored the cue.

"I promise." Leopold bent over and sniffed the nasty green water in the bucket. He stood up again, shook his head violently and coughed. "That'll do it every time. I'm wide awake now."

Thomas shook his head and laughed. "I do have to get going." He extended his hand to Mr. Cavanaugh. "If Clara ever talks about putting you away again, I want you or Mrs. Cavanaugh to get a hold of me at once."

Mr. Cavanaugh looked sheepish but grateful. "I thank you from the bottom of my heart, sir."

Thomas smiled. "I told you before, call me Thomas. I'm nobody's sir."

Leopold shook his hand. "You are to me, Thomas. You are to me."

Chapter Fourteen

The following Sunday began full of promise as the late morning sunshine streamed in through Brigid's tiny bedroom window. All Brigid could think about was spending the day with Thomas. Just the thought of him sent a thrill through her, that she never felt with David. Then came the familiar pang of guilt. She brushed aside the sad feelings.

She stood in front of a full-length mirror and inspected her new dress, a soft, green-diamond print provided by Mrs. Ransom. Although only a day dress, the frock was one of the nicest she had ever owned other than the ones David had bought her, and Clara confiscated. The sleeves were in the newest fashion, three-quarters in length. A delicate edging of white lace adorned the buttoned collar. Brigid liked the way the fitted waist accentuated her curves. She had pulled her long hair into a braid at the nape of her neck, coiled it into a bun and pinned it into place. It was the best she could manage having only a few pins, and fingers that trembled from either excitement or nerves.

Satisfied that she could do no better, she glanced again out the window, this time rewarded to find Thomas standing next to his parked automobile, one hand in his pocket, the other behind his back. She smiled, not only because he cut quite the handsome figure in his single-breasted waistcoat, striped dark trousers and broad, felt-banded hat, but also because he'd followed her instructions and hadn't called for her at the servants' door. She didn't want anyone knowing her business, especially those two busybodies, the frail and pale Anna, and rotund Ruthie. Thomas was her only friend, and Brigid didn't need any gossip flying about to ruin her happiness.

She reached to the bed for her hat and coat. "Good luck to you, then, Brigid Mary!" she said to her reflection in the mirror. Although she thrilled to spend the day with Thomas, she couldn't stop her heart from racing, for she'd soon be meeting his mother. She simply couldn't bear being looked down upon again.

With coat in hand and her hat securely atop her head, she hurried down the back stairwell, across the courtyard and to Thomas. He smiled brightly and pulled a bouquet of daisies from behind his back. As he presented them, Brigid blushed from head to toe.

"Thank you, Thomas," she said, accepting the bouquet. "They're beautiful."

"Well, they're not Oreos." He grinned. "But I hope they'll do."

Brigid inhaled the spring aroma. "I love them."

"We're not expected at my mother's until two," he said. "Would you like to go to one of the orphanages on Mrs. Ransom's list and search for Tobias? I know it's a long shot, but we need to start somewhere."

"That is a good idea," Brigid said, relieved to delay meeting Thomas's mother, but happy because she knew Mrs. Ransom would be eager to hear progress was made in the search for her son.

Thomas pulled an envelope from his pocket and handed it to her. "I have information for you to give Mrs. Ransom surrounding Tobias's death. I wrote it down for her, but I can fill you in during our ride."

Brigid took the envelope. “Bless you! It’s only been three days since I told you about the baby. Where did you get this information?”

“At the hospital where Tobias died,” Thomas said. “I told you I had connections.” He winked.

“Mrs. Ransom will be so pleased,” Brigid said. “Does the information confirm anythin’…about Tobias being dead?” She held her breath.

“Sadly, yes. The record confirms his death,” Thomas said, but Brigid noticed his sudden frown and a furrow to his brow. “Still, some things don’t make sense to me. I don’t believe we should cast aside Mrs. Ransom’s suspicions just yet.”

Brigid felt her heart sink to hear the medical record stated Tobias died. She truly wanted the baby to be alive for Mrs. Ransom’s sake.

Thomas glanced up at Ransom house. “Come,” he said, offering his arm for her to hold on to. “Let’s talk more in the motorcar.”

Brigid nodded and allowed him to escort her to the passenger side and help her into the vehicle. His motorcar was not as fancy as Clara’s, but it was surely more comfortable. *Most likely due to the company*, Brigid thought as she relaxed against the seat, placing the flowers next to her.

During the drive to the orphanage, Thomas explained all he had gleaned from Tobias’s chart and spoke of his suspicions that Charles Ransom and Dr. Stouch had accepted the child’s death too easily.

“The record seems too impersonal, something I can’t put my finger on,” Thomas said. “And later, when I returned to my own hospital, I did some more research in the hospital library. The Ransoms never ran a death notice for their son."

"That is sad and odd," Brigid said. "How did people know he died?"

"Word of mouth, I assume. The Ransoms probably asked for privacy, so everything else must have been kept hush-hush."

Thomas told her of his meeting with Leopold Cavanaugh.

"Mr. Cavanaugh is a dear, sweet man," Brigid added. "I only knew him briefly, but I enjoyed his company."

"Was he ever violent or out of control?"

"No." Brigid looked at Thomas. "Why would you be askin' that?"

"He said Clara institutionalized him a few years back. Due to his drinking."

"She did?" Brigid sat shocked. "I can't imagine poor Mr. Cavanaugh locked away. Even when he was into his cups, he only became sweeter." Brigid smiled, remembering the few occasions she had been in Mr. Cavanaugh's company. He had made her feel like family, even after David perished. "And very talkative, too."

"Yes, I know," Thomas laughed, but grew serious again. "I barely know the gentleman, but his confinement bothers me. Then again, Clara may have done what she thought was best at the time. Or perhaps she didn't know what to do. Oddly enough, Mr. Cavanaugh's incarceration was around the same time as Clara's relationship with Dr. Stouch. Perhaps Stouch mentioned something to her about the baby or the death. She might be able to confirm a few things."

At the mention of Clara's name, Brigid cringed. She hated the idea of Thomas meeting with that woman. Then she cringed again, this time at herself. Was she *jealous*? She had no right to be! Thomas was only trying to assist her in helping Mrs. Ransom! And it wasn't like he was her beau. She pushed away a wave of unwarranted melancholy. Where had that come from?

She sat up straight in her seat and stared out the front window. "I'm not sure you can trust Clara," Brigid warned, wanting to add, "She's deceitful," but knowing her own behavior hadn't been perfectly pious since arriving in New York.

"I'll be on my guard," Thomas said, and shot her a reassuring smile. "We're nearing the orphanage. It's called Stonebridge Home for Abandoned Children. I called ahead to ensure we could see the children."

The drive took them from the city and into the country. Buildings were sparse, but an occasional home or farm popped up here or there. Thomas turned down a stony road lined on both sides with maple trees. The winding drive led to a main building with two wings. The property was enclosed by a black iron gate, which stood open.

Thomas pulled into the long driveway.

"Oh, and by the way, we're posing as a married couple that can't have their own children," he said as if simply noting that the sky was blue.

Brigid's cheeks burned scarlet, and she swallowed back an embarrassed laugh, but thrilled at the thought of being married to someone like him.

Thomas cast a sideways glance her way. "There wasn't really any other way they'd let us attempt adoption. When I called, the woman I spoke to, a Mrs. Bensen, wanted us to fill out paperwork, but I explained that I'd be short on time as I have patients to see." Thomas laughed sarcastically, but Brigid failed to understand the humor. "I told her she could check my credentials with the hospital."

"But your credentials don't show that you're married, do they?" Brigid asked impressed by how much thought Thomas had put into helping her find Tobias.

"We'll worry about that should they mention it," Thomas said. He exited the car, rounded the front to Brigid's side and escorted her from the vehicle.

Brigid took in the scenery. "It seems like a nice place, at least from the outside," she said, noticing the well-cared-for lawns and tidy shrubbery. "Not that I've ever seen any orphanages."

"Actually, this is rather decent as compared to the ones in the city. It's run by volunteers, but privately funded by the wealthy Bensen family, which is why I'm sure it's on Mrs. Ransom's list. She probably suspects Charles sent the lad somewhere decent."

"If he wanted to do somethin' nice for the lad, he should've just kept him!" Brigid said, letting her indignation get the best of her Irish temper. "Ransom House is more than decent! And Tobias would have his ma!"

Thomas smiled and nodded his head. "Yes. *If* the child is alive. Let's make certain that's the case. Wouldn't you agree, *Mrs. Ashton*?"

Brigid suppressed an awkward giggle at his calling her by her "married" name. At the same time, her heart did a wistful little flip at the sound of it.

She motioned toward the building. "After you, *dear*."

Thomas took her gently by the elbow. "We'll go together. Link your arm in mine, in case anyone looks out the window."

Brigid obliged, the close proximity of their two bodies sending a wave of warmth throughout her. She was tempted to rest her head against his arm, but refrained. No need to scare off her new husband so soon!

They walked up the stone steps, rang the bell and waited. A tall, slim woman with dark hair and kind, light blue eyes greeted them.

"Good day," she said. "Welcome to Stonebridge. May I help you?"

"Good day," Thomas answered. "We are Mr. and Mrs. Ashton. I telephoned earlier to inquire about adopting a child. Would you be Mrs. Bensen?"

The woman smiled in recognition. "Indeed I am. Please come in." She opened the heavy door wide for them. Brigid and Thomas stepped inside a long hall.

"You mentioned on the phone that we might see the children?" Thomas said.

"Yes. You're the couple looking to adopt an older child, is that right?" She looked at them both.

"Yes." Thomas and Brigid spoke in unison.

"We're looking to adopt a toddler, actually. Age two or so?" Thomas sounded more as if he were ordering a pastry from the bakery than inquiring about a child.

"That is lovely," Mrs. Bensen said, and motioned them to follow her down the hall. "Most couples only want an infant."

At the end of the hallway, she led them up three flights of stairs to the top floor. They walked down another long corridor, at the end of which Mrs. Bensen stopped before a wooden door, the upper half of which was a glass pane.

She removed a key from her pocket and unlocked the door. "This is the East Wing where the toddlers and infants are kept in two separate nurseries. The older children reside in the West Wing. It's nap time for the younger ones, which is why it's so quiet."

Brigid and Thomas nodded as if they'd known this all along.

Mrs. Bensen opened the door to a large room with sunny yellow walls, ample windows and a row of large cribs aligned against the northern and southern walls. In the center of the room was a drab-colored, padded rug with a good assortment of wooden toys strewn about.

A few elderly women cleaned dishes at a sink, or folded linens at a counter. Mrs. Bensen spoke quietly. "The children are in their cribs. You're welcome to peek at them."

"Thank you," Thomas said. Brigid smiled in appreciation.

"Well, thank *you* for thinking of Stonebridge to adopt from. So many people forget about the orphanages these days, preferring instead to have an adoption service place a child with them." She sighed, glanced at the cribs and continued. "But every one of these children is dear and deserves a home."

Her moment of sentimentality left as quickly as it came. She turned back to Brigid and Thomas, her face serious. "Just to inform you further, we don't allow for indentured adoptions from our orphanage. If you decide to adopt one of our children, they will be your *child*, not your employee. I will have you sign papers to that fact, and Children's Services will follow up."

Brigid was taken aback that people would actually adopt children to work for them, and also that Mrs. Bensen felt the need to warn "the Ashtons" not to do this. She felt indignant at the suggestion until she remembered they weren't really adopting a child.

"That's certainly not the type of adoption we're looking for," Thomas said. "We intend to love the child, not put the poor thing to work."

The passion in his voice seemed to please Mrs. Bensen. "Excellent!" She clasped her hands together, smiled wide and turned back toward the door. "I'll return to my office, but before you leave, you must see me and fill out the adoption forms."

Brigid and Thomas nodded.

"Do come in," encouraged one of the women folding towels.

Thomas led Brigid to the cribs on the north wall. They both peered tentatively into the first crib as if the babe within might suddenly spring up and shout "Gotcha!" The blonde, curly-haired little girl simply laid lazily on her back cooing, and playing with her toes. Upon noticing Brigid and Thomas, she smiled, her big blue eyes adoring.

"Let's take her," Brigid teased.

"Let's move on," Thomas said, winking and smiling.

Next crib. A Negro boy, sound asleep and sucking his thumb.

Third crib. Another girl, sleeping.

Fourth crib. A boy with reddish hair, but not disabled in any way as far as they could tell.

And so it went until Thomas and Brigid had seen babies of the wrong sex, the wrong skin tone, the wrong hair color and not a mentally disadvantaged child in the lot.

"Wouldn't this have been easier if we just called and asked if they had a baby lookin' like Tobias?" Brigid whispered, feeling the watchful eyes of the nursery volunteers upon them.

"That would arouse too much suspicion," Thomas whispered back and pointed to a child, as if they discussed his possible adoption. "Besides, Mrs. Ransom already did that and was told he wasn't here, but she wants you to check anyhow."

"Oh, that's right," Brigid answered softly. "Well, perhaps they have another wing for children like Tobias?"

Before Thomas could answer, a stout, copper-haired volunteer about Brigid's age approached.

"The little boy you pointed to is Arthur," she said. "He's eighteen months, cute as a button, and a very happy little lad." She glanced down the line of cribs. "They are such sweet children. I wish I could take them all home."

"As do we," Thomas replied quickly.

"We hope they all find homes," Brigid added, hoping to give Thomas time to think up their next move. How to leave the orphanage without actually choosing a child?

"Let's hope so," the woman said. "Stonebridge was developed by Mrs. Bensen so that orphaned children have a home but are still eligible for adoption. Our mission is to keep these unfortunate babies off the orphan trains."

"Orphan trains?" Brigid said. "What are those?" There was so much about this country she'd yet to learn.

"My wife is from Ireland," Thomas explained. "She's unfamiliar with the term."

"Ah," the woman said, and nodded, seeming happy to educate, but her smile faded as she explained. "Orphan trains take New York orphans of all ages out West to be adopted by families in those states."

"Well, that's good, isn't it?" Brigid said, but both the woman and Thomas frowned.

"One would hope so," the woman said, shaking her head. "The idea, in theory, is a good one and started with the best intent. The Children's Aid Society sends the homeless children west, their mission being to place them with good families who truly want a child to love and raise. But there are rumors that some adoptions are akin to auctions, and the children are used for free labor…or worse." The woman shook her head. "I pray every night for those children."

Brigid's heart plummeted. Poor wee mites! She would pray for them as well.

"But anyhow," the woman said, brightening. "As Mrs. Bensen said, here at Stonebridge we keep the children safe, taking care of them as we would our own, until some caring and wonderful couple such as yourselves provide them a home and loving family."

Thomas coughed and Brigid felt her face flush with guilt. They weren't here for any of those reasons. She wondered what kind of penance would be required for the deceit.

"Actually," Thomas said. "We are hoping to help the most disadvantaged. You see, I'm a doctor, and with my expertise, and my wife's loving nature…"

Brigid tried not to laugh. Loving? He should have seen her wallop her annoying younger brothers from time to time.

"…we were thinking to adopt a child with mental or physical challenges, one that other families might turn away from."

Brigid smiled. Thomas was so crafty. He worded that so tactfully. Much better than her idea of simply asking if they had another wing for the slower children.

The woman's smile faded. She seemed strained to keep the shock from her voice. "Well, that is a highly unusual request, Mr. Ashton. The feeble-minded children are not usually adopted."

Thomas bristled. "Regardless. Are there any at your fine orphanage?"

The woman shook her head and spoke in a low whisper. "No. Those children are usually placed in institutions, not orphanages, as adoption is unlikely, and their care would be expensive."

"I see," Thomas said.

Brigid made a mental note to cross all the other orphanages off Mrs. Ransom's list.

"Well, thank you for your time," Thomas said and took Brigid by the elbow.

"I'm sorry we couldn't help you," the woman said sincerely. "Godspeed to you in finding a child. They will be most fortunate to have you as parents."

"Thank you." Thomas guided Brigid from the room. They retraced their steps back to the first floor and then scurried quietly past Mrs. Bensen's office door, lest she stop them to fill out needless paperwork.

Once inside Thomas's car, and with Stonebridge far enough behind them, Brigid felt safe enough to speak.

"Well, we didn't find Tobias, but at least we learned where he won't be."

"Yes," Thomas said, sounding as dejected as Brigid felt. "We can stop searching orphanages."

Brigid looked out the side window, suddenly saddened by what she'd heard about indentured children, orphan trains, and children left to grow up in orphanages. Her own problems didn't seem quite that bad after all.

"We'll head to my mother's now," Thomas said.

At the mention of his mother and the reminder of the impending dinner, Brigid's nerves hit a high note. She'd rather think about the babies.

She glanced over at Thomas, but he seemed oblivious to her angst. In fact, he looked as if his thoughts were a million miles away.

"What are you thinkin' about?" Brigid asked.

Thomas drew a deep breath. Perhaps he was also nervous about his mother meeting her? His answer proved otherwise.

"You know, talking about the orphan trains bothers me and I can't put my finger on why, other than the obvious reason regarding the children."

Brigid gasped. "Are you thinkin' Mr. Ransom put Tobias on one of those trains?" If that had happened, they might never find him.

"No. I can't see that," Thomas said. "If the baby didn't die, I can't see a man of Charles Ransom's wealth putting his baby on one of those trains. He's too well-known to hand over his infant to someone random and have it kept secret."

They drove in silence for the next several minutes until Thomas pulled alongside a curb. With her thoughts wrapped around the Tobias mystery and the orphans, Brigid hadn't even noticed that they had driven back into the city. On her right, fashioned a tree-lined street made up of multi-storied, ornate apartment buildings. Thomas pulled the car into a parking space in front of one with a Spanish tiled roof and two imposing towers atop.

"Is this where you grew up?" Brigid asked.

"We moved here five years ago, when the building was newly built. I was about ten, when my father began to succeed in real estate, and as his fortune grew, so did his taste in housing. Before that, we were poor and lived in the South Village neighborhood with the other working class Italians."

"Ashton isn't Italian soundin', though, if you don't mind me sayin' so. Was your father?"

"He was English, but my parents had no money when they moved here. My father could get along with anybody though, so they settled in South Village where the working class Italians lived, and where my mother, who didn't speak a lick of English, felt most comfortable. My father found work in construction and worked his way up to develop affordable housing for the poor. Ironically, the more money he made, the better our own living situation became. Sadly, my father passed away right after moving to this apartment."

"I'm sorry," Brigid said, although mesmerized by Thomas's background. She had assumed he'd been a child of means all his life. But he had meager beginnings like her. No wonder he could empathize with those beneath his social standing.

"Ready to meet my mother?" Thomas said, smiling.

Brigid nodded and smoothed her dress.

The question was whether Mrs. Aston, most likely a lady of some means, was ready to meet her.

Chapter Fifteen

Brigid took a deep breath and followed Thomas into his mother's first floor apartment. She half-expected a servant to greet them, but to her surprise, there was none to be found. The house was quiet, except for soft music playing in a distant room. The air was filled with the sweet smell of tomato sauce, and Brigid's stomach softly rumbled.

"My mother must be in the kitchen," Thomas said. To Brigid's delight, he took her by the hand. She relaxed at his warm touch.

They walked through a parlor and down a long hall, past a dining room on their left and a library on the right. The modest, nine-room apartment was pretty, yet not pretentious, even with its walnut paneling, wood-beamed ceilings and mahogany doors with glass knobs. Another left turn at the end of the corridor brought them to the kitchen, from which a melodious voice hummed along to the music.

"Good afternoon, Ma!" Thomas let go of Brigid's hand, but touched the small of her back, encouraging her to step into the kitchen. "I've brought Brigid, the woman I told you about. Brigid, this is my mother, Angelina."

Brigid stepped into the room, and all her preconceived notions about Mrs. Ashton being an uppity, high-class socialite flew out the window, as the short and plump woman walked over and took Brigid's hands in her own. She wore no make-up and had flawless olive-toned skin, thin pink lips and eyes the color of chocolate. Her silver-gray hair was pulled into a net at the back of her head, and an apron covered her modest black dress. She looked Brigid up and down, and smiled.

"Benvenuto, signorina!" Mrs. Ashton patted one of Brigid's hands as she spoke. "Benvenuti a casa nostra! Welcome!" Mrs. Ashton's warm smile and the sincere kindness in her eyes radiated straight to Brigid's heart.

"Thank you," she said.

Thomas helped her with her coat and hat, and as he placed her belongings in a room off the kitchen, he shouted over his shoulder. "Ma! Si prega di parlare inglese, se potete. Brigid non conosce l'italiano."

Returning to the room, he explained. "I asked my mother to speak English. She knows it, but prefers Italian." He shot his mother a playful smile. "Sei testardo in quel modo, no?"

He interpreted his remark for Brigid again. "I called her stubborn. And I'm right, aren't I, Ma?"

Mrs. Ashton laughed and patted her son on the cheek. She turned and pulled two aprons from a nearby drawer, handing one each to Brigid and Thomas.

"And now, we cook," Thomas said, removing his morning coat to reveal a crisp white shirt and suspenders. He draped his coat across a chair and rolled up his sleeves. He looked playful and charming, and Brigid knew she'd have a hard time concentrating on her work because of it.

"We make the ravioli," Mrs. Ashton said, pointing at a round lump of dough on a wooden, flour-coated cutting board. "I show you. But first, you wash your hands."

Thomas and Brigid obeyed and walked to the sink. Thomas turned on the water as Brigid stepped up to the basin.

"Oh!" She couldn't help but gasp and stare at the mass of live snails slithering about in a colander.

Thomas laughed. "Sorry. I forgot to warn you about the snails."

She didn't want to seem rude, but she'd never seen live snails in someone's kitchen sink before. The garlic hanging in front of the window she understood, it was used for cooking. But live snails?

"My mother adds them to her sauce," Thomas explained.

"Ah." Brigid tried not to grimace.

He pushed the colander to the side. They washed and dried their hands and returned to the table.

Over the next several hours, Mrs. Ashton taught Brigid how to roll the homemade dough to the appropriate thickness and how to cut the dough into perfect circles by pressing down on it with the edge of a round glass. They filled each ravioli with just the right dollop of ricotta cheese mixture, covered it with another circle of dough, and pressed the edges closed with a fork, sealing the round pillows.

"This seems similar to bakin' pies," Brigid said, swiping flour from her forehead with the back of her hand. "Except we're makin' hundreds of little ones."

Between making so many ravioli and chatting with both Thomas and his mother, who did indeed speak decent English when she wanted to, the time flew. Mrs Ashton told Brigid how she grew up on a sheep farm in Calabria and how she met Thomas's father when her family moved to England. Her father had hired the young man to paint their house. The dashing, blonde-haired, blue-eyed John Ashton swept the dark Italian beauty off her feet. They had married young and sailed to America, where John sought his fortune and promised to make Angelina happy.

"But no," Mrs. Ashton said, shaking her head. "I did not like New York. Too busy. Ugly. But I loved my husband, so I stayed. And then, I had my Tomaso." She smiled and glanced at Thomas. "Someday, I go back to my beautiful Italia." She sighed.

Brigid understood Mrs. Ashton's longing for home. But then again, maybe someday she'd have a husband and a baby to keep her here. She glanced at Thomas but forced her thoughts back to the present. "Your name is Tomaso?"

"It's my given name," he explained. "Tomaso Roberto Ashton."

"Very Italian!" Angelina said, beaming. "But his father said, 'No. In America, he will be *Thomas*'." She patted her son's hand. "But he is Tomaso to me."

Thomas smiled at his mother, and Brigid warmed at their affection for each other. A pang of longing for her own mother threatened to surface, but she defiantly pushed it back. She would not allow her sadness to ruin this happy afternoon.

"It's my goal to send Ma to Italy, someday," Thomas said as he and Brigid cleaned the table and Mrs. Ashton placed the ravioli in boiling water. Brigid watched as Thomas's mother then took the colander of live snails from the kitchen sink and threw them into a second pot of water.

"My father was a good man and took care of us, but he was adamant about us staying in America. He said our future, our prosperity, was here." Thomas and his mother exchanged sorrowful glances, and Brigid guessed that it wasn't in memorium for the snails.

"But I'm working on getting her to Italy," Thomas said. "I can't send her now, as the money is tied up. My father's will stated that upon his death, his savings should pay for housing, the car and fund my education. We also get a household living expense each month. I can't touch the rest of the money until I've graduated from medical school. The minute I have that diploma in hand, however, Ma is going to Italy!"

"Tomaso is a good boy," Mrs Ashton said as she grabbed a wooden spoon and beat an escaping snail back into the pot.

Dinner proved as delicious as it smelled. Greens tossed with oil, vinegar, garlic and salt were also served, along with fresh slices of mozzarella and preserved meats. Dessert was sweet bakery cannoli, and not too soon after, Mrs. Ashton presented a tray of fruit, nuts and homemade coffee. So as not to seem impolite, Brigid sampled a bit of everything. By the time she sipped her last bit of coffee, she felt as if she might burst out of her dress.

Thomas yawned, and fatique engulfed Brigid as well. They stayed a bit longer, however, to clean up the dinner dishes for Mrs. Ashton.

When Thomas finally brought Brigid's coat and hat to her, she thanked Mrs. Ashton for the wonderful dinner, friendly company and happy afternoon. To her delight, the dear lady kissed her on both cheeks. "Si prega di visitare nuovamente!"

"You're welcome back anytime," Thomas interpreted with an exasperated look at his mother's lapse back into Italian. Brigid stifled a giggle, but thanked her again. Thomas kissed his mother. "I'll be back shortly."

The May evening was cool but comfortable, and as Thomas drove her back to Ransom house, Brigid's heart was light. Dining with Thomas and his dear mother reminded her of what being part of a family was like. It felt good.

"Your mother is the nicest lady," Brigid said. "She's givin' me hope for all New Yorkers."

Thomas laughed and reached across the seat, taking Brigid's hand in his. His touch radiated through her entire body, and she was grateful that the sun had set so he couldn't see her cheeks flush with happiness.

"My mother liked you, too." His eyes left the road for a moment to catch hers. He squeezed her hand. "As, of course, do I." He paused and stared intensely at her. "Very much."

Her heart raced. Could he possibly feel for her what she'd been feeling for him?

"Thank you, Thomas. And I'm likin' you very much." She looked straight ahead, hoping she hadn't sounded too forward. Just in case, she quickly added, "How do you know your mother likes me?"

"You got dessert."

They both laughed, but Brigid's humor dissipated as they neared Ransom House. The day had been long, but now seemed too quick to end. Thomas parked the car where he had picked her up earlier.

He exited from his side, walked to hers and opened the door. Sad to have the evening end, she took her flowers from the seat, and he helped her down. As her feet touched the pavement, her body accidently brushed against his, sending little waves of electricity shooting throughout her. She took a step back and looked away.

"Excuse me." She glanced up to find those crystal blue eyes staring into hers.

He did not step aside to let her pass. Her mind became a sea of tossed emotions. Her body still tingled from his touch. She felt excited, yet safe. Happy, yet oddly nervous. Desirous, yet cautious. Wanting, yet patient.

"I have something for you." He stood so close she felt his warm sweet breath on her skin.

The streetlight illuminated him from behind, making him seem larger than life and leaving Brigid enveloped in his shadow, as if in his arms. How she wished she could be.

He reached into his coat pocket and pulled out a sealed, manilla envelope. "These are the hospital notes for Mrs. Ransom."

"Oh." He *had* mentioned those earlier, hadn't he.

She lowered her head and tried to hide her disappointment as she took the envelope and placed it in her coat pocket. "I'll be sure she gets them."

She looked up again. Why did he stare at her so? Did he know how difficult it was for her to be this close to him and not fall helplessly into his arms? She looked away. "Mrs. Ransom will be grateful, I'm sure."

"Thank you for coming to my mother's today." Thomas's eyes remained intent. He took her free hand in his. "May I see you again? I mean, outside of orphanages and entertaining elderly ladies?" He held her hand tighter. "I've grown quite fond of you, Brigid. If you don't mind me saying so?"

If he only knew!

"I don't mind." She smiled demurely, but fought the urge to shout at the top of her lungs. Happiness flooded her. Was this what is was like to finally, possibly, be in love? For real? If so, it was the most wondrous feeling she'd ever known.

Thomas continued talking and Brigid had to force herself to concentrate and listen above the manic beating of her heart.

"Unfortunately my hospital schedule is quite busy this week. I believe my professor may allow me to actually treat a few patients. Could we meet Thursday during your break and perhaps next Sunday as well?"

Joy radiated throughout her. She could not contain her smile. "I'd like that."

"Very well, then!" Thomas seemed as pleased as she felt. "May I escort you to the house?"

Brigid knew the time grew late and that the others would soon be returning from their own Sunday excursions. "I'll be fine, but thank you."

"Then I'll sadly stand here and watch until you disappear from my sight." He feigned a dejected countenance, let go of her hand and placed it to his heart.

She laughed, secretly pleased that he cared so much for her safety. "Somehow, I'm thinkin' my leavin' should not be quite that tragic."

"Well, I must admit, my motives are purely selfish." Thomas grinned. "I want to enjoy every last minute with you that I can."

"All right, then." She took a step sideways as if to leave, but he took her hand again.

"Wait," he said. "There's one more thing."

He bent and placed his lips lightly against her own. Brigid closed her eyes, and as his lips lingered, she returned the kiss, feeling her body respond as if she'd never been kissed before. And, as far as she was concerned, she hadn't. Not like this, anyhow. Thomas's lips started a slow simmer of an unfamiliar fire within her, something she'd never felt with David, or the boys she kissed back home. He made her feel alive, not only by the sensual longings his lips caused, but because this kiss reminded her that wonderful things could happen. Perhaps this was the start of a new life for her? A life without arranged marriages, secrets and running away.

All too soon, his lips pulled away. They held to each other, enjoying the quiet of the moment.

"I should go," she finally said, fearing if she didn't leave, she'd throw herself against him like a wanton hussy and beg for more.

"Until Thursday then?" Thomas stepped aside to let her pass.

"Yes."

Cursing each step that took her further from him, she walked slowly toward Ransom House.

Rounding the corner to the courtyard, she stole one last glance over her shoulder. Thomas still stood there, her shining knight under the streetlight.

She descended the servants' entrance steps and used her key to enter the kitchen hall. She removed her coat and hat and hung them on the coat rack, with Mrs. Ransom's notes from Thomas still in the pocket.

With flowers in hand, and thinking only of Thomas's kiss, Brigid climbed the steps to her room and opened the door. As she walked toward her bed, she startled to hear someone behind her. Before she could turn around, a cloth was pressed over her mouth and nose, forcing her to inhale a sickeningly sweet odor. An iron strong arm tightened around her waist, pinning her arms. Her flowers dropped to the floor. Try as she might, she could not scream, fight nor kick free from her captor. She struggled to tear away from the cloth, but strength and consciousness failed her. As her body surrendered beneath her, her mind tried to react.

An image of her family flashed. She saw her home in Ireland.

A bouquet of fresh springtime flowers.

Snails.

And finally, Thomas. She tried to call to him.

No words came.

Chapter Sixteen

From his bedroom window, Charles Ransom looked down upon the scene below. Anger surged through his veins as he watched women from all ranks of New York society walk together in the street, protesting for their rights. "Suffragettes" the women called themselves. They marched singularly or in groups, some appearing to chat with others as they went, many holding the hands of their children, some even pushing baby carriages. They dressed in white and held gold pennants with nine stars each, the flags bearing the phrase "Votes for Women", the stars representing each state already granting women the right to vote.

The pounding in Charles's head seemed to increase ten-fold with each step the women took. As if things could only be that easy! Don't have what you want? Hold a parade! Refuse to take no for an answer and *demand* that you're given your due! What a simple solution! Perhaps he would join them and demand that someone provide him with a healthy heir!

He let go of the heavy curtain, rested his aching head against the damask panels and squeezed his eyes shut as if that might make the unpleasantness of last night disappear.

Rupert had lied. Or been quite mistaken. Charles's part had *not* been quick, pleasant or easy, but it was done. Yet Charles felt worse than before the deed. Why couldn't his first child have been born right-minded? Why couldn't Eliza bear him another child? Why couldn't he have been born a man without a conscience, a man who could simply take what he needed and forget about it.

But he was not that man. Last night had been a nightmare, most likely for the maid as well, although Rupert had insured she'd be unconscious and wouldn't feel, or remember, anything. But *he* knew. Charles couldn't forget what he'd done. It was a sin against God, and against Eliza. No wonder he'd found it loathsome.

He raised his head and pulled the curtain open again.

"A rather peaceful protest, isn't it?"

Charles turned to find Rupert Stouch standing in the doorway.

"Is it?" Charles let the curtain drop and moved closer to the doctor. "I can't hear anything from here."

"You could open the window," the doctor said with an amused smile.

"Ah, yes, quite right." The idea hadn't even occurred to him.

"It is rather stuffy in here," Rupert said, taking a step into the room.

"Leave then," Charles snapped, and imediately regretted it. He had no right to be angry with the man. For years, Rupert Stouch had done Charles's bidding. Last night was just another scheme concocted by the good doctor to help Charles succeed in his goals. Stouch was always willing to help. Of course, he also got paid rather handsomely for it.

"I apologize, Rupert. Please, sit." Charles motioned to a plush recliner near the hearth.

"No, no thank you," the doctor replied, but no malice laced his words. "I just came to tell you that I'm leaving. Before the girl could regain consciousness last night, I gave her a strong sedative and another this morning. She'll sleep on and off for a good two days and not remember anything. I've told Mrs. Duffy and your housekeeper that she's taken ill with fever, should remain in bed and is not to have visitors. I'll call again in a few days."

"Good." Charles walked to his dresser and pulled a long envelope from the top drawer. "Your payment, my good man."

Rupert took the envelope and turned to leave, but stopped as he noticed the suitcase lying open on Charles's bed. He turned back. "Are you traveling? For how long? How will I contact you should our efforts be fruitful?"

My efforts, thought Charles. *All Stouch did was restrain and drug the maid, bring her to the bed and leave the room.*

"I'm going to our vacation home in Maine," Charles answered. "Alone. Eliza won't come. I've asked."

He couldn't stay at Ransom House. He'd never be able to face the girl again without remembering what he did. Granted, she'd never know exactly what happened, and if she did, she could never prove who did it. Still, that did not ease his shame. His own unfortunate circumstances had forced him to take advantage of an innocent girl. He could not erase the act from his mind, so he must escape. At least until the end justified the means.

"You can contact me by telephone at the house in Maine," Charles said. "When will you know for certain?"

"I'll send a midwife to speak with Brigid in three or four weeks time. It won't look good to have me constantly showing up. It will seem odd enough that I just happened to be here last night when... she took ill."

"You were visiting me," Charles said. "It's believable. We're old friends."

"Yes, excellent," Stouch continued. "Anyway, we'll know for certain after I speak with the midwife."

"Very good."

"And if it did not work this time, you can certainly try again," Rupert said, as if committing vile acts was an every day occurrance for Charles.

Charles slammed his suitcase shut. "No!" He would not subject himself to this guilt-ridden torture again. Not only had he fornicated with low-lying Irish trash, but by doing so, he betrayed his beautiful Eliza in the worst of ways. He could not bear the thought of hurting Eliza again.

The doctor remained still as stone at Charles's outburst.

"Forgive me, again," Charles said. "I didn't meant to shout. But I won't repeat what happened last night."

Rupert nodded.

"If it doesn't work, we'll figure something else out," Charles said, knowing full well there were no other options to secretly beget a biological heir. He could not take a mistress, women couldn't be trusted not to talk. And what if the woman wouldn't give up the baby, even for money? Either way, he'd still had a problem explaining a new child to Eliza. He'd have to trust that her thrill to have another baby would overshadow the fact that it wasn't actually hers. *He* would finally have a healthy, biological heir and *that* was what should matter.

Rupert placed the envelope inside his coat. “We’ll cross that bridge, should we come to it.”

“Yes. Well then, good day to you, my friend.” Charles walked back to the window.

“Good day, Charles.” The doctor exited, leaving Charles alone with his thoughts.

It was not a place he enjoyed being.

Chapter Seventeen

Thomas couldn't wait to see Brigid again, and yet it seemed the one thing most impossible to do. For the second time this week, he could not find her. She hadn't shown up the previous Thursday when she was to meet him in Central Park, and now, as he stood at the servants' entrance to Ransom House ringing the bell repeatedly, she didn't answer, nor did anyone else.

She was all he could think about since the night they kissed. He wanted to kiss her again, but at this point, he'd be happy just to see her. He had so much to tell! He wanted to share how much his mother liked her, but even more importantly, he wanted to tell her that he had finally been allowed to treat patients, albeit nothing too complicated, mostly rashes, pneumonia cases and a few broken bones.

But Brigid hadn't appeared, and he was getting nowhere again today. He couldn't understand why she didn't meet him. Or wouldn't meet him? Had he offended her by kissing her? She had seemed to enjoy it. Had something happened to her? Was she ill? Had their trip to the orphanage somehow been discovered and she'd been fired? Granted that would be far-fetched, but he had nothing else to go on as to why she hadn't shown.

He decided to try the front door. With flowers in hand, for he loved seeing the delight in Brigid's eyes when he presented her with gifts, he hurried to the front of Ransom House and ran up the cement steps. He startled as the door opened just as he reached the landing. Two men stepped out, one a butler, and the other, Dr. Rupert Stouch. Thomas halted just before colliding with the renowned doctor.

The men appeared equally surprised to see Thomas.

"May I help you?" the butler said.

Thomas scrambled to speak, his surprise at running into the doctor unnerving him.

"Well?" The butler spoke and looked at him as if he were a mangy cat come howling for a scrap to eat. He placed his entire body in the doorway in case Thomas might attempt an uninvited dash into the house.

Dr. Stouch stared at him as well, but his expression was kind. Thomas's mind became a whirlwind of thoughts. Should he pretend not to know the doctor? Should he acknowledge Dr. Stouch for the famed doctor he was? Should he mention he also studied medicine? Would being on familiar terms with Dr. Stouch give him leeway later to ask questions about Tobias?

"Sir!" The butler seemed in no mood for Thomas's stalling. "Either state your business or leave!"

Thomas swallowed and decided to keep mum with the doctor. He had yet to form any plan about what he'd like to ask him about Tobias, so best to keep quiet.

Dr. Stouch unwittingly allowed him more time to think as he addressed the butler himself. "I'll take my leave then, Henry. I left instructions with Mrs. Latimer as well."

"Thank you, Dr. Stouch." The butler turned to Thomas as the doctor descended the steps. "Now, how may I help you?"

"Yes, of course. Forgive me." Thomas offered his warmest smile. "I've come to see Brigid O'Brien."

"Who?" Dr. Stouch retraced his steps to the top of the landing. His expression had turned to stone. The butler's eyes grew wide and his face paled as if Thomas said he'd come to murder them all.

"Brigid O'Brien," Thomas repeated. "She's a kitchen maid."

"I know who she is, but you can't see her," the butler said.

"Why ever not?"

"She's il-"

"Not here," interjected Dr. Stouch.

"Well, where is she?" Thomas looked from the doctor to the butler. He was not unaware of the strange look that passed between them.

The butler cleared his throat. "That's right. She's not here. Who are *you*?" His glance fell to the flowers Thomas held.

What to say? Brigid had made it clear she didn't want the staff at Ransom House knowing her business, but Thomas figured he'd already surrendered her privacy by coming to the house in the first place. "I'm a suitor."

"Suitor?" Dr. Stouch laughed. "What's your name?"

Thomas was about to answer when he noticed an ominous shadow cross the doctor's face. He silently thanked his lucky stars that he hadn't introduced himself to Stouch earlier. Neither man seemed pleased by his presence. He decided to keep quiet about his real name. Should he get on Stouch's bad side, the doctor could ruin his medical career with just one word to the right people.

"William." Thomas glanced at the street while his mind grasped for a suitable last name. "Carr. Two r's."

"Well, Mr. Carr," Dr. Stouch said. "Miss O'Brien has left the country. So forget about her and be on your way." He shot a glance at the butler again, then shook his head and smiled as if Thomas was simply a naughty schoolboy. "Young, foolish love."

Thomas's heart dropped to his knees. "What do you mean Brigid left the country? For where?" He looked to the butler for answers. Surely he'd know what might be amiss with Brigid. But he appeared as confused as Thomas felt.

"Ireland," Dr. Stouch said. "She went back home to live."

"That's impossible!" He looked at each man as if this were some kind of joke. "Her family disowned her."

The doctor and the butler exchanged odd glances again.

"She was unhappy here," Dr. Stouch answered. "Very depressed. I was asked to see her and found her in an extreme case of melancholia. She wanted to leave, so the Ransoms paid to have her sent home."

Thomas wasn't buying it, and his ire rose. He turned on Stouch. "Why would they call *you*? You're an obstetrician!"

The minute the words flew from his mouth, Thomas knew he'd made a mistake. Dr. Stouch's eyes grew wide and his eyebrows arched nearly to the brim of his hat. A sinister smile spread from under his handlebar mustache. "And how would *you* know that, Mr. Carr?"

Yes, how *would* he know that being a single man supposedly not in medical school? Thomas thought fast. "You're famous!" Nothing like stroking an ego to change the subject. "I read an article about you in the *New York Times* a while back." It was a risky thing to say, but Rupert Stouch *was* a noted doctor to the wealthy, so there must have been something in the news about him at some point throughout the years.

"Ah yes." Dr. Stouch visibly relaxed. "You must be referring to when I delivered the Bellamy triplets."

"Yes, that's it!" Thomas said, snapping his fingers. He actually remembered the case. Triplets were so rare, and the mother was so grateful to Stouch, that she took out a full-page ad in the *Times* thanking him.

The conversation had veered off course, and Thomas wanted to reel it back to Brigid's whereabouts. "You treated Brigid?"

Stouch coughed. "Yes, but Mr. Carr, that's all I can tell you. I've told you too much already that I shouldn't have. You know, patient confidentiality and all that."

"If that's all then, Mr. Carr?" The butler placed a hand on the door, ready to slam it shut should the need arise. "I'm sure the good doctor needs to be on his way, and your business here is finished."

He had been dismissed.

"Good day." Dr. Stouch tipped his hat slightly and hurried down the stairs as if Ransom House had caught fire.

"Good day, as well, sir." The butler slammed the front door shut.

Thomas stood alone on the landing, flowers in hand, his heart as heavy as his feet, which felt permanently imbedded in the concrete. He didn't want to leave. How could Brigid be gone just like that? Without a word. She was depressed? How could it be?

They had such a good time together! She'd made no mention of melancholia or homesickness! They had made plans to see each other again!

It took all his effort to walk back to his car. None of this made sense. When had she left? His lovesick heart told him to run to the dock, book passage to Donegal and go find her. But he had no money for that, and even if he did, he should first send his mother to Italy.

Brigid was gone, but he could not accept it. He barely believed Dr. Stouch. Why would Brigid go to Ireland of all places? She wasn't wanted there. Maybe she was in some sort of trouble at Ransom House just said she went to Ireland? But why wouldn't she come to him for help?

Whether still in New York, or sailing to Ireland, Brigid remained locked in his heart.

He turned from his car and walked to Central Park. He located their bench, the one he and Brigid had shared on their first meeting and placed the bouquet on the seat.

"I will find you, again, Brigid O'Brien," he said to the sky. "I will find you."

~~~~

Thomas returned to the hospital. He hoped getting his mind back on his patients would get Brigid off of it. Or not. If her memory was all he now had, he wanted it foremost in his mind, a mental picture of their brief time together. It was all he had left of her. How could she have breezed into his life, only to vanish in an instant, as if swept out to sea? Something didn't feel right about her disappearance. Just like the disappearance of Tobias Ransom.
~~~~

Brigid was gone and the baby was supposedly dead, yet Thomas couldn't outright accept either notion. But why? Why did he want to dig up ghosts where none were likely to be found? Yet both disappearances were interrelated, for with Brigid gone, how would Eliza Ransom ever find out what truly happened to her baby?

"And why should I care so much?" Thomas thought as he walked the hospital corridors in search of his mentor.

Perhaps he needed more to do. He certainly needed better medical training. Although the new cases he been allowed to treat were a step up, they didn't inspire him. He actually felt that he did more good by searching for the baby. Another thought struck. If he spoke with Mrs. Ransom and explained that he had helped Brigid search for Tobias and would like to continue to do so, perhaps Eliza might exchange information regarding Brigid's sudden departure.

Buoyed by this idea, and with a renewed sense of purpose, Thomas hurried to find Dr. Hack. He located him in the staff lounge, reviewing charts.

"Dr. Hack." Thomas squared his shoulders and cleared his throat. "May I have a word?" He kept his voice firm.

The gray-haired doctor glanced up through round spectacles. "Make it quick."

Thomas drew a deep breath. "Have I not done well under your tutelage?"

"Are you fishing for compliments, Dr. Ashton?"

Thomas saw his opening. "No, indeed not. Actually, I'm fishing for patients." He offered a hopeful smile.

It had no affect on the man. Dr. Hack closed his file, sat back in his chair and rubbed his eyes. "Dr. Ashton, what *are* you talking about?"

"I need more to do. I want more challenging cases. I've set so many broken bones I could do them in my sleep. I've treated so many cases of pneumonia, I'm surprised I haven't caught it myself. I-"

"Enough, Dr. Ashton!" Dr. Hack stood, but produced a rare smile. "Point made. And yes, actually, you have been doing very well. It just so happens we've had a patient admitted today with the measles. Unfortunately, I've not had the disease, have you?"

"Yes, as a very young child." Thomas didn't recall his illness, but his mother told anyone who listened how he nearly died from it.

"Excellent. Then you're not at risk of infection from our patient."

Dr. Hack pulled a chart from the top of the pile and handed it to him. "The nurses have done what they can for her. She's in one of our few isolation rooms. She's a very sick, elderly woman, plus she seems to be suffering from acute anxiety, although the cause we can't assess. Perhaps a young, good-looking chap such as yourself might be able to find out why she can't rest?"

"You want me to go and *talk* with her?"

"Procure a set of vitals if the nurses haven't recently," the doctor added. "There's not much we can do for the measles except keep the patient comfortable. Rest will be her biggest ally against her disease, yet this woman cannot seem to relax."

"Thank you, Dr. Hack. I'll report back soon." Thomas tried to hide his disappointment. He wanted to treat disease, not be a psychiatrist. Still, it was an infectious disease case, a step in the right medical direction. He'd take what he could get.

He left the lounge and headed to Room 214. He studied the file as he walked, searching first for the patient's name.

He stopped his tracks. His patient was Mrs. Grace Cavanaugh.

~~~~~~~~~~~~

Thomas entered Mrs. Cavanaugh's room. A curtain was drawn around her bed, so he let it be and walked around it. Grace Cavanaugh appeared to be asleep, a frail and pale figure covered with the telltale red rash of measles on her face and limbs. A nurse sat in a chair at her side, but rose to leave when Thomas said he'd stay with Mrs. Cavanaugh.

He quickly read through her chart; her vitals had just been taken. Mrs. Cavanaugh ran a dangerously high fever. He put the record at the end of her bed, and as he went to replace the water in her glass from a nearby pitcher, Mrs. Cavanaugh opened her red-rimmed eyes. Her sweet, round face broke into a weak smile, and she extended her hand to him.

"Mr. Ashton?" Her voice was thin and shaky. "How did you get in? Clara has limited my visitors."

"Yes, I see the restriction on the chart." He offered her his most cheerful smile and took her hand in his. "But, actually, Mrs. Cavanaugh, I'm your doctor."

"Oh!" She licked her dry, parched lips. Thomas offered her the glass of water, but she waved it away. Her hand dropped back to the bed as if the weight of holding it up took a toll. "I have measles?"
~~~~~~~~~~~~

"Yes." Thomas pulled up a chair alongside her bed and sat facing her. "Any idea where you may have caught them? Are either Mr. Cavanaugh or Clara ill?"

"No." She shook her head slowly. "They both had the measles in childhood. I didn't." Thomas noted how Grace gripped her blankets and twisted them in her small hands. "Clara thinks Leopold brought the disease home from the hospital where he works."

"If he is immune, that is not probable, Mrs. Cavanaugh. You most likely caught the disease by contact with an infected person, even a passerby on the street if they were about to come down with the disease and coughed. You may have caught it by simply sitting next to someone in church who was contagious."

Mrs. Cavanaugh reached over and grabbed his coat sleeve. "Would you tell that to Clara? Please! I'm so afraid she might send Leopold away again because of this!"

"Of course." Although he remembered that Clara had committed Leopold for his drinking, he doubted she would put her own cousin away for possibly spreading the measles. He'd have to find Clara and sort this story out. It could be, that in Mrs. Cavanaugh's feverish state, she misunderstood Clara's intentions.

Thomas empathized with Grace's stress however, but despite his attempts to sooth her worries, tears welled in the dear lady's eyes. He knew there wasn't much they could do for her beyond keeping her hydrated and comfortable, but she wouldn't recover quickly under this much anxiety and worry.

He could feel the heat from her feverish hand on his skin. He reached for the water cup again. "You need to keep drinking water, Mrs. Cavanaugh."

"No!" Her grip on his arm tightened. "You must find Clara now! She left here a little while ago. I don't know where she went, but I'm afraid she's going back to the house. I'm afraid for Leopold!"

Afraid? Clara might put on airs, but he never took her as one to be feared. Pitied, yes. Feared, no. Was Mrs. Cavanaugh delirious due to her high fever?

He tried his best to calm her again. "I've met Clara, Mrs. Cavanaugh. At dinner at your home, remember? What is there to be afraid of?"

"I told you! She's going to send my husband away! She wants Leopold silenced!"

Thomas tried to remain stoic at her statement, hiding his shock at her words. "Silenced?"

She turned her head away.

He certainly didn't know what Mrs. Cavanaugh was talking about.

"Do you mean that he's been drinking again?" He patted the hand that still held his arm. "I ran into Leopold at Baybridge Hospital when he was working. He told me Clara had him committed once."

"Yes!" Mrs. Cavanaugh faced him again, her eyes brightened and she appeared to regain some energy. "That's it exactly, and she's looking for a reason to do it again. But I've kept Leopold from the drink when he's home so she can't commit him."

She began to cough from excitement, and Thomas insisted she take a few sips of water, most of which dribbled down her chin. He gently wiped her face with a cloth.

As she rested back against the pillows, Mrs. Cavanaugh offered an imploring look. "Dr. Ashton, Thomas, my friend…"

"Yes?"

"The other doctor told me that there's nothing you can do for me here, that I could be at home, because the disease must run its course. But Clara insists I stay here, even though I've heard her refer to hospitals as dirty, germ-infested houses for the underprivileged. Why would she put me here then? I think it's so I can't interfere with her sending Leopold away!"

"But if he's not been drinking at home, why would she do that?"

"Leopold saw something years back. He told me about it at the time, and I waved it off as his imagination or a drunken hallucination, but when he confronted Clara about it, her reaction and the way she has treated him since makes me think he was right."

"What did he say?"

"He was at the train station seeing a friend off on a trip out west. Leopold swears he saw Clara there."

"That's not so odd…"

It seemed to take every ounce of her strength, but somehow Grace Cavanaugh pushed herself into a sitting position.

She looked Thomas straight in the eye.

"Clara was holding a baby and boarded a train."

Chapter Eighteen

The following Monday, Brigid finally felt well enough to return to her duties. She'd spent most of the last week sick in bed. But now, as she stepped into the kitchen, she realized she was still slightly light-headed and dazed, as if she'd been in a cocoon.

For the little she remembered, she may as well have been. She remembered her wonderful time with Thomas and their kiss and returning to Ransom House. Memories were a blur after that, but when she did come close to a memory of the previous week, it came as a inexplicable flashback of confusion and fear.

Dr. Stouch had visited several times during the course of her illness. He had explained that when she hadn't shown up for work last Monday, Ruthie had checked on her and found her in bed and out of her senses. Dr. Stouch said how lucky she'd been that he happened to be visiting Mr. Ransom at the time. He pronounced her sick with the flu and quarantined her to bed for the week. She had no visitors other than himself and Mrs. Latimer, the housekeeper, who tended to Brigid's personal needs.

Brigid had been horrified with embarrassment when Mrs. Latimer later told her that, at the same time she'd fallen ill, she'd also started her monthly course. Brigid found that odd, as she hadn't been due for at least another two weeks. And although her flow seemed to leave as quickly as it came on, Brigid still suffered a slight discomfort in her lower abdomen and womanly parts.

"Well, there's our girl!" Mrs. Duffy smiled wide upon seeing Brigid and scurried over to offer her a quick hug. "I was so worried about you!"

Brigid gently pulled from the woman's well-meant embrace. Funny, hugs never used to bother her.

Mrs. Duffy seemed nonplussed at Brigid's retreat. "I'm so happy you're back! You've missed a lot of the goings on."

"Thank you, Mrs. Duffy." Feeling a bit weak, Brigid accepted a chair the cook pulled out from the table.

"I've given Anna and Ruthie the baking duties this morning," Mrs. Duffy said, glancing to the hallway. "They should be down shortly. I told them to sleep in an extra half-hour. I wanted to tell you the latest!"

Mrs. Duffy walked to the stove and poured Brigid a cup of coffee. She returned to the table and placed the steaming cup in front of her. "You drink that while I talk." She pulled out a chair for herself. "You're as pale as a ghost!"

"Thank you for the coffee and yes, I'm still feelin' a bit off, but I'm happy to get back to work." Brigid wrapped her hands around the warm, black cup.

"Well, here's something to put a blush into those cheeks." Mrs. Duffy leaned in close and dropped her voice to a whisper. "Ruthie finally admitted that all her weight gain is because she's having a baby!"

Brigid's eyes flew open with surprise. "She's so young! She must be worryin' herself to death."

"You'd think!" Mrs. Duffy slapped the table and frowned. "Turns out she's happy about it! Stupid girl! Seventeen, not married, with a babe on the way, and she's dancing around here like she's got not a care in the world!"

"Who is the father?"

"Hold on to your coffee for this one, Brigid." Mrs. Duffy's eyes went wide, and her voice fell to a whisper as if she might reveal the secret of the universe. "Jimmy Pugh, the delivery boy! Turns out she's been seeing him on her days off, and oh, supposedly they're in love and when they get enough money, they're going to get married, raise their baby and live happily ever after." Mrs. Duffy slapped the table again and returned to her normal voice. "She's living in her own little made-up fairy tale, I tell you!"

Brigid knew things could be worse. She'd seen enough foolish girls in Donegal unmarried, pregnant and disowned by their families. If what Ruthie said was true, at least Jimmy loved her and wanted to marry her.

"I think we should be happy for her, if she's happy about it," Brigid said, and sipped her coffee. It warmed her insides and she felt better than she had all week. "Will she be stayin' on with us?"

"Just until the baby is born, which is fine by me. She's not much for work these days anyhow with her head all in the clouds about her future. If you ask me, she ruined her life getting herself with child at such a young age."

Brigid nodded in agreement and thought of her ma who had her first child at eighteen. Now, at age forty-three, her ma was bone-tired and her youngest, little Liam, was just six. Bearing seven children in nineteen years had drained her youth and aged her beyond her years.

A pang of guilt ran through Brigid. If she hadn't left Donegal, she could have continued helping with the younger children. Then again, her parents had planned to marry her off to start her own brood with that old farmer.

A woman's choices were never easy. She loved her ma, but didn't want to end up like her. So she had left, hoping for a better life. But now, she thought of Thomas, as she had a million times throughout the past week. What had he thought when she was unable to meet with him? She needed to see him again and tell him how sick she'd been.

"Mrs. Duffy, has anyone called for me while I was ill?"

"No, can't say that they have." Mrs. Duffy rose from her chair.

"Any telephone calls?"

"No, who were you expecting?" Surprise and curiosity marked the woman's face, and Brigid remembered that servants weren't allowed telephone privileges.

"No one." Brigid tried to hide her disappointment. Didn't Thomas wonder why she hadn't shown at the park last Thursday? Had she been too forward accepting his kiss? Maybe he didn't want to see her again. But, how could that be? They'd had such a wonderful time together. And that kiss! Brigid startled. Maybe she inadvertently gave him the flu!

Mrs. Duffy snapped her fingers. "Oh, I nearly forgot. Mrs. Ransom scared us all to death by coming down to the kitchen one morning. She's never done that before. I thought she was going to fire the lot of us! But, she only inquired as to your whereabouts and seemed quite agitated by your absence. We told her you were ill, and she wanted to know why your bedroom door was locked. I explained you were quarantined."

Mrs. Ransom! Brigid had completely forgotten that Eliza would wonder what Thomas had discovered about Tobias. She suddenly remembered the note in her coat pocket. Was it still there? Had anyone else found it?

She pushed her coffee to the side and stood. "I should probably go see Mrs. Ransom at once."

Mrs. Duffy shook her head. "She doesn't rise until later in the morning. We really should get to work."

"Oh, yes, I'm supposin' you're right, but I still need to check something." She hurried to the hall. Her coat remained on the hook where she left it, and the envelope was still in the pocket and sealed. She pulled it from her coat.

Thomas's handwriting on the envelope caused tears to well. She missed him and worried why he didn't inquire after her. Should she contact him? That might prove difficult.

"Brigid, are you coming?" Mrs. Duffy hollered from the kitchen.

"I'll be right there." Her head hurt from worrying about Thomas. She decided she must just be patient and wait for Thursday, go to Central Park, find their bench, and hope he was there.

Satisfied with her plan, she turned toward the kitchen, but the room began to spin, and her vision blurred. Collapsing against the wall, she cried for help.

As Brigid once again slipped from consciousness, the image of her mother, pregnant and ill, flashed across her mind.

~~~~~~~~~~~~
~~~~~~~~~~~~

She woke in her bedroom, lying in her bed. Her head ached something fierce. She recalled feeling faint in the servants' hall.

"How are you feeling, dear?"

A familiar voice spoke beside her. Brigid turned to find Eliza Ransom sitting at her bedside. The lady didn't appear quite so ghostly in the daylight. In fact, she was quite beautiful with her dark auburn hair drawn into a fashionable twist. Small ringlets framed her face, and her large gray eyes filled with concern. Brigid wondered why she'd come.

"My head hurts somethin' awful," she said, her voice weak. "I thought I was better, but I'm supposin' not now."

"This flu can be quite difficult." Mrs. Ransom smiled kindly. "I'm sure another day or two of rest and all will be right."

Brigid wanted to believe her, but from the way she felt, she wasn't sure another two days would be enough.

"Are you feeling well enough to talk?" The concern in Mrs. Ransom's voice seemed genuine.

"Yes."

It took all her strength, but Brigid managed to sit up. Mrs. Ransom stood and plumped the pillows for her. Brigid tried to hide her surprise. Since when did the lady of the house help a servant?

"Thank you." Brigid's cheeks burned with embarrassment at the kind gesture. "My head feels better now that I'm sittin'."

"Very good." Mrs. Ransom pulled an envelope from her dress pocket. "Mrs. Duffy found this in your hand and gave it to me as my name was on it."

Brigid recognized it as Thomas's letter regarding Tobias.

"I read it." Mrs. Ransom's voice dropped to a whisper, and her eyes welled with tears. "From the chart notes, it sounds as if my baby is truly dead. I had held out such hope. Just this morning I read in the paper that two small boys survived the sinking of the *Titanic* and were reunited with their mother. I thought it was a sign that miracles could happen."

"We're still lookin'." Brigid tried not to offer false hope to the dear lady, yet she wanted her to know that she and Thomas hadn't given up yet.

She noticed that her bedroom door stood ajar. "Should we close the door in case someone hears us?"

"There's no one here," Eliza said. "The staff are downstairs preparing the afternoon meal, and Mr. Ransom has gone to Maine for a spell."

The pounding in Brigid's head suddenly returned and her stomach lurched. Her skin grew clammy and her heart raced.

"I need to lie back down."

"Of course!" Mrs. Ransom rose and helped her lie back.

Just as she laid flat, an image of Mr. Ransom on top of her, sweating and panting, the veins in his sweaty forehead bulging as he panted above her… flashed into memory. She cried out in terror.

Mrs. Ransom backed away. "Oh dear! Brigid! Whatever is wrong? Did I hurt you? Are you in pain?"

"Please leave!" Brigid cried, trying to push away the awful scene that kept replaying in her head.

"I'll call for the doctor!" Mrs. Ransom headed for the door.

"No!" Brigid thrashed her head from side to side despite the painful throbbing. "No!" She didn't want a doctor! She hadn't been sick! *She knew what happened to her.*

"Please just leave me," she begged. She couldn't bear to face Eliza Ransom with this unholy image of the lady's husband in her head.

"Brigid, I must get you help," Eliza insisted. "I won't leave you like this!"

Brigid forced herself to calm down. She must stop Mrs. Ransom from going for help. "I need water."

"Of course!" Mrs. Ransom hurried to the water pitcher on her bedside table. As the lady poured, Brigid willed herself to stop shaking and tried to collect herself, if only for the moment.

Mrs. Ransom brought her the glass and held Brigid's head up so she could drink.

"Thank you," Brigid said, as she rested against the pillow again. "I suffered a pain in my head again, but I'm better now."

Mrs. Ransom stood staring at her, glass in hand, obviously doubtful as to what to do. Finally, she relented. "If you're certain?"

"Yes. I'm sorry to be scarin' you."

"I'll send Mrs. Latimer with an aspirin."

"Thank you."

Brigid wished the woman would leave, but Mrs. Ransom seemed reluctant to go.

"I came here this morning to thank you for all you've done for me," she said. "Perhaps once you're better, we can talk again. I hope you and your friend can find my Tobias, but if you discover otherwise, at least my heart will be at ease knowing for certain."

Brigid nodded, wanting nothing more than to be alone. Sadly, Tobias had become the least of her concerns.

Mrs. Ransom finally departed and closed the door behind her. Brigid let loose a flood of rage and tears. Every time she thought of Charles Ransom, the realization of what he did grew more profound and clear. It hadn't been a dream or a hallucination from fever. It was a real life nightmare.

And *why?* Why did he do this to her? He'd hurt her and left her as damaged goods. Who could she even tell? Who would believe her word against the wealthy Charles Ransom? She couldn't even prove it.

And Thomas. He'd never want her now. Even if she never told him what happened, he'd know on their wedding night. She cried harder. A wedding night. She'd never have that now either.

She turned her head into her pillow and screamed her rage. Once again, all that was found was lost. She could never face Thomas with this shame on her soul. And if her relationship with him was over, so was his help in the search for Tobias.

And poor Mrs. Ransom! How could Brigid stay here knowing what she'd done, albeit unwillingly, with the lady's husband?

Poor Eliza. Poor little Tobias. Poor her. What would become of her now? Where would she go?

Once again, she had no one.

Chapter Nineteen

A week and a half later, on a rainy Thursday, Thomas attended the funeral mass for Grace Cavanaugh. His empty heart ached. He grieved not only for his dear patient who lay in the casket at the front of the church, but for Brigid as well. It still pained him that she'd left with no note or call, and he doubted he'd ever see her again. He'd gone back to Central Park several times in hopes of finding her there. The flowers he had left on their bench lay wilted and dead. One day, he simply threw them in the trash and never returned.

Stouch's story that Brigid went to Ireland bothered him. Perhaps she had left town, but Thomas doubted she had the means or will to return to Donegal, where she wasn't wanted. Then again, perhaps he didn't know her as well as he thought.

The mystery surrounding Tobias Ransom also weighed heavy on his heart, but with the hospital now assigning him more patients, he hadn't time to delve further into the matter. It was as if, in one stroke, he'd lost Brigid, lost Grace and would never know the truth about Tobias. He felt useless, alone and ineffective.

He hadn't even been able to help Grace Cavanaugh see her husband one last time before she died. Thomas remained her doctor through her illness, not only because he truly cared for the kind lady, but also because he hoped to run into Clara and question her about Leopold's whereabouts and her train trip a few years back.

But Clara Cavanaugh seemed to abandon Grace to the hospital staff. If she visited her cousin at all, it was never during the hours Thomas was on duty. The nurses had telephoned Clara, updated her on Grace's condition and asked her to bring Mr. Cavanaugh to visit, but neither she nor Leopold came.

Thomas had planned to go to Cavanaugh House and check on Leopold. But on the very day he made the decision, Grace died. She died alone, without her relatives or friends, without her husband, and with the worry of Leopold's whereabouts following her to the grave. Thomas had been with Grace at the end, and he vowed to find Leopold.

He didn't have to go far.

As Thomas now sat in a middle pew in Sacred Heart Catholic Church, he was relieved to find Leopold Cavanaugh present and accounted for. He sat beside Clara in the front pew. Mr. Cavanaugh's head hung low, and from time to time, he shuddered and wiped his eyes with a handkerchief. Clara, dressed entirely in black, her face hidden by a matching veil, sat stone still and appeared to offer him no consolation whatsoever.

Thomas glanced around the crowded church. He hoped to find Brigid there. She had almost married into the Cavanaugh family and had talked highly of Grace. He knew she'd want to be here if she could. But, she wasn't, of course. She'd gone away.

The mass ended, and Grace's friends and family filed out of the church. Thomas held back, to offer his condolences, and to check on Leopold's well being. He also hoped to set in motion a plan to get Clara to confide in him about the mysterious baby. Given what he'd learned about Clara and Dr. Stouch's former relationship, he wondered if the baby that Leopold supposedly saw Clara with could possibly have been Tobias Ransom. Chances were slim, yet Thomas knew that the time frame of Clara and Stouch's relationship, and the date of Tobias's birth and death, neatly coincided. Unfortunately, a lot of other possibilities existed too. Leopold may have been mistaken; perhaps it wasn't Clara he saw at the train station. Or, Clara might have been there, but perhaps what she held wasn't a baby. Given Leopold's drinking problem, his vision may have been blurred. The most realistic possibility, however, and the one which he, Thomas, hoped wasn't true, was that Tobias *had* died shortly after birth, and he was on a wild goose chase invented by the possibly crazed Eliza Ransom.

Leopold, Clara and the priest stood at the coffin for a few final moments and then turned to leave. Leopold's face was red and puffy from crying, and although he seemed to have a hard time walking, Clara offered him no support. She stood a good foot away from him, her veil now lifted, her dark eyes dry, her expression stoic.

As they neared his pew, Thomas stood to summon their attention. Leopold suddenly lurched forward in a stumble. If Clara even noticed, she did nothing to help. Thomas hurried from the pew and caught the elderly gentleman before he fell to his knees.

"Mr. Cavanaugh, are you all right, sir?" He helped Leopold into a pew, knelt beside him and held onto his arm. Leopold's cologne, mixed with the scent of gin, did not go unnoticed.

Clara seemed to awaken from her trance and hurried over. "Cousin Leopold, are you unwell again?"

"Has he been unwell?" Thomas raised his glance to Clara. She appeared surprised to find Thomas at her cousin's side, as if she hadn't noticed that he saved Leopold from a fall.

"Mr. Ashton," she said, her voice surprised but strained. "I didn't know you were here."

"Lucky for me, he was!" Leopold blurted between heavy breaths. "You'd have let me fall on my face!"

"I'm so sorry, Leopold!" Clara extended a gloved hand past Thomas and patted her cousin's shoulder. "I'm just so terribly disoriented today. I forgot how ill you've been."

"Has he been ill?" Thomas asked again, turning inquiring eyes to her. "With what?"

Clara seemed taken aback at his inquiry. "A mild case of the flu. What concern is it of yours, Mr. Ashton?"

Assured that Leopold would be fine sitting for the moment, Thomas stood and faced Clara. He kept his voice to a whisper. "It's *Doctor* Ashton, Miss Cavanaugh. I was Grace's doctor, and if her husband is also ill, that is of great concern to me."

He expected Clara to rebuff him or become embarrassed about her absence at the hospital as Grace lay dying, but instead her features softened, and her eyes moistened.

"Forgive me. Of course, I remember you telling me at our dinner that you were in medicine. I didn't realize you were Grace's doctor. The nurses didn't mention you by name. Thank you for all you did. I wanted to be with her more, but then Leopold fell ill, and I needed to care for him." She turned away. "We called the hospital a few times, but Grace was always sleeping."

Thomas looked at Leopold, who nodded in agreement. "Clara tried several times to help me out of bed so we could visit Gracie, but I just couldn't manage."

"Our family doctor said Leopold had a moderate case of the flu, not the measles, which I thought he brought home to Grace. I couldn't take care of them both myself, so I sent Grace to the hospital, as she seemed worse than he did."

Thomas was stunned. If what Clara said was true, she may never have intended Leopold to be committed to a sanatorium a second time, as Grace thought; she just couldn't manage two elderly sick people simultaneously.

"Did Grace know you were sick, Mr. Cavanaugh?"

"He fell ill right after she did, but Leopold didn't want Grace to know," Clara interjected, but her words fell kind.

Thomas didn't know what to say. Grace thought Clara would commit Leopold. He saw his opening to further question Clara.

"Miss Cavanaugh, you look exhausted," he said, noticing for the first time the deep circles under her eyes. "Can we sit and talk for a moment?"

"Yes," she said, allowing him to sit next to Leopold while she sat on Thomas's other side. "I really don't wish to see anyone outside right now."

"Understandable." Thomas spoke quietly, as they were still in church. He turned to Leopold, only to find that he'd fallen asleep, his head resting against the top of the pew.

Clara noticed and turned a pale shade of pink. "I'm sorry about Leopold. I allowed him a few drinks before the service, just to help him through. Normally, I wouldn't, but this has been horrible."

"I know about his drinking," Thomas said.

"You do?" Her face flushed crimson. "How?"

Thomas omitted telling her about his run-in with Leopold at Baybridge Hospital. He didn't want her knowing more that she had to. "Grace told me. She was terribly worried that you might place him in a sanatorium while she was hospitalized."

"Oh, no!" Clara's hand flew to her mouth, and she hung her head. "Oh no, no. My poor Grace." She looked at Thomas, as her tears welled. "You must think me horrid."

"I don't know what to think, Miss Cavanaugh," Thomas said. "Are you going to commit Leopold?"

"I don't want to," Clara said, with a sigh as heavy as lead. "But I don't know how else to help him. With Grace gone, he's going to be so melancholy. We all are. I can't see him not finding a way to drink, and I don't know how to stop him." She turned to Thomas. "I do love Leopold, and I did love Grace. You must believe me. If I could have taken care of them both at home, I would have."

Thomas believed her. "I think I may be able to help. Would you allow Leopold to be in my care?"

"You would do that?" Clara pulled a lace hanky from her sleeve and dabbed her nose.

"Yes."

"I have become a woman of means. I could pay anything you ask."

Thomas was surprised by Clara's offer. She must truly want to help Leopold if she was willing to offer up any amount of money asked for. Unfortunately, it wasn't money Thomas wanted.

"There will be a fee, of course," Thomas said. "But not mine. You'll be charged for the care I find for him. At the hospital where I work, the treatment is quite different from the sanatorium, and more successful. That's not to say that Leopold doesn't have a long and trying road ahead."

"Yes, of course."

Thomas chose his next words carefully. "I need to assess his state of mind, in particular, his intellectual clarity. For instance, he told Grace some things that worried her."

"Oh?"

Thomas shifted in his seat. "She said she was afraid you'd commit him again to stop him from telling others that he once saw you taking a baby onto a train." He feigned a laugh. "Isn't that odd?"

Clara didn't laugh. Instead, she fidgeted with her handkerchief. "Not quite." To Thomas's shock, she began to cry - deep heavy sobs that unnerved him. For some reason, he didn't think Clara *could* cry.

"Miss Cavanaugh, I'm so sorry." He reached for his own handkerchief and handed it to her. "Did I say something wrong?"

Clara violently shook her head and wiped her tears, her hand shaking as she did. "No, no. I'm all right. I've just had so much on my mind. Too many deaths and too much loss. First my father, then David and now, Grace. My life just gets lonelier and lonelier." She looked at Grace in her coffin awaiting a later, private burial.

Thomas didn't speak, giving Clara time to compose herself. After a few quiet moments, she spoke forthright.

"Grace was correct on one account. I didn't want Leopold talking about seeing me at the train station. I was helping out a friend; the trip was supposed to be secret. But I would *never* commit Leopold for seeing me there! When I sent him to the sanitarium the first time, it was because I thought it was best, and as I said earlier, I had no one else to turn to."

"So, you *were* at a train station with a baby about two years back?"

"Yes." Clara sniffled. "But what does that have to do with anything? The trip was just another of my pathetic attempts to do a favor for someone I loved, and as usual, it backfired."

"How so? Would you like to talk about it?" Thomas would offer his consolation and friendship as long as Clara kept talking. But suddenly, she seemed to realize she'd said too much.

She turned on him, her sad, tear-filled eyes again sizzling black as coal. "Why do you care? What do you care about *me*? You cared about Grace, and you care about Leopold, and you even seemed to care about that pea-brained Irish wench that my brother loved."

At the mention of Brigid, Thomas's heart lurched. He wanted to bite back at Clara's comment about Brigid, yet he knew that if he didn't put Brigid from this thoughts, his heart would rule his head, and he could halt the progress made with Clara.

"Brigid went back to Ireland." He tried with all his will to act as if his heart wasn't being torn apart by his own words. "At least that's what Dr. Stouch said." He had dropped the doctor's name into the conversation so casually, he nearly impressed himself.

Clara's eyes flew wide open and her cheeks enflamed with color. "How did Rupert Stouch know Brigid O'Brien? And how do *you* know him?"

"I know him through my studies."

"Oh yes, of course, forgive me."

"And as for Miss O'Brien, she worked at Ransom House after you kicked - she left your home." Thomas squashed his inclination to chastise Clara for what she had done to Brigid. That wouldn't get him the information he needed.

"You've been in touch with her?"

Thomas paused. He certainly wasn't about to expose his true feelings to Miss Cavanaugh.

"We encountered each other a few times after we met on the pier."

"I see." Clara seemed satisfied with his answer.

"Anyhow," Thomas continued, trying to act as if his "few encounters" with Miss O'Brien had meant nothing. "She's gone. Stouch says she left the country."

Clara's sadness was replaced with a disdain all her own, and to Thomas's surprise, it wasn't aimed at Brigid. "Yes, *Rupert Stouch.*" The name rolled off her tongue as if a foul taste. "He has a way of making people disappear."

Thomas feigned surprise. "I'm afraid I don't know what you mean." Had Stouch made *Brigid* disappear?

Clara clammed up. Her hand flew to her lips as if she might stop the words from flowing from them.

"Who else did he make disappear, Miss Cavanaugh?"

"Me."

It was not the answer he expected. He scratched his head. Clearly Miss Cavanaugh became agitated at the mention of Rupert Stouch, but how far could Thomas press for information without her walking out?

"You haven't disappeared," he said.

"In a manner of speaking," Clara said, almost to herself. "And that poor little baby..." She looked away and spoke as if lost in a memory.

Thomas's heart raced. So, Stouch *was* involved in Clara's train trip with baby in tow!

"Whose baby was it?" He anxiously awaited the name.

"I don't know."

"You don't know?"

"No." Clara sighed. "As I said before, the trip was supposed to be secret, so he didn't tell me whose baby it was or why I was bringing it to an orphanage." She started to cry again. She turned to Thomas. "You must forgive me. I just can't stop my tears. I'm horribly embarrassed, but this last death has put me over the edge. And I had no idea Grace thought I'd put Leopold away! I wouldn't have done that just to keep Rupert's secret."

"You've been through a lot lately," Thomas agreed, thrilled to have gleaned the information that the baby went to an orphanage somewhere. "Perhaps if you just tell me everything, I can help. I am a doctor."

"I could use a friend more than a doctor," Clara said.

That would be pushing things, but Thomas knew he'd have to agree if he wanted this conversation to continue. "All right."

Clara managed a tiny smile that disappeared as soon as it appeared.

"Now, then." Thomas offered her his most charming smile. "Just how did Dr. Stouch make you disappear?" He really wanted to talk about the mystery baby, but Clara seemed to open up more when the conversation centered on her.

"You see, when I returned from the trip, Rupert had proposed to another." She looked down at her hands. "Just like that, I was nothing to him. Before I left, malicious gossips said he was only marrying me for my future inheritance, but Rupert said he loved me, and I believed him. I suspected he might be after my funds as his practice was not thriving, and had we married, I would have been more than happy to help him financially. But, when I returned, he'd somehow come into his own windfall, secured some wealthy patients, and found himself a nineteen-year-old fiancé."

Before Thomas could probe further, Clara spewed forth the rest of the story, as if it been a volcano lying dormant inside her these past two years.

"He used me. I've had a long time to think on this, and I believe he was going to marry me for my money. Then he used me to take that baby to the orphanage and once that was done, and he found funds elsewhere, he didn't need me anymore."

Thomas knew to stay concerned about Clara's sad plight, but she'd digressed from the information he most needed.

"Where did he send you?"

"Broken Angels Orphanage in Chicago."

"Why Chicago? There are plenty of fine orphanages here." Thomas thought of the nice orphanage he toured with Brigid. "Did he tell you the baby's name?"

Clara rubbed her forehead with the back of her hand. "You're asking me too many questions at once, Dr. Ashton." She studied him. "Why are you so concerned about this baby?"

Thomas backpedaled fast. If Clara suspected he was using her for information, just as Stouch used her for her money and to transport a baby, she would clam right up and not tell him anything.

"I'm more concerned about you, Miss Cavanaugh. Did you have a safe trip to Chicago and back?"

"Yes, and luckily the baby was well-behaved. You see, the infant was practically a newborn, and I had to take care of it on that train for twenty hours! I'd never even held an infant before!"

A newborn! He chose his words carefully. "That must have been very trying," he soothed. "Why do you think Dr. Stouch wanted you to keep the trip secret?"

"I have no idea," Clara said, weariness lacing her words. "I didn't ask. I just thought it had something to do with the baby being deformed. Maybe Rupert was embarrassed about delivering a less-than-perfect human? I wouldn't put it past him."

Thomas swallowed hard and tried to keep his breathing steady and his voice calm. "The child was deformed? How so?"

"A mongoloid baby." Clara offered a bittersweet smile. "That's why the baby was being sent to Broken Angels in Chicago. It's an orphanage for children unlikely to be adopted due to deformities or mental retardation. At least, that's what Rupert said. But this baby was cute as a button, just the same. I enjoyed taking care of him and holding him made me so anxious to return home, marry Rupert and start my new life." She looked away.

Thomas tried to register all he'd been told, yet continue to console the sad, forlorn Clara. He now understood the anger in her life, but he still couldn't forgive her for how she treated Brigid.

"Did the baby have a name?"

"Joseph."

Joseph? Could Stouch have made the name up to cover for the baby being Tobias Ransom? That would make sense.

A noise near the altar drew his attention. Father Donald appeared and walked down the side aisle toward them.

Thomas nudged Leopold. He awoke with a grunt, a snort, and utter surprise to find himself still in the church.

"I'm sorry to interrupt," the priest said as he reached their pew, his voice kind, his eyes compassionate. "But we'll be moving Grace to the cemetery now. Will you join us there?"

"Oh, yes." Clara looked at Leopold. "Cousin, are you up for this?"

Leopold wiped his face with his hands. "Yes."

Thomas, Clara and Leopold rose from the pew.

"Will you join us, Dr. Ashton?" Clara said, her face now relaxed and her eyes dry. It was as if their conversation relieved her of her cares, if only for the moment.

"Thank you for the offer, but I do have to return to the hospital."

"Of course." She turned to Leopold. "Come, Leopold. I'll assist you."

"Allow me." Thomas offered her his arm. "I'll walk you both out."

"I would like that," Clara said, and as Thomas took Leopold by the elbow, she linked her other arm through his. She stood a bit too close to him for his comfort, but if this was what she needed at the moment, it was the least he could do in exchange for the information she had inadvertently provided.

Lost in conversation with Clara and helping Leopold walk, Thomas did not notice Brigid run from the entry lobby of the church and out the front doors. Nor did he see her tears.

Chapter Twenty

Brigid's hand flew to her mouth as she tried to stifle a gasp. Her plan to wish Grace Cavanaugh goodbye privately after the funeral mass had not gone as she'd hoped. She had thought to sneak into the church at the end of the service, sit in a back pew and say a few prayers for Grace's soul. Encountering Clara Cavanaugh had *not* been in the plan.

She had been shocked and saddened to read Grace's obituary in the paper. Her heart would not be still until she'd gone in person to say prayers for the dear woman who had been so kind to her at Cavanaugh House.

Brigid had arrived very late because her cab driver got lost; the mass had been over for a while. A few mourners milled around outside the church and spoke in quiet voices. They paid her no mind as she climbed the church steps and entered the vestibule. She paused and glanced into the church before entering. She could see Grace's coffin in front of the altar, a closed casket with a huge floral spray on top. The scent of woodsy incense filled the air, and other than three people sitting in a middle pew talking to a priest, the church was empty.

As Brigid was about to step into the aisle, those last mourners suddenly stood. They turned in her direction, and she immediately recognized Clara. She would never forget that wicked woman as long as she lived. She ducked behind the vestibule door and wondered how to make her escape without Clara noticing. She peeked around the wall. She could see Clara and the men clearly now as they headed toward her. Lost in conversation, they did not see her, which was a good thing, for Brigid's mouth fell open and her eyes grew wide with shock. Clara walked arm in arm with *Thomas*!

Nausea rose at the sight of them together, walking as if lovers, albeit with Leopold Cavanaugh attached to Thomas's other arm.

So that was why Thomas hadn't called for her. He'd dropped her and latched onto Clara quicker than she could blink! Brigid turned and fled from the church, a sob daring to escape in one heart-wrenching gasp. She darted down the church steps and around the corner. Halfway down the block, she hid behind a wide-trunked tree, tried to catch her breath, and glanced back. Thomas, Clara and Leopold must not have seen her, for they headed in another direction.

Brigid let loose a torrent of sobs. She bent to her knees, trying to make herself as small as possible, and wished for the earth to open up and swallow her. Not only did the sight of Thomas and Clara together rip her heart in two, but now she knew, without *any* doubt, that there was *no one* she could confide in about what Charles Ransom had done to her. She had decided to tell Thomas about it. She knew she risked him not believing her, or worse, not wanting her, but something in her heart told her he *would* believe her. He'd been so kind. He knew her. She had hoped he'd tell her what to do. After all, he liked to help people. He had wanted to help the *Titanic* survivors. He wanted to help Mrs. Ransom. Surely, he'd help *her* if he knew what had happened.

But not now. She'd been wrong about him. She must have misread his intentions or mistook his interest in her to make him drop her like a hot rock and take up with Clara Cavanaugh of all people!

Brigid shed a few more tears and then her anger surged like floodwaters at a broken dam. How *dare* Thomas trick her into believing he had feelings for her! How *dare* Clara kick her out after David died and she had no one! And how dare Charles Ransom think he could do what he'd done to her and get away with it!

Brigid pulled herself up from the ground and swiped away a few last angry tears. She was *done* feeling sorry for herself. *Done* wanting Thomas, or any man, for that matter. *Done* thinking anyone in New York, perhaps excluding Mrs. Duffy and Mrs. Ransom, had a soul or conscience. *Done expecting help.*

Realization dawned like a bright new day. That was the gist of it, wasn't it? She had relied on everyone but herself. And when they all let her down, she never fought back. She'd run away from her parents instead of standing her ground. When Clara kicked her out of Cavanaugh house, she simply accepted it and left. When Charles hurt her, she hadn't told anyone, hadn't even *tried* to get someone to believe her.

Brigid knew that to save herself, she'd need to take immediate action. Charles Ransom would soon return home, and he might come after her again. She must leave Ransom House, the sooner the better. Then, and only then, could she start over.

She walked back, having had only enough money for a one-way cab ride. A dull cramping began in her lower abdomen, but she ignored it. The familiar ache had come and gone over the last two weeks, a sick reminder of what happened and its possible horrid consequence. But, she wouldn't think about that now.

She couldn't add the nightmare of a possible pregnancy to her growing list of problems.

She had feared she might be pregnant the moment she collapsed a week and a half ago. She had recognized the same light-headedness and dizziness her mother suffered throughout her many pregnancies. Brigid observed her mother's symptoms one too many times to not know the signs, although she also knew it was much too soon to be certain of anything.

What she did know was that she did not want Charles Ransom's baby. Abortion was a sin, so if worse came to worse, and she prayed to God that it wouldn't, she would deliver the child and place it in that nice orphanage she and Thomas toured.

Brigid recalled how that ended with that wonderful kiss. But it had obviously meant nothing to Thomas, and she needed to forget it.

What she wanted most was to go back to Donegal and her family. But her mother had made it clear that she could not return to them; she had disgraced them, and her aunt in England as well. Perhaps she'd move to Connecticut. Mrs. Duffy once said it was nice. If only she knew where Connecticut was.

She would *not* stay in New York. Nothing good happened here, and if it did, someone or something quickly snatched it away. But she had very little money saved. What she did have might provide enough for a week or two at a women's boarding house, but then what? She'd need a job. She'd overheard some of the housemaids talking about employment agencies that hired maids out to the rich. Perhaps she'd start there.

Brigid reached Ransom House. She was due back in the kitchen in a half hour, certainly enough time to pack her bags, collect her money from under her mattress and leave. She'd heard of a rooming house down on East Twelfth Street or West Fourteenth. She'd have to walk; she couldn't afford to spend any more money on cabs. Her only regret was that she would leave Mrs. Ransom without answers about Tobias.

Brigid hurried to her room. She pulled her valise out from under her bed, placed it on top of the spread and turned to retrieve her dresses from the wardrobe. As she turned back, another severe cramp caused her knees to buckle. Hanging onto the bed, she pulled herself back to her feet, and as she rose, she felt a familiar dampness in her undergarments.

She fell to her knees in thankful prayer. She wasn't pregnant, or, if she had been, she no longer was. Relief overwhelmed her like a tidal wave.

"Where are *you* goin'?"

Brigid startled and stood as hurriedly as she could, trying to mask her pain. Ruthie stood in the doorway, obviously pregnant, her eyes wide and fixed on the valise.

"Oh, Ruthie!" Brigid said, and wiped droplets of sweat from her brow. "I didn't see you there."

"I was just on my way down to the kitchen," Ruthie said, still eyeing the bag. "Are you coming to the kitchen? Or are you going somewhere?"

Brigid quickly shut the valise and tucked it back under her bed. As she slowly rose, she felt another gush of blood. She squeezed her legs together. "Oh, no, I'm not going away. I was just airing that old thing out. Something smells funny in my room, and I thought it might be the valise."

"Oh." Ruthie seemed to accept the lie.

"I'll be down in a minute." She hoped Ruthie would be on her way, but the girl remained in the doorway. Brigid hurried to her wardrobe to retrieve fresh undergarments and sanitary towels, only to find she had very few towels.

She turned to Ruthie. "By any chance, do you have extra feminine towels I might have?" She tried not to stare at Ruthie's prominent belly. "I assume you must."

"Yes. I'll be right back." Ruthie turned to leave, and nearly collided with another woman who appeared in the doorway.

The woman looked vaguely familiar, but Brigid could not place her as a member of the household staff. She was of medium stature with light brown hair and dark eyes. She wore a dark overcoat, matching hat, and carried what appeared to be a physician's bag.

"Who are you?" Ruthie looked the woman up and down.

The woman smiled at Ruthie, but spoke to Brigid. "You probably don't remember me, Miss O'Brien. I'm Rebecca Fields, a nurse and friend of Doctor Stouch. I checked in on you a few times for him when you were ill with the flu."

"Really?" Brigid's ire accelerated. She knew damn well she hadn't had the "flu". Did this woman know what *really* happened to her? Did Doctor Stouch?

"You weren't conscious when I visited," the woman continued. "But I've returned as a favor to Doctor Stouch. How have you been feeling?"

Oh, what Brigid could spew about how she'd been feeling! She offered up few words. "I'm fine. I don't need a nurse nor a doctor anymore." And, thankfully, she wouldn't be needing one in the next nine months either.

"I see," the woman said, seemingly nonplussed at Brigid's rudeness.

"I'll get those pads for you," Ruthie said, and hurried to her room.

"Are you in need of feminine supplies?" Miss Fields seemed only too willing to help. "I have some on hand."

"I don't need yours," Brigid said, suddenly uncomfortable with the curious expression on the woman's face. "Ruthie has extras."

"Certainly." Rebecca Fields smiled again, but Brigid couldn't relax. She didn't trust many people anymore.

"You're still here?" Ruthie glared at the woman as she returned with the supplies, her hefty form nearly knocking Miss Fields from the doorway. She handed the towels to Brigid.

"So, Miss O'Brien, it seems as if everything is right and regular with you then?" Rebecca said, as she eyed the towels.

"Yes." Or it would be, once this woman left and she could clean up and lay down for just a few moments to relieve the God-awful cramps.

Ruthie spoke the words on the tip of Brigid's tongue. "She had the flu. Ain't it kind of odd you inquirin' after her womanly stuff?"

The woman shrugged and offered an apologetic smile. "In all honesty, I think it's odd too, but Doctor Stouch asked me to make sure *everything* was fine with Miss O'Brien. He's a very thorough doctor."

"I bet," Brigid said.

"But, as long as you say you're well, Miss O'Brien, I'll report back to Doctor Stouch that you've made a full recovery."

"Thank you." Brigid wished she would hurry and leave so she could use the washroom. "Good day."

"Good day." The woman nodded to Brigid and Ruthie and took her leave.

"How very strange." Ruthie walked to the door and watched the woman walk down the hall. She turned back to Brigid. "Are you sure you're all right? You look a bit pale."

"My monthly pains," she answered. Brigid warmed to Ruthie's concern. In the entire time she'd been at Ransom House, she had never had a friendly conversation with any of the scullery maids other than to give them orders or greet them in passing. "I'm fine, but I do need some privacy to change."

"Oh, of course," Ruthie said.

She left Ruthie and went to the hallway bathroom to clean up. Once there, she was shocked at the amount of blood she'd lost, and the cramping that continued. She tried to wrap her head around that she might be losing a baby, but since she didn't want any baby of Charles Ransom's anyway, she could accept whatever this was and with gratitude to the Lord above. Still, the shock of it all left her stunned and weak.

On return to her room, Brigid was surprised to find Ruthie sitting on her bed. She plastered on a casual smile not wanting to alert the girl that she was anxious to pack and leave.

"I thought you were headed downstairs," Brigid said.

Ruthie toyed with the bedspread. "I am." She paused. "But it's just so difficult. I hate the way Mrs. Duffy and some of the others look at me. You'd think I was the first girl in the history of the world to find herself unwed and havin' a baby."

Brigid offered the hurt girl a compassionate smile. "Well, you *are* the first maid at Ransom House in this condition, I hear."

"I suppose. Still, I don't know how I can stand it while I wait for Jimmy to get me out of here."

"Quittin' isn't possible?" Brigid suggested with a pang of guilt. Here she was about to run off and leave Mrs. Duffy short a kitchen maid, and if Ruthie left, the poor cook would be minus both a kitchen maid *and* a scullery maid. Brigid pushed away the thought. She had to stop caring. It got her nowhere.

"I can't quit." Ruthie sighed so heavily that Brigid feared they might both fall through the floor. "Jimmy wants me to make as much money as I can before the baby is born, 'cause once I have it, I'll be taking care of the babe."

"Yes, you will," Brigid agreed. She guessed that Jimmy and Ruthie were in no financial situation to hire a nanny. "Could you ask Mrs. Latimer to assign you lighter duties, like the ironing? That would get you out of the kitchen."

"I wish," Ruthie said. "But Mr. Ransom has to ultimately approve everything, and he won't be back for another week."

Another week! Brigid thrilled to hear it. She hadn't known when the bastard was going to return, but she wanted to be gone before that. If she still had another week, however, she could stay and earn a bit more money.

"I just don't know how I'll stand it." Ruthie's dark eyes filled with tears. "They're actin' like I'm some harlot. I love Jimmy and he loves me."

Brigid sat next to her on the bed. "That's what you need to remember. You *are* gettin' married, which is more than a lot of girls can say." *Myself included*. "And that Jimmy. He's a handsome devil, isn't he?" Brigid didn't really think much of the tall and lanky blonde boy, but Ruthie obviously had.

Ruthie nodded and wiped away her tears. "You're right. I've got more goin' for me than the lot of them!"

She's got more goin' than me.

"Yes, yes you do." Brigid stood and straightened her skirts. "Now what do you say we be gettin' ourselves down to the kitchen, put wicked smiles on our faces and make them all wonder what we've been up to?"

Ruthie allowed Brigid to help haul her whale of a belly off the bed. Ruthie smiled wide. "You know, Brigid O'Brien. You're all right."

Brigid returned the smile. She *would* be all right.

Chapter Twenty-One

Charles returned to Ransom House exactly one week and one day later, on a wicked- weathered Friday morning. Storms rained and thundered, and the wind blew fierce, doing nothing to help Charles's dour mood. The time spent in Maine had calmed his nerves somewhat, but returning home triggered his conscience again. It didn't help that only bad news greeted him.

The staff reported Eliza to be in better spirits, yet she still refused to acknowledge or talk to him. His arrival only sent her spiraling back into her melancholia. Charles then discovered he lost a small fortune on a bad, private racing bet. The driver he'd picked to win in the second running of the Indianapolis 500, developed engine trouble two laps away from victory. And if that wasn't enough, the morning newspaper told of the untimely death of his good friend and aviator, Wilbur Wright, the older of the two Wright brothers. Wilbur had passed away the previous day in Boston while on a business trip.

It seemed to Charles, that since his "encounter" with Brigid O'Brien, nothing had gone right, as if the deed cursed him with bad luck. And there was only one man to blame for his misfortune, the same man that now stood before him in the study, and had the gall to deliver even more bad news.

"Brigid O'Brien is not pregnant," Rupert Stouch told him, accepting a brandy from Charles. "Rebecca Fields, a nurse, confirmed it for me last week. Brigid started her menses."

Charles stared at the doctor, his blood on a slow boil. Their evil design to impregnate Brigid had been for naught. Her womb lay as empty as his hollowed out soul. There'd be no Ransom heir by the Irish maid.

"You're telling me that the plan failed and the only thing I have to show for it is sin on my soul?"

Charles could not mask his growing irritation and rage. Rupert offered no ownership of the failure, yet contemplated their next move as if they had simply lost at cards.

"A pregnancy did not occur this time with the girl, but you can certainly try again." Rupert took a sip of the brandy. "Damn fine liquor, I must say, Ransom."

Charles clenched and unclenched his fist. He spoke between gritted teeth. "There isn't going to be *a next time*! Do you really think we can keep drugging the girl and assaulting her, and she won't catch on? Poor doesn't equal stupid, Rupert!"

He couldn't believe Stouch could be so daft. Plus, he would never, *ever* do something like that again. It had been the act of an irrational and desperate man, at least that's what he convinced himself in Maine. He wasn't that man anymore. Yes, he was desperate to have an heir, but not crazed enough to attempt *that* again.

"I suppose." The doctor sounded less than convinced.

Charles put his hand to his aching head and sat in one of the wingback chairs near the fireplace. "There's got to be another way for me to have a biological child. Eliza will inherit after I die, which is fine, but with no heirs, the fortune will go to her side after she dies. I can't have that. Eliza's family is all a bunch of lunatics."

Rupert sat in the chair opposite him. "You should consider the mistress idea again - impregnating some woman and paying her off for the child and her silence. And, there is always adoption." He took another sip of brandy.

Charles ire rose. Why was Stouch treating this like some ordinary man's problem? He was no ordinary man. His problems were not simple, and therefore usually, neither were the solutions.

"I've *told* you!" He stood and began to pace. "Women *talk*! No mistress could be trusted to have *my* child, hand it over and not tell. Adoption is out. I didn't give up one mangled child only to adopt another! Adopted children have problems, which is why they're given away. Or they're from horrible backgrounds and poor people, and God only knows what their lineage would bring. At least O'Brien was attractive and healthy, and that baby would be half *mine*. I want a normal, child. You, of all people, should know that!"

Rupert nodded. "Yes, yes, but if you don't want to be with the maid again, and you don't want a mistress, I don't see how you're going to have a biological child. I'm not a miracle worker, Charles."

"But, isn't that what I pay you enormous sums of money for?" Charles could not keep sarcasm from his words. How could his friend fail him this badly? He *always* got what he wanted, and if he didn't, he could pay someone to get it for him. It irked him that Rupert had the nerve to suggest defeat.

He walked over to Rupert, grabbed the brandy glass from him and tossed back the amber liquid. His throat burned and his eyes watered, but he didn't care. His mind relaxed, and he could think. He handed Stouch the empty glass.

"*You,* Stouch, have all you want. I have paid you well for your ideas, your services and for your silence. And don't forget, your *new money* keeps your pretty, young wife quite satisfied with her marriage."

"I beg your pardon!" Rupert slammed the brandy glass onto the side table. "Are you saying that Louisa only married me for my money?"

"No, she married you for *mine*! May I remind you, that before I paid you to help me with the…problem, you couldn't afford to marry and keep the Twyne heiress."

"There's nothing wrong with making my wife happy." Stouch straightened and adjusted his tie.

Charles bellowed. "You're being *paid* to make *my wife* happy! *She* needs a baby! *I* need an heir to inherit my fortune! While y*our* wife now struts about in the finest fashions that New York City salons offer, I'm still childless! Where is *my baby*, Stouch?"

Rupert paled, but Charles could care less. He had paid Stouch plenty to get him a replacement for the child, and Stouch failed. "Well?" He tapped his foot. "What's your next *incredible* plan?"

Rupert stared at the fire, his voice soft and shaky. "If you're going to continue to shout at me, I won't discuss this with you, Charles. I'll return your money if you wish, but I refuse to be insulted in this manner."

Charles rolled his eyes. Oh for Heaven's sake! He didn't have time to deal with injured pride, yet he needed Stouch. He stared at the wounded man, swallowed his rage and tried to quiet the demon in him that threatened more verbal fireworks. He returned to his chair and cradled his head in his hands. "Forgive me."

When he glanced up, the color had returned to the doctor's cheeks. "Please sit." Charles motioned to the chair across from him.

Rupert picked non-existent lint from his pants. "I do have another plan, but it will take compromise on your part."

"Then it will take compromise in your pay." Charles mimicked his condescending tone. He couldn't help it. He was temporarily a mad man trapped in a refined man's body.

The doctor didn't flinch. "Fine." He seemed as resigned to ending this problem as much as Charles.

"What is the plan?" He would try to keep an open mind, but if it involved the molestation of another woman, he'd fire Stouch right then and there.

"Let me ask you this," Rupert said, cautiously. "Why are you so determined that this must be your biological child? It's not like you're the King of England."

"Is that the compromise? That the child won't be biologically mine?"

"Yes."

Charles sat back in his chair and ran a hand through his slick hair. He remained calm, but it took every ounce of energy he possessed. "Well, the thought of my money going to some child that isn't really related to me, doesn't sit well."

"But the child *would* be *yours*," Rupert pleaded. "You'd come to love it as your own. And think how happy a new baby would make Eliza!"

Charles had to admit that making Eliza happy tipped the scales in Rupert's favor. Charles sighed. "Well…I would need to know who the parents are. I can't risk ending up with another deformed child or one of low intelligence."

"And that's another reason to adopt, Charles. Since Tobias *did* have a deformity, it might be best if the child wasn't from your lineage."

Charles exploded. "Tobias's problems came from *Eliza's* side! Have you met her family? Have you?"

Rupert shook his head. "Can't say that I have."

"Then you have no argument! *I did not cause Tobias to be as he is.*" Charles sat back in his seat, huffed and stared at the fire. A moment of silence passed between the two men.

Finally, Rupert cleared his throat and shifted in his seat. "Very well, then. Getting back to adoption and the infant I have in mind. I do know the parents."

Charles sat up straight, his anger turning to curiosity. "You know of a healthy couple willing to give up a child?"

"I know such a couple," Rupert said. "Both parents are of good health. The child isn't born yet."

"Who are they? Do I know them?"

"Yes." Rupert smiled. "It's your scullery maid, Ruth Benton, and her boyfriend, Jimmy Pugh, the kitchen deliveryman. Their baby is due soon. They're not married and both dirt poor, so I'm positive they'd hand over their unwanted burden for the right sum."

Charles knew of the maid "Ruthie" and her condition. She brought disgrace upon his house, and he counted the days until she left. He would have fired her the moment he learned about her pregnancy, but the girl had begged Eliza to keep her on, and Eliza, being Eliza, had agreed.

"And you're sure they want to give up the baby? What if they change their minds and want to keep it?" Charles was not about to get caught in another ill-fated scheme. This time, he'd have assurance of the outcome.

"Then we'll take the infant," Stouch said without hesitation, as if kidnapping was part of his profession. "Ruth can't afford medical bills. I'll offer up my services free of charge. 'Employee benefits', I'll say. When she's in labor, I'll put her to sleep, just as I did Brigid, and take the baby. When she wakes, I'll tell her the child was stillborn."

Charles tried to sort out the plan. *It's almost like we did to Eliza. Is my desire for an heir so great that I'd ruin the life of yet another woman? Could I love Ruthie's baby as my own? Does love even matter?*

Jimmy Pugh. He's decent enough looking, and Ruthie is pretty enough.

And what of Eliza? How will she react when I bring her a strange child? Won't it cheer her to finally have another baby to love? A normal baby! Why should it matter to her where it comes from? Once she holds that baby, she won't be able to refuse it.

"All right."

"All right?" Rupert's eyes glittered with hope. "We have a plan?"

"Yes." Charles let out a deep breath. Hopefully Ruthie would take the offer and hand over the baby, keeping things simple, yet a nagging doubt lingered.

"What if something goes wrong?" Charles asked. "For instance, what if Ruthie won't give up the baby and then tells someone you wanted it?"

"I've thought of that." Rupert smiled as if he were the smartest man in the room. Charles knew better. "Even if she refuses to surrender the child, I'll pay her for her silence. At least, that will be what she thinks; that she's getting paid whether she gives up the child or not. But, of course, I'll still deliver the baby."

"But won't she be suspicious when she wakes and the baby is gone? Will she really believe it's stillborn after you offered to adopt it from her?"

"You really doubt my intelligence, Charles." Rupert frowned, but his eyes stayed bright. "I've thought of that. If the maid shows any doubt about what happened to her baby, we'll pack her off to the place Brigid was to go after having her baby."

Charles smiled for what felt like the first time in weeks. Rupert had thought the entire thing through. It sounded like a fail-proof plan. "Splendid idea!"

A crash outside the door silenced the two men.

Charles stared at the door. "Who's there?"

The door opened, and to Charles's shock and horror, Henry held Brigid O'Brien by the arm. Charles and Rupert stood as Henry dragged the protesting woman into the room. As Charles's eyes met hers for the first time since the assault, the blood drained from her face, and her eyes filled with terror. She looked at him as if he was a monster. He turned away, her expression and his own memories of the event, making him sick.

"Look who was listening at your door!" Henry shoved the girl his direction. She stumbled, but caught herself and stood next to Rupert. Charles thought quickly. He would fire her on the spot. But, what if she'd heard all that was said?

Before he could speak, she answered his worst fear. Her eyes burned into him as if she might set him on fire. He almost wished she would.

"I know what you're both plannin' to do to Ruthie!" She trembled with each word, but an earthquake roared in Charles's brain at her next statement.

"And I know what you did to me!"

Her words were a million tiny daggers ripping into his flesh. His head pounded, and his knees grew weak. He held onto the chair for support.

Stouch grabbed her arm and turned her roughly toward him. "You know *nothing*!"

The girl pulled from Rupert's grip and ran back to the butler. "Henry, you must help me! These are evil men. They're goin' to-"

Charles stood numb as the scene before him played out in slow motion: Rupert hitting the girl on the head with the fireplace poker, Brigid crumpling to the floor like a rag doll, and Henry looking as shocked as Charles felt.

"Good heavens!" Henry hurried to help Brigid, but Stouch stopped him.

"Leave her!" Stouch ordered. "She's been nothing but trouble since the day she was hired."

"But, sir, she might be seriously injured!" Henry looked aghast from Stouch to Charles, and back to Stouch again. Charles remained silent, his own bewilderment unnerving him.

"She'll be fine!" Rupert snapped. "Charles, dismiss this man!"

"Henry, leave us at once!" Charles barely recognized his own voice. It came out harsh and sinister as if it belonged to someone else, someone vile. "And don't repeat a word of this."

"Or you'll be fired," Stouch added, as if Charles hadn't made himself clear enough. Charles bristled. Henry had always been a loyal servant. He knew that the happenings at Ransom house were never to be repeated. How dare Stouch threaten *his* butler! The doctor seemed to be getting a little too confident for his own good.

Charles would have to deal with that later. For now, Brigid still lay unconscious on the floor.

Henry left, shutting the doors behind him.

"What now?" Charles's heart raced, and beads of sweat formed above his brow.

Rupert knelt at Brigid's side. "She's alive, thank God. I didn't mean to knock her out, only to stun her." He looked up at Charles. "We must carry on with our plan at once. As for her," he nodded toward Brigid. "It seems she'll be taking a little trip after all."

Chapter Twenty-Two

Thomas stood outside Chicago's Union Depot, his hands heavy with luggage, his heart burdened with guilt. Not only had he left his mother alone in New York, but he'd also bought his ticket using the money he'd saved for her trip to Italy. He might have found a cheaper ride, but not a faster one. The luxurious Broadway Limited got him to Chicago in only twenty-hours, and time was of the essence. He needed to be back in New York in three days, and he required enough time in Chicago to visit Broken Angels Orphanage, and hopefully, find Tobias Ransom.

Not only did he feel guilty for using the money, he also wondered if deep down, his search for Tobias was a way to quell his unceasing desire to find Brigid. No matter how many times he told himself that she'd gone to Ireland, he couldn't shake the feeling that she hadn't. It didn't make sense for her to leave without telling him why. Each day he woke vowing not to think of her, yet he'd find himself standing at the Ransom's front door. His ring was never answered, although he swore he heard someone moving on the other side. He called out once, but still, no answer. He had even tried the servants' entrance, ringing the bell repeatedly, yet no one answered, although he saw heads peep to look out the window to the side of the door. He called to them, but again, to no avail. He had to suspect that instructions had been given not to answer his call. But, *why*? He thought to wait for a servant to come out the door so he might inquire about Brigid, but his schedule didn't allow him the time to wait.

Eliza Ransom might know what happened to Brigid, but Thomas couldn't just telephone this wealthy woman. The Ransom staff would never put a stranger through to her; he knew how the wealthy worked. He certainly couldn't explain to the staff that he needed to talk to Eliza because he was searching for her supposedly dead baby. They'd hang up on him faster than they could blink. Had Brigid even told Mrs. Ransom he was helping in the Tobias search? If not, she wouldn't know him from Adam. He couldn't even be certain Brigid gave Mrs. Ransom his letter. He couldn't tell her about this upcoming trip either. What if he found nothing? The news might greatly upset her, and he heard she was of fragile mind. He would only call Mrs. Ransom if and when he found Tobias. Then, perhaps, she might tell him where Brigid had gone.

Eliza Ransom had become Thomas's last hope, and unbeknownst to her, he had become hers.

Finding Tobias, however, was another shot in the dark. Thomas's mind raced with crazy, yet possible, scenarios he might encounter. Since the boy would be about two now, he might have been adopted, which would be good for Tobias, but bad for Eliza as she'd have a hard time locating him and having him returned. Another scenario, Tobias might be at Broken Angels, but what if he couldn't recognize the child? Or worse still, what if the boy Clara took on the train wasn't the Ransom child at all? And finally, what if Tobias *had* died at Broken Angels? If the baby had passed away at the orphanage, it would be extremely difficult for Thomas to find that information.

With these thoughts in mind, Thomas hailed a Yellow Taxi Cab to take him to Broken Angels.

Whatever the outcome, he knew he couldn't afford to return to Chicago again, nor take more time off from his studies. He'd been allowed time away from Cranston Hospital by telling Dr. Hack that he'd taken an interest in pediatric medicine and would like to study the unfortunate children at Broken Angels and its affiliated hospital. Dr. Hack had remained skeptical about the trip until Thomas said he'd pay for it himself and present a lecture of his findings for the other students. Only then had Dr. Hack's interest piqued. If advancements were being made in the specialized care of disabled children, Dr. Hack wanted his hospital to access the information first.

The taxi pulled to the curb. Thomas got in and told him the address of Broken Angels in Oak Park, a small town just outside the city limits. A short while later, the driver pulled up in front of an expensive, three-storied Victorian house.

"Excuse me, sir," Thomas said. "This is Broken Angels?" He couldn't believe an orphanage existed on this tree-lined, well-kept street that sported such grand homes.

"Yes, sir." The driver repeated the address back to Thomas. "That's the address, right?"

Thomas nodded and paid the man. He glanced again at the massive gray house with the white wrap-around front porch, long driveway, and well-maintained front lawn. He saw no sign anywhere stating that this was Broken Angels Orphanage.

He departed the taxicab, walked up the pavement and stairs to the door and rang the bell. He tried to peer in through the door's stained-glass window, but the view was blurry.

The door opened a moment later by a woman holding a little girl with metal braces on her legs who appeared to be about two. The woman kept the upper chain bolted, so only two inches were allowed between them for speaking.

"Good day," she said. "May I help you?"

"Yes. I'm Dr. Thomas Ashton, from New York. I spoke with a doctor, Marvin Hughes, by telephone a week ago and arranged to visit Broken Angels." He tried to peek past the woman and into the home. "Have I come to the right place?"

The woman smiled and unchained the door. "Oh, yes, that's right. Dr. Hughes mentioned your visit. Unfortunately, he was called away on an emergency." Still holding the curly-haired girl, she opened the door the rest of the way. "Do come in. You must forgive me. The children have been in a high state of excitement after their outdoor play. But it's nearly rest time, and they're upstairs trying to settle, thank goodness!" She extended her hand. "I'm Mrs. Victoria Cole, owner of Broken Angels."

Thomas shook it gently. Mrs. Cole appeared to be in her forties, with grayish brown hair pulled into a loose knot at the back of her head, and close-set, dark blue eyes. Her dress was plain, a light blue frock covered by a white and slightly smudged apron. She seemed exhausted, but pleasant.

She shifted the little girl to her other hip. "Allow me to put Cynthia down for her rest. Then we can talk, and I'll give you a tour. I'll help with your questions about Broken Angels and the children, as I'm not sure when Dr. Hughes will return."

“Yes, thank you.” Thomas removed his hat.

They stepped from the foyer into a long hall that opened to two playrooms, one on his left and another slightly ahead on the right. Cribs, toys and play mats littered each room. He guessed from the gated hearths in each room, that these used to be parlors. To his immediate right rose a massive staircase covered with plush, light brown carpet.

Mrs. Cole seemed to notice his gaze at the stairwell. “We keep it carpeted in case the children fall coming up or going down.”

“Ah,” Thomas said, pleased to see such a nice safety precaution installed.

Victoria started up the stairwell. “Please go on ahead to the kitchen. It’s at the end of the hall, on the right. Mrs. Proccio, our cook, should have some coffee brewing. We always have biscuits and muffins at the ready."

Thomas smiled appreciatively. "Thank you kindly.”

As he searched for the kitchen, he noted two handrails on each hall wall, about two feet apart in height. Again, he was pleased to see that Broken Angels thought of simple accessibilities that would aid children who had difficulty walking.

At the end of the hall, a door stood open. Thomas peeked in and found a bathroom complete with tub, stepping stools and a cabinet full of clean, cloth diapers. To his left was a dining room with a hardwood floor, and high chairs in each corner.

And, as instructed, he located the kitchen on his right.

A short and stocky woman with gray hair tucked neatly into a net stood at the stove transferring freshly baked biscuits from sheet to plate. Thomas cleared his throat so as not to startle her. She turned, spatula in hand.

"Don't let me interrupt you." Thomas offered a friendly smile. "Mrs. Cole sent me in. I'm Dr. Thomas Ashton, from New York." The smell of sugar biscuits caused his stomach to growl.

"How do you do?" the woman said, but returned to her baking, and talked over her shoulder. "Have a seat. There's coffee on the table. You can pour yourself a cup. We don't have time to stand on ceremony here, as you might imagine."

Thomas laughed. "No, I would think not. Thank you. I can indeed pour my coffee."

As he reached for the pot, Mrs. Cole entered the kitchen. She wiped a wisp of hair from her forehead and tucked it behind her ear. "The children were a handful today."

Thomas placed his hat on an empty chair and pulled out one at the head of the table where Mrs. Cole was about to sit. She nodded her gratitude to him, and after she sat, he poured coffee for them both.

"Oh, thank you." She smiled, and her eyes crinkled at the corners. "My, a gentleman!"

"I try." Thomas smiled and sat himself to her in one of the few chairs not occupied by pillows, safety belts or crumbs. Mrs. Proccio brought over a plate of biscuits and warm, blueberry muffins and placed it before them on the table.

"I'll be in the dining room, Mrs. Cole," she said, and made a hasty retreat.

"You seem to have made a wonderful home for the children, Mrs. Cole," Thomas said, as he reached for a biscuit. "Do you manage the children all by yourself?"

“Oh goodness me, no!” She laughed lightly. “I could never do it alone. I have three other women who help. Unfortunately, one is under the weather today, and the other two are upstairs helping the little ones get to sleep.”

"How many children are there? I’m surprised to find that Broken Angels is a house, rather than -"

"- an institution?" Mrs. Cole said. "I know. I worked in an institution in my younger years. I wanted to do better for children such as these, but for now, this is the best I can do. I’d love to have a larger place and help more children.”

“How do you decide which children to take in?” Her answer might tell him straight away whether Tobias could be here.

She smiled, but her eyes grew sad. “And that, Dr. Ashton, is the question, is it not?” She took a slow sip of her coffee and then continued.

"I only have room and enough help to care for eight children and four infants. I try very hard to take in the child with the least chance of being adopted. My children not only have handicaps to deal with, but they may be hard to place for secondary reasons as well. For instance, we have a little girl here who not only was born with deformed arms, but she is a Negro. Do you know of any married Negro couples, Dr. Ashton, with enough money to adopt her and pay for the care she’ll need now and in the future? And sad to say, no white couple gives her a second glance. And so, she’s mine.”

“How do you keep this place running?” Thomas immediately realized his rudeness. “I’m so sorry. That’s none of my business.”

Mrs. Cole shook her head. "Oh, no, that's quite all right, Dr. Ashton. I provide what I can from an inheritance my parents left me and another from the estate of my late husband."

Thomas felt even worse that he asked. "My deepest condolences."

"Thank you. And, of course, Broken Angels has kind benefactors."

"Benefactors?" Thomas reached for another biscuit.

"Yes, anonymous men and women who agree with my mission and support my work."

"And that is enough money to cover expenses?"

"It's enough. Dr. Hughes and his hospital offer my children medical care at no cost to me."

"That's wonderful," Thomas said. "And wonderful of you, for the work you do."

A faint blush rose in her cheeks. "Thank you, but I'm happy to do it. It grieves me to know people give up a child simply because he or she was born slow or deformed. I don't understand how a parent can pretend a child never existed."

Thomas thought of Charles Ransom. "I agree."

Mrs. Cole looked him straight in the eye and sat tall in her chair. "If you ask me, Dr. Ashton, these are the children who need me the most. I provide them with a good home, but most of all, I give them the thing they'll never get from those parents…unconditional love."

Thomas knew it was time to test the waters. "I know of a man in New York whose child was born disabled. He told his wife the baby died and sent the baby away."

Mrs. Cole nodded. “I’ve heard of that happening,” she said, but gave no hint that she linked the story to any of her children.

Thomas tried a different approach. "Why don't you have a sign out front?"

She wrapped her hands around her coffee cup. "There used to be one, but the neighbors asked me to take it down. They felt it lowered the neighborhood image. Can you imagine?”

Thomas shook his head. “The audacity.”

"Agreed.” Mrs. Cole smiled warmly. "So, Dr. Ashton, how did you hear of Broken Angels all the way in New York?"

What to say? He didn't want to raise suspicion that he might be here looking for a particular child. Yet, this lady wanted the best for these children. Would she understand if he told her he was trying to reunite a mother and child? He hated lying to her. On the other hand, she seemed so protective of her children; he couldn't be certain how she'd react if he told her his real mission.

He stuck with his lie. "Well, word travels amongst the medical community when advancements happen in the newer specialties such as pediatrics and pediatric surgery. I read that Dr. Hughes has made great strides in orthopedics, and childhood diseases brought on by inadequate nutrition. He wrote an article in which he mentions helping a child or two in your care."

That last part wasn’t a lie. He'd done his homework and came prepared with background information on the famous doctor.

"Yes." Mrs. Cole nodded. "That article was quite recent. Cynthia, the little girl you saw me holding, was one of those lucky children. We hope one day she'll be able to walk."

A commotion in the hallway caught their attention. Thomas turned to find a woman about twenty standing in the doorway. She held a dark-skinned girl about four years old who had a stump for one arm with little fingers protruding off the end. She didn't have a second arm. But she did have large, almond-shaped dark eyes, a shock of curly black hair and the sweetest of smiles. Thomas couldn't help but smile back.

Standing next to the woman, and grasping tightly to her long skirt, was a little boy about two, with a shock of red hair and a sprinkle of freckles across the wide bridge of his nose. But what drew Thomas most to the child were his eyes. They were the heavy lidded, slanted eyes of a mongoloid child, but the most amazing sapphire color. The same as Charles Ransom's.

Thomas's heart raced, and his stomach tightened. Could this be Tobias? The child certainly fit the physical description Eliza gave to Brigid.

"I'm sorry to interrupt, Mrs. Cole." The woman in the doorway smiled apologetically. "But Charlotte and Joey don't seem to want naps today."

"Let them in, then," Mrs. Cole said, and opened her arms wide to hug each child. Thomas hid his astonishment. The baby Clara transported was named Joseph. The coincidences were just too striking for the childe not to be Tobias. If this child bore the heart-shaped birthmark on the inside of his left wrist, Thomas would know for certain.

Mrs. Cole addressed the other woman. "Agnes, please set the children at the table, and let's try some warm milk for each."

Mrs. Proccio returned to the kitchen and set about pouring the children's milk. Thomas tried to catch a glance of Joey's left forearm, but it was impossible to see under his long-sleeved, oxford shirt.

"Now then," Mrs. Cole said, after the children were settled, and the cook and Agnes left the room. "How may I help you, Dr. Ashton?"

Thomas swallowed, wiped his mouth and began. "I'm interested in pediatric medicine, especially surgery, to help children with deformities."

"Why come all the way to Chicago for that?" Mrs. Cole said. "Don't tell me New Yorkers all produce perfect children?"

Thomas laughed. "No. I chose Broken Angels because the children here are orphans." Thomas paused. It wasn't a lie. "I'm interested in helping these children more so than non-orphans because it will give them a better chance to be adopted." As Thomas spoke, he realized that he really *would* like to help these children. "It's tragic that no one wants them, when they need the most care."

"I want them."

She sounded a bit defensive. Could she give one up if she had to?

"But I agree, Dr. Ashton. They need more than most couples can give. What breaks my heart most is that some people abandon these children *only* because of their deformities."

Thomas saw his opportunity to ask about Joseph. He dangled the verbal worm in front of her. Would she bite? "I can't imagine abandoning either of these children," he said and nodded toward the two quietly eating their biscuits.

"Charlotte's mother was a single woman who died after childbirth. A hospital down south called Dr. Hughes about her, and he called me. As for darling Joseph, his arrival was mysterious."

Thomas tried not to act overly interested. He kept his voice steady. "How do you mean?"

"I received a telephone call from a doctor in Boston who said he had a mongoloid child to place, that the mother died in childbirth, and the father couldn't handle the burden of caring for him." She glanced at Joey and smiled. "Can you imagine calling this sweet boy a burden? I find him a joy."

Thomas also smiled at the little boy. Joey smiled back and offered him his biscuit, but with his right hand.

Thomas's heart melted. "Oh, no thank you, Joey. You eat that biscuit, my belly is full."

"Yum," Joseph answered, his face full of crumbs.

"You were saying?" Thomas turned back to Mrs. Cole.

"This doctor wanted to place the infant in my home, and I had openings at that time, so I said yes. I asked, as always, that all Joseph's medical records be sent with him, but a woman delivered him here and had no such papers."

Clara, Thomas thought, hoped, prayed.

"I tried to telephone the doctor," she continued. "But the number he provided wouldn't connect. I wrote to him at the Boston hospital he was affiliated with, but they returned my letter, saying no such doctor worked there. Finally, I asked Dr. Hughes if he knew of a doctor named William Berkley, and Dr. Hughes hadn't. Eventually, I just gave up. But one day, a messenger who would not identify himself delivered a package to me. He handed it to me and immediately left. I opened it to find a letter and a sizeable amount of money. The letter had no return address, but contained specific instructions that the payment was to cover Joseph's care. Well, let me tell you, Dr. Ashton, that money not only covered Joey's care, but the needs of other children here as well."

Thomas shifted in his seat. Everything pointed to this boy being Tobias Ransom. William Berkley had to be Rupert Stouch. If only he could find the birthmark.

"Look at him," Mrs. Cole said. "He is the dearest child, but he wasn't wanted. He belonged to someone with money, and that breaks my heart. If they are wealthy people, they'd be able to afford care for him."

Thomas saw an opening. "I heard that some men, when faced with a feeble-minded child, send the child away and tell the mother it died." The Ransom case wasn't unique, unfortunately. Dr. Hack had told him of other similar situations.

Mrs. Cole shook her head and looked at her hands. "I can't imagine."

Thomas cleared his throat. He was treading in deep water, but it was time to sink or swim. "Mrs. Cole," he began, trying not to sound like a lawyer. "If you found out you had such a child, would you willingly return it to its mother?"

The look Victoria rewarded him with could have frozen Hell. "Dr. Ashton." She paused as if contemplating her next words. "What do you think? Of *course* I would, given enough proof that this was indeed that person's child."

Thomas tried to sooth the rough waters he churned. "I know, of course you would." He straightened his tie for no reason. "I believe you. I just…"

He wondered how far her kindness stretched. If she knew the truth about Joseph, about himself, and the real reason he was there, would she understand, or would she call the authorities and have him arrested for posing as an imposter trying to obtain a child? Unfortunately his own schedule and pocketbook didn't allow him a second trip to Chicago to win this woman over in a series of visits. If he was to act for Eliza, and for Tobias, the time was now.

Before he could speak, Mrs. Cole pushed her chair away from the table and stood, startling the children who looked up at her with wide, frightened eyes. Thomas panicked. Was she going to leave? Did she suspect why he came?

"Mrs. Cole," he began, nearly begging. "My intentions are as noble as your own."

She remained silent and stared him down. He felt like a defendant on trial.

"What I'm about to say is going to sound strange, impossible even, but I've come here under false pretenses."

Her eyes remained hard, her voice harder. "I figured that out two minutes ago, Dr. Ashton, if you're even a doctor?"

"I am. Well, a medical student, actually." He suddenly felt like one of the children. A naughty one.

"Mrs. Proccio." Mrs. Cole said to the cook who attended the oven again. "Please, come get the children."

The cook turned with a heavy wooden rolling pin in hand, as if she might beat him. Thomas spoke rapidly.

"Ladies, please don't be alarmed! I am who I say I am!"

Little Charlotte began to cry. He felt awful.

"I'm so sorry for the disruption." He searched for the right words to explain. There was no turning back now; Mrs. Cole was on to him.

"Why *are* you here?" She gripped the table in a vise-like hold. Mrs. Proccio kept the rolling pin in hand, and picked up Charlotte.

Thomas gathered his courage and reminded himself of the reason he'd come. "I'm looking for a boy who was given away two years ago by his father." He took a deep breath. "I think he may be Joseph, in fact, after being here, I'm about nearly positive about it. You see, I know a woman, Clara Cavanaugh, who brought a boy to you. She was told not to tell, but obviously, she did."

Victoria Cole's stern expression remained unflinching. "I think you should leave. I will report you to the authorities if you don't!"

Thomas stood, not to leave as ordered, but to buy himself some time.

"Please," he begged again. "I honestly believe that Joseph is Tobias Ransom, the son of a wealthy gentleman and his wife, both of whom are very much alive!"

Mrs. Cole laughed sarcastically. "You're telling me that Joseph is the son of Charles Archibald Ransom, the millionaire banker? Incredible!"

"Think on it, please, Mrs. Cole! I found Tobias's medical file and supposed death certificate, but things in it don't add up. I believe Charles Ransom and his doctor faked the boy's death and brought him to you."

"Jesus, Mary and Joseph!" Mrs. Proccio said, as she rocked Charlotte back and forth.

"Mrs. Proccio, please take Charlotte to Agnes upstairs," Victoria ordered. "And forget everything you heard just now."

Thomas waited for the cook and little girl to leave and then continued, his words flying at a frantic pace. "I copied what I could from the records, but I sent them through a friend to Eliza Ransom, otherwise I'd have brought them here to show you, which was stupid of me not to think of doing, but I have another way to prove I'm telling the truth." He knew he rambled, but couldn't stop himself.

"This is a lot of speculation you wish me to believe, Dr. Ashton. Perhaps I shall show you to the door."

Thomas had only one last card to play; it was all or nothing now. "Does Joseph have a birthmark on the inside of his left forearm near the wrist?"

Mrs. Cole's face went ashen. The room became deadly quiet. Still gripping the table, Mrs. Cole, ever so slowly, sat back down.

"He does." Her voice was quiet. "How do you know that Dr. Ashton?"

"Mrs. Ransom told my girl-, my friend Brigid, who worked for her, that although she only held her baby once, she saw the birthmark and remembered it because it appeared to be heart-shaped."

Mrs. Cole looked as if she might faint. Thomas sat down again, his heart beating a mile a minute. Mrs.

Cole rose from her chair and walked over to Joey, who looked up at her and laughed. She smiled at him and reached for his sleeve.

She rolled back the material and turned the boy's pudgy arm to Thomas.

"There it is, Dr. Ashton," she said, her eyes misting over, her voice weak. "The birthmark, just as you said."

She paused and then whispered. "In the shape of a heart."

Twenty-Three

Thomas returned to New York exhausted, but exhilarated about finding Tobias, yet he couldn't shake the sensation that since arriving home, he was being followed. Whether walking down the street, driving in the car, or working at the hospital, he felt as if someone lurked only a few steps behind at all times. He'd turn, only to find no one there. Weariness added to his paranoia, and he wondered if somehow Charles Ransom knew he'd gone to Chicago and sent spies to follow him. He knew a good night's sleep would show how irrational this idea was, but his work schedule prevented that rest.

After the hurried three-day Chicago trip, he had immediately resumed his medical training. His mother also needed help around the house, and he kept a constant watch on Leopold Cavanaugh's care; the elderly man had been hospitalized in a special ward at Cranston to "dry out." The man was in good hands, but had a long, hard fight ahead of him. While reviewing Leopold's chart, Thomas discovered a nurse's note that Clara Cavanaugh would like Thomas to contact her. He bristled at the request, still not trusting Clara's intentions. Still, he took the note, folded it and tucked it in his trouser pocket. He would telephone her soon, but foremost on his mind was informing Mrs. Ransom that he had found Tobias.

He couldn't wait to tell Eliza the good news, yet therein lay the problem. Eliza had no idea who he was, and since no one at Ransom House would open the door to him, he knew going there and introducing himself was out of the question. Plus, the butler already thought he was "William Carr." He couldn't suddenly reappear and say he was Thomas Ashton, and so, a telephone call, it must be. He just had to hope that whoever answered would put him through to Eliza. Once he told her the news, however, she'd have her work cut out for her.

Victoria Cole had agreed that the toddler in her custody was most likely the Ransom child, but she wanted more proof. She was loath to let him go without one hundred percent certainty that Joey was Tobias, and Thomas didn't blame her. Mrs. Cole said she'd only give the child up if provided with a medical record saying the boy hadn't died but was legally surrendered to Broken Angels. Thomas couldn't blame Mrs. Cole for protecting herself from becoming a knowing participant in Charles Ransom's scheme.

With these thoughts heavy on his mind, Thomas treated each of his patients and then checked on Leopold one last time. He looked forward to a short rest and light meal at home before returning to Cranston to write up his findings about Broken Angels, as he'd promised Dr. Hack.

As he exited Leopold's ward, an elderly nurse stopped him. "Dr. Ashton, I'm sorry to interrupt you, but Miss Cavanaugh is on the telephone again."

He remembered the note in his pocket. "I suppose she's calling for an update on her cousin," he said, trying not to sound as weary as he felt.

"I don't think so," the nurse replied. "We've been keeping her updated twice a day." She rolled her eyes heavenward. "Sir, if I may speak my mind, the woman is a pest."

Thomas laughed lightly. "Well, better to have a relative care too much, than too little, I suppose."

"I suppose." She didn't look too convinced. "But now she keeps telephoning for *you*."

Thomas sighed. There'd be no trip home just yet. "Very well. I'll talk with her."

"Thank you!" she said, visibly relieved. He followed her to the switchboard area of the nurses' station, and she handed him the receiver.

"This is Dr. Ashton, Miss Cavanaugh, how may I help you?"

"Thomas!" Relief flooded Clara's voice. "Finally! Where have you been?"

He ignored that question. The fewer people knowing he went to Chicago, the better.

"How can I help you?" he repeated, trying to maintain a formality between them. "I believe the nurses informed you that Leopold is doing well, considering?"

"Yes, yes," she said, her voice urgent. "But, there's something I think you should know."

Thomas turned toward the nurses' desk to find the same nurse straining to hear his conversation. "Just a minute, Miss Cavanaugh." He picked up the phone, carried it to a desk as far away as the cord allowed, and sat facing the wall. He spoke quietly. "All right, continue please."

"A man came to my house two days ago and frightened me out of my wits!"

"How so?"

"I was walking up to my house, and he appeared right in front of me as if he'd been hiding in the bushes waiting to ambush me!"

"Are you all right? What did he want?" His own paranoia suddenly returned.

"At first, I thought he had something to do with me telling you about that baby I transported. But, it turns out he wanted to know the whereabouts of that woman, Brigid O'Brien."

She had his full attention. Clara had no idea of his involvement with Brigid. "Did he say why he was looking for her?"

"No." Clara nearly wept into the phone. "I was so frightened by him and his thick ugly Irish accent, that I didn't think to ask that, or even for his name! I just said that Miss O'Brien wasn't here anymore, and that Grace said she went to work for Mr. Ransom, and the last I heard, she'd gone back to Ireland."

Thick Irish accent? Could this be the farmer Brigid was supposed to marry before she fled her home? If so, and if Brigid had returned to Ireland, why would he look here for her? Her mysterious disappearance became even more confusing.

"How did this gentleman even know you knew Miss O'Brien?"

"Oh my goodness, Thomas, I never thought to ask him! I was just so frightened at the time!"

He tried to reel her thoughts back to the stranger and away from herself. "What happened next?"

"He asked me where Charles Ransom lived. I was shaking so badly, and I couldn't think straight. I wondered if he might hurt me if I didn't know the answer!"

Thomas rolled his eyes and fought to keep his voice calm. "But, *did* you answer him?"

"I think I eventually rattled off something about Fifth Avenue."

"Yes, that's correct," he said. "But, Brigid isn't there anymore as far as I know. Dr. Stouch says she went home to Ireland. I told you that at Grace's funeral."

Silence met him on the other side of the line. He waited, thinking he may have said too much, but then Clara spoke again, the panic in her voice replaced with ice. "*And just how would you know that*? Why would Rupert tell you about Brigid?"

Thomas sighed. Dealing with Clara was like befriending Dr. Jekyll and Mr. Hyde. "She and I became friends."

Dead silence again.

"What did the Irish gentleman look like?"

Clara clammed up. "It doesn't matter." Nor did she sound very upset about the incident anymore.

He tried another approach. She might have lost interest in the conversation, but he hadn't. "Well, what did he do after you told him the address?"

Her words came clipped. "He took off his cap. Thanked me most kindly and walked off."

"I see." Thomas said, confused and worried. If Brigid hadn't returned to Ireland, had Charles Ransom known that Brigid searched for Tobias and sent some thug after her?

"Well, thank you for informing me of the matter."

"I just thought you might want to know about the incident, as you seemed so interested in the Ransoms at Grace's funeral." She didn't seem in any hurry to hang up.

"Yes, good of you to think of me. Is there anything you'd like me to do? If you're still nervous, I'll call the police and have them send someone over." *Which you would have done, if you were truly scared.* "Or, I could write you a prescription for a sedative."

"No." She paused again and Thomas waited. "Don't worry about me. I'll be fine. As always."

She hung up.

He replaced the receiver, stood and returned the telephone to its original spot.

"Is everything all right?" the nurse asked. She must have noticed the confused look on his face.

"Oh, oh yes," he said, although he still wondered who the man inquiring after Brigid might be.

"That Cavanaugh woman sure is a piece of work, isn't she?"

"You have no idea," Thomas replied, only half aware of what he said.

He bid the nurse goodnight and headed to his car. Although he looked forward to dinner with his mother, Clara's conversation still weighed heavy on his mind. On the drive home, he glanced over his shoulder from time to time, in case he was being followed. Nothing.

As he turned into the driveway, he made a conscious effort not to let Clara's telephone call make him more paranoid than he already was. A good home-cooked meal would set his mind right.

And then, after dinner, he would telephone Eliza Ransom.

Chapter Twenty-Four

Charles Ransom did not like being ignored. It was bad enough to have his own wife act as if he didn't exist, but when the kitchen servants wouldn't even answer his call, well then, something must be done. He stormed down to the kitchen with jaw set, fists clenched, and set to demand attention.

He stopped in the arched entryway to the kitchen and bellowed, "*Why isn't anyone answering my call?*"

Mrs. Duffy, who stood in the scullery with her back to the doorway, turned quickly and sent a bucket of soapy water crashing to the floor. Hot liquid splattered everywhere, but mostly on Mrs. Duffy.

"Oh! Oh!" she cried. "My heavens, Mr. Ransom! You scared the devil and his disciples out of me! Look at what I've done!" She stared at her wet skirts and sopping floor.

He could care less. He stepped into the kitchen and glared into the scullery. "Just mop it up! Why haven't my calls been answered? Is the bell system not working?"

Mrs. Duffy stared at him as if he'd slapped her. He certainly wanted to slap somebody.

"I heard the bells, sir, but if you have a look around, I'm the only one here!" She nodded in the direction of the empty kitchen. "Which is why I'm doing the cleaning. There isn't anyone to help!"

His strident tone set him off. "You could still have answered me!" he thundered. "Think of the time I've wasted coming down here!"

Mrs. Duffy huffed and crossed her arms in front of her chest as if he were nothing more than a bothersome child.

"Mr. Ransom," she said, her tone nearly as irritated as his own. "I have been busy cleaning up the kitchen from the midday meal so I can start the evening meal. I'm unable to answer your calls if you hope to eat on time and expect your food to be warm when it arrives. Why did you come in person, may I ask? Where is Henry?"

Normally Charles wouldn't allow a servant to talk to him in this manner; in fact, normally he wouldn't be talking with a kitchen servant at all. He'd allow Mrs. Duffy's insubordination this one time however, for he was as exasperated as she was, and he needed answers.

"Henry can't help me with this problem," he said, finding some humor at the thought of asking his valet to bear him a child. "I wish to speak with Ruth, the scullery maid."

"Well, as you can see, Ruthie isn't here and neither is Anna or Brigid. Anna's mother took ill, and Anna took her break to visit her, and no one seems to know where Miss O'Brien is. Do you, sir?"

He didn't answer and she seemed not to notice. "So I'm working alone all of a sudden."

He had no time for this woman's problems. If the kitchen wasn't cleaned properly or the evening meal was late, she'd be sacked, end of story. Amen and good riddance. Poor women looking for work were a dime a dozen.

"I don't care where *Anna* is," Charles said. Actually, he had no idea who Anna even was. He'd avoid mentioning Brigid. The less said, the better.

"Where's Ruth? Is she out as well? When will she be back?"

"Never." Mrs. Duffy headed for the broom closet and retrieved a mop.

"What do you mean never?" Ruth couldn't be gone. He needed her. Well, he needed her baby.

"She left yesterday to go live in Boston with her beau, Jimmy. He was our delivery boy, so we're short one of them too, now. He received a job offer from a relative there. He told Ruthie to pack her things, and off they went."

Charles felt as if his head might explode. Hell, life might be easier if it did. Ruth was gone? And the baby? Gone! Ruth was his last hope to get a healthy child. Now what to do? Where was Stouch when he needed him? Charles had last seen him days ago when the doctor whisked Brigid away. He should have returned by now, but Charles hadn't heard from him. Stouch would pay for this, another of his failed ideas!

"What did you want with the girl anyway?" Mrs. Duffy asked as she mopped the floor. "Is it something I can help you with?"

Charles laughed snidely to himself. *As if.*

Mrs. Duffy twisted the wet mop into the bucket. "Will we be getting more help now that Ruth is gone, or do you know if Brigid will return?"

He didn't like this cook woman one bit, but he needed her to believe that what happened to Brigid was for everyone's good.

"Miss O'Brien will not be returning. She carries typhoid and has spread it within my household."

"Oh, pish!" She laughed.

Pish? Charles felt as if he'd been slapped. How dare his cook disrespect him in this manner! Why wouldn't she believe what she'd been told?

"That girl never gave anyone typhoid!" Mrs. Duffy mopped the floor with a vengeance. "Who told you that?"

"Dr. Stouch said the maid Anna was sick with it," Charles said, his heart racing, his skin growing warm under the collar. He never was a good liar. Even about Tobias. He had to have Stouch tell Eliza the lie about the baby dying. "The doctor confirmed that Brigid infects others through her contact with food."

"Anna was getting sick *before* Brigid arrived." Mrs. Duffy placed the mop against a worktable and faced him square on, her round face red from exertion.

"And *I* believe you're incorrect, Mrs. Duffy." He stared her down, willing her to believe him.

"And *I* know I'm not, Mr. Ransom." She wiped the sweat from her brow. "I know typhoid. My late husband died in 1906 from the disease."

"My condolences," he said flatly.

"Anna's illness resembled the flu, not typhoid. My husband, who *did* have typhoid, suffered agonizing fever and headaches, severe nausea and a terrible cough. And that was just the *beginning* of his illness. Shall I go on?"

"That won't be necessary." He was in too deep. But, how to exit the conversation? The woman kept yapping on and on.

"Anna was not that sick. And she recovered. How many patients with typhoid recover to be as healthy in body and spirit as Anna is today?"

He wouldn't know. He didn't know Anna. Where the *hell* was Stouch?

"And further more, Mr. Ransom, if Brigid could spread typhoid, why didn't the rest of us get sick? Or your family? We all ate the same food, including yourself!"

"*I'm not a doctor, Mrs. Duffy*!" He didn't mean to shout, but the woman was acting like some upstate lawyer. "Dr. Stouch discovered she was infectious. Brigid assisted you with the food preparation and therefore needed to be put away for our good and her own good."

"Pish!"

Charles felt like a naughty school child caught in a lie and yet he couldn't stop the fibs from flying. "Dr. Stouch thinks Brigid was infected with the disease when she came over from that filthy, Godforsaken, Ireland. Lord knows how many people she killed over there!"

Mrs. Duffy picked up the mop and stormed toward him. "Mr. Ransom, you're a liar! Brigid O'Brien did nothing but her best to do her job!"

Charles backed up against a wall.

"I noticed the way you eyed Miss O'Brien." Mrs. Duffy stopped a few feet away and shoved the mop handle toward him. "What really happened to her?"

Some lowly, suspicious servant would not undo him. He somehow managed to keep his voice calm while his heart raced. "Are you *threatening* me?" He called her bluff. "Are you *accusing* me of something, Mrs. Duffy?"

His words were the panacea to her anger. She seemed to awaken from her fury, conscious now of her actions and words. He expected her to back away, kowtow and beg forgiveness. He might even give it, allowing she'd never again mention the matter.

"You're an evil man." She retracted the mop and backed away.

Not the expected answer. "And you're fired, Mrs. Duffy."

He straightened his shoulders and tie and left the cook standing with her loud mouth agape.

"Fine, but I'm taking Anna with me," she yelled as he ascended the steps to the upper floors.

Charles walked to the dining room and poured himself a stiff brandy from the snifter on the Chinese sideboard. His nerves were firmly rattled from his encounter with the cook, or perhaps it was from the lying. Should he have fired her? Could she actually prove Anna never had typhoid? He'd talk to Stouch directly on the doctor's return and sort out the details. Stouch should have explained the entire plan before he left, but he had to hurry to get Brigid to the boats.

The brandy had begun to work its magic when Charles heard a rustling of dresses in the hall. He turned toward the door in time to witness Eliza and her lady's maid, Jean, shuffle by.

"Eliza!" He couldn't believe she'd left her rooms. Where on earth could she be going?

She stopped as he joined them in the hall. Jean startled at his sudden appearance, yet Eliza seemed cool, almost detached. She placed a gloved hand on her maid's arm as if to calm her. So strange, this behavior of Eliza's. Shouldn't she be the one in need of calming?

"Where are you going, darling?" He reached to touch her, but she pulled away.

"Out." Her expression remained stoic, those huge, haunting eyes that he fell in love with years ago, determined.

"But darling, you haven't left the house in two years," he said, as if to a child. He looked to the maid. "What's this all about?"

"I can speak for myself!" Eliza said, the first full sentence she'd spoken to him in two years.

"Eliza! You're talking!"

"Not to you," Eliza said. "Except to inform you that you will most likely be in need of a lawyer."

Charles shook his head. "I don't understand."

"No, but you will." Eliza offered a small, but quick, thin-lipped smile. Had he blinked, he might have missed it.

She turned toward the door. "Come, Jean."

The maid dutifully followed her mistress, not even acknowledging Charles with an obligatory curtsy.

"But where are you going?" he called, confused and feeling slightly crazed by the afternoon's events. "Eliza!"

She stopped at the door and turned back. "I'm leaving for a bit, Charles. But, if I were you, I'd get used to my absence."

He watched in stunned silence as Eliza and her maid walked out the door.

He stood in the hallway, alone. What had happened? In the course of a few days, he'd lost a kitchen maid, a scullery maid, and fired the cook who would now take the other scullery maid with her. Stouch had disappeared. He had no doctor, no kitchen staff, no baby and now, what was Eliza alluding to? He wouldn't have a wife? Impossible!

Sulking, he tramped back into his office, downed the remainder of his brandy and poured himself another. Brigid O'Brien! She was to blame for this mess! Everything had gone wrong since he'd first laid eyes on that woman. If anyone was to blame for his ills, it was she. She couldn't carry his child! If she'd succeeded, he'd have his beloved heir, and Eliza wouldn't have any reason to walk out the door.

He reminded himself of his remaining assets. He had a fine house, a few remaining servants and a nice bankroll. All was not yet lost, for money talked, and Stouch listened. When the good doctor returned, they'd find another way to get Eliza back.

Yes, as long as he had money, he was still Charles Archibald Ransom, a man not to be fooled with.

Charles Ransom could and would have what he wanted.

Chapter Twenty-Five

Brigid held on to the side of the small boat and tried to quell the nausea that rose as each choppy wave sent the vessel rocking. She sat next to the repugnant Dr. Stouch, who remained silent and stoic the entire trip, not even bothering to answer when Brigid begged him to tell her where they were headed and why. He sat upright and tight-lipped, staring straight ahead as if she didn't exist. Two muscular men rowed them. A few other passengers filled the boat. One, Brigid surmised by his medical bag and fine suit, to be a doctor, and the other two, mostly like his patients, as they appeared quite ill, and produced heavy and congested coughs into the relentless wind.

Thankfully, the ride wasn't long. After the boat docked, Dr. Stouch, still silent, gripped Brigid by the arm, and whisked her to the island hospital. They waited in a small, white-walled room until another doctor, a tall, broad and older man with a full head of white hair, and round spectacles, arrived. He also ignored Brigid, introducing himself to Dr. Stouch as Dr. Horace Mantel.

"This is Brigid O'Brien, the patient I telephoned you about," Dr. Stouch said, with a nonchalant nod toward her. He handed Dr. Mantel a folder of papers. "Her test results are all there. She is a danger to any community she serves, as she refuses to admit that she carries disease."

"What disease?" Brigid interjected.

"See?" Stouch said.

Dr. Mantel glanced quickly through the papers, nodded and coughed. "Yes, yes, thank you."

Dr. Stouch lowered his voice, but not enough. Brigid could still hear him. “The money is there in an envelope as well.”

“Excellent.”

Dr. Stouch glanced at his timepiece, stood and headed for the door. “If that is all, I’ll leave her in your care.”

It seemed he could not exit fast enough, leaving Brigid and her small valise of quickly packed items with Dr. Mantel.

“What do I have?” Brigid demanded.

“You carry typhoid.” Dr. Mantel answered sternly, but looked away. “You’ve infected the Ransom household with your slovenly hygiene.”

Brigid’s eyes flew open wide. “The hell I did!” Her face burned crimson with anger and embarrassment.

Dr. Mantel startled at her cursing and stepped backward. It almost made her laugh, this giant man, afraid of her.

He shuffled the papers and cleared his throat. “You’ll be housed here, on North Brother, until we can cure you, but as we’ve not found a cure for our other patients, it may be…a while.”

“You can’t cure me of somethin’ I don’t have! I’ve never had typhoid!”

The doctor slapped the papers with the back of his hand and looked her square in the eye. “This paperwork proves otherwise. You carry typhoid.”

“Then, those aren’t *my* tests! No one’s been testin’ me for anythin’!”

“Miss O’Brien.” The doctor removed his spectacles and rubbed his eyes. “Keep your voice down.” He lowered his own. "You must realize you are *lucky* to be here. Worse has happened to your kind."

"My *kind*?" Brigid's blood boiled. "What is my *kind*?"

"A sick, Irish immigrant. Mr. Ransom could have had you thrown in prison for what you've done, and no one would have thought twice about it."

Prison! A chill ran up her spine. "But, what have I *done*? I'm *not* sick, and I swear that no one in the Ransom household has typhoid!"

Dr. Mantel looked away again. "According to the paperwork, you spread typhoid to another maid and then knowingly remained on as a cook."

Brigid shook her head. This made no sense. The only one who had been sick while she worked there was Anna, and Anna had the flu.

"I've never had the disease, and I don't have the germs! I swear on the Holy Mother and all the angels and saints above!"

How had this happened? Why had she ended up here? She vaguely remembered being hit on the head with something in Mr. Ransom's study. On the boat ride over, she had tried to collect her wits and remember, but battling nausea from the unforgiving waves commanded all her attention.

But now, she remembered that afternoon most clearly. She had overheard Mr. Ransom and Dr. Stouch talking about what Charles had done to her and their plot to take Ruthie's baby! Henry had caught her listening and dragged her into the study. She awoke later in her bedroom with a bump on the back of her head. Dr. Stouch was in her room, packing her valise.

Then, despite her protests, he pulled her from the bed and hurried her down to the boat docks.

Dr. Stouch. He'd been the one to examine her on her arrival at Ransom House, and declared her healthy! He had never tested her for typhoid; he'd been more concerned with the regularity of her monthly courses.

Which made nightmarish sense now. She had often wondered why Mr. Ransom made her a kitchen maid when she had no experience cooking American food. She wasn't there to be a cook. There was another purpose for her. Charles Ransom had tried to get her pregnant! But her body had either rejected the pregnancy, or she'd never become pregnant, either way fine by her, and thank the blessed Lord for that!

How *convenient* for them to use her as a kitchen maid. What a perfect ruse to accuse her of spreading typhoid once she was no longer of use to them.

She could barely concentrate as Dr. Mantel droned on. "We've arranged for you to have a very nice cottage down near the water. You won't be bothered by anyone."

Realization hit her like a wall of water. Was sending her to North Brother Island the plan all along? Was this where she was to go after she had the baby? Had she been hired solely to give Charles Ransom a child? And what had become of Ruthie?

Dr. Mantel rambled on about her living quarters, but Brigid tuned him out. Everything became crystal clear, but she needed to tell someone who would believe her! Someone who could save Ruthie in time! But who? Certainly not Dr. Mantel. He'd been paid by Dr. Stouch to keep her here, silenced forever.

And poor Mrs. Ransom! Brigid prayed Thomas would continue to help her find Tobias. She also hoped that Thomas cared enough about her to realize she would never have left him of her own choice. She had to believe that *someone*, somewhere, searched for her, too. She hoped that someone was Thomas.

~~~~~~~~~~~~~

Brigid stood on the porch of her new home and gazed across the East River, just as she had each day since her arrival. Like most days, she was able to discern the skyline of New York City. For a city she hated so, she'd now give anything to return there. Dr. Mantel hadn't lied when he said no one would bother her on North Brother. Absolutely *no one* talked to, or visited her save for the middle-aged man who brought her food. Yet even he didn't knock on her door; he left her items in a box on the porch.

She knew she should be grateful to live in one of these bungalows instead of quarantined at Riverside Hospital. Her modest cottage consisted of a living room, kitchen, bathroom and the modern conveniences of gas, indoor plumbing, and electricity. Still, Brigid could not help but fear that she'd become a prisoner here.

No one, save Dr. Stouch and Charles Ransom, knew she was here. And they didn't care. She wished she had pencil and paper, but it wasn't supplied. She wanted to write to Mrs. Ransom, to tell her she didn't leave on her own accord, and that Eliza should try to contact Thomas. Mostly, she wanted to write to Thomas.

Thomas. How her heart still ached for him, his friendship, his smile, his kiss.
~~~~~~~~~~~~~

Tears threatened again. Brigid blinked them back and turned to go inside. She had noticed a few books in the living room and thought to give them a try.

"Wait, don't go!"

Brigid turned to see a woman emerge from the house next door. She had long, wavy blondish-brown hair that blew freely behind her as she raced in her long, dark skirt down her cottage steps.

"Are you new here?" She called to Brigid over the wind, and pulled her knit shawl tight against her chest.

Excited that someone took an interest in her, Brigid nearly yelled. "Yes!"

The woman reached the bottom step, gasped for air, but smiled. "I live next door. I'm Abigail Langford." She reached out a hand for Brigid to shake. "I've been under the weather for about a week, but better now. I'm from the Bronx, you?"

Brigid walked down the three wooden steps and shook the woman's hand. It was red and chapped, but warm and firm. Her accent sounded funny. Door sounded like "doe-ah."

"I'm from…" Brigid paused. Was she really from anywhere anymore? "New York."

"We're all from New York, honey," the woman said, with a laugh. "You've got an accent. Irish?"

"Yes. I came over in April."

"That explains it." The woman looked her up and down without the least amount of embarrassment.

"Explains what?"

"Why you're here. You'll find lots of Irish here. The city got overrun with the poor and sick, especially the Irish, and farmed them here."

"Are you Irish?" That accent certainly didn't sound Irish.

The woman laughed. "No, Polish. Grabrowski was my maiden name. Langford, my married. But I was born in the Bronx."

"Oh."

"How old are you?" The woman eyed her again, but her smile remained kind.

"Twenty-three."

"I figured you to be young. Why are you here?"

Brigid sighed. "They say I spread typhoid." She expected Abigail Langford to turn and run screaming, but she stood her ground and shook her wild-haired head.

"So, did you?"

"It was news to me." Brigid sat down on the porch steps, swishing her skirt beneath her knees. "If I do have typhoid, no one seems too concerned about it. I haven't seen a doctor since I arrived."

"Oh." Abigail studied her as if she could discern whether Brigid was truly sick or not. "I *do* carry typhoid." She spoke as if it was only a simple cold. "Didn't know it until my kids started getting sick. I had it when I was fourteen. Thought I was fully recovered, but according to the doctors, it hides in my bowels." She paused and looked out to the East River. "One of my children, my Stanley, died."

Brigid gasped. "I'm so sorry."

"I was the only one taking care of my children of course, so they tested me, and sure enough." Her voice dropped, and Brigid noticed Abigail's eyes mist up.

"But why are you *here*?" Brigid was aghast. "Couldn't they help you at a city hospital so you could be closer to your family?"

"You'd think. But see, my illness was a stroke of good fortune for my husband. Unbeknownst to me, he had a girl on the side, so it was convenient to have me out of the way." Abigail motioned to the steps. "Mind if I sit?"

"Please do."

The woman sat only a few inches from Brigid, as the three wood steps were not very wide.

"Whose takin' care of your children?" Brigid asked.

Abigail wiped away a tear. "That bastard of a husband sent them to Poland to live with my parents. I guess that's best, as he's got no child-raising smarts at all."

Abigail's comment about her children caused Brigid to suddenly miss her own brothers and sisters. She had tried to put them all from her mind. It was easier than missing them. But now, as she realized she truly might never see them again, she could not deny her longing to see her parents, her brother Simon, who was a year older than she, and the younger ones, Cecelia, Mary, Joseph, Danny and little Liam, only six. Lord, she missed them.

"I have a lawyer though," Abigail said.

Hope had replaced her tears. "If the doctors here cure me, I will most likely get my children back. Do you have a lawyer?"

Brigid shook her head. She had nobody.

"Oh." Abigail glanced away. "It's not too bad here, actually. We have it better than those kept at the hospital."

"I suppose." Brigid wondered if it was too soon to ask this kind lady about borrowing pencil and paper from her, if she even had any.

A noise from a bungalow further down caught their attention. Brigid hoped it might be another friendly woman or someone coming to save her, but instead it was a bird flapping its wings and building a nest under the cottage's peaked roof.

"Who lives there?" Brigid asked.

"As far as I know, just the bird," Abigail said. "I think they're keeping it vacant in case they catch Mary Mallon again. She used to live there until a couple years ago."

"Mary Mallon?"

Abigail gave her a quizzical look. "You've never heard of her? The doctors here refer to her as Typhoid Mary. Do you recognize that name?"

"No."

"She infected many people with the disease. She tested positive for typhoid and was held here for about three years. They finally let her go because she promised to never work as a cook again, but rumor has it, she's back at it."

Brigid pondered this. She shifted on the uncomfortable step. "Do you think, even though I still swear I don't have typhoid, that if I promise the doctors never to cook for anyone, that they'll let me go?"

Abigail placed her hand on Brigid's knee. "Oh honey, after Mary Mallon, I doubt they'll ever take a chance like that again."

Brigid shivered. Abigail had confirmed her worst fear. “How long have you been here, Mrs. Langford?”

“Three years.” She sighed. “In all fairness, the doctors are trying to cure me, but just haven’t discovered how yet. Once my tests come back without evidence of disease, I can leave.”

Brigid’s anger rose. “Well then, why don’t they test *me*? Why are they just goin’ by what Dr. Stouch said? If they would just test me, they’d see I don’t have it! No one has even taken my blasted temperature!”

Abigail offered a sympathetic smile. “Honey, haven’t you figured it out yet? You’re not here because you’re sick. Someone wanted you out of the way, just like I’ve been put here, except I handed them the excuse.”

Brigid realized she’d sealed her fate when she confronted Charles Ransom. “Do you think I’ll ever be freed?”

Abigail’s silence told all Brigid needed to know.

Chapter Twenty-Six

Thomas raced up the steps to Sacred Heart Church, the meeting place designated by Eliza Ransom, and the same church where Grace Cavanaugh had her funeral mass. His heart beat wildly as he wiped beads of sweat from his brow. He took a moment in the vestibule to stop, remove his hat, and try to collect his thoughts. Yes, he was excited to share his news about Tobias with Mrs. Ransom, but more importantly, he hoped to find Brigid here.

He had finally reached Mrs. Ransom by telephone two days ago, stating that he was a doctor with dire medical information about someone in her family. He was put directly through to her. He then explained who he actually was, how he came to help Brigid with the search, and of the events that led to locating Tobias in Chicago. Eliza Ransom had wept with joy and gratitude.

He had wanted to tell her more, but Eliza said she couldn't stay on the line much longer without arousing suspicion. She suggested they meet. Thomas explained that his hospital schedule left him little free time but Mrs. Ransom had agreed to meet this evening, two nights later.

"I'll sit two pews back from the altar," she had said. "On the left side of the church. Oh, and I'll see if Brigid would like to come along."

"I'm sorry, what?" He must have misunderstood her.

"I'll ask Brigid to accompany me. She's been so kind asking you to help me. I haven't bothered her about the matter since she's been ill, so I'm glad you continued the search."

Thomas's mind was a whirlwind of confusion. "She's been *ill*?"

"Yes, didn't you know? She had the flu a few weeks back from which she recovered, but then relapsed and was quarantined for her own good, I was told. She's better now, although I still haven't disturbed her. I figured if she knew anything more about Tobias, she'd tell me."

Thomas hadn't known what to say. If what Mrs. Ransom said was true, Brigid was still at Ransom House, but ill or not, she hadn't contacted him. And, if Mrs. Ransom was correct, why was he told she went to Ireland?

"I really must hang up, Dr. Ashton. We can talk more at the church."

The last thing Thomas had wanted to do was end the call. He wanted to know more about Brigid. He wanted to talk with her! "Mrs. Ransom, I-"

Before he could finish, she hung up.

The last two days had dragged as he waited for this meeting and the chance to see Brigid again. He thought to call her, or visit her at Ransom House, but pride stopped him. It was she who hadn't made an effort to contact him. Then again, had she been too ill?

So many feelings swirled through him. Longing, anger, confusion, and then more longing. He had never missed anyone he'd known for so short a time so intensely. Even if Brigid only appeared at the church to tell him goodbye, it would be more than he had now, nothing but unanswered questions.

He drew a deep breath and walked up the aisle. Even though he had never met Mrs. Ransom, he knew what she looked like from the society page. She sat exactly where she said, dressed entirely in black as if still in mourning for her baby.

Mrs. Ransom was alone. Brigid was not with her. Disappointment hit Thomas like a falling boulder. He stopped to quickly glance around the quiet, candle-lit church. Only a few other people sat apart or kneeled in pews, none of them Brigid. He turned and looked behind him. Could he have missed her? He hadn't.

Thomas felt as if a light dimmed in his heart. It took every ounce of his strength to continue his journey forward. He still had a job to do. If he couldn't be happy, at least he could make Mrs. Ransom happy.

He passed a young, dark-haired man who glanced up at him and then away. A few pews ahead, a younger woman sat. She also noticed him as he passed.

Eliza Ransom turned as he approached and lifted her dark veil. Her beauty was all it was noted to be, ethereal and mystifying with wide, haunting gray eyes, alabaster skin and wavy, dark auburn hair.

"Dr. Ashton?" She whispered his name as if it were a secret code.

"Yes." He nodded and motioned to the pew. "May I sit?"

She glanced back at the woman Thomas had passed. Eliza nodded, and the woman left to find another seat several pews back.

"My lady's maid," Mrs. Ransom explained. "Please sit." He sat next to her, trying not to be inappropriately close, but near enough so their voices would not carry.

Thomas placed the paperwork he'd brought on the pew and placed his hat in his lap.

They turned and looked at each other. Mrs. Ransom's eyes were full of hope, while he tried to hide the disappointment in his. He didn't want to give the wrong impression that he had bad news, but it was hard to mask the sorrow etching away at his heart.

"I'm pleased to make your acquaintance," he said, his voice a hushed whisper.

"Have you truly found my boy?" Those huge eyes misted over.

"Yes. As I said on the telephone, he's in good health and well cared for."

"And you're certain it's him?"

"The evidence would prove it true." Thomas refrained from patting her hand. This lady of such refinement might find it too forward. "The child called Joseph is a mongoloid, is about two and a half, and has the heart-shaped birthmark on his left, inner wrist."

Mrs. Ransom gasped, but smiled. "You told me that he's with a Mrs. Cole at her orphanage in Chicago. Will this lady agree to let me have him?"

Thomas paused. Now came the tricky part. He leaned in closer to her. "Mrs. Ransom," he started.

"Eliza, please, I hate formality."

Thomas smiled. "Eliza." He cleared his throat. "Mrs. Cole agrees that Joseph is most certainly Tobias. But, you must understand that Mrs. Cole is an extremely caring and cautious woman."

"Meaning?" Eliza's hopeful smile faded.

"Meaning that she's more than willing to place him back with his true mother, but she wants more evidence that the boy is indeed Tobias."

"What evidence?"

He could feel Eliza's frustration and disappointment as if it were his own. In a way, it was.

He drew a deep breath. "She wants to see Tobias's medical records, which isn't the problem, I have those." He patted the file beside him. It had been easy to remove the record from Baybridge Hospital. He'd gone back there on the ruse of needing to sign out records for his case study on disabled children and simply slid Tobias's chart in between two others he checked out.

"Then what is the problem, Dr. Ashton?"

"Thomas, please. I don't stand on formality either." He offered her a warm, comforting smile as if that might soften the upcoming blow.

"All right. Thomas."

"Mrs. Cole wants Tobias's death certificate revoked. She wants Rupert Stouch to issue a live birth record acknowledging that the child lived and was placed by him or your husband in her home."

"Rupert will never do that, it's akin to admitting a felony," Eliza said, her thoughts mimicking Thomas's exactly. Retrieving Tobias would not be as simple as they hoped.

"I don't know the doctor well," Thomas said. "But my suggestion would be that you agree not to press charges against him if he'll change the certificate and write the letter to Mrs. Cole." He put his hat aside and turned to her. "I know this is difficult, Eliza, but you have to understand that Mrs. Cole needs to protect herself too."

"Oh, I do understand," Eliza said. "It's just that even if I didn't press charges, I don't believe Rupert will admit to this, less he suffer the wrath of my husband. I can't believe what Charles has done to my son!"

"I can't believe he could do this to you," Thomas said, truthfully. "If it would help, I'll go with you to confront Dr. Stouch." He saw his opening. "And perhaps Brigid should come too?"

Mrs. Ransom fell silent just at the time Thomas most needed her to talk.

"Eliza-" he began, but she held up a gloved finger.

"I'm thinking on how this shall all work."

Thomas waited. He glanced around the church. Eliza's lady's maid remained at the back of the church, but the dark-haired man had moved closer to them. He glanced at Thomas again and nodded. Thomas nodded back out of politeness, but turned back to face the altar. He supposed it strange that the man changed seats, but all he could concentrate on was Brigid.

Finally, Eliza spoke. "I must get away from Ransom House before we confront anyone. I will pack when I get home and leave during the night. I'll go to my sister's in New Rochelle. Once there, I'll contact you, and we can devise a plan to talk with Rupert. I don't want Charles knowing a thing about this."

"Understandable," Thomas said, waiting as patiently as he could for an answer regarding Brigid.

Mrs. Ransom stood. Thomas stood as well. He turned to find Mrs. Ransom's maid rising from her pew, as did the mysterious man.

"I must get back." Eliza placed a gloved hand on Thomas's arm. "Thank you for everything."

He stepped from the aisle to let her pass. As she neared the end of the pew, she suddenly stopped. "Oh, and about Brigid..."

Finally! "Yes?

"I discovered she's not employed with us anymore. She left a week ago." Mrs. Ransom seemed sad at the news. "A few others are gone as well. It's a mystery to me what has happened."

"Brigid worked for you up until a week ago?" Thomas was more confused than ever. This didn't make sense. "I was told she went back to Ireland."

"When?" Eliza appeared stunned.

"On May twelfth!"

"No, when did she go to Ireland? Maybe that's why I haven't seen her in a week?"

"The last time I saw her was May 5th. I visited at the house May twelfth and was told by Dr. Stouch and your husband that she went home."

"Thomas, that was untrue. Brigid worked at Ransom House until at least last Friday."

He stood dumbfounded. He didn't know whether to be happy, angry, hurt or some combination of all three.

Eliza started towards the vestibule, and Thomas followed. As they passed the dark-haired man, he nodded to Eliza, but Eliza didn't respond, turning instead to glance over her shoulder at Thomas.

As he passed the man's pew, Thomas became keenly aware that the man followed him a few feet behind. He could not deny that something strange was definitely going on. He recalled his recent telephone conversation with Clara about how she'd been startled by a dark-haired, Irish fellow inquiring about Brigid. Could this be the same man?

As they proceeded from the church and into the vestibule, Eliza turned to say something to Thomas, but the man reached them and interrupted.

"Pardon me." He held a workman's cap in his hand. "May I be takin' a moment of your time, ma'am?"

Thomas noticed he had the Irish accent Clara mentioned. Eliza automatically reached to open her purse, but the man held up his hand.

"No, it's not a handout I'm after. Might you be Mrs. Ransom, though?"

Thomas quickly sized him up. He stood a half a head shorter than Thomas's six-foot stature, but appeared broad and fit through his white workman's shirt and suspenders. His gray pants were clean, but worn, his laced boots, scuffed. His face was tan from the sun, his expression one of worry, not malice. Thomas felt pretty confident he could take the young fellow if need be, but didn't think it would be necessary. The man appeared more disheartened than angry.

"What do you want with the lady?" Thomas said.

"I just need to be knowin' if this lady is Mrs. Ransom."

"I am," Eliza said, with no quiver or quake to her voice. "And who may I ask are you, sir?"

Recovering from her mistake in offering money, Eliza now treated this fellow with every respect given that to one of her own class. Thomas liked her even more for it.

The man bowed low.

"Pleased to be makin' your acquaintance, Mrs. Ransom."

He straightened up and looked them both in the eye, his countenance serious and determined. "I overheard you talkin' about Brigid O'Brien with the mister, here."

He nodded toward Thomas. "She's my sister. I'm her brother, Simon."

He looked imploringly, but firm, at both Eliza and Thomas.

"I've come to bring Brigid home."

Chapter Twenty-Seven

An hour later, Thomas sat directly across a table from Simon in a local tavern. He'd invited the fellow out for a drink and to talk. Perhaps together, they might shed some light on Brigid's whereabouts.

Eliza and her maid had returned back to Ransom House to pack. Upon parting, she and Thomas agreed that Clara Cavanaugh needed to be included when they confronted Dr. Stouch. After all, she was the one to actually transport the baby to Chicago. Thomas volunteered to call on her. He figured if anyone could sway her to join them, he would be the one. Once they had Clara on board, they would agree on a time to approach Stouch.

Although matters had progressed regarding returning Tobias to Eliza, things were now more confusing than ever about Brigid. Simon confirmed that she had not returned to Ireland, at least not to her hometown, the surrounding counties or to her aunt in England.

"So how have you come to know my sister?" Simon said, as he accepted a draft of ale from the barkeep. He sipped the beer, but his piercing green eyes never left Thomas's face.

"I met her on the pier when she waited for David Cavanaugh to arrive on the *Carpathia*." Thomas shifted in his chair. "After that, we became…friends." They could have been more. He had wanted more. He'd thought she'd wanted more, but then she was gone. He couldn't tell Simon that. He didn't know Brigid's brother well enough and wasn't sure how he'd react to Thomas's interest in her.

"I see." Simon took another sip and wiped his mouth with the back of his hand. "You've taken a fancy to her then?"

"Excuse me?"

"You like my sister?"

Thomas couldn't keep from smiling. "Very much, actually."

"Hmph."

It wasn't exactly the reaction Thomas hoped for. But then again, he wasn't here to please Simon O'Brien.

Thomas drummed his fingers on the table. "Brigid told me she wrote your parents and they said she couldn't come home. So, why are you here for her now?"

"Our father has passed," Simon said matter-of-factly, as if reporting the weather. "And good riddance to him. Bloody, drunken sot."

"Oh. My condolences." Thomas wasn't sure Simon actually needed them.

"It's his own fault." Simon emptied his mug, and Thomas called for another. He, himself, sipped slowly as he had patients to check on yet this evening.

"Knockin' me poor ma up every other year and then he gets caught with another farmer's wife in the barn." Simon spoke into his beer, but Thomas listened intently.

"Good God!"

"The farmer caught him and shot him. The bastard lived a few days, but then infection set in."

"So now that he's passed, it's all right for Brigid to go home? I thought she was disowned."

"That's the rub, ain't it?" Simon gripped the handle of his mug so hard Thomas thought it might splinter. "Da kicks her out because she disgraced the family, while he's running about pokin' stray skirts. He was the one who didn't want her back. It broke Ma's heart to write that letter to her."

"Brigid will be relieved." Thomas looked out the window and spoke softly. "Once we find her."

"I thought she'd be at the Cavanaughs'," Simon said. "That's where Brigid's letter was sent from." Simon finished his second beer and pushed away his mug. "Now, Clara Cavanaugh. There's a fine lookin' lass if ever I saw one!"

"Well," Thomas said, stalling for the right words as Simon's taste in women obviously ran opposite to his own. "You certainly made an impression on her." Clara acted as if Simon was a thug.

"Did I now?" Simon smiled for the first time since approaching Thomas and Eliza in the church. A twinkle gleamed in his eye. Thomas noted Simon appeared a lot less menacing when he relaxed. But as quick as his demeanor softened, Simon's eyes filled with worry and he frowned.

"So you're not knowin' where my sister is?"

Thomas shook his head. "I'm hoping Brigid spoke to someone at Ransom House. Now that I've met Eliza Ransom, I hope she might talk to the rest of her staff to see if anyone knows where Brigid went."

"Was she happy here?" Simon asked. "Do you think she'd come home with me? My ma and the children miss her." He glanced out the window. "We all do." He looked quickly back at Thomas. "And Ma could surely use her help."

Was Brigid happy here? Thomas didn't know how to answer. He thought she'd been happy with him, but then everything went wrong.

"I suppose we'll know that when we find her." He had a few questions of his own. "How did you know Mrs. Ransom would be at Sacred Heart this evening?"

"I followed her." Simon offered a sheepish grin. "I tried to call on her, but couldn't get past that butler fella at the door. When I told him I was actually lookin' for Brigid, he said he didn't know anyone named Brigid and shut the door in my face. But Miss Cavanaugh had told me Brigid went to Ransom House to work, at least that's what her aunt told her, so I knew that butler was lyin'. I sat in wait for someone to come out. I assumed she was Mrs. Ransom by her finery and havin' a maid along."

"You got blasted lucky, my friend," Thomas said. "Mrs. Ransom hardly ever leaves the house, so I hear."

"So, anyhow, I followed Mrs. Ransom, hoping to talk with her. She went into the church, and then you arrived, and as I got closer I could hear the two of you talkin' 'bout some babe, but then one of you mentioned Brigid."

Thomas sighed. "Yes, except Mrs. Ransom has no idea to Brigid's whereabouts either."

"Well, I ain't the most learned man, Dr. Ashton, but if it's brawn and might you need to get that doctor to confess and someone to tell us where Brigid is, I'm your man."

"I hope that won't be necessary, Mr. O'Brien," Thomas said. "But I do believe it might help to have you along. After all, you are Brigid's brother." Another thought crossed his mind. "Where've you been staying?"

"A men's boardin' house, but money is runnin' tight. Which is why I must find my sister soon. Got to hang on to what I saved for our passage home."

Thomas thought of the extra bedroom in his mother's house, and then a devilish idea developed. If Simon ran out of money, he couldn't buy Brigid a ticket back to England. Thomas shook the evil thought away. "My mother has a room."

Simon shook his head. "I appreciate the offer, but I don't accept charity, thank you, kindly however."

"It wouldn't be charity," Thomas said, truthfully. "The house needs work that I can't get to due to my studies. I'm sure my mother would keep you plenty busy in exchange for a bed and home-cooked meals."

Simon grinned from ear to ear and held out his hand. "I won't say no to that! I could use a decent meal. Looks like the good Lord above is on my side to find my sister all right."

Thomas shook on the deal. "Another?" he offered, nodding toward Simon's mug.

"No, I'm finished, thanks just the same." Simon pushed the mug away. "I'm not my da. I ain't here to carouse. Just here to find my sister and bring her home."

Thomas's heart lurched. He wanted to locate Brigid as much as Simon did. Yet, Simon threw a wrench in his plans. He hoped to one day be reunited with the beautiful Brigid O'Brien, and that there had been just some horrible misunderstanding between them which they'd quickly resolve. She'd then fall happily into his arms and promise never again to leave. Nowhere in that scenario, however, did she hop on a boat with her brother and sail away!

"Then again," Simon said, looking away. "Perhaps she doesn't want to be found."

Thomas's heart shattered.

Yes, and then, there was that.

Chapter Twenty-Eight

Three days later, Thomas stood outside Cavanaugh House accompanied by Simon. Staying true to both their words, Thomas had offered up a room at his mother's house, and Simon repaid the favor by helping Mrs. Ashton with chores around the house. Simon turned out to be a rather likable fellow, quick with a joke, a helping hand or a sympathetic ear for Angelina Ashton, who pined for her beloved Italy.

Before they left Ransom House, and for no reason Thomas could fathom, Simon picked a handful of tulips from a neighbor's garden. Thomas thought to tell him that wasn't acceptable in America, but Simon seemed so pleased with himself, Thomas let it be. Simon had also showered, shaved, combed his hair and laundered his clothes. Thomas had to admit that the fellow cleaned up well, and with his dark hair and startling green eyes, he might be considered handsome by the ladies.

Eliza Ransom met them at the entrance to Cavanaugh House. She dressed casually and far below her station in a plain skirt and high-necked white blouse, but donned a large purple hat with a wide, unadorned hat that concealed most of her face. She explained to Thomas that she hoped not to be recognized. The last thing they needed was Charles questioning why she might call on Clara Cavanaugh. She grasped Thomas's arm so tightly, he feared she might fall over if she let go. He couldn't blame her nerves, however. A lot rode on obtaining Clara Cavanaugh's help.

Thomas rang the bell. As they waited, he noticed a familiar scent in the air. Simon stepped closer.

"Simon," Thomas said, amused. "Did you use my shaving soap this morning?"

"I borrowed some." Simon coughed nervously and straightened his cap. "I didn't think you'd mind as we're vistin' a lady, after all."

The lady in question finally opened the door. Her eyes became the size of saucers as she glanced from face to face, but as they settled on Simon, she frowned.

Thomas spoke on behalf of the three. "Good morning, Clara. I hope you don't mind, but I've brought friends."

"This is the man who approached me the other day!" Clara shrilled as she pointed a long, accusing finger at Simon.

"Yes, I'm aware. May I present Simon O'Brien, Brigid's brother." Thomas cocked his head toward Simon.

Simon tipped his cap and shoved the flowers her direction. "Here. I picked them for you to 'pologize for startlin' you so the other day."

"*Brigid's* brother?" Clara stood stone still as if she'd been introduced to the devil himself. "Dear God. Another O'Brien!"

Simon remained undeterred. "Take the flowers, lady!"

Startled, Clara slowly reached for the bouquet. She looked at the assortment of haphazardly bunched tulips of varying colors as if they were an oddity. It was as if she'd never been given flowers before. Thomas thought that, sadly, maybe she hadn't.

He cleared his throat. "And Miss Cavanaugh, may I present Mrs. Eliza Ransom."

Eliza let go of his arm and greeted her kindly. "How do you do, Miss Cavanaugh?"

Clara nearly dropped the tulips as recognition and shock marred her pale features. "Oh! Mrs. Eliza Ransom! What an honor!" She appeared totally flustered. "You must forgive my surprise. I thought Dr. Ashton would be alone." She cast a disapproving look his way. "To discuss…" she looked at Simon and back at Mrs. Ransom, and her voice trailed off.

"Clara, I apologize for not telling you about Mr. O'Brien and Mrs. Ransom joining us," Thomas said. "But I was afraid you would decline to meet if you knew the real reason why we must talk."

"Well, I-," She looked again from one face to another. "Why *are* you all here? Thomas?" Her frightened stare remained fixed on Eliza. Realization dawned. Her hand flew to her mouth. "Oh, dear Jesus."

Eliza gently touched her arm. "Miss Cavanaugh, please be assured that I'm not here to blame you for anything. We simply need your help." She turned and glanced to the street where people strolled and cars whizzed past. "Could we talk inside? In private?"

Clara's eyes grew wide again. "Oh, oh yes! Forgive my manners!" She stepped aside and motioned with the flowers for them to enter. "Please, do come in!"

Thomas allowed Eliza to enter first, and then, Simon.

"You're lookin' most lovely today, Miss Cavanaugh." Simon removed his cap.

Clara turned her attention to a redheaded maid. “Betsy, please take Dr. Ashton’s and Mr. O’Brien’s hats.”

“Simon.” He straightened the tie he borrowed from Thomas.

“Excuse me?” Clara asked.

“My name’s Simon. That’s what you should call me. Mr. O’Brien was my father, and he’s dead.” He shot her a playful wink. “May I be callin’ you Clara?”

“No.” Clara ignored his charm and bustled past. “Please, everyone, come into the parlor where we can talk and have tea.”

“How lovely your home is, Miss Cavanaugh,” Eliza said as she entered the room and perched delicately upon on a light green Victorian parlor chair. Thomas sat across from her in a matching one, and Simon stood by the fireplace in front of the grate. Clara ignored Simon and selected the green chair farthest away from him.

“Thank you, Mrs. Ransom,” Clara said, a blush rising in her fair complexion. “I’ve bought some new parlor furniture with my recent inheritance, but surely, this can’t compare to Ransom House.”

“Believe me.” Eliza cast her eyes downward. “This home is a far nicer place to be.”

The maid brought in the tea, and once everyone had been served, Thomas settled into the matter.

“Clara, again, I apologize for the intrusion,” Thomas said. “And for not telling you the entire matter on the telephone.”

“Yes, I was under the impression that we were to talk about Leopold coming home,” Clara said.

"Yes. I'm sorry to have misled you, although Mr. Cavanaugh is trying his best to get well. The real reason I'm here is two-fold, one being about where Brigid O'Brien might be." Thomas noticed Clara's face harden again. "The other regards the infant that Rupert Stouch asked you to transport to Chicago."

"I believe that baby was my son," Eliza said, her voice soft and gentle as if trying not to scare Clara off.

"Your *son*? But…but…" Clara looked to Thomas for help. "I thought the Ransom baby-"

Thomas tried to calm Clara's rising panic. "- had passed, yes, that's what we all thought."

"Not me," Eliza said. "I always felt my child was alive somewhere."

Thomas went on to explain how he and Brigid came to be involved with finding Tobias. Simon stayed silent, while Clara emitted tiny gasps as her controlled demeanor evaporated.

"And so," Thomas concluded. "We are going to confront Dr. Stouch about the baby he sent to Chicago with you, but we would like you there to corroborate our suspicions."

Eliza set her teacup on a table. "Miss Cavanaugh, on what date did Rupert give you the baby?"

"January fourth." Clara's hands trembled so badly she also put down her tea. "I remember it clearly because I missed a wedding I dearly wanted to attend."

"My son was born January second. And the baby had a shock of red hair?" Eliza spoke gently like a lawyer leading a terrified witness.

"Yes." Clara hung her head. "Rupert said the baby was not wanted by his parents due to being a mongoloid. Mrs. Ransom, I am so sorry." She looked up, her eyes moistening. "I had no idea."

"No one blames you at all, dear," Eliza said. "We were both victims of this horrible scheme of Rupert's to do away with my imperfect child. I have no doubt my husband was involved as well. I could tell the minute Tobias was born that Charles was horribly disappointed in him."

"That's putting it gently!" Thomas blurted, unable to contain his disgust with Charles Ransom and Dr. Stouch. "He led you to believe your baby died!"

"Ah," Eliza offered a quick smile. "But I never did."

"And Rupert promised *me* we would marry when I returned from Chicago," Clara said, shaking her head. "I believed him. But once I returned, he married another."

"That's for the best," Simon said, and then swallowed his tea in one loud gulp. He clanked the cup and saucer upon the fireplace mantel. "I mean, it's for the best you not marryin' that..." he stopped himself. "Well, I won't say what he is in front of the ladies, but, anyhow, Miss Cavanaugh, you hang in there. You'll find a decent fella, one who's hard workin' with no designs on stealin' any infants. I'm thinkin' an Irishman is what you're needin'. We don't go around stealin' babes. We make our own."

Clara blushed so fiercely Thomas thought her face might catch fire. He stifled a laugh. "So, Clara. Will you help us?"

A tense minute passed as Clara remained silent. Thomas glanced at Eliza. She sat on the edge of her seat, her gloved fingers knitted tightly together.

Clara cleared her throat and smoothed her dress. “I’ll help.” She offered a quick smile to Eliza. “It’s the least I can do.”

Eliza sighed, leaned back in her chair and unlaced her fingers. “I am so grateful, Miss Cavanaugh.”

“Another nail in that quack’s coffin!” Simon pounded his fist into the palm of his other hand.

Eliza turned toward Thomas. “But now, about Miss O’Brien.”

Before Thomas could begin, Simon spoke, his eyes suddenly sad, but still fixed on Clara. “My sister’s gone missin’. She’s not at Ransom House like you said.”

Clara startled. “Mr. O’Brien, I’m not to blame for her disappearance from Ransom House. I promise I didn’t transport her anywhere, I simply kick-” she stopped suddenly and hung her head. “I’ve been a horrible person all around.”

“What in the heck are you talkin’ about, woman, er, Miss Cavanaugh? I thought you found her employment at the Ransoms’?” Simon furrowed his brow, but his voice remained even.

Thomas knew Clara could not lie about the matter, because he knew the truth. Clara would have abandoned Brigid to the streets if Grace hadn’t interfered and sent her to Ransom House.

“I was in such a state after my father and brother died.” Clara stared down at her hands and picked invisible lint from her skirt. “I didn’t want Brigid getting any of my inheritance since she never rightfully married David. And, I felt she never truly loved him.”

Thomas blinked and held his tongue. Clara didn’t know how right she was about that, except that Brigid wouldn’t have taken any of his inheritance. She had just needed a little help to go home to Ireland or find her bearings in New York. That's what she had told Thomas, and he believed her.

Clara's next words were barely audible. "I was awful to Brigid. I was still angry about Rupert using me and then marrying someone else. I didn't think she deserved more happiness than me, so I made her leave with nothing but the clothes on her back and a few other items. That's all I knew of what happened to her, until my aunt told me Brigid worked for the Ransoms."

Simon stood, walked over and pulled one of Thomas's handkerchiefs from his trouser pocket. He offered it to Clara. Not only was Thomas surprised that Simon had borrowed his personal item, but he was equally amused that Clara did not shun Simon's offer of it.

She dabbed at a few stray tears. "Thank you, Mr. O'Brien. I'm so sorry as to how indecently I treated Brigid. She'd been nothing but kind to me."

Simon knelt on bended knee in front of her, bringing them nearly eye-to-eye. "Miss Cavanaugh," he said, his tone mock serious. "If you weren't a lady, I should bloody you one on behalf of my sister."

Eliza gasped and Thomas jumped up, but Simon raised a hand to halt him. "But that would be somethin' my father would do, not me. I'm a gentleman, Miss Cavanaugh, and I don't strike women."

Clara cast a worried expression at Thomas. He let Simon continue.

"We all do things we're sorry for later, especially when we are grievin'. Why, when my father recently passed, I had his body burned and never told my mother."

Simon's entire captive audience gasped, including the maid, Betsy, who had returned to collect the teacups. Thomas handed his over, and then Clara shooed her from the room with a wave of her hand.

"My mother, praise the saints above, never knew my father's coffin contained nothin' but his ashes." Simon rose from his knee, turned and addressed them all. "Yet my mother, bless her heart, still forgave my father for all his transgressions against her. Just forgave him outright as the first mound of dirt hit his coffin."

He turned to Clara again. "And therefore, Miss Cavanaugh, if my own blessed mother can forgive my bast-, er, devil of a father, I forgive *you* for mistreatin' my sister."

Clara sniffed and wiped another tear. "Thank you kindly. You're a good man, Mr. O'Brien."

"Simon."

"Simon." She smiled.

He returned to the others. "Well! Now that Miss Cavanaugh knows me for the gentleman I am, how are we goin' to find my sister?" He shot them a quirky grin.

Eliza shifted in her seat. "It's my turn to apologize. I believe her disappearance may be due to her involvement in the search for my son."

"How so?" Thomas asked, happy to return to the subject of Brigid.

"Over these past days at my sister's, I've been talking on the telephone to Charles's valet, Henry. It seems there's been more than one employee fired or leaving of his or her own choosing, and of course, there's Brigid's mysterious disappearance. I asked Henry why Brigid and other kitchen staff had left. It turns out that Henry was also about to resign, but he was silent as to the reason, that is, until I bribed him." Mrs. Ransom smiled. "With Charles's money, of course."

Thomas chuckled.

She continued. "It was then that Henry said he had misgivings about working for a man who would allow the maid, Brigid, to be hit on the head by Dr. Stouch. Later, he witnessed Rupert escorting Brigid from the house."

"Christ!" Thomas jumped up and paced the room. "That bastard! And all along he had me thinking she went to Ireland!"

"Where did he take her?" Simon said, clenching and unclenching his fists.

"Henry didn't know, but the next day he was told that Brigid was forced to leave because she carried typhoid."

"Impossible!" Simon balled up his fists again. "She's never been sick a day in her life!"

"And she passed inspection after disembarking from our ship," Clara said.

"And no one at Ransom House, family or staff has had typhoid!" Eliza straightened in her chair. "I don't think Brigid had typhoid. I think Rupert somehow found out that she was looking for Tobias."

"But how could he know?" Thomas said, stopping his manic pacing to scratch his head. "It doesn't make sense."

"I concur, Thomas," Eliza said. "We were very discreet. But why else would he send Brigid away under the pretense of typhoid?"

"And to where?" Simon said.

Thomas thanked his lucky stars he'd chosen to go into the medical profession.

"I think I know."

Chapter Twenty-Nine

Brigid placed a small wooden chair in the center of her bungalow's living space. She walked around it, deep in thought, her fist curled under her chin. After circling around the chair a few times, she stopped and turned to Abigail, who had watched her silently with an amused look upon her face.

"You don't have a hammer, do you, Abigail?"

"If I did, I'd use it on one of these idiot doctors and escape with you off this island." Abigail stared at the high pile of wood, boards and planks Brigid had collected and stacked in the corner throughout her long, dull days on North Brother. "You really think you can build a boat out of all this?"

Brigid stared at the chair like a lion sizing up its prey. "If only I could figure out a way to get the nails out of this chair, all the parts could be of good use."

"You're serious about building a boat?"

Brigid sighed and sat on the chair. She rested her hands on her knees. "Look, Abigail. No one is comin' to rescue me, and I don't have a lawyer like you do to plead my case to anyone. I don't think anyone, other than that bastard Dr. Stouch knows I'm here. You don't know how many times I've walked over to the hospital beggin' for someone to listen to me, to test me for typhoid, but they all ignore me. They just stare at me like I'm mad! I'm never leavin' this island, unless I find a way to do it. And it's a long, cold swim back to the city!"

"But, even if you knew how to build a boat, it will take you forever." Abigail glanced at another pile of tree branches and thick sticks Brigid collected on her walks.

"I've got nothin' but time." Brigid hung her head and tried not to cry. Nearly a month had passed since her entrapment on the island, and she thought she was all cried out. Yet, at least a few times a day, uncontrollable tears streamed down her cheeks. "I need somethin' to do - somethin' to concentrate on. Somethin' that gives me hope of seein' my family again."

"And that handsome doctor you told me about?" Abigail pulled up a chair beside her.

The dull island days had provided the two women plenty of time to get to know each other. Brigid had told Abigail about Thomas and her feelings for him and about her suspicions that he now courted Clara Cavanaugh.

Brigid placed a wayward strand of her hair behind her hair. She wore it loose these days, as Abigail did. No need to dress fashionably for anyone.

"I'm certain Thomas doesn't care for me anymore. He must have thought me brash and forward the night we kissed. I never heard from him after. Didn't even call on me when I-" she halted as she hadn't told Abigail all that happened to her. "When I fell ill."

Abigail patted her leg. "We'll just keep praying, Brigid. It's all we got." Abigail glanced at the pathetic piles again. "Let's just say you somehow manage to build this boat and oars to go with it. Just how you going to get it into the river without anyone seeing?"

Brigid smile. "I've thought about that. I'm not goin' to haul it to the docks. The nurses here only peek in on me once a day in the mornin' to make sure I haven't escaped or died. I'm hopin' to haul my boat down to the nearest shore and slip it into the river. That is, if I can get the thing over the rocks without it breakin' apart."

Abigail rose. "Honey, if you actually build that boat, I'll help you get it into the water." She walked toward the front door. "I'll see if I can find anything in my place that might help remove those nails."

"Thank you, Abigail." Brigid walked her onto the porch, and watched as her friend went next door. As they waved to each other, Abigail went inside.

Brigid had hung her washed skirt, blouse and undergarments over the wooden porch rail, and as she reached to get the now dry clothing, she realized that she could probably use half her front porch for the boat as well.

Buoyed by the idea, she quickly grabbed the clothing, but as she turned toward the door, the skirt caught on a loose nail and tore.

She cried aloud at her misfortune. Dr. Stouch had only packed her two skirts and blouses - the set she wore, and the ones just washed. And now, that skirt was ruined. She had no sewing supplies. What on earth was she supposed to do without decent clothes? Brigid stomped her foot in frustration and threw down the torn skirt. She was sick of being ignored and living off the tiny provisions supplied.

She slammed her front door shut and stormed down the steps toward the path leading to the hospital. She needed help, and she was done being ignored. If she had to sit outside Dr. Mantel's office day and night to get help, this time she would.

Brigid neared the island's main grounds. The hospital where Stouch brought her was up a ways to the left, and on her right, she recognized the pier at which she and the doctor had arrived. A small rowboat, nearly a quarter of the size of the vessel she and Stouch had arrived in, sat tied by a rope to the pier and bobbed up and down in the choppy water.

Brigid's heart raced. Why build a boat when you could just steal one? She glanced back at the hospital. A few people milled about outside, but no one glanced her way. She looked longingly at the boat. The pier had been a hub of activity the day she and Stouch arrived, but today it was quiet except for the boat bumping up against it every few seconds. A few men stood chatting on another pier a ways away, their attention caught by a capsized rowboat run ashore. Could she slip unnoticed onto the unoccupied pier and reach the rowboat? What would they do to her if they caught her? Imprison her for life? She knew no difference in that.

Without another thought, Brigid darted for the boat.

~~~~~~~~~~~~~~~~~~~~~~~~~~~~

"I'm only going to say this one more time, Dr. Ashton. There is no Brigid O'Brien on North Brother."

Thomas shifted in his chair and tried yet another approach. He and Simon had been in Dr. Mantel's office for the better part of an hour stating their suspicions that Brigid had been sent there erroneously.

"Perhaps she is here, but under a different name." Thomas tried to keep his voice calm although his agitation with the uncompromising Dr. Mantel grew with the doctor's every denial.
~~~~~~~~~~~~~~~~~~~~~~~~~~~~

"Impossible!" Dr. Mantel said. "I have documented medical records on each of our patients, and there is no one here by her description."

"But what if you were tricked?" Simon said from the chair next to Thomas. "Maybe she was wearin' a wig when she got here?"

The doctor ignored Simon. "Dr. Ashton. It is you who is here under false pretense. I agreed to see you because you're a medical student and you said you wanted information on how our facility runs. Now that I am aware of your deceit, unless you have proof that a Miss Brigid O'Brien was sent here, I have nothing further to discuss." He started for the door.

Thomas jump up. "Dr. Mantel. Where is your heart? A woman is missing!"

Dr. Mantel turned and glared at Thomas as if he'd spit on him. "An *immigrant* is missing, Dr. Ashton. Immigrants go missing daily from the city, especially young women. Have you tried searching the brothels or the Hudson or East rivers?"

Simon flew from his chair as if to box the man's ears. Thomas held him back by the arm, although he as well thought to slug the doctor a good one for the comment.

"Dr. Mantel. You are mistaken about this girl. She was working for a well-to-do family." He loathed naming names at this point fearing a slander and libel suit should the doctor tell the Ransom's about his visit. "They accused her of having typhoid and sent her away. Wouldn't this be the logical place for her to come? Have any young, blonde, Irish women been brought here in the last few weeks?"

Something in the doctor's demeanor flickered, as if an insect of some sort crawled up his leg. He seemed suddenly uncomfortable and antsy, and his voice cracked slightly.

"I repeat. *She is not here*. There is nothing more I can or will do for you. Good day, sir."

Thomas knew he could do no more without being physically thrown out on his ear. He signaled to Simon that they were leaving, but addressed the doctor one last time. "I will return." Without another word, he and Simon left the hospital.

"You should have let me beat the truth out of him," Simon said as they stood outside the hospital entrance.

"Then you'd be in jail, and I'd have *two* people to rescue," Thomas responded without humor.

"I say we go back into that hospital and storm our way through each room lookin' for her," Simon said.

"And again, you're looking at jail time, my friend." Thomas ran a hand through his hair, opting to leave his hat off in the warm summer sun. "I think we need to confront Stouch as originally planned. If we threaten to spill what we know to the police about the Ransom baby, Stouch might tell us where Brigid is in return for our silence."

"And that would be blackmail, now wouldn't it?" Simon said, squinting in the late afternoon sun.

"Why yes, Simon, it would be."

Simon grinned from ear to ear. "You're my kind of man."

In better spirits, the men followed the path leading to the docks. As they neared, Simon smacked him hard on the arm to get his attention. "Someone's stealin' our boat!"

Thomas shaded the sun from his eyes and saw a woman working hastily at the ropes anchoring boat to pier. "I'll be damned, you're right! Come on!"

They flew toward the boat as Simon bellowed, "Stop right there woman! That's *our* boat!"

The woman did not stop or look up. She worked the ropes even faster, but she was no match for the quick men. They reached the dock, panting and nearly out of breath.

"Stop!" Thomas yelled, gasping.

The woman looked up. Her eyes grew wide and her hand flew to her mouth.

"Brigid!" Thomas said, frozen in his tracks.

"Praise the saints above!" Simon ran to his sister, pulled her into his arms and swung her around. As he set her down, her tears streamed.

"Jesus, Mary, Joseph and all the blessed saints, Simon!" She ran her hands up and down his arms. "I feared I'd never be seein' you again!"

She looked past his shoulder, her voice riddled with confusion. "Thomas?" She stifled a sob, more tears brimming.

He hadn't moved, his mind swirling with emotion from the shock of actually finding her. He willed his legs to move, and his arms to reach for her. But the look on her face stopped him dead in his tracks. She didn't appear happy to see him. She seemed shocked, her eyes wide with an emotion he couldn't pinpoint. Was she scared? Angry? She almost looked betrayed. She glanced at him for only a minute, as if any longer might scorch her. He stayed in his place, but his heart beat wildly.

"Someone's comin', and they don't look all that pleased!" Simon said, pointing toward land.

Thomas and Brigid turned to see Dr. Mantel and a few orderlies storming to reach them with the demeanor of an angry mob. All they needed were pitchforks.

"Into the boat, now!" Simon yelled and wasted no time scooping Brigid into his arms and setting her in the boat. Thomas quickly worked the ropes. Both men jumped into the vessel, grabbed an oar, and pushed away from the pier with all their strength. They paddled as fast as they could against the incoming waves.

They were a safe distance from shore when Dr. Mantel and his henchmen reached the pier. They expected to be followed in hot pursuit, but to their surprise, the men just watched them row away.

"They're lettin' you go, Brigid," Simon said.

"They probably forgot who I am," she said, quietly.

"If they ever really knew in the first place," Thomas added, noting the way her golden hair hung loose, and softly framed her face and shoulders. He'd never seen it in this fashion, and as the late afternoon sun glittered upon her, she looked like an angel.

He couldn't believe she sat across from him. He wanted to reach out and touch her, but feared her reproach and that her protective brother might deck him.

"What did they call you?" he asked, trying to decipher if the doctor had truly known who she was or not.

"No one ever called me by a name," Brigid said, her voice flat and void of emotion. "They only spoke to me that first day. When they checked in on me in the mornin', it was always 'miss.'"

Thomas could not stop looking at her, afraid that if he did, she'd be gone when he glanced back. She looked anywhere but at him.

"This is a miracle!" Simon rested an oar, slapped his knee and gave his sister another quick kiss on the cheek.

Brigid jumped as if suddenly realizing that her brother sat in the boat. Emotion in the way of surprise finally found her. "Simon! What are you doin' in America? How did you meet Thomas? How are Ma and Da?"

Simon was about to speak, but Thomas but interrupted. He couldn't have Brigid knowing her mother needed her and that her father was dead. Not yet. He realized he was being selfish, but he wanted time with her first. Time to tell her how much he had missed her, that he had realized he loved her, and that he'd move all the mountains in Europe to keep her with him.

"There will be time for all that later, Brigid," he hurriedly said. "Simon has a lot to tell you, but there are things you must tell us, too." He smiled. She remained tight-lipped. But why? She must be so relieved to be off North Brother. "We thought you might be here, but Dr. Mantel said you weren't."

"We didn't believe him," Simon said.

"Yes, we're going to have a good long talk with Dr. Stouch," Thomas said. As he and Simon rowed, he explained how they figured out where Brigid might be. "So, you see, now that you're back, and we know what Stouch did, we can blackmail him with what he did to you and get Mrs. Ransom's baby back."

Thomas smiled at her again, but she only looked down and gripped the seat.

Her voice came pained and angry.

"Unfortunately, you don't know the half of what happened to me!" She looked up as tears rolled down her cheeks once more. "There's more."

Chapter Thirty

Brigid didn't get the chance to explain further as the boat ride back to the city was short. As she, Thomas and Simon exited the boat and pier, Thomas suggested he take her to the hospital immediately to be checked over.

Brigid waved away the suggestion. "I'm just lookin' worn and thin due to a poor diet," she assured. "Once I get a good meal of meat and potatoes, I'll be better in no time."

She sensed Thomas was about to protest, but an elderly man walking by suddenly clutched his chest and fell to the ground. His lady companion called for help.

"Wait here," Thomas said to Brigid and Simon. They could only watch as he hurried off toward the couple. Thomas assessed the ill man, spoke to the woman and then returned to Brigid and Simon.

"I need to get this man to the hospital," Thomas said, his expression apologetic but serious. "I'll drive him in my automobile. That'll be faster than waiting for an ambulance. Brigid, I insist you come as well."

"And, I say no." She tried not to sound harsh. "The last place I want to be is near another hospital. I'm feelin' all right, truly."

Thomas glanced from her to the man on the ground. "Well, fine, but I don't like it." He quickly reached into his trousers' pocket, pulled out some money and handed it to Simon. "Get a cab, and take Brigid to my mother's house. I'll telephone once I get to the hospital."

He smiled at Brigid. "I'll meet up with you later. I'm so sorry about this." He touched her arm, as if to comfort her, and it was all she could do not to pull away. She must ignore the tingles he sent coursing through her body, for he belonged to another.

Simon linked his arm in hers. “Come on, sister! We’ve got lots of catchin’ up to do!” He guided her to the street while prattling on about how he met Thomas. Without coming up for air, he continued on about how they and Mrs. Ransom had put two-and-two together to find Brigid on North Brother.

Although happy to find her brother in America, Brigid could barely pay attention to his ramblings, her thoughts returning instead to the moment she saw Thomas on the pier. Her heart had leapt with joy, only to have reality squash it back to its rightful place. She could not push the image from her mind of Thomas comforting Clara at Grace’s funeral.

What she did not understand, however, was the way he stared at her on the pier and in the boat, as if she were some rare diamond he’d searched for and finally found. He had appeared shocked, but jubilant. For an instant, she felt he might take her into his arms and swear he cared only for her. But it wasn’t what happened, just as nothing she hoped for since leaving Ireland had come true. David died. Clara was not whom she seemed. Her employer had drugged and raped her, and she’d been kidnapped and shut away on an island. Was God punishing her for disobeying her parents? Would all be righted if she returned to Ireland begging absolution?

These thoughts still plagued an hour later as she and Simon sat in Mrs. Ashton’s kitchen, sipping hot tea and eating hearty bread smothered in butter and honey. It was the best meal she’d had in over a month. On North

Brother, she ate canned goods, rice and beans. Even if Mrs. Ashton had served up those odd snails again, she'd have devoured them with gusto.

"Thank you again for everything," she said to Mrs. Ashton who sat with them.

Mrs. Ashton nodded. "You are welcome. My Tomaso, he missed you. Where have you been?"

Brigid set down her teacup. It was obvious that Thomas hadn't yet told his mother about Clara.

Brigid told Mrs. Ashton and Simon about her time on North Brother, and how she'd mistakenly been accused of having typhoid. She purposely omitted the truth about why she'd been sent there, not wishing to worry Mrs. Ashton or Simon further, nor wishing to revisit those incidents in her mind. Also, she wasn't sure how much Simon, Thomas or Eliza Ransom really knew about what happened to her.

"Some doctor made a mistake?" Mrs. Ashton seemed to understand the gist of Brigid's absence. "You are not sick?"

"That's correct, Mrs. Ashton. I do not have typhoid," Brigid said, as the hall telephone rang.

Mrs. Ashton went to answer the telephone, and after a moment or two of speaking in Italian to the caller, she motioned to Simon. "You. Come talk to Tomaso."

Brigid tried not to care that Thomas didn't ask to speak to her. Simon walked over and took the receiver. Mrs. Ashton returned to the table, bringing with her a platter of fruit, and saying something in Italian that Brigid couldn't understand. Mrs. Ashton's chatter only served to distract her from listening in on the telephone call.

As Brigid bit into a crunchy apple, Simon returned to the table.

"Well, it's all settled." he said, reaching for a pear. "Thomas is stuck at the hospital, but Brigid, you'll be spendin' the night at Eliza's sister's as I'm in the extra bed here, and she's got room. Eliza is sendin' a car for you. Thomas called her when he got to the hospital, so your ride should be here any minute."

She wasn't sure if she should be delighted that Thomas thought of her welfare, or heartbroken that he was sending her away. Then again, she had to admit that staying under the same roof with him, here at Mrs. Ashton's, would be dreadfully awkward.

"I've been stayin' here," Simon continued. "Takin' care of things for Ma Ashton while Thomas works."

"Oh!" She hadn't realized her brother and Thomas had become so close. She wasn't sure how she felt about that, but supposed it mattered little, as she and Simon would most likely leave for Ireland in a few days.

The doorbell rang. Mrs. Ashton rose, as did Simon. He held up his hand. "No, Mama, you stay put. Let me answer. You never know who might be callin' this time o' the evenin'."

Brigid stifled a smile. It was obvious he'd grown close to Mrs. Ashton. Of course, she was a lovely and kind woman, easy to grow close to.

"He's a good boy," Mrs. Ashton said, as if reading Brigid's thoughts.

"Yes." Brigid smiled.

"It's the car, sister!"

Brigid hurried to the living room and peered out the window. A black, luxury car parked curbside. The driver, an elderly, harmless looking gentleman, stepped down from the driver's side.

Brigid thought to get her things, but then realized she had no things to get. Mrs. Ashton joined them at the door, handing Brigid a basket covered with a plain white kitchen towel. "Cookies, bread, sausage. You take."

Brigid wanted to cry at Mrs. Ashton's kindness. She accepted the basket and kissed Mrs. Ashton on the cheek. Mrs. Ashton smiled.

"Thomas and I will stop by Eliza's sister's in the morning to see you and discuss further plans," Simon said as Brigid turned to him next. "Also, I've got bit more news for you."

"What is it, Simon? Why didn't you tell me earlier?"

"You've been through enough for one day," he said. "You get a good night's rest and we'll talk in the mornin'."

She knew her brother wouldn't tell her more if he set his mind not to, and she *was* exhausted and facing a long ride back to Eliza's sister's home. Whatever Simon's news was, she'd wait.

She turned to Mrs. Ashton. "Thank you kindly for everythin', Mrs. Ashton. I will repay you one day."

"No!" Mrs. Ashton took Brigid's hand between her two plump, warm ones. "No. You must only make my Tomaso happy." She patted Brigid's cheek. "That's all." She smiled and padded back to the kitchen.

Basket in hand, Brigid kissed Simon goodnight and thanked him for everything. As she walked to the car, Mrs. Ashton's words tore at her heart. She'd love to make Thomas happy, to be part of this loving family, part of this world, but that it would never be.

Thomas had Clara, and she was going home.

Chapter Thirty-One

New Rochelle, where Eliza's elder sister, Natalie Markeson, lived, was only an hour or so outside of the city, but to Brigid, the quaint town may as well have been another country. Gone were the ugly tall buildings, the crowded and dirty streets, the unwanted smells and bustling noise of the city. Brigid found herself instead in a quiet little community with attractive homes, winding roads and tall trees.

Arriving at the Markeson home and exiting the motorcar, Brigid breathed in the fresh country air. The June evening was warm and smelled of freshly cut grass, a recent rain and chimney smoke. In the vast expanse between estates, fireflies flickered and overzealous crickets serenaded her with their lovely song. Compared to the damp chill, musty odor and bleak atmosphere of North Brother, the Markeson estate seemed like Heaven.

Eliza greeted her at the door, and nodded to Brigid's driver who had waited for her to enter the home. As he drove away, Eliza introduced Brigid to her sister, who might have passed for Eliza's twin had she been a tad taller and slimmer.

Brigid handed Mrs. Markeson the basket of food from Mrs. Ashton, happy to have something to offer in return for her stay.

"Oh, thank you kindly," Mrs. Markeson said, accepting the gift. "But, I'm only too happy to help you out, Miss O'Brien. Eliza has told me of your dreadful ordeal on that island."

"I promise, I won't be stayin' long. As soon as I'm able, I'll be leavin' with my brother for Ireland."

It hurt to say it, but Brigid knew it had to be. Without any money, she had no other choice, and she could not keep living off Mrs. Ransom's charity.

"Come, come." Mrs. Markeson nodded toward a room off the hall and on the left. "Let us gather in the reception parlor and get to know each other, shall we?" She handed the basket to a maid, asked her to bring them some tea and escorted Brigid and Eliza into the parlor.

Although the hour grew late, and Brigid longed for the comfort of a bed, she sat with the sisters and told of her stay at North Brother. Both women seemed captivated by her survival and escape.

She tried not to yawn as she spoke. She wished for nothing more than to go to bed, but then the maid arrived with the tea.

"You look as if you could use some, dear," Mrs. Markeson said.

She was painfully aware that she still wore her dirty, worn skirt and tattered white blouse. Although she had managed to pull her hair back into a braid at Mrs. Ashton's, she knew by now that her unruly tendrils loosened, and she must look a fright. Especially when compared to these well-dressed, refined ladies.

As the maid poured tea, Brigid noticed that Mrs. Ransom looked healthier and happier than ever. Her cheeks were aglow with color, and her dark auburn hair was fastened atop her head with a bejeweled comb. Her huge gray eyes sparkled with life; so different than the deadened expression she wore at Ransom House. Gone were the haunting nightgowns she used to walk about in, replaced instead by an elegant white lace dress cut square in the bodice, accentuated by sparkling neck beads and earrings. She looked like the heiress she was, not the ghost of a woman Brigid had met at Ransom house. Natalie Markeson, who sat next to her sister, shown equally as brilliant in a red and black dress of a similar fashion, accessorized with a dazzling black teardrop choker and matching earrings.

Mrs. Ransom informed Brigid of all that had occurred while she was away. Brigid was relieved to hear that Ruthie left with Jimmy before she gave birth, but shocked to hear that Charles fired Mrs. Duffy for being insubordinate, and that Anna left with her. Most intriguing to Brigid, however, was that Mrs. Ransom seemed unconcerned about the sudden reduction in her household staff, and didn't seem wanting for a reason. She wasn't sure what Mrs. Ransom did or didn't know about what had occurred under her nose, so Brigid decided to speak cautiously around her, afraid that the knowledge of all Charles's crimes might shatter they lady's sanity.

Mrs. Ransom continued in her musing. "I just don't understand why Charles and Dr. Stouch would take such drastic measures to send you away for simply helping me. How patently absurd!"

Just the thought of Charles Ransom made Brigid's stomach twist and the bile rise. Her heart pounded, and she grew sweaty. Brigid knew she could not tell Mrs. Ransom what her husband had done. She could barely face it herself.

"Brigid, are you all right?" Mrs. Ransom hurried to her chair, but Brigid politely waved her away. "I'm fine, thank you. It's just been a long day."

Mrs. Ransom fiddled with her beads. "Indeed! How thoughtless of me! You must be exhausted. Allow me to accompany you to the room Natalie has had made up for you. You shall rest."

"Thank you, kindly," Brigid said, relieved to end the conversation. She bid Natalie Markeson good evening and followed Mrs. Ransom into the reception hall and up a polished stairwell to a room on the second floor. Mrs. Ransom opened the door.

Brigid gasped. She'd never seen a room so lovely. She'd been used to sleeping in her empty box of a room at the Ransom's, and upon a hard cot on North Brother. It was as if she'd forgotten what comfort was. She walked to four-poster bed, running a hand over the soft quilt of a delicate rose-colored floral pattern. A matching canopy hung above. Braided round rugs adorned the shiny hardwood floors and tapestries in the same floral pattern as the bed hung floor to ceiling. The wallpaper was a cream and pink print, and vases filled with miniature pink roses and baby's breath decorated the dresser and bedside table. Brigid was positive now that she'd been sent to Heaven, and Eliza and Natalie were her guardian angels.

A fresh nightgown and robe lay ready for her. Brigid didn't think she could want for more until Eliza walked to another door and opened it.

"Natalie asked the maid to draw a bath. You'll find soap, shampoo, oils, whatever you desire."

Brigid fought back grateful tears. "I'm overwhelmed by her kindness, and yours as well, Mrs. Ransom." Eliza and Natalie could not be more generous, and yet she harbored a secret that could make them despise her. Still, she could not fight fatigue or the thought of how profoundly filthy she must appear, so she allowed vanity to rule the moment.

"I'd be very much in need of a bath," she said. "Thank you."

"It's the least I could do for you, Brigid," Eliza said over her shoulder as she exited the room. "Thanks to you and Thomas, I know that my son is alive."

Thomas. Her heart ached at the thought of him, and the loss of what might have been.

Brigid stripped off her stained and worn clothing and stepped into the warm, clear bathwater. She pushed away all thoughts of Thomas, Charles and whatever else tomorrow might bring. For now, she'd enjoy this one, wonderfully luxurious moment.

It might be her last.

Chapter Thirty-Two

Brigid slept as if she hadn't slept for hundreds of years. Tucked between lavender-scented sheets, her head resting on a down pillow, she slumbered so deeply she didn't wake until nearly eleven the next day. A maid woke her with a cheerful "Good morning!" and a tray of boiled eggs, thick bacon, toast with orange marmalade, and coffee. She served it to Brigid in bed, and Brigid thought she'd died and gone to Heaven. As she finished the very last morsel, the maid returned with three dresses in the latest fashions. She also brought a pair of delicate, cream-colored shoes with crisscross ankle straps. She placed all in the wardrobe.

"The mistress wanted you to know that the clothes are yours to keep, miss," the maid said, as she proceeded to pull back the heavy, tasseled curtains and let in the summer sun. "Compliments of Mrs. Ransom. She had your other clothes disposed of."

Brigid's eyes opened wide. Eliza had bought her dresses? When had she the time? Guilt festered in her like an infected boil, and her breakfast suddenly turned sour in her stomach. She could not continue to accept Eliza's charity. She would have to wear one of the dresses, however, as she had nothing else, but she'd choose the simplest. Then she'd march downstairs, tell Eliza the truth about Charles, and pray that Simon would take her away as soon as possible. She was certain that once her secret was out, neither Thomas nor Eliza would want anything to do with her. They would also have enough information to do what they wanted with Charles and Dr. Stouch. She dreaded hurting Eliza, but she couldn't accept any more undeserved generosity, and no one would be the worse-for-wear if she left.

After the maid helped her fashion her hair into a stylish bun at the nape of her neck, Brigid decided on the blue and white pinstriped skirt with matching blouse and jacket. The shoes were a bit large, but she wouldn't complain. Stepping into the dress reminded her of her trip over on the *Olympic* and the wardrobe David had bought her. She'd felt like a proper lady then. But now, as she looked into the full-length, oval mirror, she felt a fraud, as if dressing for a part in a play, knowing she was the understudy without a chance of actually performing.

A half-hour later, Brigid sat in Mrs. Markeson's parlor, her back straight, her fingers laced tightly together in her lap. Simon and Thomas had arrived, and joined her in the parlor. She was eager to hear Simon's news, especially about finding Tobias.

"Look at you all dolled up and fancy lookin'," Simon said. He turned to Thomas. "Ain't me sister a beauty, there, Tom?"

"You look splendid, Brigid," Thomas answered.

She felt herself blush from head to toe and then burn crimson as Thomas's eyes trailed from her fancy shoes, up the length of her dress and met her eyes. His stare lingered with an intensity that unnerved her, yet excited her at the same time. In the months they'd been separated, Thomas had become only more handsome. He mesmerized her with his heavy-lidded, transparent blue eyes, and the same wanting expression he wore the night he kissed her.

She looked away. What game did he play? She knew of his affections for Clara, so why look at her as if he desired her? Also, if he knew what had happened to her at the hand of Charles Ransom, he would not want her for long.

"Good morning. Shall we sit?" Eliza's entrance into the parlor broke the awkward silence between them, and Brigid was grateful. Thomas and Simon sat in chairs at opposite ends of the hearth. Brigid sat next to Eliza on a red patterned loveseat.

"Brigid," Eliza began, patting her hand. "Your brother has news from home."

The sudden grim expressions on the faces before her signaled that this news wasn't good. Simon then told her of their da's death, the circumstances surrounding it and concluded with the better news that their ma fervently wished for her to return home.

Brigid sat shocked to her core.

"Da is dead? He was shot? He was foolin' around?" She didn't know which of the statements upset and disturbed her more. Her poor da! Then again, that nasty bastard cheating on her ma! Her ma wanted her home?

She cast a quick glance Thomas's way. He appeared grieved, as if her sorrow was his own, but she knew her da's death could not have affected him as it did her. Something else was wrong, and she knew what it was. He would soon tell her of his devotion to Clara, and that he only went with Simon to North Brother because Simon asked him to.

Then again, it mattered not what Thomas said, for she knew, deep down, that she would return to Ireland. It was for the best. Even if Thomas wasn't with Clara, could he accept her having been with another man, even if it was against her will? And how could she stay here, accepting the kindness and generosity of Mrs.

Ransom and her sister, knowing she'd been with Charles? Mrs. Ransom was rumored to be of fragile mind, although Brigid found that hard to believe. Would telling Mrs. Ransom about what Charles did send the sweet lady spiraling into despair? Then again, didn't Mrs. Ransom deserve to know what an evil brute her husband was, or did she already conclude that based on what he did to Tobias? Perhaps it was best to go to Ireland and leave the awful truth unsaid. She just didn't know.

She'd have to sort it out later, however, for Thomas and Eliza were anxious to inform her, and she was anxious to hear, how they found Tobias. Thomas reiterated the story, starting back with Grace being hospitalized, the knowledge he gleaned from Clara Cavanaugh and his successful trip to Victoria Cole's orphanage.

Brigid was joyous that the babe had been found, but at the same time she wondered if Thomas's dealings with Clara had been what drove them together. She felt her blood boil. Helping Mrs. Ransom had been *her* mission, not Clara's.

If Thomas ever meant to tell her about Clara, however, he'd have to find away to interrupt Simon, who now rambled on about their mother, their siblings and the farm. Perhaps she should be grateful that Thomas wouldn't have the chance to humiliate her.

"I'm going later today to purchase tickets for our voyage home as soon as we know Mrs. Ransom will be gettin' her boy," Simon said. "That'll give you a few last days to visit with Thomas and Mrs. Ransom." He smiled a mischievous smile. "I'd like a bit more time to see someone as well."

"Who do you know in New York?" Brigid asked, Simon's strange statement diverting her thoughts away from her own problems.

Her brother grinned from ear to ear. "It's a lady I met! And she's warmin' to me, too."

Thomas snapped to attention. "Please remind your lady, Simon, to be on the ready for when we confront Dr. Stouch and Charles."

Brigid's mind swirled with confusion. So now there was another woman, some lady friend of Simon's, involved in the plot? She knew she should be able to put two and two together, but she still didn't seem to be thinking right after a month's isolation on North Brother. Add to that, the knot forming in her stomach at the thought of confronting Dr. Stouch and Charles Ransom again. The last thing she wanted to do was to return to Ransom House.

Thomas turned to Eliza. "I'm sorry this couldn't be simpler, but we can't blame Mrs. Cole for wanting to protect herself and the child. Stouch will need to change Tobias's records to prove that the boy has always been alive and he was told to send him there. She's afraid someone will accuse her of something unsavory, such as kidnapping, if he's not who his records say he is. The records must show that Tobias didn't die. Everything needs to be on the up and up before she hands over the child. Until then, she still considers your child as Joseph Green."

"I understand." Eliza smiled. "Mrs. Cole seems to be a very caring and intelligent woman. I wouldn't want any harm to come to her." She looked away. "She's taken good care of my child for the first two years of his life."

Eliza dabbed at her eyes with her handkerchief.

Thomas cleared his throat. "Speaking of Tobias, we should set a time to go to Ransom House and inform Charles of what we know." His eyes lit with excitement. "I can't wait to see the look on their faces when they see you again. With what we know about what they did to you, and Clara's information about taking the baby to Chicago, they can't refuse our demands to fix Tobias's records. We'll threaten to tell the authorities."

"Do I really need to be goin' with?" The words flew from Brigid's mouth before she could stop them. She sounded whiney and unwilling to help, and she hated herself for it, yet she just couldn't face Charles Ransom.

The room fell silent as the others stared at her as if she'd lost her mind. Thomas spoke. "But Brigid, you're the key to this whole thing! Why wouldn't you want to show them you've returned? You started the search for Tobias. It's why they sent you away."

It was all Brigid could do to not shake her head and scream. That was *not* why she was sent away, but fear of the truth held her tongue. Clara would be joining them when they went to Ransom House? This whole ordeal was fast becoming her worst nightmare. Being stuck back on North Brother suddenly looked pretty damn good.

The room turned stifling hot, and her breakfast sat like a massive lump in her stomach. She rose. "I need air." She could blame the morning heat for her queasiness, but the real reasons, Thomas and Clara, and seeing Charles again, would remain hidden. For

Christ's sake, why was her brother sitting there looking like a lovesick puppy? Her stomach lurched again.

"Excuse me," she said, addressing Eliza. "May I sit on the front porch?"

"Of course, dear."

Thomas rose as well. "I shall accompany you."

She didn't have the strength to protest, yet the last thing she wanted was to hear about him and Clara.

They stepped out onto the wrap-around front porch and over to a white wicker bench with green cushions.

"May I join you?" Thomas motioned to the space beside her on the bench.

She squinted up into the morning sun. His hair shimmered and his light eyes twinkled in the new day. She longed for him more than ever, now that he was not hers, and it hurt. "Suit yourself."

His smile faded, but he sat.

His nearness unnerved her, yet she remained silent, waiting for the final blow that would send her sailing straight back to Ireland.

As if reading her mind, Thomas spoke softly from her side. "Are you truly thinking of returning home?"

She looked out onto the lawn of the Markeson estate. The lush, emerald-colored lawns reminded her of the Donegal hills in springtime, and the ebony bark of the trees recalled the cliffs that guarded the sea. She missed home, but she also longed to stay right where she was. "It's for the best all 'round, I'm supposin'."

Thomas shifted in his seat. "We were just getting to know each other when you disappeared." He cleared his throat and looked away. "I was hoping to continue our…friendship, to become closer. I thought you wanted that as well?"

She did, but she spoke with her mind, not her heart. "What does it matter?"

"What does it *matter*?" He turned to face her, his expression marred by frustration.

"You're here! You're back!" His eyes softened and searched her face. "Might we try again?"

Brigid's eyes flew open wide. *The audacity*! "How dare you be playin' with my affections this way, Mr. Ashton!" She would not honor him further by calling him 'Thomas.' As far as she was concerned, there'd be no more familiarity between them.

"What *are* you talking about, Brigid? I've missed you so. I've never stopped thinking about you!"

"Except when you've been courtin' Clara Cavanaugh!" She crossed her arms defiantly, but watched him from the corner of her eye.

He jerked as if she had slapped him. "*Clara?* Clara Cavanaugh and I?" He shook his head. "I never-"

"Don't deny it!" Brigid felt her Irish temper enflame, and her face felt as hot as a roasted beet. "I saw you two together at Grace Cavanaugh's funeral! I was in the back of the church!"

"Grace's funer-" Thomas stopped. "I was there to *console* Clara in hopes that she'd tell me about the baby she took to the train station!"

"What?" She wanted to believe him.

"Before Grace died, she told me that Leopold saw Clara with a baby at a train station. As I explained earlier, the baby turned out to be Tobias."

Brigid inhaled quickly and held her head in her hands. "Oh, blessed Jesus. I give right up. I was in such a state that day, I just assumed." She looked up and wiped her brow. "Oh, you don't be wantin' me

Thomas, I'm just a stupid, stupid woman!" She put her hand to her forehead as if to shield her embarrassment. "Could you ever think to forgive me for my assumption?"

"Nothing to forgive!" He took her hand in his and smiled at her, his eyes boring into hers. "And besides, it's *Simon* who has taken a shine to Clara, not me!"

"Holy Mary, Mother of God, *no*!" But Brigid started to laugh, picturing her funny, brawly brother taking a liking to the rigid, no-nonsense, doomed-to-be-a-spinster, Clara. Her laughter seemed foreign to her, and for some inexplicable reason, she began to cry.

"Christ! What's wrong?" Thomas held both her hands.

"Nothing, I'm happy, I think." She offered him a half-smile and quickly wiped her tears.

Thomas moved closer on the bench and offered her a handkerchief from his vest pocket.

"I've missed you, desperately," he said. "I searched for you when you didn't show up at the park that day. I went to Ransom House, and Dr. Stouch told me you went to Ireland. For the life of me, I couldn't figure out what I did that sent you home."

"You did nothin'!" She didn't mean to shout, but she couldn't believe that Thomas would blame himself for her disappearance. She accepted his handkerchief and dried her eyes, determined to stop the silly tears.

"I was happy bein' with you!" There. She said it. "I still am." Her heart leapt. It was what she dreamt of telling him, and yet, she felt conflicted. Could she be with him again without telling him of her despoiling at the hands of Charles Ransom? Did he know her well enough to believe that she'd been an unwilling participant? After all, she had enthusiastically kissed Thomas back that one night. Would he think she somehow led Charles to desire her?

"Brigid. Simon says you need to go to your mother, but do you want to? I realize you want to help her, no one would ever fault you for that, but do you wish to stay here for any reason?"

Hope grew in his eyes, and she didn't wish to dash it. In a dream, she'd say 'yes' in a heartbeat, but the sledgehammer of reality pounded her desire into smithereens.

"I have no money."

"I'll find you a job at the hospital."

"No!" Her answer was more abrasive than she meant, but the thought of running into Dr. Stouch in any capacity sent shivers up her spine. She realized she sounded ungrateful. "You're very kind, but…I don't like hospitals."

"Oh! Forgive me for not thinking of what you've just been through."

She shook her head. "It's not that."

Thomas squeezed her hand, sending pleasant tingles coursing through her body. She was reminded of their kiss. Her desire to stay with him in New York heightened, yet tears welled again as he spoke.

"If it matters any to you, Brigid, I'm asking you to stay. I'll do whatever I can to help you."

How she longed to consider it! She found warmth and comfort in his mere touch, a sense of protection she hadn't felt with anyone, ever, not even David. Yet Thomas deserved to know the truth before he chose to be with her. It was only fair.

"Thomas," she said, mustering all her strength. Her heart beat so fast, she felt as if it might explode from her chest. "I know you would help me. And if I could find a way to stay, I would. But there's somethin' you must know before you decide that you want to continue our…friendship."

"There's nothing you can't tell me."

She drew a deep breath. "I was sent to North Brother because-"

"Because Stouch and Ransom found out that were you were searching for Tobias. Yes, I know."

"No, Thomas." She shook her head and talked slowly as if each word might soften the next. "Charles Ransom didn't know I was helpin' Eliza."

"Then why'd he send you away?"

"I overheard him and Dr. Stouch talkin' about takin' a servant's baby and passin' it off as Charles's."

Thomas laughed. "How could he get away with that?"

"I think he could get away with whatever he wanted." Brigid looked away.

"But he didn't get that servant's baby, right? Eliza would have known."

"No, he didn't get that child." Brigid looked at her hands, holding tightly to his handkerchief that housed her tears, her hands protected within his once again. "Eliza never knew about that." She drew another deep breath. "Eliza doesn't know any of this." Her voice dropped and she trembled. "You see-"

The screen door slammed open and banged against the porch wall. Brigid and Thomas startled.

"We've go to go!" Simon boomed, storming out onto the porch.

Thomas held tight to Brigid's hands. "Where? What are you talking about?"

"My sweet, dark-eyed bonnie, Clara, just telephoned. Stouch is leavin' town with his wife on a trip. They're leavin' this afternoon."

"How would Clara know that?" Thomas asked.

Brigid silently cursed both Simon and Clara for their ill-conceived timing. She'd been so close to telling Thomas the truth.

"Clara was at the hat shop and ran into his wife," Simon said. "I guess the wife was braggin' about how they were off to Paris in a few hours. Clara asked where Dr. Stouch was, and the wife said he'd gone to collect on some money from Charles Ransom."

"Christ!" Thomas wrapped an arm around Brigid's waist and gently helped her to her feet. "If we're going to confront them together and get Stouch to change the medical record, we have to leave now."

"That's what I'm sayin'!" Simon turned and yelled back into the house. "Hurry, if you can please, Mrs. Ransom!"

Thomas turned to Brigid. "We'll continue our conversation later, all right?"

Brigid faked a smile as her heart wilted. She knew she'd never again have the nerve. And now, she must face her assailant. She could think of no excuse as to why she couldn't go, plus they needed her help. Dr. Stouch and Charles Ransom needed to see she'd been found.

Most importantly, she needed to go for Eliza and Tobias, for if she and Thomas might never be together, at least a mother and child would.

Chapter Thirty-Three

Brigid sat next to Thomas in the front seat his motorcar, while Eliza and Simon followed in her chauffer-driven automobile. It was a place Brigid both wanted, and did not want, to be. She loved sitting alongside Thomas, but feared their destination - Ransom House.

But first, both vehicles stopped in front of Clara Cavanaugh's house, and Brigid watched Simon bound from Eliza's car and up the front steps. Before he could ring the bell, however, Clara stepped out, clothed in a drab-black dress, hat and parasol.

"You're a vision of loveliness today, as always, Miss Cavanaugh," Brigid heard Simon say. She was surprised as he offered Clara the crook of his arm. She turned to Thomas in disbelief.

"Well, I'll be," Thomas said, as Clara linked her arm through Simon's. "I do believe she's taken a liking to your brother." He turned and winked. "Perhaps she'll be your sister-in-law after all, Brigid."

"And I've got no lady-like response to that," Brigid said, still digesting her brother's behavior. "So I'll just be pretendin' I didn't hear you."

Thomas laughed, but Brigid could not entertain humor at the moment. "I don't understand why we had to stop for Clara. She's got her own chauffeur." She talked in a whisper as Simon and Clara walked past them to Eliza's automobile. Clara looked up and nodded politely at Brigid, but Brigid ignored her. Simon grinned like he owned the city.

Thomas patted Brigid's hand. Any other time, she'd long for his touch, but the knot in her stomach was so tight, nothing could soothe her.

"Simon insisted we pick her up," Thomas said. "He didn't think she'd come otherwise, but I believe that was just Simon's excuse to spend more time with her."

"Yes, considerin' she's the one who telephoned about gettin' over to Ransom House right away, I would think she'd show up!"

"I think he's on a mission to win her over before he has to leave." Thomas shot her a quick smile, returned his hand to the steering wheel and pulled the car back onto the street.

Brigid rolled her eyes, but turned her head away so Thomas would not see. Yes, she was happy how things had turned out between her and Thomas, but the situation ahead squashed any momentary romantic notions. She hated seeing Clara again, and as they neared Ransom House, the more agitated she became.

They parked a block away from the residence so that Charles wouldn't see them arrive. No one spoke on the short walk to the mansion, but Thomas held Brigid's hand. It brought little comfort however, as her anxiety accelerated with every step.

Simon and Clara strode side-by-side behind them. Eliza walked a few paces ahead and led them to the servants' entrance, pulled a key from her sleeve and opened the door. She raised her index finger to her lips and motioned for them to stay quiet. "We shall take Charles by surprise," she whispered.

Like dutiful sheep, they followed her into the hall and up the back staircase. They waited there while she searched the living quarters for Charles. Brigid's heart pounded so hard she was sure half of the city heard it.

"You're trembling," Thomas whispered. "No need. It will all work out."

Brigid doubted that, and she could not help but heap more internal resentment upon Clara. She had yet to acknowledge the woman. She couldn't help but feel that if Clara hadn't tossed her out on the streets, all these horrible things wouldn't have happened to her. Then again, if she *hadn't* come to Ransom House, Eliza might not have found Tobias. Had God sent Brigid to help Eliza? Surely The Almighty wouldn't have put her in the situation knowing what Charles would do. Then again, the Lord had not given her a child by Charles, so he definitely wasn't on Charles's side. Either way, if ever she needed the Heavenly Father's protection and strength, it was now. Eliza had returned, and it was time to face the devil.

"Charles and Rupert are in the study," Eliza whispered. "The door is slightly ajar. Henry is polishing silver in the dining room, but we needn't walk past there. Let me enter the study first. I'll call for you when I need you. Just listen outside the door."

"I think we should go in with you," Thomas whispered back. "I don't trust that man not to hurt you."

Eliza smiled serenely. "Charles would never lay a hand on me. Despite what he did to my child, he loves me. The problem is that he loves himself more."

They stepped softly through the back of the house and down a hallway to the study. The familiar smell of old varnish and musty air made Brigid's stomach roll.

Everything about this place reminded her of Charles. She willed herself not to shiver in revulsion.

They paused outside the half-open study doors. Charles and Dr. Stouch were in the middle of a rather animated conversation.

"You're departing for Europe in a few hours? When did this come about?" Charles was saying to Rupert.

Rupert sounded agitated. "I need not consult you if I wish to take my wife abroad."

"But we have unfinished business," Charles said. "I've paid you handsomely for something you did not deliver. I do not have a child, and Eliza has left me!"

Rupert sighed so loudly, those listening at the door heard it. "I believe our business is finished. We've tried several times to secure a child and failed. I was paid for my help in each endeavor, but frankly Charles, I'm tired and simply wish for a vacation. Sadly, if it's true that Eliza has left you, there's no need for another child."

Charles's voice bellowed throughout the room and hall. "But I don't have Eliza, either! *You*, Stouch, need to do something! Think up something else!"

"Charles, I'm done. I spend more time with you lately than I spend with my wife or at my practice. If you could please reimburse me the money I spent to secure placement on North Brother for the O'Brien maid, I'll be on my way. Our ship sails in two hours."

With no response from Charles, Dr. Stouch continued. "I'll be gone several weeks so I've brought you my baseball tickets for the next month. Great seats, I must say! Word has it that the team will do splendidly this year. Great pitchers!"

"I'd like those tickets," Simon whispered. "Never saw me a real baseball game."

"Shh," Brigid warned.

The sound of something heavy, perhaps a crystal goblet smashing, startled them all.

"I don't want your blasted baseball tickets!" Charles's voice boomed. "I want my wife back, and you have failed me in that!"

"I did not! How long will this go on Charles?"

Brigid could hear heavy footsteps on the hardwood floor; she figured it to be Charles, pacing.

"Your grand ideas failed each and every time. Eliza has *left* me. When was *that* ever in the plans? I have no idea where she is or why she left. Does she *know* something, Stouch?"

"Yes, I do, darling," Eliza whispered out of the men's earshot, but not the group's.

"No, how could she?" Stouch responded.

"Ha!" Eliza said, peering inside the door.

"I've paid you handsomely, Stouch! And what do I have to show for it? There's no child to lure Eliza home. That pregnant maid ran off before we could offer to take her brat, and the O'Brien wench failed to conceive!"

Brigid's heart cannonballed into her stomach. Shock filled the faces of those around her as they turned to stare at her. Thomas's expression broke her heart. He looked completely stunned, or appalled, or angry. Possibly all three.

Brigid shook her head in protest of what they must think. Clara's eyes were as big as saucers. Simon appeared confused.

The color had drained from Eliza's face, and she held on to Thomas for support. "Brigid, did my husband hire you to conceive his child?"

Brigid crumpled into a heap in the corner. Words stuck in her throat, but as she tried to answer, the argument between the two men in the study heated to a fevered pitch.

"It's not my fault that the maid didn't get pregnant!" Stouch said. "I rendered her unconscious. The rest was up to you!"

"Oh, Christ!" Thomas said, louder than needed. Inside the study, all fell quiet.

"It's time," Eliza said. She walked to Brigid and knelt beside her. "My dear girl."

Brigid could not stop the tears from streaming down her cheeks. "I'm sorry, Mrs. Ransom." She looked to Thomas. "I'm so sorry."

He didn't answer, but his eyes held a rage she'd never witnessed before. His breathing came heavy and his face burned crimson. She looked away.

"Come, my dear. Everything shall be all right." Eliza assisted Brigid in standing, linked her arm in hers and walked to the door. She motioned to the others to follow them. They entered the study to the shocked expressions of Charles and Dr. Stouch.

"Hello, Charles." Eliza held tighter to Brigid. "Look who we found."

Brigid couldn't raise her eyes to him. But when Thomas stood next to her, and Simon and Clara stood in back of her like a human fortress, her courage grew. She slowly lifted her eyes to glare at the man who had forced such shame and terror upon her and then imprisoned her like a criminal.

Charles would not meet her stare. Dr. Stouch developed a facial twitch that caused his mustache to rise and fall on one side and his mole to bounce up and down.

"What the-" Dr. Stouch began, but one sharp look from Charles, and he folded into a shadow of himself.

No one spoke as they awaited Charles's reaction. He looked from person to person, as if trying to solve a puzzle. Then, just as quickly, his expression turned to stone with no hint of any emotion.

He cleared his throat and drew a deep breath. His sudden smile seemed forced. "Eliza, darling! I'm so happy you've returned, but what's the meaning of all this? What is Miss O'Brien doing back here? I nearly didn't recognize her out of her servant's clothing. She's been ill, you know, typhoid."

It was then that Brigid laughed, a sharp, loud and obnoxious laugh. She didn't even recognize it as her own. It seemed to come from some hideous creature living within her. Thomas touched her shoulder, and it calmed her.

Eliza let go of her arm. "Let's not play games, Charles. Brigid is not ill and never was. The only sick person in this room is you, and perhaps Rupert, although I suspect his malady is greed. Let me introduce you to my friends, Charles." She reached across Brigid to squeeze Thomas's arm. "This is Thomas Ashton. *Doctor* Ashton is a dear friend of Brigid's and will prove she doesn't have, nor did she ever have, typhoid."

Brigid noticed a small drop of sweat trickle down the side of Dr. Stouch's face.

"Dr. Ashton has in his possession our son's record from the hospital," Eliza continued.

Charles inhaled sharply "Why should he have that?"

"Why indeed, Charles. But, we'll get to that." Eliza spoke calmly as if introducing dinner guests. "The other gentleman with me is Simon O'Brien, Brigid's brother. He came all the way from Ireland to find her. You see, Charles, Brigid is a *person* with a family and people who love her…" Eliza paused and squeezed Brigid's hand. "…not only in Ireland, but here as well. She wasn't here for your use, or to be discarded when you no longer needed her."

Charles's jaw set and his words sounded tight. "Eliza, I don't know what you're getting at. Have you been taking your medication?" He glanced at Rupert. "At least she's talking again, but she's nonsensical. Am I correct, Dr. Stouch?"

Brigid found the courage to look Dr. Stouch straight in the eye, but he glanced away quickly. He did not respond to Charles, but swallowed hard, causing his Adam's apple to bulge in his skinny neck.

"We've been listening outside the door, Charles," Eliza said, her voice hardening. "*All* of us."

Dr. Stouch cleared his throat and seemed to summon the courage to finally speak. "I do have a boat to catch. Please forgive me, but I must leave." He started for the door.

Charles's voice boomed. "You're not going anywhere! My wife has returned to me, and she obviously needs help!" He shot Rupert a look that Brigid could only interpret as desperation. "Eliza's delusional. Do something, Stouch!"

The doctor stopped dead in his tracks.

"Yes, please stay, Rupert." Eliza smiled. "You won't want to miss this." She walked over to Clara and took her by the hand, moving her a step forward. "Rupert, I do believe you remember Miss Cavanaugh, who, under the pretense of your marriage proposal, delivered an infant boy to Broken Angels Orphanage in Chicago."

"Oh, Christ!" Charles turned on Rupert. "You had your *intended* transport the baby?"

Rupert's twitching intensified. He looked so comical, Brigid nearly laughed maniacally again.

"Yes, Charles." Eliza said. "Clara told us everything, and Dr. Ashton, on Brigid's behalf while she was away, put the pieces together. He even found Tobias in Chicago. You see, while you had your own designs on our dear Brigid, I had plans of my own. I asked her to find my son."

"I never touched that girl!" Charles bellowed.

"Liar!" Brigid's voice rang loud and strong. With Thomas by her side, and Simon and friends present for support, her courage blossomed like a latent seed finally watered.

"We heard you admit to tryin' to impregnate her, you feckin' gobshite!" Simon said, and tried to bulldoze his way to Charles, but Thomas caught him and held him back.

"It was all Rupert's idea!" Charles said, motioning swiftly at his friend.

"Oh no, don't you blame this on me, Charles!" Rupert's head swiveled back and forth so violently Brigid thought it would fly off. "It was *you* who didn't want the infant, and *you* who asked me to get another."

If looks could kill, the glare Charles shot Dr. Stouch would have laid him flat. Just as quickly, he turned on Eliza, his expression now one of apology and remorse.

He's a trickster, Brigid thought. *An evil, disgusting, trickster.*

"Eliza," Charles cajoled. "Everything I did was for you!"

"You sent my child away!"

"He wasn't -. Oh, Eliza. He wasn't *right*."

"He was *mine* and he was *perfect*!" Eliza spoke with a world of anger and heartbreak. Her voice cracked, yet she remained firm.

"We need a child we *both* could love," Charles said. "Tobias was-"

"*Is*." Thomas interrupted. "Tobias *is*, Mr. Ransom. He's a vibrant and beautiful, red-haired, blue-eyed, two-year-old. And yes, he is a mongoloid. You're going to have to accept that."

Charles ignored him. "Eliza, Rupert felt you wouldn't have more children, so I found us someone who could!"

Brigid felt nauseated again. She tried to speak, but couldn't. Hearing Charles admit to what he did made it all real once more. Her heart pounded so hard that she thought she might die right there.

"O'Brien didn't conceive, so no harm done." Charles had the audacity to smile.

Brigid gasped and Thomas tensed beside her, his breath coming quickly, his face turning an angry shade of fire. Brigid was pretty sure he might deck Charles himself, if he wasn't stopping Simon from doing so.

"No harm done?" Thomas said between clenched teeth. "You *raped* her, you bastard!"

The insult seemed to simply bounce off Charles.

"You're going to prison, Charles." Eliza spoke matter-of-factly. "And most likely, the 'good' doctor as well. The fact is, I no longer love you. I never will again, and I don't care what becomes of you."

The blood drained from Charles's face. "Eliza. You're not in your right mind. Just come back to me. Besides, it will be the maid's word against mine in a courtroom, and who do you think will be believed, an upstanding wealthy business man like myself, or a poor immigrant trying to earn some fast cash?"

Brigid gasped at the lie. Simon took another start toward Charles, but Thomas's grip held him firm.

"We have no intentions of going to court, Charles," Eliza said. "We can prove the other matter outright which would send both you and Rupert to jail."

"What other matter?" Charles looked at Rupert who wiped the sweat from his forehead with an already soaked handkerchief.

"You sent my son away and declared him dead. You falsified his record. I believe that's kidnapping, at the very least."

Charles motioned toward Dr. Stouch again. "Rupert signed the death certificate. He'll swear the boy is dead." He turned to Rupert. "Tobias died, didn't he?"

The doctor didn't answer, just stood cowering as if before a firing squad.

"*Didn't he, Stouch*?" Charles yelled.

Thomas didn't wait for an answer, but stepped forward, wearing a calm smile. "Well, the irony of the situation is, Mr. Ransom, that the supposedly dead child is on his way to New York as we speak." Brigid knew that not to be true, but she understood where Thomas led. He turned to the doctor. "And Dr. Stouch, my *esteemed* colleague, I happen to have Tobias's medical chart right here." He slapped the folder with the back of his hand. "You signed off on the child's death. Imagine the shock amongst your fellow peers when the dead child walks into a courtroom!" Thomas held his hand to his chin. "What will you say in your defense, I wonder. Will you say you made *a mistake*, Dr. Stouch? That you can't tell the difference between a living and a dead infant? Will you allow yourself to appear *incompetent* in your chosen field? Or will you admit that you can be bought and that you're nothing but a low-life leech when money is involved? That you allowed Eliza Ransom to suffer for years so that you could take vacations to Europe!"

Dr. Stouch twisted the handkerchief in his hands. "Why are you threatening *me*, Dr. Ashton? I was only helping a friend!"

"Oh, believe me, Dr. Stouch. We have every intention to exonerate you from this situation entirely." Thomas let go of Simon with a warning look to stay put, and took a pen from Charles's desk. "That is, if you'd be so kind as to rewrite Tobias's records the way they should read. You will write in the record that the baby was sent away at the request *of his father and unbeknownst to his mother*."

"If you're getting the child back anyhow, why should I have to do this?" Dr. Stouch crossed his arms in front of him, but his shaky voice and defeated posture defied his bravado.

"You told Mrs. Cole that the child was Joseph Green. She wants the truth."

"And if I refuse?"

Clara took a step forward. She spoke loud, strong, and full of the venom that Brigid remembered was once aimed her way. "You *won't* refuse, Rupert. I, alone, have enough information to put you away for a long, long time. Let's start with the child I took to Chicago. I know now that he was Tobias Ransom. He was a newborn, a mongoloid, had red hair and that birthmark on his wrist."

"I'll deny giving you the child."

"My cousin, Leopold, saw me with him."

"Cavanaugh's a drunk. No one will believe him."

"He's doing much better," Thomas interjected. "He'd make a very fine witness."

Clara smiled wickedly. "Even so, Rupert, do the names Esther Greenfield and Carrie Cartwright strike your memory?"

All eyes turned on Clara. It seemed that no one, Brigid included, knew what she spoke of. No one, except Rupert, who now crumpled into a fireside chair and held his head in his hands.

"What on earth is wrong with you? Get up!" Charles demanded.

"He killed those women through botched abortions," Clara said. "He told their families they died from severe miscarriages. I know the truth, because he was so distraught after each one, that he drank himself into a stupor and stumbled to me for comfort. At the time, I loved him, so I kept his nasty little secret. But I'm more than willing to testify to it now. You're a sham of a doctor and a man, Rupert Stouch!"

The doctor did not raise his head from his hands. His shoulders shook, and Brigid realized he was crying. She held no pity for him.

"I could easily have an inquisition done into each case," Thomas added. He offered Brigid a reassuring smile and walked over to Dr. Stouch. "Now, will you rewrite Tobias's file and admit to sending the child away?"

Rupert raised his tear-stained face. He stared at the folder and then reached for it.

"Don't you *dare*!" Charles took a step toward Thomas as if to grab him, but Simon rushed forward and restrained Charles's arms behind his back.

"Let go of me!" Charles roared and struggled, but was no match for the muscular Irishman.

Rupert grabbed the file, opened it and wrote.

"Now, Charles," Eliza said. "Why don't you sit down?"

"Good idea," Simon said. He slammed Charles into another velvet armchair and stood over it, daring him to move.

"Thank you, Simon." Eliza walked to Charles's desk and removed a checkbook from the drawer. "Charles, you have some writing to do as well."

She threw the checkbook and pen in his lap. "I'm leaving you, of course, but I'm sure you would rather not have a *lawyer* dragged into this, now would you?"

Charles didn't answer, although his eyes held fire, and his breath came heavy.

"The first check shall be made to me. I have figured out the amount I require to raise and care for Tobias for the rest of his life." She told Charles the number. He flinched, but wrote and handed Eliza the check.

"Good. The next check shall be made out to Brigid O'Brien."

Brigid gasped again, and Eliza turned.

"Oh, I'm sorry, Brigid," Eliza said. "I really should have consulted with you first. It's your call, dear. Would you like to prosecute Charles for his crimes against you, or can I persuade you to accept his apology and guilt through a sizable payment that will not only set you up in New York, if you choose to stay, but also be generous enough to send a portion to your mother?"

Brigid swallowed. Could she accept money as an apology for what Charles had done to her? Would that be right or simply make her a paid…

As if reading her mind, Thomas spoke. "A trial would be ghastly, and no one here would think any less of you for avoiding it."

The others, Clara included, nodded.

Brigid looked at each encouraging face. She really didn't want to relive the horror of what happened to her. She didn't care about the money for herself, but her mother could certainly use it now that she was left alone with all the children yet to raise. But, how would she ever explain where it came from?

Simon took her hand. "Take the money, love. We'll tell Ma that you're just one hell of a maid."

Brigid couldn't help but laugh and cry. This was all too much.

"Write the check, Charles," Eliza said. When Brigid heard the sum, she went weak in the knees.

With checks in hand, Eliza waited while Rupert finished redoing Tobias's record. He handed it back to Thomas.

"Thank you, Dr. Stouch," Thomas said. "And just so you know, as long as I'm in the medical profession, I'll be watching you."

"Our business here is nearly finished," Eliza said. "I believe Simon has something for Charles however, in his sister's honor."

Charles rose quickly from his chair, but not quick enough. Simon grabbed him by the lapel and pulled back his fist to deck him, but Thomas stopped him. Grasping Simon's arm, he nudged him to the side and handed him the folder.

"Please. Allow me." He said to Simon and laid a fist into Charles's gut so hard it knocked him to his knees. He socked him, this time in the jaw.

Brigid's eyes flew open wide. Thomas took down Ransom for her.

He glared down at Charles. "If you ever so much as look at Brigid again, I'll kill you."

"And then, I'll kill you a second time!" Simon shouted.

Thomas turned, walked to Brigid and took her hand. He smiled. "Your nightmare is over, my dear."

She felt it truly was.

As Dr. Stouch shook in his chair and Charles writhed in pain on the floor, Brigid, Thomas, Simon, Eliza and Clara left Ransom House for good.

Chapter Thirty-Four

"Brigid." Thomas's voice interrupted her thoughts. They cuddled together on the Markeson's porch swing, holding hands and stealing sweet kisses. "You seem a million miles away." His soft voice returned her to the present.

She sighed, but smiled. "I know, forgive me."

Indecision weighed heavy on her heart. Although she missed her mother and siblings terribly, she knew she couldn't commit to returning home permanently. She'd found Thomas again, or rather, he found her, and she didn't want to let him go.

His attention to her since the Ransom House visit had been unwavering. When he wasn't working, he either called on her at Eliza's, or Brigid visited with him and his mother at their home. Thomas brought her candy, bouquets of Forget-Me-Nots, and other mementos of his affection, her favorite being a simple gold bracelet. She thrilled at each gift, but knew, even without the gifts, she had fallen in love with him. She hoped he felt the same.

The past few days had been a whirlwind of happy activity as she and the others awaited Tobias's arrival. Eliza and Natalie had invited her to remain at their home for as long as she needed; Simon chose to stay with Thomas and his mother.

Thomas squeezed her hand. "Simon says he's going to be returning home soon, possibly within a few days time. Says he's got some business to finish here first, and hopes by then that you'll have made up your mind."

"I know." She rested her head against his arm.

Simon was scarcely about these days, choosing to spend his remaining time with Clara. Brigid could only shake her head and try to understand. She wasn't sure what redeeming trait Simon saw in the woman, but she figured there must be one, as Clara was David's sister and Leopold's niece, and they were both wonderful men.

"I'm torn as well," Thomas said.

"How so?" She looked up, still finding it hard to believe that this handsome, wonderful man wanted to be with her.

"Brigid, you must know that I desperately wish you'd stay in New York. I don't want you to leave, but it's truly selfish of me to keep you from being with your mother."

Brigid covered her hand with his. "Well then, I'm more selfish than you, because she's my ma, and although I'd like to see her, I am happier here."

Thomas grinned. "I'm so glad to hear that you are considering staying."

Although her heart fluttered at his response, she could not enjoy the moment entirely, for she knew the time had arrived to discuss the pressing matter between them. She'd made earlier attempts to discuss it, but Thomas would interrupt and tell her she needn't talk about it if it upset her. What upset her more, however, was not knowing how he truly felt about what happened between her and Charles Ransom. He didn't seem bothered by it, but surely, this must be discussed. She needed to know that he didn't think less of her, or that her morals had been tainted. She wanted him to understand that she was the same woman she'd always been.

"Brigid, by now, you must know how I feel about you," Thomas said when she didn't answer.

"I do and I don't," she responded, truthfully. She tread delicately. "I've changed since we first met."

"Of course you have." His words came kind. "How could you not, given what you've been through?"

"Has your opinion of me changed?" There, she asked it.

"Yes."

"Oh." She looked away. Then it *did* bother him after all.

He turned, took her chin in hand and made her face him. "I see you now, Brigid Mary O'Brien, for the heroic woman you are. You've gone through Hell and back, and come out still pure of heart. You're the bravest and sweetest woman I know."

"Oh, you mustn't say that." She felt a slight flush color her cheeks as she removed his hand and pressed it to her cheek. "It's kind of you to say, but hardly truthful. I barely stood up for myself in front of Mr. Ransom. I felt so frightened, I thought I might faint."

"And yet, you didn't."

"Thomas, you must know how deeply I care for you. But I come before you a changed woman and not in a proper way."

"Not in any way that matters to me, Brigid." He took her hand and kissed it. "You arrived in New York with high hopes and a grand future. Everything was taken from you in an instant. You were penniless and knew no one, and despite your problems, you agreed to help Eliza. You have a kind heart and beautiful soul, Brigid O'Brien, and no one has stolen *that* from you."

He paused to catch his breath. "Because of you, Eliza shall have her son."

"*You* did most of the work getting Tobias back," Brigid said, not feeling half the woman Thomas proclaimed her to be.

"That's because I wanted to spend time with *you*," he laughed. "I did want to help Eliza too, don't misunderstand. So, you're beautiful and brave, and I'm selfish and hopelessly in love."

Hope lit her heart. "Are you truly in love with me? Can you be?" She feared to wake from this wonderful dream.

"Every day I grow to love you more. I want to be with you, Brigid. I want to protect you, take care of you, love you."

She felt the heat rise in her cheeks.

Thomas's smile faded. "But I can't do those things if you leave."

Brigid glanced down at their hands mingled together. Hers fit perfectly inside his warm, protective ones. She looked back up into his crystal blue eyes. How she longed to be able to stare into them forever.

"I love you, too." The words flew from her lips automatically. It was all she knew. Thomas bent to kiss her, but was interrupted by a car horn.

Clara's chauffeured automobile pulled up outside the gate of Natalie's estate. Simon emerged from the back seat, ran around to the other side and helped Clara from the car.

They hurried up the walkway, nearly out of breath as they approached the porch.

"Where's Eliza?" Simon said.

"Well good day to you too, brother," Brigid said, hoping the flush in her cheeks didn't give away what she and Thomas had been doing on the porch.

"Well, someone go get her!" Simon exclaimed. "There's another automobile a'comin'! We passed 'em on the way here. There's a child and a lady in the backseat."

"Oh, blessed be to Heaven!" Brigid jumped up with Thomas right behind. "It must be Tobias. They're early. How wonderful!"

"I'll get Eliza." Thomas lightly touched Brigid's arm as he passed and went into the house. If her moment with Thomas had to be interrupted, she was glad it was because of Tobias.

Simon and Clara ascended the steps to where Brigid stood. She acknowledged Clara with a nod, but said nothing. What could she say that would be kind? Nothing. So she remained tight-lipped.

Simon, however, was having none of it. "Brigid, Clara has somethin' to say to you."

Brigid shot Clara an annoyed glance.

Clara smoothed her dress. "Miss O'Brien, Brigid, if I may? I have acted most unkindly to you in the past."

"That's puttin' it lightly," Simon said.

Clara shot him a look that immediately quieted him. "Simon, please. I know what I've done."

She turned to Brigid again. Her dark eyes seemed softer than Brigid remembered, and a few wrinkles etched the corners. She appeared tired, but calm and resigned. "After David died, I was very afraid. Leopold was a drunk, and Grace was too elderly to work. I felt I needed to protect my inheritance, and in my grief and illogical thinking, I assumed you would stake claim to David's half."

Brigid remained quiet.

"All I knew was that I had bills to pay and three people to support, myself included. You became another mouth to feed and someone who'd take my money. I couldn't have that, so I made you leave."

"I am aware of what happened." Brigid looked away. When she looked back, Clara's eyes glistened with tears. She really didn't want to feel sorry for Clara Cavanaugh.

"When I heard that you found employment at Ransom House, I was relieved, actually. By that time, I had come to my senses and seen the error of my ways, but I felt you'd done well for yourself." She dabbed a tear with a handkerchief. "Now that I know what happened to you there, I blame myself for abandoning you. I am so very, very sorry."

"She's really a good woman," Simon added quickly as if Clara's confession hadn't tugged at Brigid's heartstrings enough.

"Jesus and Ma would want you to forgive her," he encouraged further.

Brigid snapped. "Simon! Enough!"

"Sorry." He hung his head like a shamed puppy.

"I don't expect you to forgive me," Clara said. "I don't deserve it. I just hope that, at some point, we might become civil to one another." She looked at Simon and offered a slight smile. "You see, I've become quite fond of *your* brother now."

It was all Brigid could do not to scream. Yes, she wanted Simon to be happy, but with *Clara*? Before she could pick her jaw up from the porch floor, a second automobile arrived.

"Oh my goodness," Brigid said, completely forgetting that Clara awaited a response. "Tobias is here."

The porch door opened and Eliza, Natalie and Thomas stepped out. Natalie and Thomas seemed excited beyond all measure, but Eliza appeared pale and shaky. She held on to Thomas's arm. Brigid didn't blame her a bit. Eliza had waited for this moment for two-and-a-half years.

Tobias had come home.

Chapter Thirty-Five

Brigid and the others watched from the porch as the driver exited the car and opened the rear door. A well-dressed woman stepped out.

"That's Victoria Cole," Thomas told Eliza.

Victoria grasped a tiny hand and helped the young child out of the vehicle. The driver reached in and pulled out a small valise and teddy bear. He handed the valise to Mrs. Cole and the teddy bear to the child.

"Oh!" Eliza gasped, and her hand flew to her heart. "My baby." Her voice was but a whisper as tears trailed her cheeks.

"Shall we go meet him?" Thomas asked.

"Wait. I don't want Tobias to see me crying." She quickly wiped her tears with the back of her hand.

Clara handed Eliza her handkerchief as Victoria escorted the toddler up the walk.

Eliza approached them as the others held back. No one said a word. Eliza smiled at Victoria, touched her arm in appreciation and knelt in front of the red-haired, two-year-old dressed in a navy and white sailor suit and Buster Brown shoes. He donned a curious expression as he studied Eliza, then pointed and said, "Mama."

"Yes, yes. I am your Mama," Eliza said. She glanced at Victoria with emotion welling in her eyes.

"I taught him "Mama' on the way over," Victoria said, smiling. "I explained that we were going to meet a great and beautiful lady who was his mama, but had been away."

"Thank you." Eliza's voice was barely audible. She turned back to Tobias. "I have missed you so very much. May I give you a hug?"

"I like hugs," Tobias said, and extended his arms. Eliza pulled him to her, held him and stroked his soft red hair. "I've waited a very long time to find you."

Tobias pulled away. "Joey want dog."

Everyone laughed through his or her tears, and Eliza looked questioningly at Victoria.

"Dear me, I apologize." Victoria placed the valise on the ground and held up her hands. "He's obsessed with dogs. Our neighbors have three. I told him about coming to a new home to live with the lovely lady, and all he talks about is a dog."

"A two-year-old has priorities," Thomas whispered in Brigid's ear.

Eliza stood up. "Oh, I'm sorry I've confused you, Mrs. Cole. I wasn't worried about his wanting a dog. It just dawned on me that he calls himself Joey." She took Tobias's hand in hers.

"Yes." Victoria nodded. "That was the name given to me by Miss Cavanaugh."

"Rupert Stouch said that was the infant's name. Joseph Green," Clara explained.

"Joey," Eliza said, as if mulling the name over.

"Yes?" He looked up expectantly. The little boy's response made them all laugh again.

Eliza smiled at her boy. "I think Joey is a fine name. Tobias was nice, but someone who we all know and detest liked it far better than I did."

She turned to the group, her eyes glistening again.

"My dear friends. May I introduce my son, Joey Markeson? I'll be changing my last name back to Markeson as well."

Brigid and the others stepped forward to greet little Joey. As they each, in turn, said hello and shook his little fist, Brigid noticed the heart-shaped birthmark on Joey's wrist, the sure telltale sign that this was indeed, Eliza's son. Pride surged in her heart, knowing she'd been instrumental in this wondrous and joyful moment in Eliza's life. Perhaps Thomas was right, just because Charles Ransom tried to inflict evil upon her, it hadn't changed the core goodness in her soul. He didn't take that away. At least, she'd like to think so.

Eliza addressed Victoria again. "I cannot thank you enough, Mrs. Cole, for taking such wonderful care of To-, I mean, Joey." She let go of Joey and took Victoria's gloved hands in her own. "Won't you please come inside and sit a spell? I'm sure you'd like more time with Joey before you return?"

Victoria smiled, but shook her head. "Thank you, Mrs. Ransom, but I think the sooner I leave, the easier it will be for both Joey and me. I am so very happy that he's been reunited with you, but I shall miss him, as will the other children in my home. He's a dear boy." She patted his head and placed her hand upon his shoulder for a moment. "Mrs. Ransom-"

"Eliza, if you please," Eliza interrupted.

"Eliza, then. You will write me and keep me informed as to how Joey fares?"

"Of course. Every week if you like."

"One moment, Mrs. Cole." Thomas turned and quickly ran back to the porch and retrieved a manila envelope off the swing. He returned to the group and handed it to her. "The corrected documentation regarding the boy's birth is inside," he explained. "His record no longer declares him deceased but states that he was sent to your fine orphanage. I also added a note with my signature that says the child was returned to his mother. That should render you free from any accusations of wrong doing in the child's new placement."

'Why thank you, Thomas," Victoria said. "Well, then. I should depart. I do have a train to catch." She picked up the valise, handed it to Thomas, but addressed Eliza again. "Those are Joey's belongings, and I've included his schedule and other incidentals you'd like to know about this precious little boy." She smiled at Joey again. "Of course, please feel free to telephone me, Mrs. Ransom, with any questions or concerns."

"Thank you, Mrs. Cole, you've been ever so kind and helpful." Tears of gratitude welled in Eliza's eyes.

"I'll see you to your car, Mrs. Cole," Thomas offered.

"No need, Thomas. You enjoy the welcome home party." Victoria bent down to Joey and gave him a quick hug. "Joey, I'm going to leave you now with your Mama. But she's going to write me and let me know how you are. When you're big enough, you can write me letters, too."

Joey seemed confused, but said "Bye-bye".

Victoria stood and offered the group a bittersweet smile. "He's been a joy to care for." She turned and walked to the waiting car.

As the car drove off and disappeared from view, Joey looked up at Eliza.

"Pitty," he said.

"Pity?" Eliza cast a worried glance at the group.

"I think he means 'pretty'," Natalie said, with a laugh. "As in, his mama is pretty. Right, Joey?"

"Yes, pitty." He smiled at everyone. "Dog?"

"If someone doesn't get the boy a dog, I will!" Simon bellowed but chuckled. The rest joined in the merriment.

Eliza turned and scooped Joey into her arms. "Would you like to see your new home, Joey?"

"Yeth." Joey pointed toward the house. "Home."

"Yes." Eliza pulled him close, tears wetting her cheeks again. "My darling boy is home."

Chapter Thirty-Six

A few hours later, Natalie took Joey up to his room for a long overdue nap. Per Eliza's request, the adults regrouped in the parlor. Tea and biscuits were served, and a pall fell over the group as usually happens at a party's end.

Brigid felt it deeply as there was now nothing holding her back from making a decision regarding her future. Even with money available to her, the decision to stay or leave was still difficult, and it pained her heart to have to choose between Thomas and her mother.

Before she could sit down, Simon pulled her aside.

"I need to talk to you about makin' a decision, Brigid Mary," he said, his tone light and his eyes twinkling. How could he be merry knowing he forced her to choose?

Eliza joined them at the fireplace. "Friends, please join the others. I have something very important to say."

"I was gonna tell Brigid somethin' important too, but I guess it can wait," Simon said.

Brigid wasn't sure she cared for all the mystery hanging about. She was tired of upheaval and secrets. She longed for a life void of surprises, at least bad ones. She sat beside Thomas on the loveseat, and he took her hand in his, its warmth radiating through her, making her wish to never let go.

Eliza stood before the group, her smile radiant.

"I want to thank each and everyone of you for helping me find my son. You can't imagine the joy in my heart today."

Thomas squeezed Brigid's hand.

"I have no intentions of ever returning to Charles, I assure you all of that." Her smile turned bittersweet. "I have removed my inheritance money from our accounts, and together with what Charles is paying me for my silence regarding Joey, I have enough money to live quite comfortably and to see that Joey has the best care available."

Brigid wondered why Eliza should want to tell them her financial business. Everyone looked a bit uncomfortable.

"You all, in some way, have helped bring Joey home to me, and I wish to repay you for your kindness and generosity of time and spirit." She pulled a few envelopes from atop the fireplace mantel. She handed one to Thomas. "Thomas, this should be enough money to send your mother home to Italy."

Thomas's eyes went wide. He shook his head. "Oh, Eliza, this certainly isn't nec-"

Eliza cut him off with a look. "Don't argue with me, you will not win." And then, she smiled.

Eliza handed Clara the next envelope. "Miss Cavanaugh, I know you most likely do not need any help from me, but perhaps you might use this to pay for your cousin's ongoing care."

Clara took the envelope, a surprised look upon her face. "I'm flabbergasted, Mrs. Ransom."

"And I am grateful to you for not arguing about it," Eliza said, casting Thomas another amused glance.

Another envelope was handed to Simon who tried to wave it away. "I didn't do nothin' to get your boy back, ma'am," he said. "Give this to Brigid."

"Just having you at Ransom House with us was a help, Mr. O'Brien. I felt safe with both you and Thomas at my side. Besides, the money is not for you, entirely." Eliza placed the envelope on Simon's knees. "Give the money to your mother and all those young children she's raising."

"No, Simon," Brigid interrupted, knowing of her brother's hopes and dreams. "You use that money for yourself to expand the farm as you wanted. I'll be giving Ma my money from Mr. Ransom."

"Eliza," Thomas said. "You must allow me to protest. Your gifts are most generous, but not necessary, really." His stunned expression reflected the way the Brigid felt. Eliza was too kind, too generous, too…Eliza.

"I insist." Eliza's face grew serious. "I won't take no for an answer from any of you. If I can't return the kindness done for me, what good am I?" She turned to Brigid. "Dear, you are welcome to stay with Natalie, Joey and me as long as you wish, but we are also willing to help you find your own home, should you desire to stay in New York."

There it was again, the looming painful decision.

"Well," Clara interrupted. "If it helps matters any, I was hoping Brigid might stay at *my* house."

Brigid nearly fell off the loveseat. Clara had to be out of her mind to think she'd live with her. She remained stoic as she tried to form a polite, yet outright rejection of that idea.

"That's what I wanted to talk to you about, Brigid," Simon said, a boyish grin lighting up his face.

Simon wanted her to live with Clara? He too, must be out of his love-struck head. She'd never, *ever,* live with Clara.

"I don't think-," she began.

"Oh, I won't be there," Clara quickly added.

"You won't?" Thomas said. "But I hoped to release Leopold to your care."

Clara clasped her hands together. "That is good news!"

"But he can't stay there alone," Thomas added, a frown forming.

"Oh." Clara looked at Simon. "I guess this changes things, then."

"Nothing has to change," Simon said. "That is, if Brigid lives in the house."

"What are you all talking about?" Brigid said, more confused than ever. Everything was suddenly so absurd. Eliza was handing out gifts like it was Christmas morning, Leopold was coming home, Simon and Clara seemed to share some big secret, and everyone assumed she would stay in New York.

Simon stood. "Brigid, Miss Cavanaugh is doing me the honor of travelin' with me back to Donegal to meet Ma."

Brigid's mouth dropped open. She heard Thomas chuckle and wanted to deck him.

Clara hung her head, but Brigid noticed a coy little smile spread and a blush rise in her cheeks. When she glanced up, happiness colored her eyes, and Brigid noted she nearly looked pretty.

"Yes, I have agreed to accompany Simon, propriety be damned!" Clara said. She addressed Brigid. "Simon and I know you need time to decide about moving back home, so we thought you might like to stay at my house while I'm gone. I would have peace of mind that the house was secure, and you would have a place to live -"

"- closer to Tom!" Simon added.

Before Brigid could respond, Thomas interjected. "I like that idea for another reason as well." He smiled at her. "Although 'being closer to Tom' is my favorite reason."

Now it was her turn to blush.

Thomas continued. "Brigid, if you stay at Clara's, she can travel with Simon and you can care for Leopold."

All eyes turned expectantly on her. It felt as if the decision had been made for her, but it was one she actually liked. Not only could she be near Thomas, but she truly liked Leopold Cavanaugh and helping him would make her feel useful.

But she still missed her mother.

"What would Ma think?" She turned to Simon.

"I'll tell her that you'll be along when you can and that you're doin' swell," Simon said. "Send a letter with me. As long as Clara and I are there to help her, you needn't come home right away. Ma's main concern was that you were all right."

"And I am, now." She smiled up at Thomas. "I've truly never been happier. Tell her that."

Thomas turned and took both of her hands in his. "If you stay in New York, I'll be the happiest man on earth. If you haven't figured it out by now, Brigid Mary O'Brien, I love you."

"I love you too, Thomas Ashton." She looked deep into those loving eyes of blue. "I'll stay."

And suddenly, New York City was a very beautiful place to be.

Epilogue

Thomas proposed to Brigid in Times Square on New Year's Eve just as the ball dropped. They married in New York City in the summer of 1913. Their honeymoon was a trip to Calabria, Italy to bring Angelina Ashton home to her beloved Italy, and a visit to Donegal where Brigid was joyfully reunited with her mother and siblings.

Brigid and Thomas made their home in New York City, selling the Ashton's home and buying Cavanaugh House from Clara. Leopold Cavanaugh came to live with them, and under Thomas's and Brigid's care, he refrained from the drink…mostly.

Brigid spent her early-married life raising Thomas's and her two sons, and becoming a respected society lady. She employed Mrs. Duffy and Anna but always treated them as friends rather than staff. Thomas finished his medical studies and became a renowned specialist in the newly established field of pediatrics. After Thomas retired, he and Brigid spent their days with their grandchildren and, during times of peace, traveled the world. They died within hours of each other in a New York nursing home in 1960.

Simon and Clara married and settled in Ireland. They helped Simon's mother raise the children and worked the farm. Clara, out from under the constraints of society, was never happier and found her greatest pleasure tending the sheep and working the land. She loved her newfound family in Simon's brothers and sisters. Simon and Clara had no children, but were content solely with each other - Simon finally found a woman willing to put up with his brash and brawn, and Clara found a man and family of good heart to love her.

Eliza Ransom never remarried. She lived with her sister and son in the Markeson home. Joey grew up happy and well cared for by his loving mother, aunt and godparents, Thomas and Brigid. Joey died unexpectedly at age thirty from pneumonia, and Eliza died two years later of a broken heart.

Abigail Langford was never cured of typhoid and died on North Brother Island three months after Brigid's escape. Brigid paid for her funeral and had her body shipped back to Poland for burial.

Rupert Stouch and his wife left New York in the winter of 1912 to live in England. In 1915, he boarded the *Lusitanian* to travel back to the States. He died when the ship was torpedoed by a German U-Boat and sunk. His young wife had not been on the trip. She remarried soon after.

Charles Ransom pined for Eliza for the rest of his days. He remained at Ransom House with only his valet, the ever-faithful Henry, and an elderly cook. He lost much of his vast fortune in the Stock Market Crash of 1929, but was able to retain his home and "good" name. One day, in the summer of 1950, Charles rose from breakfast, looked at Henry, grasped his chest and collapsed to the floor. He died hours later from a massive bleed in the heart.

Oh, the irony! Who would have thought Charles Ransom actually had one?

The End

Other novels by Linda Schmalz can be found at:

Amazon.com, Smashwords.com, Barnes and Noble.com and wherever other fine e-books are sold.

Contact Linda Schmalz at: lindas319@yahoo.com, Twitter: Mattsma, and Facebook: Linda Siedelmann Schmalz